P9-DMI-663

UNCONVENTIONAL

UNCONVENTIONAL

J. J. Hebert

MINDSTIR MEDIA

Unconventional is Copyright © 2009 J. J. Hebert.
All rights reserved.

This is a work of fiction. Names, characters, places and incidents are products of the author's imagination or are used fictitiously and should not be construed as real. Any resemblance to actual events, locales, organizations or persons, living or dead, is entirely coincidental.

No part of this book may be used or reproduced in any manner whatsoever without written permission, except in the case of brief quotations embodied in critical articles and reviews. For more information e-mail all inquiries to: info@mindstirmedia.com.

Printed in the United States of America.

ISBN-10: 0-981964-80-X
ISBN-13: 978-0-9819648-0-5

Library of Congress Control Number: 2009901524

Published by Mindstir Media (USA), www.mindstirmedia.com

Cover and Interior Design by: Jeremy Robinson
www.jeremyrobinsononline.com

Visit J. J. Hebert on the World Wide Web at: www.jjhebert.net

For the love of my life

ACKNOWLEDGMENTS

Contrary to popular belief, producing a novel isn't a one-person project. Sure, I spent countless hours writing and polishing *Unconventional*, but many people helped along the way.

I am grateful to Brook and K. L. Going for editing, critiquing, and proofreading. Both of you offered invaluable advice. I'm a better writer because of you.

I am also thankful for Jeremy Robinson, a great author *and* cover designer. Working with you is an honor.

Gemma Halliday, thanks for being one of the first to read this tome. Your kind words mean more to me than you know.

Last, in no particular order, thank you Mom, Dad, Jennifer, Corky, and the Hannons. You've shaped my life.

PART ONE

CHAPTER ONE

"The greatest and most inspiring achievements are not produced by those who conform to society's idea of normal, but by those who courageously adopt the unconventional." Mitch's eyes brighten behind oval-shaped glasses, then he smiles the way he used to when I got a hit or struck someone out when I played on his Varsity team a couple months ago. "Tell me, James," Mitch continues, "have you adopted the unconventional yet?" Grinning, Mitch takes the first step toward Robert Frost's house, the white museum, leaving his Cadillac behind on the gravel driveway.

I follow Mitch as a shadow, and two long strides later, I'm walking alongside him. As Mitch repeats the preceding question, I feel like he's the teacher, I'm the student, and he's giving a pop quiz. At the rusty metal mailbox affixed atop a tree stump, Mitch stops and faces me, waiting for a reply.

I come to a halt, and instead of keeping my eyes on Mitch, I examine the mailbox to his left. **R. FROST**, painted in black, decorates the box's side. The flag is down, the lid open a crack. "I *think* I've adopted the unconventional," I say, the words ambivalent, then I turn my gaze to his aged face.

"You *think*?" Mitch's eyes show hints of disappointment. "James, are you unconventional or not?"

I consider the question. His face blurs as I focus on the house behind him. "Yeah, sure, I'm unconventional."

His tone is vivacious. "*Well?* Let's hear some examples for once."

As though I'm back in school, pondering A, B, C, and D, I choose what I believe is the correct answer: "While most kids in school were worrying about superficialities, I was working on my poetry anthology."

"Uh-huh," Mitch says, dissatisfied.

I see Mitch's face clearly now. "I penned a new poem each week, instead of drinking or partying or—"

"Okay, okay. James Frost wants to be *Robert* Frost." Mitch puts his hand in a front pocket of his khakis. "That's all nice and sweet, but I'm looking for something deeper."

I incline my head. Apparently, I'm failing this quiz. "Deeper? Like what?"

"Writing isn't necessarily unconventional," Mitch says. "In fact, most people have written poetry and quite a few have written short stories and novels. So, what is it that's made writing an unconventional choice for you?"

"I'm not sure."

"What have you overcome?"

I flash on Brad from Langwood High School. "Ridicule. Pessimism."

"Care to expound upon that?" Mitch adjusts the collar of his Izod shirt.

Maybe I can pass the quiz after all. "There was this jerk in school named Brad. I can still picture him with his malevolent grin and spiky blond hair and expensive clothing and unkind eyes. He was part of the so-called *cool crowd*. The elite. . . . One day, Brad and his following sat next to me in Study Hall. I had my notebook spread open and I was writing a poem. Brad looked over and saw what I was writing and he started to laugh. Before I could close my notebook, he tore the sheet out and proceeded to read the poem aloud in an effeminate voice. Brad's friends laughed and he called me a loser and a sissy."

"*Then* what happened?"

I think of the poem-filled binder on the floor in Mitch's Cadillac. "I didn't let Brad steer me away from writing and—"

"You made the unconventional choice." Mitch smiles. "Very good, James." He hands out an A in his own words.

Mitch spins around, waving me forward, and begins walking toward the barn behind the house. At the barn, he points to the mountains in the distance, and together we admire the view. "Just think," Mitch says, "Robert looked upon these same peaks."

Inside the barn, we watch a slideshow about Robert Frost in Franconia, New Hampshire. One particular slide depicts Robert in a drab suit sitting in a Morris chair (an antique recliner) with a writing board across his lap, fastened to the armrests. The image doesn't leave my mind as we exit the barn and go inside the house.

My heart hammers as we walk to a Morris chair similar to the one in the photograph, and I imagine Robert sitting in it, fountain pen in hand, his face taut and ghostlike. I see him vividly: a wide nose, intense eyes under thick eyebrows, wavy, brown hair, and pouty lips. On the wooden board over his lap sits a sheet of paper, corners curled up. He jots down a few words on the sheet, stops, and holds the pen poised over the paper. Idly tapping a booted foot, he stares into the sheet for a couple of seconds, then he begins writing again. I feel as though I can reach out and touch the legend, speak to him even.

Outside, in the wake of the buildings, we walk a half-mile trail through the woods, birds warbling and squirrels chittering from every corner of the path. Every now and again, we encounter plaques of Robert's poetry posted on trees along the trail. We stop at all of the plaques and read the poems. We take pictures and talk about Robert's poetry. Then, after some silence, Mitch brings up college. I roll my eyes. He says, "Well, do you think you'll ever go?"

I tell Mitch that I can't fathom being confined for another four years, under the thumbs of professors, told where to go, and when, and how to get there—wherever "there" may be. "I can't imagine becoming a collegian clone," I elaborate, picturing scores of college kids, each with a bottle to their lips, pie-eyed, neglecting consequence.

I feel ill, thinking of how contradictory I've been. Last month, I crossed paths with some acquaintances from school. They invited me to a party where we smoked some weed, and I even got laid, which was a terrible sexual experience, to say the least. Weed doesn't exactly enhance a certain piece of the male anatomy. I was like Bob Dole before the little blue pill. Afterward, the images and emotions attached to sex with Molly were almost too much to bear. I vowed to stop acting the part of cloned adolescent and inadequate presidential candidate.

I promptly severed all communication with those people and walked away intact, before I became a drug addict. Before I woke up in jail, before I impregnated someone, caught an STD, or died. I didn't get away unscathed, though. My self-esteem is shattered due to the Molly episode, and I've done something totally unconventional: I've deleted sex from my life. No sex again until marriage. I know, I'm like a walking abstinence brochure. *Don't have sex because . . .*

"Any idea what's next for you?" Mitch asks.

"I think I wanna try my hand at a novel."

"Really?" Mitch sounds both excited and surprised.

I nod. "I've been going to the library lately, and I've fallen in love with the genre of fantasy. When I read that genre, brilliant otherworldly landscapes, elves, gnomes, and giants suddenly surround me, and I'm able to escape the mundane."

Mitch says, "Good. We all need to escape sometimes."

At the end of our hike, we amble to the Cadillac, and I pull out one of my typed poems from the binder.

Mitch slants his head. "What are you doing?"

"You'll see." I wink, then walk to Robert's mailbox, a man on a mission.

Making sure no one is looking other than Mitch, I pop the poem into that venerable gray box, close the lid, lift its flag, and take a step back, coming to grips with the fact that my poem is in the same place where Robert's award-winning poetry once sat. Wherever my unstamped poem ends up, I don't care. My reason for submitting this poem is out of hope that whatever amount of lingering magic remains in the mailbox, it will rub off on my writing and, eventually, on me.

When I return to the car, Mitch pats my shoulder and says, "I'm sure Robert will enjoy your poem." He pauses, then grins. "I know *I* did."

I let out a laugh. "Thanks. I hope so."

The magic of the moment makes me think of fantasy. Ideas swirl in my mind. Thoughts mushroom out of control. If I don't start writing my novel soon, I'm going to burst.

CHAPTER TWO

I've written six drafts of my fantasy adventure novel, *The Forsaken World*. Each draft is about one hundred thousand words, four hundred manuscript pages. I pay an editor, Arthur, every now and again to have a look at my work and polish it. He says I have a bright future as a novelist. I hope he's right.

My life is currently no fairytale. For a living, I mop floors, scrub toilets, and carry out other janitorial chores, having no formal education beyond high school. I still live at home with Dad. I'm twenty-one-years-old, three years removed from school, and I hope to play pretend on paper for a living someday. I guess some people consider that a pipe dream, but they just don't understand.

It's partly because of my decision to adopt Mitch's idea of unconventionality—and because of a plethora of other decisions, for sure—that ultimately I find myself in this car. We've been on the road for nearly nine hours, an eternity. My legs are cramped behind the passenger seat; the air-conditioner is busted, so I'm sweating and the back of my shirt is stuck to the leather seat; and nausea is beginning to form in my stomach, a touch of carsickness. I'm six-foot-two, long and lanky, and I'm a trapped animal. I'm trying to think of a way to get out of this cage. Maybe I'll escape at the next stoplight. I could walk the rest of the way. I'd be able to stretch my giraffe-like legs, take in some fresh air, and get the nausea under control before it takes a turn for the worse.

I'm full of it. I'm not bold enough to throw this door open at a stoplight and jump out. It's not going to happen. I'm not Tom Cruise in one of his action movies; I wouldn't land gracefully on the pavement, hair unruffled. I look over at my best friend, Sam, who's sitting in the seat to my left. His forehead glistens with sweat but he doesn't appear uncomfortable. He has much more foot room than I do because his father, the driver, was considerate enough to bring his seat up a bit when we began our trip in New Hampshire, unlike Sam's mother, the person perched in front of me. Sam is also shorter than me. When we stand side by side, we look like DeVito and Schwarzenegger in that movie. *What's it called? Not the one where Arnold's pregnant. The other one . . .* Sam's height works to his advantage in this case. He's in First Class and I'm in Coach.

Our destination is Pennsylvania but it feels like we're traveling the world. Here I am, a modern day Columbus, save the ship and mythic persona. So far, Sam and I have discussed music, movies, and other superficial topics—and, of course, we've cracked countless jokes. At the moment, he and I are silent in our own worlds. His parents, on the other hand, are talking about politics, mostly regarding their respect for Bush and their unwavering faith in the Republican Party. A couple minutes ago, they discussed religion, their love for Jesus, and their belief based on Biblical prophecy that these are the End Times. Before that, the topic was work. And prior to work, they chatted about Sam's high school years, the whirling blur of events.

A hush finally falls over the car and I look out my window, swallowing hard. I feel like an awful person. Why can't I be completely happy for Sam? My self-centered side experiences no feelings of joy, no unspeakable elation. I think about what Sam has said numerous times: *I don't belong in New Hampshire . . . I need to leave and start over with a clean slate . . .* Here is his big chance. College. Part of me, the selfless side, does rejoice for his dream. Sadly, at the moment, that side pales in comparison to the other.

I close my eyes, trying to keep the queasiness at bay, and imagine him in his new life, the people he will meet, new girls and new friends. Sam is the last of my friends to leave for college, all the others having set off on journeys of their own.

"So, James, when are we going to take *you* to college?"

His mother's voice rouses me from my thoughts. I open my eyes and turn away from the window. I speak to her headrest. "College isn't for me, you know?"

"Yeah, okay, James. Whatever you say," she says, unconvinced.

Sam's father looks at me in the rearview mirror. "Weren't you writing a book? How's that going?" His tone telegraphs skepticism. I know he doesn't really care about my novel. As far as he's concerned, I tinker with words and nothing is going to come of it. He's probably never seen magic in his life. People like that, the play-it-safers, feel threatened by the unconventional. They share an idea that if magic didn't happen for them, it can't happen for anyone else.

He continues to stare at my sallow face. Judging by his knotted brow, I suspect it bothers him that I haven't answered yet. A portion of me waits for him to say that I'm wasting my time with the idea that I will ever be published.

I focus on his reflection, those tufty eyebrows and his lined forehead, and finally respond, "Yeah, a sample's sent off to publishers in New York and a bunch of agencies. I'm waiting to hear back. Hopefully I'll get some good news." I can't see his eyes, but I notice him nod.

"What is it about your novel that'll make people want to read it? It's fantasy, right?" Sam's mother joins the conversation, cynical.

I jump into defensive mode but respond devoid of anger. "I think people will read it because it's fresh. There isn't anything quite like it."

Sam watches and listens. It bothers me that even though he's read excerpts of my novel, and claims he really digs my work, he says nothing to his parents now to assure them that I have talent and I haven't squandered my time.

Sam's father shifts his hand on the steering wheel. "But what happens if the book doesn't do well?" He glances up into the mirror. "*Then* what are you going to do?" His eyebrows lift, then drop back into place. "I mean, it's a tough business to get into. Thousands of books are published. Your odds aren't good that you'll sell millions of copies." His eyes settle on the road. "You don't want to become a starving artist, do you?"

I lower my head and look at the floor. What does he want to hear from me? *Yes, you're right, Mr. Nuggett. It's a tough business to get into. I should give up. I should conform to society's idea of normal by following in your son's footsteps and going to college. It's the only way. The conventional way.* I release a barely audible sigh. What I want to say is—*Odds are based on averages, and I'm not average.*

Sam's mother clears her throat. "I guess you could always fall back on your father's company," she says. "I suppose that's all right as a last resort." She chuckles; her husband follows suit; Sam remains silent, afraid of defying his parents.

I don't respond to her familiar sardonic witticism. The thought of working for Dad's janitorial company for the remainder of my life churns my stomach.

CHAPTER THREE

We arrive at Sam's college and we're greeted in the parking lot by an upperclassman. He shakes my hand. We exchange names. His name is Fred, and he asks if I'm Sam's brother. He wants to know if I'm going to attend college with Sam. I tell Fred that Sam and I aren't brothers and I won't be taking classes here.

Fred puts a hand on his hip. "What college do you go to?" he asks, falsely interested.

I feel my face flush. "I don't go to college," I say. With a piece of luggage in my hand, I lean against the back bumper of the car. This is my least favorite part about meeting people.

"Oh, then you work?" Fred asks, slipping his hand into a front pocket.

I can feel him judging me. "Yeah, I work." Three words. I have no desire to socialize with him. I glance at Sam, who stands to my right with bags in his hands. Behind him, his parents stand proudly, speaking quietly to one another. Then I bring my eyes to Fred again. I know it's wrong to judge a book by its cover or in this case, a person by his appearance, but I judge anyway. Fred is wearing Gucci sunglasses, a sparkling silver necklace, diamond studded earrings, and designer clothing that would take me weeks to pay for. *Surely*, I think, *there's no way this guy paid for all of these possessions on his own. Daddy and Mommy had to have assisted.* I want to ask Fred if he knows what work is, but out of respect for Sam, feeling that Fred may be some bigwig on campus, and also because I know I'm hypocritical for judging him as I think he judged me, I bite my tongue. Maybe he does work. Or maybe he leeches off his parents. I can't be sure either way.

"Well, what do you do?" Fred looks on me through dark lenses.

"I'm a brother, a friend, a son . . ." I pause to let it sink in. "And what do I do for work? Is that what you're asking?" I see him nod. "I work for my dad's company," I say, awaiting more prying questions.

"What kinda company is that?" Fred asks.

"The R.O.T.C.," I say. As always, I smile without revealing my decayed, disgraceful teeth. I've never been to a dentist and only recently—roughly three years ago—started to take care of my set. Flossing, brushing twice daily, once in the morning and once before bed, and swishing with mouthwash that sets my cheeks and gums on fire. I've been doing everything in my power to keep from losing these brown Chiclets, but I fear no amount of maintenance can reverse the damage already done. I find it humiliating that I may have to wear dentures before the age of thirty. Or walk around toothless is more likely; I can't afford a visit to the dentist, never mind false teeth.

Fred's forehead creases. He wakes from silence. "R.O.T.C.? Doesn't that have something to do with the Army?"

Smiling, I shift my attention to Sam. I languidly wink at him. Then I throw a stare in Fred's direction. "The Royal Order of Toilet Cleaners. Haven't heard of 'em?" I watch Fred, imagining the confused eyes underneath his dark lenses. "I do janitorial work, to put it bluntly."

Sam lets out a nervous laugh and looks at me with widened eyes. Sam isn't part of my bloodline, but he might as well be my brother. I can tell he wants me to shut up. I'm embarrassing him, so I refrain from any more clever jokes. That's a shame, too, because it's fun toying with Fred, the Gucci man.

Without cracking a smile or saying a word, Fred lifts the sunglasses from his face and sets them on his head. He looks up at me as though I've rolled around in manure. Because of my job as janitor, Fred—a fine representation of society—wants me to be or believes me to be an uneducated imbecile whose only lot in life is to clean up after the white-collar population of America. I'm assuming things, possibly; assumptions are, I admit, one of my flaws. I want to tell Fred that I'm not an idiot and I'm not a slave and education isn't only about a piece of fancy paper.

"I see," Fred says finally, looking me up and down. I think he means "I see" literally. He can see that I do janitorial work. I'm not wearing anything fancy over my thin frame—ratty jeans, a tee shirt— and I haven't done anything to my mop of ash-blond hair, so I probably fit his image of a janitor. He turns to Sam, dismissing me, and says, "Let's get you moved in." I watch as Fred takes Sam away.

* * *

Sam and his parents are at an assembly on campus for college newcomers. Darkness fell over the campus about ten minutes ago and I'm sitting in silence at the wooden desk in Sam's dorm room, his new home, staring into space. I've known Sam for seven years, give or take. For the first four or so, while we were neighbors, we hung out almost every day. Memories swirl through my mind: Sam and I play wiffle ball and flag football in his backyard with the local kids; he and I build forts outdoors; talk about girls; discuss life, the future; we laugh together; cry together; and grow together.

With a sinking heart, I lean back in the chair. I will miss Sam Nuggett. I stand and scan the room, noticing posters on a far wall that once decorated the walls at his house. The posters look foreign in this environment.

I think of Donovan, my other best friend, and the sickening feeling I discovered when he left for college last year. I didn't go with him to see him off, but I went to his lake house to say "see you later" before he left; I didn't want to say goodbye because, as I've heard, that's something you only say to someone you are never going to see again. I hugged him and didn't want to let go, didn't want him to leave. Of course, he left anyways. But I couldn't blame him, just as I can't fault Sam for leaving. Our paths are different.

I turn away from those posters and sigh. I get tired of being emotional, so I look for a diversion and find Sam's laptop perched on his bed. I grab it up and swipe my forefinger over the touchpad to bring the laptop out of hibernation. I know he won't mind. I sit on the bed, check my e-mail, then sign in on MySpace.com, an online community where I registered last week. I bring up my page on the screen and read over the About Me section, the part I filled out: *Hey. The name's James Frost. I'm from New Hampshire, and I hope to one day get published. I like baseball (played varsity both junior and senior year), football (mostly enjoy watching it), and writing.*

Most people on MySpace give a hint about their occupation and some come right out and mention the job title—and details of their job—on their profile, but no way will I reveal my job to the world. *Hey. The name's James Frost. I'm from New Hampshire, and I hope to one day get published. I work for my dad's janitorial company, and I can be seen scrubbing toilets with an oversized toothbrush.* I chuckle to myself. There are some things about me that strangers don't need to know.

I sign in on AOL Instant Messenger; instant messaging addicts refer to the program as AIM. A message pops onto the screen at once: *Hey James, how ya doin?* It was sent by Erica, a girl who I dated for a period of about three weeks. Our little fling ended a couple days ago. Even after the alarms went off in my head telling me that we weren't a good match, I still stayed with her until it got to the point where I couldn't trust her anymore. There's an old proverb that I came across: *Where there is no trust, there is no love.* I thought of that line when I broke up with her in Dad's living room. I told her that she had lied to me too many times, and that the trust was gone. After she graced me with a dozen or so consecutive f-yous, she stormed out of the house and sped away. I ate ice cream and threw a solitary party. *Bye-bye, Wicked Witch.*

I focus on the laptop's screen, on the message box that I think of canceling. I don't initially want to respond to her, especially because of the things she said to me before she left Dad's house that day, but I start to think: *Who am I gonna hang out with when I'm home? Dono-*

van's gone. Sam's gone. Everyone's gone. Except . . . I poise my fingers over the keys, then type: *Hey.*

"Hey, man."

Sam's voice rips my attention from the laptop. I look up and see him, DeVito-like, brown hair instead of baldness, standing alone in the doorway.

"Hey." I sit the laptop on the sheets, the screen aimed toward him. "How did it go? Meet anyone cool?"

He comes in and sits next to me. "You wouldn't believe the girls here, man. They're so hot." He smiles. "It'll be a good year." His eyebrows dance.

I can't help but feel a little jealous. Sam has thousands of girls to choose from, and who do I have? Erica. The Wicked Witch. *Yippee.* "That's good, Sam. Maybe you'll get lucky."

His smile grows. "Maybe."

I fold my hands over my legs. "Pretty good odds, I'd say."

He notices the laptop on the other side of me. His eyes light up, and he raises an eyebrow. "Why are you talking to her, man?"

I shoot him a serious look. Sorrow tugs at my heart. "Once I leave this place, who else do I have? What do you expect of me? Am I supposed to talk to my walls or paint a face on a volleyball and talk to that?"

Sam puts a hand on my shoulder. "You can talk to me. Plus, you have your dad."

"Don't make promises you can't keep," I say.

Sam appears baffled. "What do you mean? We'll still talk."

I cross my arms. "I know how it goes. It happens the same every time someone goes away." I look down at the carpet, dirt and paper scraps strewn over the surface, a janitor's nightmare. "They give me the we'll-stay-in-touch speech, but then their new life kicks in and they don't have time for me anymore. I become last on the priority list, and whatever we had fades." I think of my relatives in Nevada— Mom and Sis, brother-in-law and niece, and I feel an explosion of anger as I flash on how this occurred: the divorce between my mother and father, the segregation in our family, miles between us hindering our communication, awkward phone calls once or twice every few months.

After a couple seconds of pondering, stiff in his upright position, Sam says, "But that doesn't have to happen to us." His voice discloses his concern. "We're like family, like brothers."

I veil my sadness with a smile. "I know." I hold out arms to hug my brother. "Let's do this now, so we don't have to later."

I hear the *ding* of an incoming message on the laptop as he wraps his arms around me. I ignore that sound. This takes precedence. "I love you, man."

"Love you too." His voice cracks. "See you later."

A sickening feeling swells in my stomach. I hold on tightly, not wanting to let go. Grief crashes down on my heart like thunder, or maybe like a large river wave teeming with flesh-eating piranhas.

* * *

We're on our way home, Sam's parents and I, the radio on a station with talk only, and we drive by New York City. I stare out the window, thinking about the publishers and literary agencies. Their businesses are situated among those countless glimmering lights, the kaleidoscope of colors in the distance.

I imagine I'm a fly on the wall and I see an editor laugh and cry and smile as she reads my novel at her teakwood desk. I'm invisible in an agent's office and he, the literary expert, can't put my novel down; the elegant prose and genius plot magnetize him. Every agent I observe wants to represent my work. They expect a six-figure deal. Predict it'll become a best seller. I see myself at Dad's house, walking straight to my landline phone. The answering machine blinks twelve. I listen to the messages. *The publishers and agencies love me. They really love me.*

I rest my head against the window, my reverie twisting. I see Sam socialize with his new friends. He wears an exuberant smile. Around every corner, he meets a new girl. He's not in New Hampshire anymore. He's starting over with a clean slate. His dream has come true.

I half-smile, feeling simultaneously pleased and miserable; satisfied because Sam got what he wanted and awful because of his departure. My buddy of all those years is no longer just a couple towns away.

I think of my own dream, wonder if it'll come true, if I'll get to start over fresh like Sam. I close my eyes and pray, pleading with the Maker. *Please, I need to get published. Please, I don't want to be alone.*

CHAPTER FOUR

Another school year turns up. I find it difficult to believe this will be my third year working for Dad. This must be a nightmare I'll wake from at any moment. The car I'm driving—a black 1989 Ford Escort, white scuffs on the front and rear bumpers, and clusters of rust on various spots of the driver's door—evokes reality. This is no dream. I paid off this vehicle last month. Fourteen hundred dollars returned to my father. It feels liberating to live without the burden of repaying Dad, but that feeling doesn't shrink my hatred for this ill-favored car.

I pull into the school's parking lot, reducing my speed to fifteen, the limit for this area. I drive toward the front of the palatial brick school. As expected, elementary-aged children stand scattered near the main entrance, waiting for their buses and parents to arrive. Some of the kids, backpacks slung over their shoulders, point at my car, laugh, and plug their wrinkled noses, like this is a garbage truck or something, and others smirk or smile as I roll by. These types of reactions aren't uncommon. No doubt, they point and laugh because of the noisiness of my car's loud grinding and pig-like squealing sounds. They smirk and smile for the same reason. They squeeze their nostrils with a different motive—to keep out the smell of burning oil.

I turn a corner, away from the horde, isolating myself, and park the car near a side door. I'd get this piece of junk fixed but I don't possess the proper funds. I brought this ole block of metal to a repair shop last week and they quoted me a price of eight hundred bucks. The manager looked at me as though I had ten heads when I laughed and told him I'd have to pass. According to him, I need new front and rear brakes and some other parts indecipherable to me. I can't afford to sink hundreds of dollars into my car. Bills—like car insurance, gas, rent, food, editing fees owed to Arthur, and my laptop that I'm *still* paying for through a credit card—give me little choice in the matter. I could get the car fixed and charge the bill to the same credit card, but I don't wish to fall further into debt.

I yank the keys out of the ignition, body tense, frustration washing over me. There's a baseball bat in my trunk—a wooden Louisville Slugger, thirty-four inches—which I used during practice in my Varsity baseball days. I'm tempted to pop the trunk, get out of my car, take hold of that bat and, allowing my hatred for this vehicle to feed my strength, swing like a madman at this joke-of-a-car. I would take delight in releasing my frustration on this inanimate object, but to bash this car would only draw attention to me. I don't crave attention. Not that type. The perception people have of me is negative enough already—*imbecilic janitor who drives a noisy car from hell.* I don't need to provide them with more ammunition by beating my car to a pulp in broad daylight. *Imbecilic,* psycho *janitor who drives a* dented, smashed, *noisy car from hell.* I shake my head, opening the driver's door, drop my car keys into a front pocket, and proceed to the building's side door. As I step through into the vestibule, I accidentally brush up against a departing teacher. "Sorry about that," I say, standing still.

She doesn't stop or even glance back in my direction. She darts out the door, leaving one sharp word in her trail: "*Yep.*"

I turn to the door as it slams in my face. Did she think I purposely ran into her? Did she expect that from me? Maybe she had a bad day. Maybe she was in a rush and didn't have time to talk. Possibly she didn't think I was worth her time, this person responsible for cleaning up after her.

I step out of the vestibule and onto the faded green hallway. I stroll down the hall, peeking in the classrooms as I pass. Nothing new today. Another day in paradise. The floors, carpeted or tiled, littered with dirt and dropped pens, pencils, crayons, markers, crumpled pieces of paper and more, cause outright disgust in me. To an outsider, it would appear that at some point throughout the day, bombs containing writing utensils and paper exploded in each room. To me, an insider, it's evident that the children behaved as their usual disrespectful selves and the teachers, as in days prior, held no control over them. If only teachers were allowed to bring back rulers like in the days of the knuckle-swatting nuns.

I get to the last room at the end of the hallway and notice Mrs. Fredricks sitting at her desk, her crooked nose deep in paperwork, wearing a customary scowl on her crinkly face. She reminds me of a nun, with only the penguin getup and ruler missing. I avoid the classroom and retreat quietly to the center of the hall, the place of my closet. I unlock and open the door labeled JANITOR and roll out the cleaning cart—containing a vacuum, bathroom supplies, and an attached wastebasket. I push it up against the adjacent wall.

First step is to round up the garbage. I grab an unused, oversized garbage bag from the cart and start in the classroom across from Mrs. Fredricks's room. As I approach the wastebasket next to the teacher's desk, I notice a new poster on the wall to my left, above the room's sink. Mister Hutchins, the teacher who molds young minds here, must have hung this poster earlier today. From my spot in the middle of the room, near a couple student desks, I find the poster effortlessly readable. In large bold letters across the top, it says **I WANT TO BE A . . .** Underneath, photographs appear in four separate columns. The top left column portrays a doctor with a stethoscope around his neck. The top right depicts a female dentist with a giant, cartoonish toothbrush in hand. Bottom left, the image of a male chef grips a spatula. Neighboring that, a police officer smiles, gun in his holster, his hand raised, frozen in a wave. Below the four photos, the words **WHEN I GROW UP** finish the poster's message.

I step closer to the poster, pondering this thought: *No kid ever says I want to be a janitor when I grow up.* I peruse the images on the poster once again, then glance down at my trash bag. Anger knifes through my body. *How did I end up here?* It'd be easy to pass the blame onto my parents. Neither one of them pushed me to do much of anything. Their guidance was, to put it nicely, scarce. In hindsight, their parenting was far too lenient. Nonetheless, I can't blame them. I ought to take personal responsibility for the outcome of my life. We are all products of our own choices.

All that aside, I'm financially handcuffed. At this time, I can't make more money anywhere else than I accrue at this job: eight dollars per hour. That's fact, not illusionary, because I've tried to get a new job before, but to no avail. I went through the tedious process— wrote cover letters, constructed résumés, sent them out, but no businesses offering more than eight bucks would hire me. Minimal skills, no ornate piece of paper indicating a college degree.

A diminutive voice in the back of my mind speaks as I return to the wastebasket. *My only chance to get out of this situation, my only ticket, is not to find another menial job, but to get my book published.* No, I'm not demon-possessed. The voice spoke of inspiration, not harm, and it was *my* voice inside my head, not a gruff hi-I'm-the-devil-with-a-spinning-head-about-to-vomit voice. I drop the small, rank bag into the oversized one, tie a knot in the large bag, then hoist it over my shoulder. The voice was correct. Becoming published remains my only hope, which is why I worked so diligently on my novel, sacrificing much, at many junctures. *Sorry, Sam, I can't go to the movies tonight because I have to work on my novel. Sorry, Donovan, I can't watch the game with you today because I need to write.*

Apology. Excuse. Sacrifice. Time and again.

As I start toward the door, balancing the bag, I begin to muse. Old, unwise choices placed me here. Theoretically, recent, improved choices—to write nightly and send my manuscript to the publishers and literary agencies—ought to plunk me in an enhanced setting, an environment that doesn't include performing mindless tasks like collecting fetid waste, washing soiled toilets and gunk-filled sinks, mopping grimy floors, and vacuuming trashed carpets.

I'm about to step into the hallway when I hear Mrs. Fredricks conversing with someone from her room. The word "college" piques my interest. I stop in the doorway and listen attentively to the conversation echoing across the corridor. Another teacher joined Mrs. Fredricks while I contemplated the poster. Fredricks talks about her two sons, Will and Steve. I didn't know she had any kids but, according to what I hear, they're twins. Will attends college, has a bit of a drinking problem, she says, and Steve, a married man, works full-time. The two teachers joke about their own college years, how they partook in the occasional alcoholic beverage. They have no knowledge of my nearby presence. Laughing, they say that many of their peers drank more than they studied but that there is no B.A. in Alcohol Consumption, the last time they checked. When the hilarity wears out for them, Fredricks expresses her pride in Will—she sees herself in him, and is pleased with his college selection. She claims his drinking isn't detrimental, providing he continues to thrive in college. Her voice, while she discusses Steve's mediocre life, as she calls it, implies her disrespect for his choices. "I wish he could be more like Will," she says.

I shake my head, repulsed. What is Fredricks thinking? From what I've gathered, Will is the one with the drinking problem. He's probably an alcoholic, for all she knows. But he's in college, so that somehow cancels out the alcoholism? Steve, he works full-time, supports his wife, doesn't, according to her, have a drinking problem, and nothing about him makes her proud? Why? Because he doesn't participate in college to cover up his troubles, whatever they may be? Enraged, I drop the garbage bag and walk away, up the hallway and into a bathroom.

I lean in over the sink, palms flat on the white porcelain on either side of the faucet. I shut my eyes and imagine myself standing next to Will, the collegian alcoholic, Fredricks's pride and joy, whatever he looks like. I picture Fred (Fred—Fredricks? Maybe a connection here?), Sam's new college friend, the uppity Gucci man. Mrs. Fredricks has Fred and me in front of her, while she sits in her high-backed chair, examining us. She looks at him, smiles, glances at me and shoots her trademarked scowl. The other teacher, a nondescript individual, asks, "Which one is going to be successful, Mrs. Fredricks?"

Fredricks looks at Fred. Like a queen from her throne, she points a bony finger his way. "This one—he'll be successful," she announces.

Mrs. Nondescript asks, "Why not the other?"

Fredricks smiles, lowers her forefinger. She shifts her royal gaze to me. "This boy is uneducated. He's nothing more than a servant."

My hands ball into fists. I open my eyes, wanting to punch at the sink, knock it off the wall. Fredricks doesn't know me. This culture doesn't know me. I do janitorial work, but I'm living a secret life. I don't show the real James Frost. *They wouldn't understand my writing life, so why should I tell them about it?* I'd rather they not know; I can do without long stares, squinting, disbelieving eyes, whispers, and gossip that tends to generate when one dares to be different. I can live without derisive comments from those bent on smothering my go-getting fire and from those who don't believe in dreams or in magic. I wouldn't want them as friends, these people who mask everyone around them with stereotypes.

I step away from the sink, shaking my head. Wow. I'm such a hypocrite. I've probably judged a few people in my lifetime, too.

* * *

The only people who remain in the school are Dad, Randy—a coworker who has worked here three years longer than I—and me. It is 8:30 PM and I just completed my designated cleaning area. I stand at Mrs. Fredricks's end of the hallway, hands in the front pockets of my jeans. I look down at either side of the hallway, double-checking the doors (are they shut? Yes), then I take a step backward through a set of open doors to Randy's elected cleaning area. I can hear the distant roar of his vacuum.

Feet planted on a gray carpet runner in Randy Land, my back to his province, I observe my hallway. The ceiling lights glint on the waxy tiles, creating an illusion of ice. I nod at the hall, think *job well done*, and shrug my shoulders. Another day. Another dollar. I turn and begin to walk down Randy's hall, thinking of Sam. *What's he up to these days?* Whatever he's doing, I'm sure it's more glamorous than the work I've just completed and the work I'm about to do. I should call him. In his position, plenty can happen in a few days. He could have met his future wife by now. For me, a few days doesn't amount to much. This colorless world in which I dwell doesn't often change or offer stimulation. I'm jealous of Sam at the moment. The longing to hear his voice, the familiarity of the tone, is nothing compared to the envy I feel. I conclude, out of spite, perhaps, that if he wants to talk, *he* can phone *me*.

I reach the final classroom in Randy Land and hear his vacuum come to a stop. The silence breaks abruptly owing to his heated voice: "College-educated idiot."

I attempt to sneak past the room without his noticing, but he spots me. He steps out of the classroom, vacuum in hand. I stop so as not to come across as rude or arrogant.

"Ooops." He laughs like a hyena. "Did I say that out loud?"

I face him, the man of sixty who never grew up. His eyes are bloodshot, his peppered-gray hair slovenly and greasy. I make solid eye contact, despite my desire to turn away from his leathery face. As long as I've known Randy, he's never—and this may or may not be an exaggeration—had anything genuinely nice to say about anyone. Frankly, he gets tiring.

"How are you?" I ask him.

"Been better." He puts the vacuum down on the carpet behind him, leans against the doorframe. "First it was you-know-what smeared over the walls in the boy's bathroom, and then it was this dumb teacher," he says, pointing over his left shoulder. "Come here. Take a look at this." He waves me into the room. "Where'd the idiot get her degree? A Cracker Jack box?" He chortles.

I inspect the carpet, speckled with numerous colors of glitter, from the doorway. "Another party, huh?" I say. This sight doesn't surprise me.

His nostrils puff out. "I vacuumed this rug twice. I ain't doin' it again. Forget that. They wanna throw crap all over the floor, then that's their problem!" His tone brims with fury. "It won't all come up." The veins in his neck are about to pop.

I defuse his anger by a change of subject. "The weekend isn't far. Thank goodness. Got any plans?"

He morphs from *Hulk* to normal, non-green, alcohol-lusting Randy. "Gonna have some friends over and get hammered." He smiles. "My type of weekend. Should be great."

No, Randy, not great. Awful. I work not to roll my eyes.

Randy nods at me. "What about you? Any big plans?"

I know what he wants to hear: *Oh, yeah, Randy, I'm gonna get sloshed, man. My type of weekend. Should be great . . .* but that isn't me, so I say, "I'm gonna do some writing."

He squints. "Still working on that book, huh?"

"Yeah."

"Who do you think you are—*Hemingway?*" He laughs derisively.

I don't find hilarity in his wisecrack. He's like Carrot Top, props absent—not the least bit humorous. That Hemingway reference is a great example of why I don't mention my writing as often as I'd like. I've told him about my desire to be published, to get away from the cleaning scene, but no matter what I say, he never takes it seriously.

Randy quickly puts on the I'm-just-playing-with-you/I'm-a-jerk look. "I better be nice to you," he says, "because you'll be signing my checks one day." He winks.

I want to shove my thumb in his eye. He knows that I don't want to take over Dad's business, but he offers me that line all the time—more proof that he doesn't think I have potential as a writer. I try not to take it personal, considering the source—a child in an alcoholic man's body. I glance down at my wristwatch. "Oh, man," sounding surprised, "I gotta go sweep the gym."

"Aight, bro," he says, then turns back toward the room, that glittery carpet, and mutters something.

"Catch you later," I say, but I'm thinking *I'm not your bro.* I walk away, turn a corner and sigh, continuing into the gym, where I grab the dust mop and begin to sweep the filthy floor.

Walking the dust mop up and down the court, I flash on my grandfather, the geezer who never had anything to do with me. Stan was his name, Dad told me, and he drank religiously. For the longest time, Dad used Gramps as an example.

"You don't wanna become like Gramps, do you?" Dad would say. "Alcoholism's in our blood. Stay away from the booze, James."

I never formally met my grandfather. According to Dad, I was a toddler when we saw him at his trailer. Dad told me about the deal he had made with Gramps. Dad and Mom would bring my sister and me to the trailer only if Gramps swore to stay sober for the visit. Gramps agreed. When we arrived, though, that one time, Gramps opened the front door drunk out of his mind, slurring his words. Dad was heartbroken. We didn't step foot in the trailer that day or any other. Dad continued to give Gramps ultimatums from time to time, but Gramps never admitted to a drinking problem and, thus, never stopped. He died six years ago, alone. A neighbor found his lifeless body sprawled across the couch, reeking of alcohol, with dozens of empty beer bottles on the rancid floor.

That was also about the time Dad turned into a hypocrite and took up drinking. As with any addiction, it started off slowly, virtually unnoticeable. One beer turned into two, which turned into three, which turned into four and five and six . . . I remember witnessing this downward spiral, watching Dad drain the cans on the sofa, at the kitchen table, on the recliner. I thought: *Alcoholism's in our blood. Stay away from the booze, Dad.* He was what some would call a "quiet drunk"—vacant stares and pure silence. It's no great wonder that his relationship with my mother fell apart and she left him. If he hadn't been so sly, and if the judge could have determined that my father was a drunk, I would have had no choice but to leave him, too.

Dad showed up at court in a neat suit, sober for once. He smiled a lot, spoke smoothly throughout the case. When asked about his drinking, he told the judge, "I have a drink here and there. Nothing overboard." In the end, the judge had no proof of substance abuse (even with my mother's testimony) or abuse on his family—Dad had maintained a solid work history and neither my sister nor I could recall our father hurting us—and so the judge gave us kids an option. When the judge asked me who I wanted to live with, the answer was simple: "Dad." When the judge asked my sister, she said, "Mom." The judge granted the divorce on grounds of irreconcilable differences, I've come to learn.

And so I understand why Randy bothers me. When I look and listen to him, I'm looking and listening to Gramps and to a younger, drunk and un-rehabilitated version of Dad. Randy's presence, although negative at times, is primarily a gift to remind me of what I don't want to become.

What I *never* want to become.

CHAPTER FIVE

It's midnight, the long work night behind us, and I sit at the kitchen table eating dinner—lasagna, garlic bread, corn—with Dad. Our house is small, a one-story modular home, two bedrooms, with a one-car garage. Basically a trailer on a cement foundation. This kitchen table doesn't actually reside in the kitchen. It sits on russet-colored carpeting next to the sliding door, underneath an unimposing chandelier, a few feet behind the couch. The couch acts as a barrier between the living room and the dining room. *Open concept* is the term, I believe.

I take a bite of lasagna, savoring the flavor, and look up at Dad, the maker of this meal. He raises a glass of soda toward me and says nonchalantly, "To sobriety."

I set my fork on the plate, lift my glass to his, say, "Cheers to that," and we clink our glasses of Coke together. I drink. He says, "Thanks to AA," and winks. He smiles, then drinks and puts his glass back on the table.

I have never attended an Alcoholics Anonymous meeting, but I feel like an expert on the matter. The Twelve Steps and the Twelve Traditions—I've heard about it all from Dad. He went to his first meeting a little over a year after the divorce, after he woke up one morning and realized that he had turned into his father. For several months, I knew nothing of his meetings. He would disappear every now and again and I would ask him where he went, but he wouldn't tell me. One evening, I came across some AA literature in the house. I confronted my father about it, and he broke down and wept. The big, buff man actually cried. Then he told me where he had been. "Alcoholism's in our blood. Stay away from the booze, James," he said. As of now, I am the only family member he has told about AA.

"Anything new with you?" In between bites, Dad initiates conversation.

I sit my fork on the plate. "Not really. Sam's gone, but you already know that."

Dad glances up at the clock on the wall over my head. "I gotta call Christy in ten minutes."

Christy is his new woman, his latest addiction. He has a fresh woman every time I turn around. He's gone from alcoholic to woman-holic. Last month, he dated Amanda. The month before, he dated Cindy. Ever since his divorce from Mom, he's been searching for the perfect woman . . . or for the perfect *something* to, once and for all, replace his nagging desire to drink. I've been told that most recovering alcoholics deal with the urge on a daily basis, regardless of how many years it's been since their last drink.

"She's really great." Dad brushes dark, graying hair away from his face. "We're hitting it off big time. It'll be interesting to see what happens."

I smile. This is how it always begins. She's great initially, then he gets to know her and realizes she's imperfect. *Wow, what a shocker.*

Dad pulls the fork from his mouth. "She works out four days a week," he says, chewing. "You should see her. She's *hot*." He smiles at his emphasis of the last word.

"Four days a week? That's good," I say, sounding impressed. I take a swig of soda, speak again. "Blonde or brunette?"

Dad leans back in his chair. "Wanna see a picture?" He pats his stomach once, an I'm-so-full pat, then folds behemoth arms over his chest.

I don't respond to his question right off. I feel like I have loads to tell him, but nothing I have to say ought to be discussed in a matter of a couple of minutes.

Dad notices my hesitation. "I can show it to you some other time." He glances at the clock again. A couple minutes remain in the Countdown to Call Christy. "Are you all right?" he asks.

I shrug. The tick of the clock emerges, reminding me of the passing of time. *Thirty, twenty-nine, twenty-eight, twenty-seven, twenty-six . . .*

I love my father. Always have. Always will. Unconditionally. Beneath his brutish exterior lies a tender heart. I know this because of the love he displays. For instance, this nice meal he prepared. I presume that when he said, "There's too much lasagna here for just me, so you can have some if you want," he was actually trying to say that he made the meal for the both of us, out of the kindness of his heart, out of the love he has for his son. I would like to believe that.

Twelve, eleven, ten, nine . . .

"I'd be lying if I said I'm not nervous," I finally say.

Six, five, four, three, two, one.

Dad's eyes gravitate toward the clock yet again. He fidgets in his seat.

Zero.

I continue to talk despite the time constraint. "The publishers and the agencies I sent my stuff to, I don't know what's gonna happen with them. The anxiety's killing me."

He dismisses my concern: "Ahhh, don't worry about it." He grins, reaching for his plate. Stands, plate in hand, and starts toward the kitchen.

I stand, my plate in hand also. I join him at the sink. "I can't *not* worry about it," I say.

Dad sets his plate in the sink. "I'm sure it'll be fine," he says.

I follow suit. "Hopefully." *Gee, Dad, thanks for the encouragement.*

"I need to go make my phone call, okay? Don't wanna keep her waiting."

"Okay. That's fine." Not really, but I say so anyways. "I need to go write some more."

"Why? Your book's done. Your baby's out in the world." He gradually backpedals out of the kitchen.

"A writer doesn't have a choice whether to write or not. A writer *has* to write, like a painter has to paint and a musician has to make music."

He tilts his head. "Interesting," he says, uninterested.

We go our separate ways. I go to my bedroom, my writing sanctuary, feeling like Dad isn't as supportive and enthusiastic as I'd like for him to be. I'm aware that, internally, I'm still a little boy yearning for Daddy's attention, for his love.

I sit at the desk in my room, lit only by a small lamp behind my back. Unmoving, I focus on the laptop, its screen. I wait impatiently, tapping a foot (like Sonic the Hedgehog) beneath the desk.

The file finally opens, my entire novel, the fruition of countless hours slapping at the keys of this worn keyboard. I stare at the text, marveling at my masterpiece, the piece of work I haven't laid eyes on for almost two weeks. As I read, the words seem foreign, like they could have been written by someone else. As I read on, entire paragraphs don't match up to my memory. For the first time, I'm able to look on this manuscript objectively, virtually unattached to the creature I created. My eyes dart left to right over the screen, word after word. *Smooth prose.* I read on. *Proper grammar.* I read further. *A fast-paced tale. Dynamic. Magical.* I continue to read for about an hour.

I stop at the end of a chapter, smiling inside and out. The characters are surprisingly three-dimensional, the dialogue succinct and meaningful. The settings are brilliant, believable, and otherworldly. *Nonstop action!* The scenes hang, forcing the reader to turn the pages. Suddenly, I'm a book reviewer.

I shake my head, chuckling. What am I worried about? Rejection and failure? *What if they don't like it? What if it's not good enough?* My mind flips to the literary agents and the publishers, the mysterious individuals. Doubts come in waves, but not one crashes on me now. Truth is: I'm pretty good at formulating a story.

There aren't many things that make me feel this way. Actually, I can't think of *anything* that makes me feel this way. Pride swells within me, love aimed at the living, breathing story I birthed. I imagine this is how other artists feel while they gaze at their finished work: paintings, songs, sculptures . . . I wonder how Robert Frost felt after he completed a poem.

The image of him sitting at his Morris chair comes into focus. His face carries a beaming smile. He crosses his arms, pen on the writing board beside his written-on piece of paper, and he knows. He doesn't think or hope what he's written is quality. He knows.

I'm glad I submitted this novel to those bigwigs in New York. Even through all my insecurities, I know now I made the correct decision. I've always worried about the questions, *What if they don't like it? What if it's not good enough?* Currently, I think this instead: *What if they* do *like it? What if it* is *good enough?* The positive spin I choose to take. I *will* hear back from those agents and publishers, each with their own rendition of "I love your novel."

The smell of lasagna wafts by my space, tapping at my memory. I glance at the blank wall above the screen and flash on dinner, then on Dad, and his face, his well-groomed goatee, elongated nose, and saddened brown eyes. He was a talented baseball player, an all-star in each league in which he participated. He could have gone somewhere with baseball, maybe the big leagues, but he quit. He withdrew because he didn't believe he was good enough.

Every time he watches baseball, I see pain etched in his face, the anguish of an abandoned dream. He'll never get his prime baseball-playing years back. One can't reverse time. I see where he is now, the owner of a janitorial company, and I never want to be him. His situation motivates me to go at this writing gig with full force.

Dad's face fades away, and my laptop's screen comes into focus. My father will scrub toilets, mop floors, and vacuum carpets until the end of time, I'm convinced. So, I'm not just glad I sent my manuscript to those agents and publishers, I'm *extremely* glad. I'm not my father. We aren't the same.

* * *

Another night at the school.

I take my fifteen-minute break. I'm eating a package of crackers when Randy joins me in the hallway, a Diet Pepsi in his hand. He asks, "How was your weekend?"

"Good." I prepare myself for his stories.

Sure enough, before I can even ask him about his weekend, he goes off about the party he hosted at his house and how the cops had to get involved because one of his friends hit another one and blah, blah, blah.

I keep eating my crackers. About five minutes go by, and he abruptly changes the topic, not uncommon for him, the alcoholic with a short attention span. "Anything exciting happen for *you?*" he asks.

I think of laughing because he's totally implying that he finds it exciting that cops showed up at his house because they needed to break up a fight. "I wrote a lot," I say finally, knowing that's not what he wants to hear.

"You really believe in that, don't you?" He looks surprised, like the concept is something new.

I nod. "I wanna get out of here."

Randy drinks from his can. "I wouldn't get your hopes up too high," he says.

"Huh?" His insensitivity shocks me, even though it shouldn't by now.

"Us common folk don't read much anymore," he says.

Speak for yourself, Randy. "A lot of people read . . ."

I think I can read his mind, and it says, *Well, none of my friends do, bro,* but then his words don't match my telepathy: "Just don't believe *too* much." His statement leads me to think that at some point, he trusted in something but that *something* didn't work out.

Then I think: *Is there such a thing as believing too much?* And I don't want anything to do with this exchange anymore, so I say, "Well, I need to get back to work," putting an end to this encouraging (not!) conversation.

We separate. I return to mopping the mucky hallway floor, and I begin thinking about the unexpected voicemail messages I recently received from Erica, her all-too-familiar perturbed tone. Apparently, she's upset because I haven't written to her since the day in Sam's dorm. It seems she thinks I forgot how badly she treated me when we were together—the lies, the verbal abuse—and now she wants to be my friend. I wonder about her motive. Presumably, loneliness, a condition that can make a person carry out practically anything. In my case, even contemplate befriending a girl who mistreated me.

Twisting the mop back and forth over the floor, I decide not to waste my time with her. I'm lonely. Sure. My friends are gone. I have nothing but an absent father, a couple mentor-like friends, and the ability to write. The latter is enough to keep me away from Erica.

I dunk the mop in the soapy bucket, wring the mop out, plop it back onto the floor, and begin, once again, to clean. I still haven't heard from Sam, the brother of mine. I'm losing hope in our friendship. Perhaps this relationship *is* like all the others: The person leaves and whatever we had fades.

Time will tell.

* * *

After work and dinner (which I prepare and eat solo), I knock on Dad's bedroom door and ask him if he would be up to listening to me read my novel. I hear him sigh from the other side of the door. I hear footsteps approaching, then they stop at the door. I hear the door handle jiggle. I watch Dad open the door inward. He's wearing boxers and a sleeveless shirt.

"Can't you read to me tomorrow?" he asks sternly.

Standing at the door, I say, "But you always ask that and it never ends up happening."

He glances at the computer behind him. "I'm in the middle of something."

"You're always in the middle of something," I say, and I wonder if he stays busy on purpose because my dream of getting away from cleaning is too threatening for him to handle. I hope that's not the case, but his lack of interest sure makes me feel like he doesn't want me to succeed. After all, in his mind, it wouldn't be fair, would it? Years and years of scrubbing toilets and his son gets to walk away from it all in a fraction of the time . . .

Dad looks at his computer once more. "I need to get back. Christy's waiting for me."

The next day, I ask, once again, for a few minutes of Dad's time, but he turns me away, says that he has things to do, that it will have to wait. I settle on never asking him again.

Never, ever again.

CHAPTER SIX

I sit up in bed, smiling, just in time to witness the morning sun slip through my window. Last night showed great promise. The dull, uneventful life I've grown accustomed to changed directions. I was on MySpace.com when I came across an attractive profile of a woman by the name of Leigh. From the looks of things, she was the complete opposite of Erica. Different hair and eye color. Different energy surrounding the posted words: language of kindness and gentleness, not of hatred and anger. Naturally, I messaged Leigh. Amazingly, she messaged me back. She said she liked what she read and saw in my profile. She wants us to talk soon.

Scary? Yes. Exciting? Yes. Scary because I may have received a message from some murderer. Exciting because if the message actually originated from a woman named Leigh, who created that nice profile, and who looks like that person in the provided photo, then I could be onto something great.

Every part of me wants to believe she's real.

* * *

Unfortunately, I still haven't received a response from any of the agents or from the publishers. Life goes on. I continue to breathe, to eat, to shower, to poop, to shave, to work, to write. To survive.

I finally crack and call Sam. He doesn't pick up. I stay on the line to hear his outgoing message. I feel ridiculous, like a teenage girl who can't get over a break-up. I don't leave a message. I'm beginning to let go. Sam's new life takes precedence. Time is telling.

I check MySpace nightly to see if Leigh, or the person posing as her, is signed on, but her status shows OFFLINE. I feel alone in this world, the trite reclusive writer. Who am I kidding? Leigh can't be real. Good things can't just fall into your lap. Attractive women don't treat me nicely, they look strangely at me and say words like "Are you kidding me?"—"Do I know you?" They think they're superior to this gaunt, tooth-decayed freak. Mutely, I concur.

* * *

Wow, I'm pathetic. I sit at my laptop on yet another night, waiting for Leigh, the specter, to sign on. The average person, the conformist, would go to a bar or a club to meet a woman, but where do I go? To a Web site. Yes, that's right. Unconventional Man himself. Complete with cape, spandex, and padded crotch region to accentuate my manhood.

My patience wears thin and I sign off. Saturday night and I'm home. My dad, on the other hand, is out on a date. Something wrong with this picture.

I'm going to sign on one last time and if she's not online, then forget it.

To my surprise and delight, when I sign on this time, I notice a message from Leigh in the inbox, an apology for zero communication. She says she feels bad and would really like to get to know me as soon as possible. She includes something I never expected: her screen name for AIM.

I open AIM and add her screen name to my buddy list. She appears online, ready to chat, ready to embark on this possible relationship. In the back of my mind, I still have doubts about her legitimacy.

The conversation begins the way most do; we discuss family, hobbies, religion, and politics. She seems genuine; the information she offers doesn't feel phony. She has a brother, a dog, her parents are still married, she's twenty-three-years-old and still living at home. She plays the piano for the Baptist church she attends. She's one of those Christian girls. Not necessarily preachy, from what I can tell, but Christian nonetheless. Something about how openly she mentions Jesus' name causes me to feel uncomfortable. She refers to him as though they are friends. One would think they have daily discussions. I know the historical Jesus existed, believe that much is true, but I don't know him. I've never seen him. We are not friends. He's a ghost to me.

Furthermore, Leigh enjoys Bush. And I don't mean shrubbery. She likes *President* Bush, the talking Chimpanzee. Talk about your conventional Christian. The man declares himself Christian and suddenly every Christ follower in this so-called Christian nation thinks he's the best thing since sliced bread. Okay, it's been established that Leigh and I are very different people. I'm not a Christian. I can't play the piano, and I don't attend church. I think Bush is a pretentious, spoon-fed, power-hungry bully. My parents are divorced. I don't have a brother or a dog. It seems our common ground is that we both live at home and we both eat, breathe, work, and live.

She is certainly nothing like any of the girls I've known. Her face isn't green and she doesn't have a long, protruding nose, and she doesn't ride a broomstick. In the past, I would have steered clear of anyone like Leigh, but I'll give this a try. I'm not stupid enough to do the same thing over and over again and expect different results.

From out of nowhere, she announces her bedtime. She proceeds by typing: *It's been nice talking to you. Let's make sure to do it again sometime soon.*

I respond: *Yeah, sounds like a plan.*

Then she does something earth-shattering—she supplies her cell phone number and types: *Give me a call tomorrow night. It'd be nice to hear your voice to make sure you're for real.*

I chuckle, Ringo tapping at my heart like it's a drum. *Leigh* wants to know that *I'm* for real?

I type: *Tomorrow night it is.*

We swap farewells. Excited, blood filling my head, I dash to my cell phone, flip it open, and enter her phone number as a new contact. For once, I have something to look forward to, a glimmer of color in my world.

* * *

Sunday night. The three-quarter moon casts a silvery glow over the porch. I lean my left elbow on the railing, right hand at eye level, gripping the cell phone, trembling. I stare into the lit screen of my phone, contemplate not calling, but decide it's only right to follow through. With the push of a button, I dial her number.

One ring.

Two rings.

Three.

Four.

"This is Leigh." The voice of an angel, tender and soothing to my senses, floats through the cell.

Those three words help me to discern her authenticity. My hand shakes, sweating. "This is James." I take a deep breath.

"Oh, hello, James!" Her tone reveals excitement, stunning me. "I hope you don't think I'm crazy," she says.

"Why would I think that?"

"Because I threw my number at you," she responds. "I don't do that for just anyone. You've gotta be special."

She obviously wants to make sure I don't perceive her as easy. "So what makes me special?" I ask, curious.

"Most guys online, they only talk about sex. You don't seem like that type." She pauses. "And, not to mention, you write for fun. Now if that isn't original, I don't know what is."

I feel my face redden. "Well, thank you." This a refreshing experience. Friendly, attractive women do exist!

"I wasn't sure what to expect," she says, "but I like your voice."

"Really? I can't stand the sound of myself." I laugh nervously.

She chuckles. "Come on now. You sound like a sweetheart."

We continue with small talk for a couple more minutes. Compliments fly every which way. My suffering self-esteem receives a mild boost. Every time she sends praise my way, though, a piece of me can't accept it. *She wouldn't treat me nicely if she were to meet me*, I surmise.

We transition into a discussion about her religion. She asks if I am Christian. I tell her I'm not. She gives a cursory glimpse of salvation: "Everyone falls short of the glory of God. We're all sinners," she elaborates, "but because Jesus died for our sins, we can be cleansed from those sins through his death. All we have to do is repent and accept him as our personal savior."

Jesus undoubtedly means a lot to Leigh. I still experience discomfort with her mentioning his name so liberally, but I think I understand now why she does. She's testing the waters. She wants to know if I have an open mind and heart toward Christianity. Consciously, I don't furnish any clues.

We move gradually to another topic. Work. She has two employers; the first, a prestigious advisory group and the second, a management company that runs local hotels and inns. I listen attentively throughout her spiel, give my two cents where appropriate, hand over the occasional "uh-huh" to let her know I'm still on the line, awake, listening. All the while, anticipation throbs in my throat. Before long, she'll want to know about my job, for sure. This thought presses on me, creating a knot in my stomach. The last piece of information on earth I want her to know is that I work for Dad's janitorial company.

I tell her about my fantasy novel, that I sent it to publishers and literary agents for review.

"Great, James," she says, impressed. "That shows a lot of devotion and persistence on your part."

I thank her. Then, unexpectedly, she goes off on a tangent about her lazy ex-boyfriend. She says she desires a man with a more diligent work ethic. "You don't sound lazy," she says, "and that's good news."

Throughout the next half-hour, I discover, while extra vigilant, that her friends no longer live close by. Suddenly this situation makes increased sense. She and I have more in common than I once thought. We're both friendless and yearning for companionship.

A tad over three hours into our exchange, our comfort level rising, she finally launches her version of the dreaded query: "I know you write, and that's awesome, but what do you do to pay the bills?"

A dishonest approach pops into mind—*tell her you work construction*—but the heart directs me away from a deceitful answer. I reveal the truth, bracing myself: "I work for my dad's janitorial company."

She doesn't laugh, chuckle, mock, or ridicule; instead, she seems interested, "When did he start the business?"

I think about her question at length. "About a year after I was born."

She pauses.

Nerves set in.

She laughs, but not at me. "My dad started his business about a year after I was born, too. Can you believe it?"

We lose ourselves in laughter, then she says, "This has been great, James. I haven't had a conversation like this in a long time. Can you believe we've been talking for almost four hours? I've gotta get some sleep."

"It went by too fast," I say, aching for more. "What would you say about meeting up sometime? In public, of course," I blurt. *Was that too aggressive? Don't wanna scare her.*

She doesn't shy away. "I think our best bet would be to give it about a week of, you know, talking and see where it goes from there."

Right. You wanna make sure I'm not an ax murderer . . . "Sounds good to me." I pause, taking in the moment. "It's been great, Leigh. Let's keep in touch."

"We will."

CHAPTER SEVEN

Gazing into her photograph online, I can't believe she agreed to meet with me today, after only five days of conversing. Her long, flowing brown hair, friendly coffee-tinted eyes, and glowing smile will no longer be visible through a mere picture on the Internet. In three hours, she will stand before me, marvelously palpable. Bernard's, a fairly well-known eatery in her hometown, Troftonfield, is the site where we will come face-to-face.

I close my laptop, the matchmaking device, and begin to pace around the house, full of anxiety and excitement. Dad's out on another date, I have been seemingly disowned by Sam, for unknown reasons, and Donovan is virtually unreachable, as busy as he is, so I have to keep these feelings to myself.

What will I wear? I think.

I mosey into my bedroom, open the closet door, and stare at the worn and tatty clothing. I think of Fred, the college guy, oddly enough, his apparel of great splendor. Truthfully, I wish the closet looked different, brimming with Ralph Lauren and Tommy Hilfiger. One will not find any brand names in this mockery of a closet. No way. I pick out a pair of no-name jeans, shake my head at the pitiable garment, and toss it on the floor. I reach deeper in and grab a pair of hole-ridden khakis, the only pair I own, and chuck them as well. For a solid half-hour, I rummage through the rest of my clothing. I come to the last clean outfit I own, a *Superman* shirt and carpenter jeans, and decide I have no choice. I visit the bathroom, gripping the outfit, where I strip from my pajamas and stand nude in front of the mirror, scrutinizing my deplorable body. I'm exceedingly skinny. I can barely look at my stick-thin arms, my underdeveloped chest (am I twelve?), the paleness of my body (am I albino?), and, of course, my rotted teeth (is my name Billy Bob?). I want to peel out of this sallow skin, find a body I halfway enjoy, and live in it. Metaphorically, of course.

* * *

I am clean, dressed, and away from the mirror. I check my watch. I have to leave for Bernard's in an hour. What to do? What to do? My car needs cleaning. I go outside with a trash bag, meet up with the rust box, and collect candy wrappers and empty soda bottles from the passenger's-side floor. I move to the back seat and set off on the same process until all the trash lies in the bag.

I take a step back from the vehicle, bag in hand, and sigh. The interior is spotless but the rest of the car is still a mess, forlorn. Unfortunately, in this society, cars disclose status. When I pull up to Bernard's in this *thing*, Leigh will develop a different impression than if I were to drive up in a Mercedes or a Beemer. BMW and Benz equal success. Dilapidated, pig-squealing Escort means failure. I don't need to add wrappers and bottles to the first impression.

I flash on children laughing and wrinkling their noses at my car, and I can see Leigh doing the same. She turns her cheek and says, "This was a big mistake. I didn't know you were so unsuccessful—and dirty!"

I shake off that reverie, pondering. Leigh doesn't strike me as superficial. She knows what I do for a living. She can't expect me to appear at Bernard's in a Benz. I need to think positive. I must leave in a half-hour.

I tie the bag and stride toward the house.

* * *

Upchucking butterflies fly inside my stomach as I drive away from the house, thinking of meeting with Leigh. I pull to the end of our road and open our mailbox. Mail is stacked inside, bound by an elastic band. I reach in the box and remove the pile. I riffle through the load. Credit card offers. Bills. Flyers. Then I spot a disparate piece of mail. The envelope bears the insignia of a publisher to whom I sent my manuscript. Slack-jawed, I throw the rest of the mail on the passenger seat and drop the publisher's envelope on my lap. For ten seconds that seem eternal, I mull over the options. To open, or not to open. Heart racing, I choose to remove the letter from its home and unfold the stationery. My hands shake as though palsied. I read the publisher's handwritten response:

Dear Mr. Frost,

Thank you for sending me chapters from The Forsaken World—*you certainly are very creative! Regretfully, though, I must say that the manuscript seemed a bit overwritten, and I will have to pass on this project.*

Beth Cinder
Editor

I'm shocked. *What have my eyes seen?* I look down at the text and reread to confirm that the largest, most exalted publishing company in the world has rejected me. They're not busting down my door to publish my tome and they're not leaving glorifying messages on my answering machine. Anger, flaming in all its fury, replaces the previous numbness.

My manuscript is overwritten? What is that supposed to mean? Overwritten. What was overwritten about it? *The Forsaken World* isn't like some of the drivel I see on bookstands these days, the books that try to find meaning in a snowflake or describe in excruciating detail settings that could easily and more effectively be explained in a couple quick sentences.

In this incensed state, I shove the letter in its envelope and throw it onto the passenger seat with the other mail. I feel like I've been attacked. I've never met Beth in my life. Never seen a picture of her, so I don't even know what the woman looks like, but I loathe her entirely. I spent an innumerable amount of hours on *The Forsaken World*, draft after draft, hour after hour, week after week, month upon month, and with one quick decision on her part—which probably took her all of ten minutes, if that—I'm stuck with a dagger in my chest. Perhaps it's good that I don't know what she looks like, this way I have no image to wrap my rage around, just a name.

I try to shake the fury by busying myself as soon as possible, shifting the car into gear, but to no avail: I remain horribly angry. I let the car roll away from the mailbox. Steaming inside, I drive down the road, gripping the steering wheel so tightly that I almost lose circulation in my hands.

"WHAT DID I DO TO DESERVE THIS?"

I press down harder on the accelerator, going twenty miles over the speed limit, body tense.

"But I worked so hard!"

Without much thought, I abruptly pull to the side of the road. Sorrow replaces anger. My heart is heavy in my chest, raw and aching, and I think of Leigh. How in the world will I go through with our meeting? What will I say if she asks how I'm doing? *"Well, Leigh, honestly, I'm having a horrible day. I just got rejected by the biggest publishing company around, which shows you that I officially suck at writing. Now what do you think of me? Still wanna get to know this person who cleans for a living?"*

Maybe I should turn this car around.

I shake my head. *No.*

I get back on the road and start driving once again. I should stick with my plans to meet Leigh today. It would be tacky to stand her up. I fight the urge to go home and isolate myself.

CHAPTER EIGHT

I sit in the parking lot at Bernard's for a couple minutes, trying to fake myself into an improved mood, so as not to appear angry and downtrodden in front of Leigh in this preliminary meeting. I understand the importance of first impressions, and I don't want her to regard me as an emotionally fragile weakling with a short fuse.

Outwardly calm and composed, I step out of the car and enter the restaurant, forcing a smile.

The hostess greets me immediately. "Smoking or non?" she asks.

I give the room a quick scan. Leigh is nowhere in sight. The first thought that pops into mind is *I've been stood up*. My fake smile fades. A no-show, now that would be the icing on the cake.

"Umm . . . I think," I stumble over my response, "I mean . . . I'm meeting someone here."

"Oh," says the hostess. She turns and nods at a booth at the far end of the room. I hadn't noticed the booth. The hostess asks, "Is this person you're meeting a woman, and does she have long hair, and is your name James?"

I squint at the backside of who I suspect might be Leigh sitting at the booth. "Yeah. Long hair, and a woman, and the name's James. How'd you know?" I ask.

"I've been informed." She winks. "Right this way, please." She motions me forward. Guides me to the booth, where she drops me off and says, "You two enjoy your meal. Your waiter will be with you shortly."

I'm taken aback by Leigh, and I forget to acknowledge the hostess. In person, Leigh encompasses all the beauty of her photograph and much more. Her brown hair flows like rippling waves down to her mid-back, her eyes welcoming and innocent.

"Hey, James," she says excitedly, standing.

"Leigh, right?" I extend a hand toward her.

She seizes it and shakes. "I hope you don't mind; I wanted to get us a good seat."

"This is great," I say. We sit in opposite ends of the booth.

"So how was your ride?" she asks, her eyes examining me. "It wasn't too long, was it? I kinda feel bad having you come all the way out here."

"Honestly," I say, "it went by quickly. Just one big blur, really." I forge a smile.

She tilts her head. "Are you all right?"

Oh, no. The feared question. "Umm . . . truthfully, I've been better. It's nice finally meeting you, though. I've been looking forward to this."

"So why have you been better?" She leans in. "I'm a good listener. Try me." She wears a concerned look.

She's gonna think I'm a loser. "Remember how I told you that I sent my book to a bunch of publishers and literary agents?"

"Of course," she says, nodding. "Hear back from any of them yet?"

"Actually, yeah, I did, and that's why I could be better."

"Bad news, huh?"

"Today, one of the biggest publishing companies in the world rejected me. I was hoping they'd want to take my manuscript on, but I guess they didn't think my novel was good enough."

"Bummer." She frowns, then brightens. "But you have all those agents that could respond with good news, right? This is just one publisher . . ."

"True." She makes some sense here, but I remain depressed. *Woe is me.*

"I bet you're an awesome writer. I wouldn't let this bring you down."

"Thanks, but I don't feel like an awesome writer at the moment." I shake my head. "Look at this, I'm bringing *you* down. . . . I'm sorry. Enough about me."

"No, no. You're not bringing me down. I told you, I'm a good listener. This is obviously a big deal for you, and I respect that."

I smile. "Tell me about your day," I say.

"Mine certainly can't compare to yours," she says. "It was very uneventful. Did a lot of cleaning around the house."

I don't intervene. I want her to keep talking, to take the spotlight off me and my situation.

"I spent some time earlier studying the Bible," she says.

I fall into my own little world of misery. The best I can do is sit here and nod, fake involvement in this conversation. In reality, I only catch a few stray words here and there, like "End Times" and "Jesus." I think this is her way of reiterating her faith. Or maybe she's trying to make me feel better. Not sure what her intention is, to be honest. She may be trying to show me that life could be worse.

I guess it could.

* * *

From what I remember, the rest of the meal was rather monotonous, although, I might feel that way because I was in a daze. I have the hardest time remembering, in detail, what we even discussed.

Now we're in Leigh's car, a black Eclipse in pristine form, definitely an upgrade from my piece of junk on wheels. I'm relieved. I won't have to expose her to the Decrepit Mobile. The opportunity won't arise for her to laugh at my vehicle or wrinkle her nose. Not today.

She glances at me. "Have you ever been to Weirs?"

I pull away from my thoughts, turn to face her where she sits in the driver's seat. "Once, I think, when I was little kid," I say.

"You'll like it." She smiles, as though she knows something I don't.

"I'm sure I will." I go to smile in return but remember my teeth, so I offer a non-tooth-bearing smile.

"What type of music do you enjoy?" She reaches her hand toward the radio and turns it on.

"Sarah McLachlan's good. So is James Blunt, Sting, and Howie Day."

Leigh nods in consent. "I just went to see Howie Day. He was great live."

My interest piques. "You *went* to that concert? Are you kidding? I was gonna go to that concert."

"Really?"

"Yeah, really. I just couldn't find anyone to go with." *Can I sound any more pathetic?*

She grins, revealing her white, unstained teeth. "I went alone," she says. "I couldn't find anyone to go with me, either."

I chuckle. "Geez, too bad we didn't meet sooner. We could've had a great time."

"Yeah, that would've been fun," she agrees.

"Do you think if I went alone, we would've bumped into each other?" I ask.

Her face scrunches, thinking. "Do you believe in fate?"

"If what you mean by fate is destiny, yeah, I believe in fate."

She checks her rearview mirror. "I think if two people are meant to meet, they will. Somehow, in one way or another, they will."

* * *

I have no prior memories of this place called Weirs. As Leigh and I amble side by side, an arm's length apart, I take in my surroundings for the first time. Gift shops, arcades, jewelry outlets, and eateries encase us. Dusk has arrived, so the lights from the arcade glow extra brightly. The moon peeks through the clouds, sending slivers of light over the road and the nearby buildings.

Leigh and I cross the road and arrive on the boardwalk, wooden slabs adjacent to a railroad track, which appears to stretch over the full length of the beach. In the distance, the lake gleams beneath the moon. Beyond the water, outlines of numerous nondescript mountains poke the dimming sky.

"It's beautiful, isn't it?" Leigh waves a hand at the glistening lake.

I nod. "Thanks for bringing me here."

She pats my arm. "Are you doing okay?" Her tone shows her concern.

"I'm here with a beautiful woman, walking along the boardwalk. I'm—"

"Sad, aren't you?" she asks. "I can feel it."

"How'd you—I mean—I'm not sad about being with you. I'm glad we met. It's just the whole rejection thing."

"Follow me," she says. "There's some place I wanna take you."

I trail her to the middle of the boardwalk, to a set of wooden stairs. We walk down the steps, end on a small footbridge with built-in seats. Anchored boats line either side of the bridge.

"Have a seat." She signals to the wooden bleachers.

I sit on a hard plank, as does she, across from me, and I say, "You're a good person for trying to cheer me up."

She blushes and shrugs. "I do my best."

We sit in silence for a long minute. The breeze picks up and blows over us. Distant lights, with the addition of the moon, illuminate this space enough for me to see her smile.

I finally break the silence. "I'm not sure what I'm gonna do next. Part of me thinks I should do another rewrite, but another part can't fathom doing that. It's times like this when I really doubt myself. Maybe I should give up on writing altogether, pick up some other hobby. Something that isn't this arduous."

"And why would you do that?" Leigh asks. "You love writing. That's obvious. You wouldn't write an entire book if you didn't love it."

I pause, get a little choked up. "I gave everything to this novel. Everything." I look down at the wood, shaking my head. I want to explode into tears, to release the anguish within. I can't, though. Not in front of Leigh. No emotionally fragile weakling here.

Silence falls over us yet again. I imagine Leigh doesn't know how to respond to my situation. Perhaps she can't relate, can't think of a time when she put every ounce of her soul into something, only to watch it fail.

I lift my head and notice she's walking toward me. She gives me a sweet smile and says, "Do you mind if I sit next to you?"

I shake my head. "Be my guest."

She fidgets in the seat until she finds a comfortable spot. Without warning, she subtly places a hand on my leg, right above the knee. I glance at the hand, pretending that this is normal, that I'm familiar with treatment like this, but internally I'm astonished.

"Everything's gonna be okay, James." Her voice calms me.

I look dazedly into her eyes, hypnotized, and something in them makes me believe, if even for a moment, that she's right.

CHAPTER NINE

It's been a day since Weirs. Last night, I couldn't get myself to talk with anyone, not even Leigh. Her comforting line didn't take long to wear off, and I spent the late hours lying in bed, feeling like a failure.

I know I should call her. Because of my lack of communication, she must believe I don't like her, that I didn't enjoy our time together. At the moment, I don't, unfortunately, have time to call her and say that I enjoyed meeting her and that I'd like to spend time with her again sometime soon. I know I should be ecstatic about this woman, but I can't feel overjoyed about anything, presently. Not after the news from the publisher.

I hope Leigh is who she appears to be. I don't want to come across any surprises: *Oh, by the way, James, I'm actually a dude. I underwent sex reassignment surgery from male to female last year and the name's really Kenny . . .*

Uh-oh. I need to leave for work in five minutes. I'll call Leigh on my break.

* * *

Vacuuming, I want to bomb this school. The building, not the people inside. Then I wouldn't have to work here anymore, since at this rate, I won't quit anytime soon because of a book contract.

Somehow, I need to continue plugging away with my writing and hope for the best with the literary agents and the other publishers. I've heard statements about letting go of anger, releasing it somehow, but how will I do that if I can't find closure with Beth, the editor who clearly thinks I'm not good enough to be published?

I know. I'll phone her at work. The publisher's phone number is on the rejection letter at the bottom of the page. I'll take some power back. I'll tell her she's blind to pass on *The Forsaken World*, that she'll kick herself for not scooping it up, especially when it becomes a bestseller in a couple years. Then I'll scream and yell at her for a couple minutes, tell her she's an idiot who doesn't know what quality fantasy is and that she should give up her job because she's no good at it.

I let out a sigh, finishing the vacuuming for this classroom. I would never actually call the publisher and harass the editor, but it feels good to entertain the idea. At least then I would achieve some sort of closure, and I'd have an easier time moving on. I suppose it's like the end of a relationship; you never want to walk away without making a closing statement, and part of you always wants to know why it didn't work out, what it was about you that didn't suit the other person.

* * *

For our second date, a week after our first, Leigh and I meet at a gas station—of all places—in a quaint town near Dad's house; it's the only landmark she knows around this area. She offers to use her car for transportation. I accept. We carpool to Portsmouth, engaging in small talk throughout the trip. We discuss the weather, the brilliant earth-warming sun, the approaching fall season, the forthcoming foliage. We chat about the seacoast, our current destination, and we both agree it's one of the most appealing sections of New Hampshire, with the Atlantic Ocean nearby, lighthouses, sandy beaches, and historic sites spread throughout.

"If I could choose any place in New Hampshire to live, it'd be on the seacoast," she says.

When we arrive in Portsmouth at Prescott Park, the sun is in the early stage of setting. We exit the car and begin our journey toward the center of the park. Along the way, we pass artists. Each of the four stands before his or her easel, brushing paint over canvas. Leigh and I hold hands, stop to watch the artists for a moment as they recreate, in paint, their subjects, the flowers planted in lines before them. Quietly, so as not to disturb them, Leigh and I express our amazement to one another regarding the talent of these people. Beyond those artists, young children take part in a game of tag around a small tree, smiling, sprinting as free spirits. Leigh and I smile. I tell her that's how I want to be. She says, "Me too, James. Me too." We keep walking. Beyond those kids, a family plays Frisbee over a lush grassy area, laughing. I tell Leigh that's what I want someday. She says, "Me too, James. Me too."

We continue exploring the park, walk by various benches (some border the adjacent roads, which are ornamented with historic homes, while other benches flank the neighboring body of water, the Piscataqua River, Leigh says, a river that empties into the Atlantic Ocean). We follow several walkways, take in the surroundings: trees, bushes, a child-sized whale statue, lampposts, a chain link fence before the water, a white Liberty Pole complete with the American Flag, a warehouse from the early 1700s. We arrive at the Formal Garden resplendent with roses, flowers, flowers, flowers, fountains, brick walkways lined with trees, white picket fencing encasing us, and more benches. Leigh takes out her camera, takes a few shots of a rose. I say, "You two must be related; you're both beautiful flowers." Leigh blushes.

We leave the park, walk up the road to a causeway with trees and lampposts and gazebos housing picnic tables and green and white benches on the point overlooking the Piscataqua.

"How's this spot?" Leigh asks, coming to a stop.

I step to the benches, eye the statue—a whale's tail with a human face—mounted on a boulder between the seats. The salty brine fills my nostrils. A breeze brushes over my face. Across the way, a mini

Golden Gate Bridge—only this one is green—stretches over the water. I think it's called the Memorial Bridge.

"This is beautiful," I say, sitting on a bench, eyeing the river.

Leigh sits next to me, hands on her lap, her silky hair blowing in a gentle wind. "I'm glad you like it," she says. "It's a very soothing area, a great place to clear your mind."

Sailboats, motorboats, big tankers, and a tour ship float by. Two tugboats are docked in the distance. Water on date one. Water on date number two. I see a definite underlying theme here. Leigh enjoys water. Lakes and oceans and rivers. Maybe she's an ex-mermaid.

"How'd you know about this place?" I ask.

"My friend and I came here last year, before she got married and was swept away." She hangs her head. For the first time, I see her down.

"You don't see her anymore?"

She sighs, looking out at the water. "Once in a great while we'll get together. We go out for coffee or whatever. It's different now that she's married. It's like everything we had went away once she put that ring on her finger. Her husband's her number one these days."

I almost choke on saliva. "You sound like me. I can *totally* relate to that. College is Sam's number one nowadays. I haven't heard from him since he left for school."

She slides closer to me on the bench and rests her head on my shoulder. "What would you say your number one is?" she asks, looking up at me with kind eyes.

"Writing, I guess. It's what I've put the most time into. What's yours?"

"God. I mean, take a look around. Look out there." She points to the water. "How could you not want the one who created that to be your number one?"

"That's a good point." I watch a blue heron walk along the shore. "I've never thought of it that way."

"Look up at the sun," she points to the diminishing sphere, "and know God created that, too. He's someone who deserves to be up on a pedestal."

A compliment comes to mind, and as corny as I feel for thinking it, I take the thought one step further and actually say it: "All I need to do is look down at your face, and know God created that, too," I say. "*That* makes him someone who deserves to be up on a pedestal."

She blushes and smiles with her pearly whites. "Do you really mean that, or do you say that to all the girls?"

I smile, revealing teeth. "I meant every word," I say, self-conscience, naked in a way. "The sun's nothing next to you," I continue, wrapping an arm around her, bringing her closer. A brief wind sweeps over us, and I catch a whiff of her perfume, an aroma pleasant as fresh flowers. Cliché, yes. But it's true. She really does smell like flowers. I'm guessing she's probably a regular customer at Bath & Body Works. Maybe next week she'll smell like fruit.

She holds my hand. "I'm glad we have each other," she says.

Her statement echoes in my mind. "Me, too," I respond. I feel at peace, somehow or another temporarily healed from her touch, her presence. The power of a goddess, if there was such a thing. Inside, I chuckle. This gorgeous woman, this angel—she likes me? I don't deserve this girl, but I'll take her. I glance down at her tranquil face. I feel like the luckiest man on the face of the earth, a healthy Lou Gehrig.

In silence, we watch the sun slip beneath the pink horizon, listening to the sighs of waves, and to the calls of distant seagulls.

* * *

Today, I'm working on optimism, on accepting the circumstances. I was rejected by one publisher. Just one. As painful as it has been, it could be much worse. I might not have met Leigh. I could have been rejected by each of the people to whom I submitted my work. I wasn't cast off by the lot. I'm grateful for that. I'm also thankful for last night at the bay, and before at Weirs, the serene lake, both occasions with the most accepting woman I've ever known.

Infatuation for Leigh, everything about her, her smell, her smile, the way she sees me for me and doesn't judge, has bestowed upon my mind a new outlook. Hope. I'm hopeful life will improve. I could be jumping the gun, but I see Leigh and me going places, moving mountains with our relationship. Merely thinking about her fills my body with warmth. A sanguine sign? Yes. I never walk away from her emotionally drained or sapped in any way. She gives instead of taking. She edifies in lieu of putting down. From what I've seen thus far, she's wife material. I can't believe I'm envisioning this, but I can see her—and I'm aware this is totally chauvinistic and conventional, but oh well, it's my vision—in the kitchen with a cute apron over her busty frame, smiling as she cooks a large meal. I can see her taking care of me when I'm sick, bringing me saltines and soup, brushing a hand over my forehead, kissing me on the cheek. I can picture her touching me passionately. She caresses my back in a circular motion. She runs her hands through my messy hair. I imagine her holding a child, singing the kid a lullaby as he or she drifts into a peaceful sleep.

I must leave for work in twenty minutes. I still hate the job; loathe it, actually. But tonight I'm going to focus on the positive.

Leigh.

CHAPTER TEN

I tried to concentrate on the positive, I really did, but the event ten minutes ago has left me furious and shocked. I'm standing in the school's library, alone, fuming. I want to go out in the lobby and kick that guy's conceited butt. Not just for myself but for anyone who's ever been looked down on. More specifically any person who does janitorial work and has been degraded in front of others while performing the menial tasks assigned.

Some baldheaded guy with an upturned nose was throwing around a kickball with children in the lobby outside this library door. Seemed innocent enough in the beginning. Mopping the floor on the other end from where they were playing, I heard the guy and the children chuckle and joke with one another, their feet squeaking across the floor, the sound sneakers make on highly finished tile.

From out of nowhere, I heard hissing, the sound of movement. I lifted my eyes from the mop. The kickball greeted my face, creating a loud *smack*. I staggered, as anyone would. Almost fell over, in fact. A silent second passed, then I heard six bone-chilling words: "Don't worry, it's just the janitor."

I shook off the sting from the ball hitting my face and stood there, shock-numb, tilting my head at the adult. *Did my ears really hear that? Did he just demean me in front of those four kids?* I stared into his cold face, those flat, ungiving eyes. He must have seen my nostrils inflate and face redden because he gave the line that most people use to try to excuse themselves from so-called jokes: "I'm just kidding."

Flabbergasted, I could only respond with one word: "Okay." I could see in his eyes that he wasn't kidding. In his perception, I *was* just a janitor. He didn't take into consideration that I have a life outside of this school. He gave no thought to my feelings. I walked away, into this room, cursing under my breath.

Blood boiling, pacing around this book-filled room, restraining myself from going out the door and beating the living crap out of that haughty man, I think of the children. How did his words impact them? Prior to his statement, I would wager they wouldn't have looked at me any differently than they look at the rest of the people in the world, but I bet every time they see me from now on, they're going to remember: *it's just the janitor.*

As those children grow up, they'll encounter many other people who perform janitorial duties. Each of those workers will look the same to those kids, lesser, below them, practically inhuman. The kids won't know why they see janitors that way, but the prejudice will exist. And not just with janitors. Each time they see someone who gathers trash, it'll be: just the trash man. Whenever they see a man or woman working at McDonald's or Wendy's, it'll be: just the burger-flipper. Whenever they spot someone who collects money at a supermarket or a person who bags groceries, it'll be: just the cashier and just the bagger.

One day, they'll wake up as adults, with children of their own. They'll be walking with their kids in a school, and their children will accidentally run into a person carrying out janitorial chores. Then, as parrots, they will recite to their children a phrase they heard years prior, unaware of its origin: "Don't worry, it's just the janitor."

Children aren't born prejudiced. They don't hate. They don't degrade. They learn these things from society. This is one of the greatest tragedies in the world: the circle of prejudice.

Saddened, I come to a stop and sit at one of the tables next to a long stretch of bookcases. That bald guy outside this room, he doesn't know what he's done, doesn't comprehend the impact of his words. This is another one of the great tragedies in the world: ignorance.

I lower my head onto the table. *When will this world ever learn?*

* * *

I can see Leigh only once a week because of our conflicting schedules. Today, Saturday, we're going on our third date. This morning, I received an e-mail from Leigh. It said:

Dearest James:

I can't wait until you come over today. I want you to meet my parents; though, Mom might not be around when you arrive. Then I was thinking we could head to Mount Fleur and do some hiking.

I miss you!

Leigh

Naturally, I'm scared breathless. The seven most fear-instilling words in the dating dictionary—I want you to meet my parents—have been uttered. I'll try to be flattered by Leigh's request, but that won't remove my fear of saying something stupid or offensive in her parents' presence, and it will not, in any way, shape or form, absolve me from the fear that they won't approve of their daughter's new boyfriend.

I'm aware that her parents are fairly strict. Leigh has told me about her upbringing. They wouldn't let her date until she turned eighteen, and even then, she wasn't allowed any alone time with the guy of her choice. Now that she's twenty-three, they've become a little more lenient, but I'll make sure to be on my best behavior when I meet her parents. No swearing. Solid eye contact. Her parents will have to like a friendly, well-mannered man that their daughter brings home, right? I imagine they'll be relieved to see me standing at the front door instead of a pierced and/or tattooed biker dude named Skull.

Whatever I do, though, I can't mention my line of work in their presence, and I won't bring up my writing. From what Leigh has mentioned, her dad is an architect, so I guess her family is wealthy. The last piece of information I want to spill on Mr. Swanson would be that his daughter is dating a person who performs janitorial work as means of income, enjoys writing on the side, and wishes to be a published author one day.

I'm also aware that Leigh's parents are devout Christians, even more so than Leigh. The thought strengthens my trepidation. So far, Leigh has represented Christianity in a very good way. She doesn't judge. She doesn't think she's better than anyone else. No self-righteousness there. I recognize that she isn't an average Christian. She is different from any other Christian I've met. I hope her mother and father are just like her. If that's so, I know I'll get along famously with them.

Leigh gave me directions to her parents' house in another e-mail about an hour ago. I grab up the printed sheet, go out to my car, run a hand through my hair, and get into the vehicle. I sit there for a minute, taking exaggerated breaths to calm my nerves. I finally decide it's time to get rolling. On the ride to Leigh's house, I practice greeting her father and mother.

"Hello. Very nice to meet you."

Or . . .

"It's a real pleasure to have finally met you, sir and ma'am."

Or, my favorite . . .

"I'm so glad to have finally met the both of you. Leigh has told me so many great things about you."

Yes. I'll use the latter. Respectful, with a perfect amount of butt-kissing. They'll eat it right up. I hope.

I arrive at Leigh's house and park the car in their spacious birch-lined driveway. Through the windshield, I stare in reverence, jaw dropped, at the building before me. The white brick house lies in its surrounding blanket of emerald grass like a Sphinx, its four-columned two-story porches thrust out like paws, securing it to the earth. This is the home of an architect.

Suddenly, I'm extremely intimidated. I knew her parents had money, but this place borders on mansion status. Absolutely opulent. I'm even more impressed with Leigh now than I was before. One would never know she comes from this kind of wealth. Her clothing is nothing extraordinary. She doesn't wear any glamorous jewelry. She hasn't once discussed money in my presence.

I step out of the car, trying my hardest to stand tall, to fake out anyone who may be observing. The walk to the front of the house is a long fifty yards, give or take, up a pebble walkway with various flowers bursting on either side, past columns, to a large wooden door. Mahogany, I think? I swipe a hand through my hair, adjust the collar of my no-name polo shirt, and reach for the doorknocker. Before I can swing the knocker down onto the door, it opens, and Leigh appears from out of the shadows, arms wide open, smiling. "Hey you," she says playfully.

I mimic her by spreading my arms, and she slips into them. "It's good to see you, Leigh." As I begin to squeeze, I glance over her shoulder and see who I think is her father. Suddenly, I feel awkward and let go. I feel my face blush and see hers do the same as she turns to the man and says, "Daddy, I'd like for you to meet James."

He takes a step closer to the door and extends his right hand. I follow suit, and with our hands interlocked, he shoots a disapproving stare in my direction.

"James Frost. Nice to meet you," I say, unlike my rehearsal.

He releases my hand and waves me inside the house. "Come this way," he says. "I'll put on a pot of coffee."

* * *

"So, James, Leigh tells me you're in the cleaning business," says her father from a billowing chair near the picture window—the largest chair in the living room, his seat of superiority.

I slouch in the loveseat. "My father owns a cleaning business," I say, tone wobbly. "It's not the most glamorous type of work, but it's honest work, and it pays the bills." With widened eyes, I glance at Leigh, who's sitting to my immediate left, then turn my attention back to her father across the room.

He says, "I'm curious. What type of cleaning is it?"

I'm shrinking. I swear, I'm melting. I take a deep breath, swallow, and reply, "I clean carpets, floors, bathrooms. Toilets are my favorite." The last is an attempt at a joke, but he doesn't crack a smile. I see humor isn't his forte.

"Where is it that you clean?" he asks, folding arms over his chest.

I don't want to answer his question, but I can't ignore it. Lying isn't an available option either. I can't lie because Leigh is right next to me, and even if she wasn't, she almost certainly told him where I work, so a lie would only backfire.

Here goes nothing: "I clean at the school a few minutes from my dad's house."

He swipes a hand through his white-streaked hair. "Oh, then you're a janitor . . ." He rubs his scruffy chin.

"I don't necessarily see that as a fitting description, actually. Cleaning's what I do for work, not who I am. I'm much more than mopping and vacuuming and cleaning toilets. Like you're much more than building things."

"I see," he says in a stern tone.

Leigh speaks up. "James is a really good writer, Daddy. He wrote a novel and it's out with all sorts of people in the publishing industry. He's gonna get it published soon."

I turn to her, shocked; she hasn't even read any of my work. I see that she's trying to help me out of this predicament, but I'm not sure this is the route in which to travel.

"A novel, huh?" her father says, his eyes suspicious. "Not bad. What type of a novel is it?"

"Fantasy." I move my right arm onto an armrest, shaking slightly. "It's called *The Forsaken World*."

"Catchy title," he says, "but, generally, I find fantasy offensive."

"What about it offends you?" I ask.

"Does your book contain sorcery or magic of any type?"

"Yeah." I think I know where he's going with this.

"You're aware of the Bible's views on sorcery and magic, right?"

"I know the Bible doesn't find either particularly appealing, but I can assure you that the so-called sorcery and magic in my novel isn't real. I delved into ancient languages—Old Norse, for instance—and picked out words that I thought sounded mystical. Then I gave those words to my characters to use for magical spells. But a lot of the book—the beginning, for instance—doesn't contain any magical elements."

Leigh intervenes once again. "He's very creative, isn't he, Daddy?"

Her dad sighs. "James, if I might ask . . . what church do you attend?"

"I can't say that I attend church, sir."

"How unfortunate," he says.

I suppose tolerance isn't one of his strengths either.

* * *

Leigh and I have been on this hiking trail for about forty-five minutes. The wind is brisk. The sun's rays cut through the color-turning leaves overhead. Streams flow on either side of us, creating peaceful splashing and spraying sounds. A green sign in front of us says SUMMIT 0.5 MILES AHEAD.

She reaches out her hand. I accept it into mine.

"I don't think your dad likes me very much," I say. Not that it should matter to me, but for some reason, it does.

She turns to me as we continue to move. "He's not an easy man to please," she says. "I'm his daughter and I can't even please him."

"He's not pleased with you?" I sound as shocked as I feel. "How could any parent be unsatisfied with a daughter like you?"

She smiles. "This isn't anything new, James. It's always been like this, since I can remember," she says. With our hands intertwined, we hop over a couple small boulders.

Continuing at a steady pace, I say, "If *you* can't please him, I don't stand much of a chance. I mean, I'm sure there are things you do that he doesn't approve of, but you mostly obey his wishes, and he still doesn't find pleasure in having you as his daughter? Look at *me*. Strike one is my job. Strike two is my fantasy book. Strike three is that I don't attend church." We cross over a thin stream, hopping on rocks until we reach solid ground on the other side. I say, "I wonder if it'd be easier to get him to like me if I had a more celebrated job or if I knew more about Christianity . . . if I fit the image he has in his mind of the perfect guy for his daughter."

"He would be the first to tell you that there isn't a perfect guy for his daughter," she admits.

We come to the end of the trail, to the top of the mountain. Below us, thickets appear spongy, roads weave endlessly through the land, and buildings and houses look pin-sized. We stand hundreds of feet from civilization, miles from a discontented father who should bow before his perfect daughter.

His face haunts me. I say, "I wish that your dad would—"

"Forget about him for a minute, will you?" She smiles and wraps her arms around my torso.

I put my hands on her waist. "Okay."

She looks directly in my eyes. "I like you," she says, "and that should be all that matters."

For a short moment, we hang suspended in time, faces and bodies frozen. She is the most beautiful woman I have ever known, physically, mentally, and emotionally.

Her eyes, the way they smile, they tug at my heartstrings. I look down at her lips. Those soft, luscious lips. I long to feel them against my own. I can't suppress the urge any longer. I break the freeze between us and move my face toward hers, heart slapping against my chest.

I hope she's ready. I hope she wants this as much as I do.

She doesn't turn her cheek. She doesn't spot my mouth, the hideous teeth inside, and pull away. I'm in awe of this woman. Our lips connect, moist and soft. I walk my hands up her back, to her shoulders, to her hair, and I run them through her tresses as our kissing deepens. Our tongues touch and caress. Warmth surges through my body. Unparalleled warmth. She nibbles at my lower lip, tugs at it with her teeth. The embrace grows stronger.

Our lips part. She looks up at me, her eyes reflecting the sky. "Are you still thinking about my father?"

I smile wide. "You like me," I say, "and that's all that matters."

* * *

Sweeping this floor has never bothered me less. When I clean the bathrooms in a couple minutes, that won't stab at me either. After yesterday, the first kiss, nothing can. I've never experienced this level of infatuation. "In love" is another way to describe my current position.

My mind won't allow me to think of anything other than Leigh. I love her radiant smile. I love her eyes, and her long, soft hair. I love her touch, her smell, the feel of her lips on mine when we kiss. I love her skin, that olive skin. I love her voice, her body, those luscious curves. I love how she makes me feel. I love her accepting nature. I love the way her nose scrunches when she laughs.

The list goes on and on.

PART TWO

CHAPTER ELEVEN

It's Saturday again, and we lie entwined on a blanket at Troftonfield Lake, gazing up at the twinkling stars. Leigh's head rests on my chest, her hair pouring over my torso. My arms enfold her delicate body. There's a chill in the air.

She keeps her eyes on the stars. "What did you think of my mother?"

I reach for an answer. "I—uh—uh—" I sound like a chanting Indian. Meeting her skeletal mother fifteen minutes ago wasn't especially delightful. She didn't seem keen on getting to know me. At one point, while Leigh and I were getting ready to come here, I saw her mother roll her eyes. My guess is that Architect Guy spoke to her about Leigh's new boyfriend, my occupation, my fantasy-writing hobby. She wasn't impressed. That's ironic; I wasn't impressed with Leigh's mother either. Especially after what she said, with a smirk, when Leigh nibbled on a peanut butter cracker in the kitchen: "You keep on eating."

"Mom wasn't your cup of tea, was she?" Leigh asks. She rolls over onto her side, looking in my direction.

"Does your mother usually make remarks about your eating habits?"

"You mean does she usually crack fat jokes?" she asks.

I nod. We're on the same page.

Her eyes darken. "Yeah, plenty of fat jokes."

I grimace. "Doesn't that bother you?"

She shrugs. "Ah, I've gotten used to it."

"It doesn't affect you at all? I have a hard time believing that."

"I don't know if I'd go as far as saying that her words don't affect me. I try to ignore her when she shoots nasty comments my way."

"So you're saying she's been cracking jokes about your weight for a while now?"

"Oh, yeah," Leigh says matter-of-factly. "She's said she doesn't know where I got my body from, that I couldn't have gotten it from her. She's called me Porky and Piggy."

"I hope you don't buy that crap," I say. "You know you're not fat, right?"

She isn't. Not even slightly.

"I don't like my body. I wouldn't mind losing five to ten pounds. I'm too curvaceous."

"Too curvaceous? You've gotta be kidding me," I say, sitting up.

She sits upright. "When I was little, let's say ten or eleven, or somewhere around that age, whenever she saw me eating a cookie or any type of snack, she made sure to let me know that I disgusted her."

I shake my head at this nonsense. I want to go back in time and stand between Leigh and her mother. I would stare into her mother's narrow face, shake her by the bony shoulders, and say, "Do you realize what you're telling your daughter, the impact it's going to have on her?" Then I would say, "If you ask me, you're the disgusting one!" Afterward, I would let Leigh eat all the cookies and snacks she wanted. I would call her Princess. I would tell her she's perfect.

I snap out of the reverie, eyes on Leigh's shadowy face. Perhaps I can invalidate her mother's detrimental words. "You're beautiful," I say. "You're a princess. You're perfect."

"Thank you," she says. "Thank you."

Silence inhabits the beach.

After a minute, I ask, "What are you thinking about?"

Through the moonlight, I see her absently rub the side of her nose with a forefinger. "I'm not sure I should say. I don't want to paint a bad picture of my parents," she says.

I smile. "Too late. Now tell me what you're thinking."

"My parents promised to get me a cat," she says. "I was thirteen and they said if I got straight A's, they'd buy me one."

"What made you think of this?" I inquire.

She bites her lip. "Bitterness," she says. "They're so thoughtless sometimes."

"They didn't get you a cat, did they?"

Her jaw clenches. "Oh, they did. A stuffed cat, that is." Her eyes glisten in the moonlight. "They knew I thought they were gonna bring home a *real* cat. They laughed and smirked when I opened the box. I cried a lot that day."

I hug her. "I'm sorry. That's awful. They should never have done that to you."

She pulls her head away from my shoulder, looks up at me. "I'm going to miss you, James."

"What do you mean? I'm not going anywhere."

"*I* am." She looks at the blanket. "My parents and I are going to the Dominican. We've had a trip planned for about six months."

"How long will you be gone?" I ask.

Her face twists into a grimace. "Three weeks."

The news punches my gut. "Will we still be able to talk?"

She sighs, looks up at me. "My cell won't work out there."

"We won't be able to talk for *three weeks?*" I ask, troubled.

"You have to understand, when we first booked the trip, I didn't know you even existed. If I had known we were going to get together, I wouldn't have agreed to go." She pauses, her eyes thoughtful. "I can't back out now. My parents paid for my ticket. They'd be outraged, considering the circumstances, dropping them for a guy, and all."

"I understand, Leigh." *They paid for her ticket? I guess they are capable of treating her kindly.*

"I'd much rather stay here with you," she says. "I want you to know that."

"I'll miss you," I say. "I want you to know *that.*" I kiss her forehead, and she smiles.

* * *

Color is progressively disappearing from my world. Leigh has been gone for six days, unreachable in all forms. No visits. No phone calls. No e-mails. I imagine her sipping a tropical drink, walking along an endless beach, basking in the glory of the sun, and I want to be there with her. I want to lie next to her on a blanket, soaking in the rays, even though the sun would bite my pasty skin instead of kissing it. I want to wade in the ocean, even though I'm fearful of water. I want to stroll the length of the shore with my shirt off, even though I have the body of an undernourished boy, and I should never be shirtless. Of course, I want to do these things without her parents tagging along.

I think of Leigh's father, his unappeasable nature. I flash on Leigh's mother, her bitter remarks. I picture the three of them on the beach, walking, talking, and Leigh is having a miserable time.

"Your bathing suit is far too revealing, Leigh." Her father expresses his displeasure.

"A girl your size shouldn't be wearing a suit that small," her skinny mother says, smirking.

It is two-thirty in the afternoon. Dad's getting his car worked on, and I have the house to myself. I revel in the solitude of this space, writing. My fingers strike the keys of my laptop. This is my outlet. When I was younger, it was baseball—how good it felt to thump the ball with the meat of the bat and watch it soar, to run those bases unhurriedly as the ball fell over the fence, to throw a knee-buckling curveball, to strike someone out looking. Now it's writing—how good it feels to create an emotionally genuine scene, to infuse pieces of myself into the characters I've created and live vicariously through them, to be all-powerful and all-knowing.

It is three o'clock, and I decide it's time to get some fresh air. I throw on a flimsy jacket because it's breezy outdoors, then I step out, crunching through the fallen leaves of the front lawn. I arrive at the end of our driveway and resolve to go a tad further. Before I realize it,

I'm at the end of our road near our mailbox. Since pulling the publisher's rejection out of this box, I haven't been checking the mail, for fear of encountering a similar situation. Today, somewhat healed from that fateful day, I open the mailbox. As when I last checked the mail, I grab a stack of letters and bills and flyers. Unlike last time, however, there are two envelopes in the stack addressed to me. The envelopes bear the return addresses of literary agencies to whom I sent my work. I don't open them here; instead, I return to the house, mind racing.

What if they didn't like it? What if it wasn't good enough?

I step into the house and dart to the couch, where I sit, tossing Dad's mail on the cushion to my left. In my right hand, I hold the two envelopes. Hands shaking, I open the first one and read the letter, which states:

James,

Sorry, no thanks, not for me.

William Lochman

I set the paper aside, head wagging. "You've gotta be kidding me." Quivering, I tear open the other envelope and read the second letter:

Dear James Frost,

Thank you for submitting your work to Fairbanks Literary Agency. Unfortunately, the provided materials didn't strike a chord with us, and we will not be offering you representation.

Sincerely,

The Staff
Fairbanks Literary Agency

I've been shot in the chest. I throw the letter on the carpet, put my head into my hands, and weep. I hear a mocking voice: *You're not good enough. They don't like you. Loser. Sissy.*

The voice sounds so familiar, but I can't place it.

* * *

I stand at the mailbox on yet another day, the wind whipping across my face, heart smacking my chest. I reach into the Vessel of Doom and remove another mound of mail. Three addressed to JAMES FROST today. I don't wait to get inside to rip the first envelope open and read:

Mr. Frost,

Thanks for your letter of inquiry, but THE FORSAKEN WORLD doesn't sound right for me, so I'll have to pass.

Marge Browner
Greck Literary Agency

Doesn't sound right for you? As in, it isn't a good story? As in, the dialogue is choppy? As in, the narrative is weak? What do you mean, Marge? You don't like the title of the book? I think it's a solid title. Short and to the point. Memorable. And the novel as a whole sounds right to *me*. It sounded right to my friend Arthur, too, and he's a professional editor. Did you even read the excerpts I sent you? I shove the letter back in its envelope and tuck it in my jacket.

The subsequent letter reads:

Dear James,

Thank you for your query. Unfortunately, this doesn't seem like something I can get behind.

By the way, is Frost your actual last name or is it a penname? You might want to change it, as there isn't room for another Frost who writes.

Cindy Deramont
Thibault Literary Agency

Isn't enough room for another Frost who writes? Actually, it *is* my real last name, and there *is* room for another Frost who writes, thank you very much. I have an idea as to what you can get behind. How about a farting horse? This letter, too, finds its way into my jacket. Once again, I hear: *You're not good enough. They don't like you. Loser. Sissy.*

The third and final letter of the day says:

James Frost:

Your book doesn't fit my list. Good luck finding an agent elsewhere.

Sincerely,

Daphne Dergan

Just like that, I've compiled six rejections total, including the publisher's rejection. At my lowest of lows, the fraudulent voice repeats the abuse, *You're not good enough. They don't like you.*

Suddenly, the origin of the voice dawns on me. I can see Brad from Langwood High School standing next to the lockers, wearing a malevolent grin, spiky blond hair and expensive clothing. I imagine myself standing before him in the school.

I stare into his unkind eyes.

He glowers at me.

I turn away, and my eyes sweep the hallway.

We're alone.

He opens a nearby locker, pulls out a heap of paper, and reads from the top sheet. *The Forsaken World, by James Frost. Chapter One. Dreco woke with a start, eyes burning, mind wrapped around the image of a bloody corpse, his latest victim . . .* Brad stops reading and throws down the manuscript; it hits the tiles, and papers scatter. He laughs and laughs, then says, *Give up on the writing, sissy.*

* * *

On another day, in the throes of depression, sitting on my bed, I open five more rejection letters. Brad comes alive, this time standing in the middle of my room like an apparition. I brace myself for more ridicule. . . .

* * *

Friendless, completely despondent, alone in this fetid car, I tear open four rejections at the mailbox. Every pleasant thought, feeling, and emotion is sucked from my soul.

Somehow I need to get to the school to clean.

* * *

Five new rejection slips. This makes twenty rejections total.

Brad appears, sporting a grin. He doesn't need to say anything.

I drop to one knee before my bed, tears leaking down my cheeks. Every single agent and publisher responded with rejection. I'm zero for twenty. What am I going to do now? I have no desire to write. I look down at my hands, hating them, wanting them removed. They did this to me. They wrote *The Forsaken World.*

I need to talk with someone. I contemplate calling Sam but know he won't pick up. I think about calling Donovan, but he's busy with his own life, and he wouldn't understand this. I ponder calling Arthur or Mitch, but I don't want to be a bother. I even consider speaking with Dad, but I don't know where he is. I want to speak with Leigh more than any of the aforementioned people, but that can't happen because she isn't back from her vacation. Actually, even if I could get in touch with her, I'm not sure I'd tell her about the rejections anyway, for fear that she won't find me appealing anymore.

As I reflect on the ideal place to obtain a gun, which type of gun to use, and what kind of bullets to purchase, my landline phone rings, nearly sending me to the floor in shock. I fumble for the phone, grab it, and press TALK. "Hello?"

"James, my boy!" Mitch's voice resounds on the other end. "I have something for you. Can you meet me at DJ's in an hour for lunch?"

"Umm—I—maybe—I—well—"

"I want you to have this letter, James," he says.

I've seen enough letters lately. "Letter? What type of letter?" I ask.

"You're gonna have to meet up with me to find out."

I place my suicidal thoughts on the backburner. "How's one o'clock for you?"

"I'll see you there."

CHAPTER TWELVE

DJ's, a diner in Moose Acres, my hometown, is nestled between a candy shop and a convenience store. As I walk through the front door, my stomach growls; I haven't been eating much lately. My appetite has been virtually absent. I'll eat a bowl of soup here and there, maybe a package of saltines, but that's about it.

The hostess greets me. "Table for one?"

I shake my head. "For two, please. The other person should be here soon."

"Right this way." She waves me toward a vacant table and seats me.

I sit alone, as always, it seems, disappearing in my thoughts, when I notice Mitch walk through the door. He strolls past the hostess, the waiters and waitresses, smiling at each of them as he passes. He joins me at the table with a wrapped box. His appearance hasn't changed. His head is still bald. No sign of Rogaine. He's still wearing those oval-shaped glasses.

"Sorry I'm late," he says, removing his brown suede jacket. He sits down on the other side of the table. "Traffic was brutal." He places the wrapped item by his side on the seat. "So good to see you, James!"

"You too." I smile. "How've you been?" I beat him to the standard question.

"Great. I got back from New York yesterday. I was at a golf show testing the market for this new invention." He pulls out a golf ball from a pocket. I swear, every time we meet, he has a fresh invention to show off. He lets the ball roll into his palm and, with palm aimed upward, moves the hand across the table, about a foot from my nose. "I haven't settled on a name for this one yet. I'm torn between three names."

"What does it do?" I look down into his hand.

He grins, excited. "This puppy travels ten percent further than your average golf ball. Everyone at the show loved it."

"Is this the final product?" I ask, directing my attention to his smiling face as he pulls his hand back.

He tucks the ball away. "Nope. Just the prototype. I'm meeting with the packager next week. We should have it ready by March, right about the time you're published." He winks behind his spectacles, clears his throat. "I'm proud of you for finishing *The Forsaken World*, James."

I smile dryly. If he only knew about the rejections, then he wouldn't feel so proud of me.

Mitch continues, "The average person can't do what you've done. You know that, right?"

Write a book that no one wants? Get rejected twenty times? Actually, Mitch, I think many people could do that.

He rests an arm on the table, his eyes fixed on my face. "I don't know if you've ever thought of this, but what I do and what you do are very similar," he says. "I invent golf balls and other sporting goods. You invent stories. In a way, we're both inventors. We each conceive an idea, map out how we're going to tackle the idea, and we bring it to fruition." He adjusts his glasses. "Many people only get as far as the first step, conceiving the idea. They don't know what to do from that point on. But you and I are so alike, James; we know how to proceed, to go full speed after our ideas."

"Full speed is right." I laugh. "I feel like I haven't breathed for the last two years."

He grins. "Once again, I can relate."

I shake my head. "It's so friggin hard."

"What is?"

I fold my hands on the table, leaning forward a smidgen. "Being different all the time," I say. "It's like an automatic strike against me. I feel so alone sometimes."

He nods, understanding. "The greatest and most inspiring achievements are not produced by those who conform to society's idea of normal, but by those who courageously adopt the unconventional." He halts for emphasis. "Sound familiar?"

"Very," I say.

"Nowhere does it say it's going to be easy, James. Being unconventional doesn't exactly make you popular. And that, of course, is why so many shy away from the concept of unconventionality. It's hard, like you said."

The waitress flits past our table, carrying a tray full of food.

I lean toward Mitch. "I swear, people think I'm crazy for writing." I pause. "Has anyone ever thought *you* were crazy?"

He laughs. "All the time, and I think it's great."

"What's great about being perceived as crazy?"

He grins. "Because one day, when they least expect it, and when you need it most, everything will come together. That's when you can point a finger in their direction and say, 'See? I wasn't crazy after all. I made it.'" He clears his throat again. "Sorry. Getting over a cold," he says. Then he carries on, "When I first got out of college, I came across a guy who taught me everything he knew about business. He took me under his wing and I worked for him for a while, selling antique bullets. After about a year and a half, the work became dry and I wanted out. One morning, while I was taking a dump, of all things, an idea struck that I felt very optimistic about. The idea was a glow-in-the-dark football. Over the course of the next year, I created a rough prototype and felt obliged to pursue the idea on a larger scale."

"You quit selling bullets, didn't you?"

He smiles. "I went up to Mr. Winger and told him that I was going to be an inventor, and that I wouldn't be able to sell bullets for him any longer."

"What'd he say to that?"

"He said, 'Kid, are you crazy?'" Out of the corner of his eye, Mitch sees the server standing at the table. He signals for another minute with a raised pointer finger. "In hindsight, maybe I *was* a little crazy," he says. "Crazy like a fox." He smiles wryly. "If I had listened to him and conformed to his idea of normal, James, look at all I would've missed out on."

"You'd be a totally different person."

"And a totally *sad* person," he adds.

Our attention gradually falls on the menus. We figure out what we want for lunch, and the waitress returns and takes our order. After she leaves, we're up and running with our conversation again.

"Mitch, I have to tell you something . . ."

"What is it? Don't be shy."

"I'm afraid if I tell you, you won't think so highly of me anymore."

"My pride in you is unmovable, James. Remember that." He leans back in the booth. "Now tell me what's on your mind."

"Everyone who I sent my writing to rejected it. I've accumulated twenty rejections." Merely stating the fact stings.

"Have you ever heard of Meranda Erickson, by any chance?"

"A writer, right?"

"The understatement of the year," says Mitch. "Meranda won the Pulitzer Prize twice and was a *New York Times* bestseller for nine of her novels. She's practically a legend in publishing." He removes a newspaper clipping from another pocket and passes it over the table. "Take a look at that article," he says. "It was in the *New Hampshire Globe* this past week. Cut it out just for you. . . . According to the write-up, she lives in Moose Acres, your hometown! She's lived here for thirteen years. She's sixty-two now."

I scan the clipping, see her picture beneath bold letters: **FANS CRY OUT FOR NEW ERICKSON NOVEL.**

Mitch says, "Take a look at the end of the article. Look at how many times *she* was rejected before her first novel was published."

I scan the article. Spot the number. "Sixty-two. Holy crap."

"Once for every year of her life. Makes your twenty look like nothing, doesn't it?" Mitch clasps his hands behind his head; I nod. He says, "She hasn't written a novel in ten years. I figure, if she's not writing, then she must have plenty of time on her hands. I'm going to try and track her down. She'd be a good person to have on your side. And she lives in your backyard." He brings his hands into his lap.

The food arrives hot and fresh. My appetite is still flagging; I can eat only a quarter of my burger and half of my fries. Mitch eats his entire plate of chicken fingers and fries, then brings the wrapped box up from his side and sets it on the table.

"That can't be the letter you were telling me about," I say.

"Why not?"

"It's a really thick box for a letter."

Mitch smiles. "When I spotted this, I knew it was meant for you." He rests his hand on the top of the box, taps at it. "Here." He pushes it my way. "Open it up," he says.

I don't waste any time. I tear the wrapping apart and open the box. I pull out a picture frame and find a handwritten letter encased behind the glass. The stationery says HOMER NOBLE FARM: LIPTON, VERMONT and the letter is dated JULY 1, 1959. The letter reads:

Dear Mr. Lonesome,

I've read your material. You're on the right road. I'll keep an eye out for your name.

Goose bumps rise on my arms as I eye Robert Frost's signature.

"Coincidence or fate?" Mitch questions. "*You* tell *me.*"

"Where'd you get this?" I ask desperately.

"You won't believe me," he says, "but I got it from my brother-in-law's antique shop."

"And where'd *he* get it?"

"I asked him that same question and he said he couldn't remember. . . . James, do you see the significance in this letter? Remember? Our trip to his house in Franconia? Your poem? His mailbox?"

"My goodness, Mitch. Thank you!" I take a deep breath, holding the frame at eye level. "Thank you."

"I think Robert's trying to tell you something." Mitch takes a drink of water. "Have another look at the name of the addressee."

"Mr. Lonesome," I say.

"Yes, James. This letter is clearly addressed to you." He winks.

CHAPTER THIRTEEN

I decide the ideal place to mount my Robert Frost letter is on the wall to the left of my bed. I spike a couple nails on the partition and hang the frame. From here, lying on this bed, all I have to do is twist my neck slightly and I can read his message. I glance at it repeatedly.

I ponder Mr. Lonesome. He was obviously a writer, and Robert Frost felt inclined to write him a letter. How old was Mr. Lonesome? Twenty? Twenty-five? Thirty? Eighty? What type of writing did he practice? I suspect he might have been a poet. Whoever he was, however old, whatever type of writing he produced, I'm sure Mr. Lonesome wasn't a real name. Could have been a moniker. Perhaps Robert was commenting on one of the writer's attributes. Sort of like when you call someone highly successful and ostentatiously confident "Mr. Hotshot."

What really gets my blood pumping is when I think about how in the world this letter found me. It appears that Robert wrote the letter while living at his farm in Vermont. I know from reading extensively about Robert that Homer Noble Farm was purchased a year after his wife's death. It was there that he felt loneliest. Maybe Robert felt a kinship with Mr. Lonesome and it drove him to write this letter. . . . Robert won the Pulitzer four times, and wrote without many breaks. I can't imagine he responded to everyone who sent correspondence his direction. He wouldn't have had time to do that and keep a steady writing schedule. I'm sold on the notion that Robert saw himself in Mr. Lonesome.

Empathy is a great gift. When we've been through something that someone else has been through. That's when we look at a person and, as from a mirror, catch our own reflection. It would be like me receiving a letter from someone who cleans and who's trying to write for a living. How could I pass on responding? If I were to ignore him, I would be discounting myself.

Back on topic: How in the world did this letter find *me*? It's decades old, and it wasn't initially intended for a person by the name of James Frost. I stare deeper into the frame. *Or was it?* In my mind's eye, a vast hand plucks the letter from Mr. Lonesome's abandoned home. God guides it through myriad channels of auctions and, through divine influence, projects a thought onto Mitch's brother-in-law to go to a particular auction and buy boxes of memorabilia, which, without brother-in-law's knowledge, contains the letter that Mitch ultimately finds.

This ought to cheer me up, but it doesn't. Brad isn't far away. The horde of rejection letters is seated neatly on the dresser to the right of my bed. My girlfriend is in another country. At the moment, I am Mr. Lonesome.

* * *

I receive a postcard from Leigh; it bears photographs of beaches and the word FLORIDA spread across the top. I read the postcard before I head to work:

James,

We're in a stopover in FL for fuel and I wanted to make sure to write you. Travel time has been longer than expected due to hurricanes and storms, but thinking about you has kept me busy—in a good way. I am so thankful to have you in my life. I can't wait to get back and see you, show you all the pics, and tell you all about the trip!

I hope your week is going well. Will be thinking of you! Wish you were here . . .

Miss you,

Leigh

My heart smarts. She may be thankful to have me in her life now, but wait until she finds out that I'm a loser, that I can't even get one positive response from an agent or publisher.

* * *

I'm staring into my laptop, trying to figure out what my next move should be. Maybe I shouldn't continue to write. I've been writing far too long to have nothing to show for it. I hoped I'd at least be published by now, if not a *New York Times* bestselling author. Maybe I should adopt the conventional—get a second job, and move out of my father's house. Could I support myself then? What type of a life would that be? I wouldn't have time for anything other than work. I'd barely get by financially, and what would I have to look forward to? Daily, I see people walking around, dead but alive, zombies. Their entire lives are devoted to making money. My life is no enchanted story right now; that's certainly been established. On certain hours of certain days, I still want to take a gun to my head and blow my brains out. However, living a dreamless life would be decidedly worse than having the occasional suicidal thought. I don't want to be eighty-years-old, sitting in a rocking chair on the porch of my shack, thinking: *I should've gone for it. I should've taken a leap of faith.* Despite the pain I feel from my unconventionality, the pain would triple if I went the conventional route, the walking-dead avenue.

Writing is part of me. Somehow, I have to keep on plugging. But in what way? Should I write a new book? *The Forsaken World* wasn't received well. Should I trek through another long and treacherous rewrite? Do I dare?

The sound of an incoming e-mail rings through my laptop, making me feel important. The message is from Arthur.

James, my ferociously ambitious protégé:

Wondering how life is treating you. Give me a call soon. We should get together over tea or coffee in the near future to discuss things. Let me know what works best for you. I want to know how the querying has been going.

Best,

Arthur

I resolve to call him right away. I tell him about the rejections, and he sounds disconcerted, not at me but at the agents, and especially the publisher, who he calls blind and obtuse. He talks me into coming over to his house tomorrow.

* * *

The story of how Arthur and I became acquainted is quite magical. When I was younger, say, twelve through eighteen, I lived in an old-fashioned settlement called Rivertown. Population, give or take, two hundred. Across the road from my house was Snake Mountain, which ironically contained no snakes, and in the center of the mountain, the Abenaki River flowed, which resembled a snake (if you were to look at an aerial shot). That mountain was visible for miles, and if you stood outdoors and listened closely, you heard splashing and rumbling sounds from the river.

While living in Rivertown, New Hampshire for those seven years, I attended two schools: Rivertown Junior High School and Langwood High School. In both stages, I took the bus to school; I didn't get my driver's license until I was seventeen. There wasn't anything particularly memorable about the bus rides themselves, except one home we passed almost daily, a Victorian home, three-story with a rounded tower and a wrap-around porch. In the front lawn there was a garden that was extremely well kept. Nearest the road, nailed onto the middle of a tree trunk, was an engraved sign that read *Arthur A. Pennington, Editor*, and it often caught my eye.

In those days, I scribbled down stories, quick tales about life— and poetry. I told myself that if I ever wrote anything worthy of an editor's professional eyes, I would contact Arthur A. Pennington. Years later, I 411'd Arthur's telephone number and called him to set up a consultation for my first novel, *The Forsaken World*.

These days, I don't look on the Victorian from a distance. Arthur A. Pennington isn't merely a name on a sign; it's the name of my editor, the white-haired, gangly person standing inside the doorway waiting for me as I exit my car and walk toward the front of his house.

"*There's* my ferociously ambitious protégé," he says, opening the door.

I chuckle, masking the pain of recent misfortune. "Hey, Arthur. Thanks for having me over," I say.

We shake hands at the door, and he invites me inside for tea and cookies. He takes me into his office, serves the most fantastic chocolate chip cookies—even better than the ones made by those elves who live in a tree—I've ever had and pours us tea. I sip as he gathers some papers from his desk in the corner of the room, then brings them to this table. He removes a pen from behind his ear, sets it on the table, pulls a pair of specs from his breast pocket, and puts them on. He looks like an old librarian. "Now, after hearing your unfortunate news, I dove back into your novel to see if I could find examples to support or, better yet, denounce, the thickheaded editor's comment about your book being *overwritten*." He shuffles through the papers, finds a page and points his pen at a line of text. "Tell me, does this sound overwritten to you? Allow me to read: 'Looking across the street, he was drawn in by the ocean's beauty, the majestic view of sapphire water spreading over countless miles of landscape—rocks in indistinct shapes, and distant islands.'" Arthur stops, looks at me for a reaction.

I set down the mug. "When I wrote it, I was trying to be descriptive. I don't see how that translates into being overwritten."

"Bingo!" Arthur's voice livens. "There's nothing even remotely too elaborate or flowery about your work. If anything, there are many points in your novel where you can amplify." He drops his pen on the table and sits back in his chair. "Do you want to know what I think?"

"Sure."

"I think she was digging for an excuse to turn you down." His tone speaks of great control, infinite good sense. "There's nothing overwritten about your writing and she knew that, but she had to give you some reason under the sun why she couldn't take you on as a client."

"Then what do you think the real reason was?"

"Could be a number of factors," he says. "Perhaps she couldn't relate to your story. Maybe you caught her on a bad day. Or she could just be an ignoramus." His tone radiates contempt at the last.

"But what about the agents?"

He leans in, tilts his head.

I persist. "They couldn't have all been having bad days, and they couldn't have all had trouble relating to my story, and they couldn't have all been dense."

His voice is dignified. "James, the country hosts thousands of agents. You'll snag one; keep on trolling."

"But what should I troll with?" I ask. "What should I use as bait? The same story? A new story?"

"Why would you go ahead and write a new story to send them when you have *The Forsaken World*?" Disbelief is evident in his tone. He doesn't provide an opportunity for response. "James, don't you dare let these rejections steer you away from a story that, deep within the chasm of your soul, you know is meant to be in the marketplace." His voice shakes.

I'm wondering why he's so fired up about this.

"If you're unsure about your novel, then revise," he says. "Revise, revise, revise," he carries on, pounding a hand on the table for emphasis.

"You don't think I should even contemplate a new story?"

"No, sir." His voice borders on laughter. "Definitely not." Then his face becomes suddenly stern, like he's about to go into scold mode. "Quitting is a disease. You quit once, it spreads into twice, and before you know what hit you, it transforms into an epidemic.

"Kiddo, I wish I could assist you beyond the editing process," he continues. "I wish I could snap my fingers and land you an agent. I can't. You know I don't have the means. But you'll find your way. I believe in you.

"It takes a lot of courage to do what you're doing." An amount of affection enters his voice. "When I was about your age, I was a writer determined to land on that esteemed bestseller's list. I wrote every day. No exceptions. Eventually, I had written a tome of my own, hundred fifty thousand words, or something like that. I sent it off to a bunch of editors and agents. Half of them didn't reply. The other half told me I had no talent."

I intone. "But I'm sure you were good."

"I didn't know that," he says. "And that was the biggest problem of all. I didn't know that I had talent, so I allowed them to steer me away from a book that was meant to be in bookstores."

"You gave up on the story?" My voice is incredulous.

"Yeah." Same tone as *duh*. "Just like that. Called it quits."

"What did you do after that?"

"I became an editor of four prominent magazines, of fiction, and of nonfiction books," he chuckles. "Those who can't do, teach . . ." Then suddenly he's serious, librarian-like, "I want you to understand something very important. Are you listening carefully?"

"Yeah."

"You are hands down the most talented writer I have ever worked with." He pauses to let it be absorbed. My head doesn't grow. He keeps on. "There are people out there in the world that would kill to have your talent, to have such a magnitude of raw talent that you can actually pick up the art of writing as you go. And the persistence aspect, James. Your drive astounds me. Your ferociously ambitious flame, it's like nothing I've ever seen or been exposed to." He stops and stares into my face, examining me, then speaks again, "I know this hurts. Trust me. *I know.* But you don't write six drafts of a novel and call it quits. The James Frost I know would *never* do such a thing. My James Frost would sit his butt back in the chair and keep on writing. He would persevere through any obstacle thrown in his path. He would most certainly, without a doubt in his mind, prove every one of those pretentious, self-righteous dunces wrong. Now isn't that the James Frost *you* know?"

I experience a gush of inspiration. "Yeah, that's him."

"That's right it is," says Arthur. "Remember, James, you can receive countless rejections, but all it will take is one agent to say yes to your novel, one of these people to actually see your work for its potential."

"You mean that?" I ask.

"You're what some would call a natural." He grins. "Some people are born to sing, some to dance, some to play the piano . . . or edit magazines and books. You were born to write."

In the back of my mind, I know I have nothing other than writing, no chance to escape my job. Having no other option, plus my passion for writing, brings me to this decision: "I'll try to somehow do another rewrite." Another factor that plays a role in this choice are the words Arthur uttered moments ago: *You are hands down the most talented writer I have ever worked with.* And the most recent statement: *You're what some would call a natural.* That coming from a man who edits for a living, means a lot.

"Did you say you would *try* to follow through with an additional rewrite? Because that's not the right attitude to assume before traveling on a perilous journey."

"I'm not sure I can do it now," I say.

"You're not sure you can do it *now?* If you don't revise your story now, when will you? When you're living out there in the world on your own, forced into working overtime in order to pay the long list of bills, or when you get married and want to devote your time to your new wife, or when you have your first child and are expected to contribute in the raising of that child, or when you have a second and third child that needs you just the same? *Then* try to execute a rewrite and see how easy it is."

He takes a swig of tea. "Don't be like I was at your age and decide against what you know you're meant to do simply because *you don't know if you can do it now*." His voice is taut. "And don't be like me and get married and have those three kids without getting back into that writing first," he says, sadness glazing his eyes. "The time is now. Time is a gift. Sit your butt down and write."

CHAPTER FOURTEEN

Here I am, sitting my butt down on my bed to write, laptop resting on my lap. Leigh should arrive home tomorrow, and I'm thrilled about that, but I need to push that thought away for the time being to concentrate on the rewrite of this novel.

A piece of doubt lingers around this revision. I'm not completely sold on Arthur's words, but they have helped me enough to at least get me to open this laptop, and stare into the text of *The Forsaken World*. His words echo in my ears: *You're a natural . . . The time is now . . .* And Mitch's voice comes into play also, drowning out any trace of Brad: *The greatest and most inspiring achievements are not produced by those who conform to society's idea of normal, but by those who courageously adopt the unconventional.* Then I glance to my left, to Robert Frost's letter, and think *Mr. Lonesome,* and through all these inspirations, surprisingly, I take the first step toward a fresh rewrite: I choose to begin.

* * *

Hooray for the weekend. It arrives yet again. Last night went fairly well, writing-wise. I accomplished what I wanted to accomplish—twenty fresh pages written. I've been increasing the suspense, trying to make the characters more believable, and I'm semi-pleased about where the revision is heading. Otherwise, the night was fantastic because Leigh got back home and we spoke on the phone for almost four hours. Unsurprisingly, the trip was a terrible experience for her, and I don't think she'll be returning to the Dominican in the near future, especially with her parents. In fact, I don't think she'll go on a vacation with her parents ever again.

Leigh said the weather the first two days was rainy and miserable, which limited them from doing anything outdoors, and therefore they stayed inside their hotel, watching television, going to the indoor pool occasionally, and bickering with one another. According to Leigh, her parents got in a rather large fight about who chose to arrange a trip to the Dominican. Her mother claimed that she wanted to go to California all along, but that Leigh's father insisted on the Dominican and booked the trip without considering the feelings of his wife.

"I felt like I was in the middle of a war," Leigh whispered over the phone; her parents' bedroom is adjacent to hers and the house's walls have ears. "Their words were going off like grenades, and they were setting each other on fire with bitterness and evil looks."

"Did you have *any* fun?" I asked.

"Maybe for about an hour."

"An hour the entire vacation?"

She sighed. "America's a great place to live, James." She dodged the question. "It takes staying in another country to see that clearly." Then she went on about the food in the Dominican, how it isn't anything like the food in America, and she provided details about how sick she got after eating a piece of a banana or some mixture of a banana and a tropical fruit. The first half of the trip was plagued with fighting and the second half was beset by violent vomiting, hot and cold chills, pains that shot through her stomach erratically, and sadness for the fact that her mother and father showed virtually no concern or care for her situation; they were determined to not let Leigh's sickness ruin their vacation, and they went out on the beach and walked and lay in the sun for hours, leaving their daughter cooped up in the hotel room to fend for herself.

"I wish I never agreed to go with them," she said. "I could've stayed here with you and . . . What is it you did while I was gone?"

Well, let's see, I got rejected by more professionals from the publishing industry, received plenty of abuse from Brad, who still lurks somewhere in my subconscious, waiting to strike again. And, "I worked. Spent some time with Mitch." I filled her in on my meeting with Mitch, his support, the Robert Frost letter, the magic in it, everything, and she seemed happy. There was one thing, however, that I didn't tell her about: the rejections. I'm not sure if I want to tell her. Girls like Leigh don't want to be with losers; they want to be with winners. Right now, I'm far from being a winner.

I'm lying in bed, trying not to think about anything. I envision a chalkboard, words scribbled over its surface, and I use an eraser to wipe it clean. For a moment, my racing thoughts slow down. Thoughts of my conversation with Leigh, of the rewrite that I'm still scared of, and of Thanksgiving tomorrow disappear. Then my mind picks back up and I'm on my way, sprinting with thoughts about that ominous dinner, the piece of the phone call that I had forgotten—the part in which Leigh, with her cute voice, charmed me into agreeing to join her family for the holiday. She also invited my father, but he'll be spending Thanksgiving with a few friends in Massachusetts, so I declined on his behalf.

Officially, I can't sleep for any more than an hour at a time; I wake and glance at the clock near the top of every hour. The last time I saw Leigh's parents, they weren't exactly kind to me. I can think of all sorts of places I would rather be tomorrow than at their home, but I agreed to Thanksgiving dinner at their place. There isn't any backing out. I suppose I could fake sickness. I could wake up tomorrow, call Leigh, and tell her that I have the flu. I could say, "I was up all night . . . with the flu." At least, then, the first half of the statement would be true.

Her extended family will be present at dinner tomorrow, which causes anxiety in the pit of my stomach, in addition to what I feel about spending more time with her parents. Leigh's brother, whom I've never met, will be in attendance. Her aunt and uncle will also join us. I have no idea what to expect from any of them. Definitely uncharted waters ahead.

* * *

I bought a pumpkin pie from the supermarket, the most conventional pie of all for Thanksgiving, and I cradle it in an arm while I walk to the front of Leigh's house, unease ripping through my body. I give the door a pound with the knocker, and there's no answer. I wait, then slam the wood with the knocker again. Nothing. Finally, I give it another knock. Five seconds later, I hear Leigh's mother's voice: "Come in!"

I open the door and cautiously step into the house, catching the aroma of turkey and stuffing, a feast. I'm unsure of what I should do next. I don't know where Leigh's mother is, let alone the location of my girlfriend. I finally decide, after much trepidation, that I should at least take my jacket off; I do, single-handedly, balancing the pie in the other hand, and I place the jacket on a coat rack beside the door.

Still no greeting from anyone, not even Leigh.

I stand still for about a minute, waiting for someone, anyone, most desirably Leigh, to walk up to me and say hello or offer some sort of direction as to what course they would like for me to head in. But waiting gets old quickly. I walk out of the entranceway and eventually wind up in the kitchen, where I see Leigh's mother wearing an apron on her stick-thin body. A skeleton with hair, she's stirring two pots over the stove, alternating between them. I should've known she'd be in here. The turkey aroma should've given it away.

I stop behind her and see what she's stirring, stuffing and gravy. "Hello," I say politely, energetically.

Leigh's mother turns toward me, her face unresponsive. "Oh. Hello." She speaks in a listless tone.

I extend the pie toward her. "Where would you like me to put this?"

She doesn't answer, only shoots her hand at me. I set the pie in her palm and she tosses it on the counter behind a pile of other desserts, treats that have obviously been made from scratch: lemon meringue pie, strawberry shortcake, and many more.

"Leigh's still getting ready," she says, turning back to her pots, fully focused on them. "Go have a seat in the living room."

"Okay. Thanks," I say, feeling mistreated but trying to remain respectful. I start toward the living room, as requested. That woman/Grim Reaper is freezing cold, and I think: *How can she be Leigh's mother? The two are complete opposites.*

I sit in the infamous loveseat. This house feels cloaked in a dark cloud of negativity. I can sense Leigh's mother seething in the kitchen because I'm here. An assumption? Perhaps. But her actions of a minute ago certainly back up the initial notion; she wasn't the least bit friendly to me out in the kitchen, and she seemed genuinely unhappy, so I can't be too far off about her being angry about my presence. *Hopefully she doesn't own a scythe.* I wonder if she or her husband wanted me here for Thanksgiving, or if it was totally Leigh's doing. The latter sounds about right. If it was Leigh's parents' way, they'd rather not open their home to a person who cleans a school.

I feel below these people, like some sort of subhuman who lives in an underground society and is here on the surface, visiting. I want to go home. I don't belong here.

Leigh steps into the room, smiling, wearing baggy dress pants and a blouse. Her hair has been straightened, and she's wearing cherry red lipstick.

"James," she squeaks, "I missed you!" She practically jumps onto the loveseat, providing a whiff of her perfume—fruit. She gives me a bear hug, slips her hand into mine, and says, "Sorry for the wait. I wanted to be ready for when you got here, but I couldn't figure out what to wear."

I smile, looking her up and down. "You definitely made a good choice. You look beautiful."

She grins, then gives me a peck on the lips. "I'm so happy to see you." Her face is half a foot from mine. "It feels like it's been so long."

"Ditto that." I initiate another hug, and we don't let go for two minutes.

"Oh, before I forget . . ." She pulls away gradually, but makes sure to grab my hand. "I meant to ask you last night whether or not you heard anything from those agents, but I was too busy blabbering on about myself. Sorry about that."

My heart drops to my feet. That's the last thing I want to talk about. I imagine her face if I were to tell her about the rejections; her eyes would squint, she'd purse her lips, and she'd laugh, pointing a finger at me, the loser. Then she'd tell me to get out of her house, her life, because she doesn't date losers, only winners.

"Hello? James?" She waves a hand over my face, snaps her fingers. "Did you hear what I asked you?" She tilts her head, rubbing the palm of my hand with a thumb. "Are you okay? Is there something you want to tell me?"

What, that I'm a loser? "Uh, I'm not sure." I shrug.

"James." Leigh's voice rises as she says my name, reminding me of my mother, the way she used to say it when I had done something wrong or when I wasn't listening.

"Leigh, how much do you like me?" I stare into her eyes.

"A lot." She smiles. "Now tell me . . . You heard from them, didn't you?"

I can't lie to her. My voice wavers. "Yes. I heard from them." I look down at the carpet.

"Good or bad news?" she asks softly.

"Bad." I look up at her, think *oh, screw it,* and spit out the rest, "They rejected me. Each of 'em. Twenty total."

Amazingly, Leigh says, "Don't let those people bring you down. They don't know what they're missing out on."

Leigh hugs me again, whispers into my ear, "I'm here for you."

I wonder if she's lying, if it's only a matter of time until she says good riddance. She's probably just trying to be nice, or maybe she does actually like me, though I don't know why she would.

Leigh pats my back and, hands still interlocked, she says, "You should read me some of your novel sometime. I bet it's amazing."

I back up my work every time I write by sending the Word file to my e-mail address. I'm ritualistic about this, obsessive-compulsive. So I respond, "That could be arranged." I feel like I need to prove my writing skills to her. I just hope that I don't inadvertently prove that I'm one of the worst writers who ever lived.

"You wouldn't mind sharing?" Leigh asks.

Actually, I'm petrified of sharing; I wish I could retract my offer, but my rewrite is decent, I think, and maybe that would impress her. "How long do we have before dinner?"

She glances at her wristwatch. "An hour or more."

"Do you have a computer nearby that we could use?"

"Yeah. Why?"

"With the Internet?"

"Yes. Now tell me what you're up to." Her voice edges toward excitement.

"Bring me to the computer and I'll show you."

CHAPTER FIFTEEN

I download the file of *The Forsaken World* onto her laptop. Leigh sits on her bed. I open the file, readying myself to read at the desk that sits directly across from her bed. I turn in the chair to see Leigh smiling. I ask, "Are you ready?" My heart's banging so loudly I bet she can hear it.

"Of course. What are you waiting for?"

I release a titter. "I'm nervous."

"Don't be." She leans forward and borrows a phrase from our earlier days. "I like you, and that should be all that matters." She winks.

I smile, appreciating the continuity, then turn to the laptop. I stare at the copy, silent, experiencing an adrenaline rush, like I could lift a car.

I start to read chapter one. Initially, my voice cracks due to nerves or maybe late-blooming puberty, but then, once I get to the second paragraph, it levels out and I start to feel comfortable with sharing my work with Leigh. I read and read. I hear her laugh at the funny parts, sniff at the sad scenes. She must be enjoying my story; she hasn't left the room yet, revolted.

Leigh interrupts. "You really wrote this?"

I turn to her. "Yeah." I give the *duh* tone, like Arthur.

"I didn't realize how good you were." She beams. "Please, read more."

I grin, then twist away from her and back to the laptop. I read where I left off—the scene in which a person is murdered and the murderer, Dreco, hatches a plan to cover it up. I read Dreco's part convincingly, husky voice and all. I read for twenty minutes—the dialogue, narrative, monologue, thoughts, everything in character. I sweat during an intense paragraph on page twenty-one, feel sympathy for the murderer's victims, and for the murderer. On page twenty-four, I stop and look to Leigh. Her eyes are wet. Her face brightens. She says, "You're incredible."

"Thanks," I say, feeling like a winner, a real champion. "It's a little rough, I guess, but it gives you a decent idea of my writing style."

"*Rough?*" She blows out air. "It was amazing . . ."

"I hope the agents feel that way," I say. "Of course, I'll have it edited before I send it their way again."

Leigh gets up from the bed and stands in front of me. She says, "They'll love it. It's so real. So genuine."

"You think so? But they still might think that—"

She sets her hand on my shoulder. "James, they'll love it. *Got it?*"

"I don't know. They could decide to be—"

"Shhhh." She wraps her arms around me, whispers into my ear, "I believe in you."

* * *

I'm officially a fish out of water, like Michael Jordan trying to play baseball. I'm surrounded by Leigh's family at the dinner table, and I haven't spoken a word for at least twenty minutes because I don't know when or how to jump into the conversation; Leigh's father, aunt, and uncle have been going on and on about politics, poking fun at the Democrats. Kerry came up, I believe, as did Gore. I'm not the only one staying out of the conversation, though. Leigh hasn't said anything and neither has her mother—who's been poking at her meal—or Leigh's teenage brother, Erick.

I take my time with the meal, turkey and stuffing and potatoes smothered with gravy, and Leigh holds one of my hands under the table; she's sitting on my left, chewing quietly. I don't know anything about politics, so the words coming from their mouths might as well be in a different language. I tune out their gibberish and try to enjoy the food, despite my desire to get up from this table, bringing my girlfriend along, to go somewhere else. Leigh could show me pictures of her trip, and expound upon the vacation, or she and I could discuss my writing in more depth. Heck, we could do both, if we were to have enough time.

I glance at Leigh's mother at the other end of the table as she plays with her food, her gloomy eyes aimed at the plate. I shift my focus to Leigh, who takes another bite of turkey, then I eye her dismal mother again, which is when I realize something big: Leigh's mother has body issues and she's been projecting them onto Leigh from the start, through fat jokes and other demeaning ways. I watch Leigh's mother set her fork on her plate, leaving large amounts of food untouched, and this hits me like a cudgel as I look at her anorexic frame: She fears that her daughter will become fat, since to the Food Poker, obesity is about as evil as Satan himself.

So, I think that when she makes fun of her daughter's eating habits, it isn't done out of hatred for Leigh; rather, I think the poking fun is done partly out of love, as warped as that is—because in the end, who wants their child to be involved with evil?—and partly out of jealousy—because Leigh has curves and yet still chooses to eat.

Leigh's mother finally makes eye contact from her end of the table, and I quickly look away, down at my own plate. I suppose I could've been more subtle. As I pretend to ponder the last bite of turkey on my plate, I think of Leigh and her mother, and I feel a seed of sadness being planted deep within my heart for the both of them, for the fact that Leigh's mother's eating disorder has obviously been ignored, and for the fact that Leigh has had to deal with the consequences for so long.

I'm beginning to loathe this dinner. I feel like I can't talk to my girlfriend because I may interrupt this political discussion yanked straight from CNN. I didn't come here to sit in silence for what seems like hours. I should've pretended to be sick; that would've kept me out of this droning situation. But then again, if I had played ill, I wouldn't have been able to read my work to Leigh when I did and I wouldn't have been able to hear those four beautiful words: I believe in you.

"James . . ."

I look up from my plate. Leigh's father is staring at me from his wife's side; he was the one who uttered my name.

"We haven't heard much from you this evening," he says. "What are *your* thoughts on voting?"

The question strikes me like a hurled rock. I collect my thoughts and say, "I'm not sure how to answer that." It's like someone cracked open my skull and punched my brain.

He rears back. "You don't know where you stand on voting?" His tone is stentorian.

"What do *you* think about it, sir?" I ask.

"I think voting is our duty as citizens of this country," he says, pointing at me, his voice edging toward rage. Bleach his hair white, give him a goatee and a top hat, and who do we have? Uncle Sam himself.

Leigh's uncle (no top hat covering his head) jumps in. "James, you don't have an opinion on this?"

They're challenging me. I have to say something. "I don't vote," I say.

Leigh's mother rolls her eyes, and her brother simpers, as do the rest, excluding Leigh, of course.

"So you're lazy . . ." Leigh's father says sharply.

I'm tired of being quiet. "Sir, with all due respect, just because I don't vote, that doesn't make me lazy."

He points at me, his face tightening. "Then why don't you vote?"

"To make a statement," I say.

The energy at the table turns belligerent. He asks, "What kind of statement?"

"A valid political statement," I say.

"How can you make a valid political statement by choosing not to vote?" Leigh's aunt joins in the fray.

I say, "Not voting makes a statement about our entire political system."

Leigh's father shows flared nostrils. "And how so?"

"The idea is this: I will not be subjugated to corrupt politicians."

Leigh's mother strikes. "A political statement from you won't make a difference."

Concurrence ripples over the table. Leigh is still holding my hand, silent, shaking slightly. I say, "So you're saying that one person can't make a difference in this political system?"

This causes everyone at the table to stop and think. Silence settles in.

"I'd like for you to leave, James." Leigh's father speaks firmly.

"Daddy, what are you—"

His tone is wrathful. "I said I'd like him to leave!"

Her eyes are wide and rounded with fear as if she's about to be spanked. She continues in a meek manner. "I think what James said makes sense, Daddy."

His nose creases. "You're letting this boy control your mind." He points his finger at her. "What are you thinking? We raised you better than this . . . and we love you! Now come to your senses. He's a—a—*janitor!*"

I stand, the last part of his statement triggering repressed rage. "My work doesn't define me, sir!" I say loudly, hands trembling.

Leigh stands with me. Her voice dithers as she says, "He's a great writer. I've read his stuff, Daddy."

He throws his arms up. "Don't you see, he's not going anywhere with his writing. No one's going to take him seriously."

I raise a hand. "Well, thanks for dinner, and sorry we don't see eye to eye." I walk to the other side of the table and tell Leigh's aunt and uncle that it was nice meeting them. They nod, avoiding eye contact. Leigh looks like a lost little girl; she trails me.

"Show your boyfriend to the door," her father orders.

She walks in front of me, leads me to the front door. Then she throws a coat on, as I do, and we step outside. We stand on the top step, face-to-face, dead leaves falling around us.

I want to crumble. "I'm so sorry. I don't know what just happened. I wanted my visit to go well. Oh, girl, I'm so sorry." I slap a hand on my forehead.

"Don't be," she says, grabbing my hand, "you didn't do anything wrong. You spoke your mind."

"You're not mad at me?"

"No one ever talks to Daddy like that," she says. "Why would I be mad at you?" She smiles. "I liked it."

"You did?" I'm shocked.

Her head waggles. "You made a good point about voting."

"A lot of good that did," I say. "Now everyone hates me. I won't be able to come back here."

She shrugs. "Then I'll come to you. Every weekend."

CHAPTER SIXTEEN

I spent the bulk of my work night thinking about last night's horrible dinner and now, sitting at my laptop, I laugh. Wasn't it supposed to be Thanksgiving? A time to be thankful? Anyhow, my anger is currently under control. It helps that Leigh is behind me one hundred percent. I'm enthralled by her support. I think Leigh has been waiting for a long time to stand up to her dad, and last night she did, not in an enormous fashion, but enough to get a taste. She needs so very badly to be liberated. Maybe I can help her with that. Lead the way, in a sense.

I receive an e-mail from Mitch. According to him, he contacted the former head of the creative writing program at the University of New Hampshire and she, Barbara Johnson, would be happy to read a sample of my novel. She'll be going on sabbatical next week for a year or so, Mitch paraphrases, and she'll be unreachable during that period of time, but she'd be glad to speak with me and provide her opinion of my novel. She has time open this Wednesday evening, and I should e-mail her a sample of my writing (the first three reworked chapters) prior to our meeting.

I didn't know Mitch had this planned. He's always full of tricks. I guess it would be nice to get some advice from a former professor of writing. She may be able to teach me a thing or two. Or she may shove the creative writing course down my throat, as instructed by Mitch; I know he would love to have me take classes at his old college. Despite his motto of unconventionality, college is one piece of the conventional that he embraces.

Two things are for certain: I'll have to ask Dad for Wednesday night off from work and I'll need to polish up the first three chapters of my rewrite before I send it to Barbara for a critique.

* * *

Dad gave me the night off from work, after much pleading, and Mitch and I are only about three miles from Barbara's home (according to his directions), traveling in his Cadillac.

"How do you know Barbara, anyways?" I ask.

He shifts into fourth gear. Directions sit in the center console over the cup holders. "My mother knows her," he says. "I asked Mom if she knew anyone that could be of help to you, the precocious writer, and she recommended Barbara."

I think of an earlier conversation. "Still no luck tracking down Meranda Erickson?" I ask.

"The writer? No," he says, "she's practically a phantom. But my mother tells me that Barbara's a great lady, always willing to help people out, and I bet she'll give you some pointers. You never know what you may learn on any given day."

I prepare myself for her critical analysis, taking deep breaths. In and out. In and out. Leigh enjoyed the rewrite, the bit of it she heard, but Barbara isn't an amateur; she knows what to look for in good fiction, knows the elements and how they should appear. I hope the polishing I did to the first three chapters will shine through. I cut the word count from about twelve thousand words to eight, concentrating on being more succinct. Leigh would be surprised at the difference.

"You're nervous, aren't you?" Mitch asks, glancing in my direction.

"I'm a little gun-shy these days," I say. "The last thing I need to hear is that the former head of creative writing thinks that I stink."

He shakes his head. "James, my boy, why do you feed yourself that nonsense? Is that really what you think of yourself?"

"On occasion." Okay, quite often.

"You need to work on that," he says. "Discontinue the negative messages and replace them with positive ones. Then watch what happens."

He's sounding like a self-help book. *I am good. I am great. I am . . . full of it.* I can't lie to myself. "What should I do then, walk around with an upturned nose, telling myself how amazing I am?" My tone drips with sarcasm.

"Forget the upturned nose part, and you've got it."

"That's kinda corny, though. Don't you think?"

"Not really." He pauses. "I do it all the time."

"Give me an example," I say.

Mitch ponders the request. "This morning, when I woke up, I felt crappy. My back was stiff and I wanted to return to bed and sleep the day away, knowing that I had a game of tennis to play later on. But instead of submitting to my primitive instincts, and instead of reminding myself how old I was feeling, I decided to supply my mind with nurturing messages. I told myself that I just needed to stretch and that my body, as resilient as it is, would be fine as the day went on. Then, as I stretched, I thought about how good my body has been to me throughout the years. And wouldn't you know it, this afternoon I was able to go to my friend's indoor court and play some tennis. The point is, James, *I* was a bit gun-shy about getting a move on, too. But with the right perspective, I ended up joining in the game." He smiles at me, turns onto a back road. "Now you try it."

"Out loud?"

"Sure. Let me hear you say something positive about yourself and this situation."

I'm not feeling this therapy session. "Okay . . . I'm a decent writer. Barbara won't think that I stink at writing, because I don't stink at writing."

"*Please*," he says, "you can do better than that."

"Okay . . . I'm a good writer. Barbara will think I'm a good writer. I don't need to be nervous about meeting her or about receiving her opinion."

"I still think you can do better."

"How's this? I'm a great writer. Barbara will think I'm a great writer. I'm worried about nothing."

"By George, I think you've got it!" We pull into a driveway. "And just in time, too," he says. "We're here."

Everything Mitch told me flies out the window when we exit the vehicle and head toward the house. My chest feels heavy, like someone's pressing on it, and an obscure image of a woman's face spins into my mind. The lips move and say, "I should never have read your novel. It was a complete waste of my time!"

Mitch and I arrive at the entrance and he takes the lead and knocks twice. I hear footsteps from inside the house, then the door swings open and a woman in her mid-fifties greets us. She has short, curly red hair with strips of gray throughout and she's much shorter than Mitch and I, five-foot-two or something close. She's wearing denim jeans and a white Ralph Lauren sweater and a modest dose of perfume.

"Barbara Johnson." She shakes our hands, and we introduce ourselves. Then she says, "I've been expecting you. Do come in." She waves us inside. "Would either of you like a cup of coffee or tea?" she asks as we make our way into the living room.

"Oh, no thank you," I say. "Never been a big fan." I smile. *What is this? A homespun Starbucks?*

She returns the smile. "Me neither. I only carry it in stock for occasions such as this." She chuckles, then looks at Mitch. "How about you? Coffee? Tea?"

"Coffee sounds great, Barbara."

She nods at the couch in the corner of the living room and says, "Have a seat. Make yourself at home. I'll only be a minute."

We tell her "thank you" and accept her offer; Mitch sits on the left of the couch and I on the other side as she leaves the room. Initially, we don't speak to one another, soaking in the surroundings: a fireplace between a couple windows to our left, a reclining chair on either side of the room, bookcases lining a far wall, a rocking chair directly in front of us with some papers on it, and no television, not even a radio. *Simple* comes to mind, as does *Amish*.

"I'm proud of you," Mitch says.

"What did I do now?"

"Your bravery, your determination, your talent. Everything about you. . . .You've grown into one heck of a man."

Before I can thank him, Barbara comes back into the living room, holding a cup of coffee, and says, "Now let's get down to business." She hands the cup to Mitch. She walks to the rocker, picks up the papers, sits with them in a mound on her lap.

"James, how long have you been writing?" she asks.

I fold my hands. "Most of my life. Some poetry and a novel, as you know."

"Mitch, did you ever read any of James's poetry?"

Mitch swallows some coffee, lowers the cup from his face. "Yes," he says, "and it was exceptional."

"Good word choice, Mitch." She smiles, like she just complimented one of her students. She eyeballs me. "Have you always been able to write?"

"For the most part. Not before kindergarten, obviously."

She chortles. "Thanks for the clarification. But seriously, it comes effortlessly to you, doesn't it?"

"I wouldn't say that. No. Writing takes effort."

She glances at the papers on her lap. "It doesn't seem that way."

"What do you mean?" Mitch asks.

She begins thumbing through the pages, skimming. "Your words appear to flow effortlessly on the page. I can spot writers like you from a mile away."

"How so?" Mitch speaks on my behalf.

She sighs, looks up. "In my youth, I took up the clarinet. At first I wasn't any good. In fact, my parents wouldn't let me practice indoors because of the offensive sounds I was emitting from the instrument." She chuckles; we tag along. "Regardless, I practiced. Practiced a little more. And I got progressively better, to a point where I was somewhat adequate.

"Cindy, one of my friends at the time, however, started playing the clarinet about the same time I did. She also practiced. Practiced a little more. But she didn't just get better. She soared." Barbara puts her arms on the armrests and starts rocking. "The difference between Cindy and me, other than our hair color, was that from the very beginning she carried with her an innate talent for the clarinet. Once she started playing, it was as though the clarinet was merely an extension of her." Barbara's eyes narrow in on me. "I want you to think about this, James. Which one are you?"

"Umm . . . I think maybe—"

"I'll tell you which one you are," she says. "You're Cindy." She smiles. "Metaphorically speaking, certainly."

"Well, thank you," I say.

"No. Thank *you*," she replies. "I've read countless pieces from students your age. I'm guesstimating here, but I'd say that only about five of those students were in the same league as you."

"That's quite a statement," Mitch responds as my representative once more.

"Here's the thing, James: If you weren't any good, I'd tell you. It would be a great disservice to make someone believe that they should continue to pursue writing when they glaringly don't have a prayer. But with you, it would be a great disservice to let you leave here today without telling you that you should definitely continue to pursue writing." She holds up the papers. "This is all the proof anyone needs. However, that's not to say that your writing is perfect and there's nothing you can improve on . . . All writers—including myself—can *always* improve." She puts the stack on her lap again. "Before this meeting, Mitch told me that you were interested in possibly taking a creative writing course."

I had a feeling. "He did?" I play dumb. I turn to Mitch, his face red. He looks up at the ceiling and jokingly whistles.

Barbara nods, then continues, "I believe that taking a writing course could speed things up for you, James. I could help you with the registration process, if you so choose, but please don't think that I'm forcing you to get involved. . . . If you choose to stay away from school, I think you would still, after some time, learn what you need to learn in order to land on the bookshelves. It is, of course, your decision whether or not you'd like to join a class, but keep in mind, James, that either way, I think you should continue with this story and never quit, no matter how much you might want to at times."

She looks down at my manuscript. "Now, I'd like to fill you in on a couple aspects of your writing that I feel need improvement." She turns a page, eyes it for a moment, then looks my way. "First, there are times when you're fairly repetitive. I believe you can avoid a great deal of this repetition—for instance, the overuse of adverbs, those words ending in *ly*—by learning to trust in the reader," she says serious*ly*. Earnest*ly*. Sincere*ly*. "This is difficult for many young writers because they want to make sure that they tell the whole story. Just remember that oftentimes less is better, and also keep in mind that implications are more effective than an in-your-face approach."

She flips to another page, studies it, nods, then fastens her gaze on me, "Second, are you familiar with the term head popping?"

"Uh . . . no, ma'am."

"Head popping is when the author chooses to enter the thoughts of multiple characters in the same scene. This can cause confusion in the reader and also detract from suspense because the reader knows what every character is thinking. If you must use multiple points of view throughout *The Forsaken World*, try to stick with one perspective per scene." She proceeds to give examples. I listen carefully, making mental notes.

* * *

I've decided that I won't be taking any writing courses. For starters, I don't have enough money. What's more, I don't have time to go to classes. Work, unfortunately, is something that must be done, and if I were to join a class, that would also limit my time with Leigh even more. Plus, I'm scared, which I hate to admit.

Thus, a course really isn't for me. But that's okay. Barbara's advice is proving sufficient as of late. I've been reworking bits and pieces of *The Forsaken World*, according to her suggestions, and it's turning out well.

CHAPTER SEVENTEEN

I'm tired of walking by the mountain of rejection letters on my dresser. I don't know why I've been hanging onto them. They shouldn't be revered as souvenirs, but you'd think that's what they are. Maybe subconsciously I've kept them here to remind myself of how bad it feels to be rejected, to motivate the writer within, or maybe I've kept them around to torture myself. Or a mixture of both.

I no longer want these next to my bed. I shouldn't be going to sleep each night with them by my side. Plus, they were wrong. They were wrong for rejecting my book. Each of those agents, and the editor from the publishing house. I'm thinking Barbara would attest to that.

I sit on my bed, wearing sweatpants and a tee shirt, my bedtime clothing, and lift the rejections onto the mattress. I spread them out over the sheets, pick up the first paper my hand lands on.

"*You were wrong.*" I voice my displeasure directly into the open letter, then I tear the sheet into pieces and chuck the remnants into a wastebasket at the foot of my bed. I grab another letter, reread the rejection, and talk into it. "I'm James Frost. You'll be hearing that name again." I toss the paper.

Over the course of about forty minutes, I read all twenty rejections, talk into them like a lunatic, and tear them to shreds. Those agents and the editor no longer have any sort of power over me. Their words have been obliterated. I will never again have to walk into my room, to my bed, and see the papers on that dresser. I will never again wake up with them by my side.

No doubt, this was an exercise of letting go, finding closure and empowerment. I'm going to let the words of Mitch and Barbara and Arthur fill me. I'm going to find inspiration in Mitch's saying, more than once, that he's proud of me and in Barbara's saying that my words appear to flow effortlessly upon the page and in Arthur's words about my being a natural. These people understand James Frost. Their words hold power.

* * *

I'm writing with a new perspective these days, one of hopefulness and optimism. As I tap at the keyboard, I take refuge in knowing that there are people in the world who believe in my writing. Truly believe. There is Mitch, there is Leigh, there is Arthur, and there is Barbara. Each has helped to mend my afflicted confidence.

Additionally, Robert Frost's framed message is never far away.

* * *

As predicted, I'm no longer allowed over Leigh's house; her father strictly forbade my presence in his home. Leigh, since that fateful Thanksgiving, has kept her word, visiting me every weekend at my dad's house. I don't have to see her family anymore. What a shame.

It's Saturday, Leigh arrived at the house fifteen minutes ago, and now I'm driving us to the mall; she wants to go clothes shopping. At first, I was nervous about driving us in this hunk-of-junk car, but the noises and the rust, none of it seems to bother her. In fact, a minute ago, when I told her that I paid this car off and that I like not having a car payment but that I'm often embarrassed by the car I drive, she said, "You shouldn't be ashamed of this. My dad paid for my car. You did this on your own. You should be proud. It gets you where you need to go."

It's flurrying, adding to the hills of snow on the side of the road. As I drive, I feel a sudden dash of self-respect. She's right; I did this on my own. I paid for this car, and it's getting us to where we need to go.

When we arrive at the mall, our common ground is hunger, so the food court is our first stop. There isn't anything extraordinary about the court; it harbors a pizza joint, Chinese food, subs, McDonald's, and Taco Bell. We roam around for a minute, studying various menus on walls. We decide on Chinese and step into line.

"I think I'm gonna get a number five. General Tso's and fried rice sounds good," I say. "How about you?"

"I'll probably just get some rice and water."

"I thought you were hungry."

We move up in the line. Leigh rocks her head and says, "I've been eating too much lately."

I study her thin frame. "You wouldn't know that by looking at you."

She half-smiles. "Thanks, but rice and water sounds about right."

I look at the menu on the wall. "Are you sure you don't want something with your rice and water? There's vegetable plates you could get."

She surveys the menu. "The chicken fingers look good and so does General Tso's, and Mountain Dew—that's what I really want." Her eyes dim. "But like I said, I've been eating too much lately. It's disgusting."

The last pokes my memory. "Is this you or your mother speaking?"

Her sad eyes descend from the menu, then cling to me. "Rice and water is about right," she says. "I'm going to go find us some seats, okay?"

"Are you all right?" I already know the answer.

"Do you wanna sit near the windows?" She eludes the inquiry.

"Sir, are you ready to order?"

I turn to the counter, to the speaker, a smiling Asian man with a strong accent. "One sec, please," I say, signaling with a pointer finger. When I turn back around, Leigh's not in line any longer; she's walking toward the multitude of tables, hanging her head.

I face the counter. "Number five, please." I lift my eyes to the menu. "And . . . give me an order of chicken fingers and rice, too, please. A Pepsi with mine and a Mountain Dew with the other."

"Coming right up."

He grabs a tray and some Styrofoam plates and fills them with the requested food. A guy my age appears from behind the server and sets the sodas on the tray. "Here you go," says the eldest. "Have a nice day."

I thank him and start toward the windows, balancing the cluttered tray. I spot Leigh at a table; she's gazing out the window to her right, her back hunched.

"Hey." I step to her, set the tray on the table.

Her head swings away from the window. "You're going to eat all that?" she asks.

I remove my jacket, hang it over the back of the seat, and sit across from her. "Actually," I say, "half of it's for you."

She angles her head, shock-faced. "But I said I only wanted rice and water."

"No you didn't. Your mother did." I pass the chicken fingers and the Mountain Dew across the table.

She stares at me for a lengthy moment, perplexed. Then I think she gets it because all of a sudden, she smiles and looks down at the food, eyes bulging. "But I shouldn't."

"But you *should*. It's okay. Let go."

She traces her bottom lip with her tongue, focusing on the plate. "It *does* look good."

I take a bite of General Tso's. "When isn't Chinese good?"

She ventures a smile. "Never," she says, stabbing a chicken finger with her fork like it's her mother on that plate.

* * *

"Thanks for lunch, James," Leigh says, smiling, as we enter one of the department stores.

"Anytime." In my mind, I hear her say, *Thank you for liberating me.*

She moves to a clothing rack. I hover behind. She swipes her hands through the garments, the clearance items, medium long sleeve shirts. She takes a white shirt off the rack, holds it up to her jacket-clad torso, shakes her head, and returns it to its hanger. We move to another section of the store, jeans folded in cubbies lining the wall. She takes a size six from one of the cubbies, then leads me to a rack of sweaters. She scans the selection, brow wrinkling, and chooses a green medium sweater.

"I'm gonna go try these on," she says, one arm full.

"Do I get to see?"

"If you'd like."

"I would."

We enter the coed changing room and I sit on the bench outside a booth.

She unzips her puffy jacket, then presents it to me. "Can you hold this, please?"

I nod, accept it into my hands and lay it over my lap. "I'm ready for the fashion show. Don't hold out on me."

She chuckles, one foot in the booth. "Don't worry." She gives a grin, then closes the door. I hear a zipper unzip, watch her shuffling feet through a slit beneath the door. Her pants fall to her ankles. Hands grab them up. The new jeans arrive at the feet, her hands around the waist. The jeans lift, her hands disappear. I hear a zipper zip. A minute passes, ample time to put on the sweater. I stare at the door, waiting for it to open.

"Are you okay in there?" I knock from the seat.

"I don't like the way I look," she says.

"C'mon. I'm sure you look great. Show me."

The door unlatches and opens. She steps out of the booth.

"*See.*" She spreads her arms. "I look like crap."

I examine her outfit. "Are you insane? You like fine."

"Just *fine?*" She puts her hands on her hips.

Silent, then: "I don't think those clothes do you justice. They're too baggy. You could easily wear a smaller size."

She snickers. "Smaller size, eh?"

"I'm serious. You're a thin girl. You don't need to be wearing baggy clothing. You've got nothing to hide."

She checks over her body. "Think so?"

"I'll tell you what . . . go back in there," I say, pointing to the booth, "and take those clothes off. I'll be back with your size."

"Okay," she says, uncertain. She steps into the booth.

I leave the dressing room, track down, over the course of two minutes, the same green sweater in a small and the same pair of jeans in a size four.

"Pssst. Leigh." I stand outside her booth with the clothing.

"Is that you?" she answers.

"I got the stuff," I say, as if I'm a drug dealer.

The door opens a crack and her naked arm pokes through. "Thanks," she says. "Give 'em here."

I hand them to her, the dealer giving a free sample. She pulls them in and shuts the door. I sit on the bench, watch her feet step into the size four jeans, hear the zipper zip. Thirty seconds . . .

She sighs. "I don't know. I think this stuff's too tight."

"Lemme see."

The door opens. She steps before me. The sweater and jeans are pasted on, her breasts well pronounced and perky beneath the sweater, her legs slender in the jeans.

My hormones go crazy. "Let's see the other side," I say.

She twirls, granting a quick view of her butt, then faces me. "What do you think? Too revealing?"

I shake my head, hormones bouncing. "Perfect," I say, grinning.

CHAPTER EIGHTEEN

I close my cell phone. *White Christmas.* I've just agreed to see the play with Leigh and her cousin, Meredith, tomorrow. The show will be in Boston. I've never attended a play. Thus, I don't know what to expect. I'm excited, unable to concentrate on my writing, fingers stationary over the keys, eyes unmoving on the screen.

* * *

Meredith was recently married and is three months pregnant, Leigh informs me on the ride to Massachusetts. Meredith and her husband, Greg, bought their first home together last month, a modest house in Revere, five miles from downtown Boston. We arrive at the house, get out of the car, lock hands, and take synchronized steps to the front door.

One, two, three, four . . . One, two, three, four . . .

No need to knock; a woman—Meredith, I presume—materializes at the door and lets us in. We stand in the humble kitchen.

"Meredith," she says, "and you must be James . . ." She shakes my hand, then faces Leigh. They squeak excitedly at one another. They hug.

"It's been too long," says Meredith from within the clinch.

"Way too long," Leigh says. They untangle.

Leigh puts her ear to Meredith's stomach and says, "Are you in there, little buddy?" She and Meredith laugh, as do I.

The laughing subsides. Meredith insists on showing us around the house. She leads us out of the kitchen and into the spacious living room, conventionality galore: TV, family photographs adorning the walls, a couch, a coffee table, lamps, drapes, a La-Z-Boy recliner burdened by a football-watching husband. Voices from the TV fill the room.

"Hon, we have company," Meredith says. "Can you turn that down, please?"

Greg grunts, eyes unblinking and glued to the television, feet elevated, a bowl of popcorn on his lap, a soda can on the round accent table by his chair.

"*Hon.*" Meredith raises her voice. "I *said* we have company."

His eyes blink, move to us. "Oh. Hey. Sorry." The zombie speaks. He mutes the TV with a clicker. He sets the bowl on the table, stands, one eye still on the idiot box. He approaches us and offers his hand. "Greg," he says. We shake loosely.

"James," I say. "Nice to meet you."

He hugs Leigh briefly, says, "Good to see you." Leigh matches the greeting.

"I'm showing them around, then we're off to the play. Are you sure you don't wanna go?" Her voice is harsh.

He glances over his shoulder at the television. He nods. "I'm sure."

Meredith sighs, shakes her head. He returns to his position on the recliner, undoes the mute with a zap of the remote, eyes fixed on the game, absent from reality.

Meredith blows out air, says nothing to him. "Let me show you the baby's room," she says, hand motioning to a nearby staircase. We walk up the flight and into a room containing a crib, which she tells us all about—where she and her husband picked it up and how its safety rating is far superior to any other crib on the market. She points out a rocker in the corner of the room and says, "My mother used to read me stories from that chair." She points to the lively walls, talking about the mural she painted over the surface: rainbows and clouds, the sun and flying birds, grasses, trees, and rocks. "I'll use it to teach my child about nature," she says.

I notice there isn't any mention of her couch potato husband in the equation. "Did Greg help with the mural?" I ask, facing it.

Meredith sighs, as before. "It was a solo project," she says, pain in her voice.

I can see myself living in a place like this, married, expecting the firstborn. I can imagine Leigh as the mother, plump and smiling. I don't sit at the boob tube, ignoring her for a game. I don't busy my-self with whatever while she paints a mural in the baby's room by her-self, brooding, building resentment. The fervor for the marriage doesn't die away after the honeymoon. It doesn't disappear as we buy our first home. It certainly doesn't dissolve upon receiving the news of her pregnancy. I envision Leigh and I painting a mural in the baby's room, smiling, hearts pleased, satisfied with our marriage.

That's how I want it to be.

* * *

The theatre's grand lobby is ornate in every sense. A chandelier hangs from the vaulted ceiling, the walls festooned with elaborate murals of angels riding on clouds. Marble columns, fourteen of them, I count, stand erect on either side of us. The checkered floor leads to a gold-encrusted staircase, which we climb. We end on a dais that blends into the auditorium.

An usher welcomes us, peeks at our tickets, and brings us to our box seats. As in the lobby, this auditorium also contains columns—more than I'd like to count. There are frescoes of clouds and Greek gods. Ornaments and arches consume the top of the stage, which is currently clothed with a blue velvet curtain. Balconies are everywhere.

I'm sitting between Meredith and Leigh. Leigh marvels at our surroundings, the pure opulence; she's eyeing the stage area, open-mouthed.

Eight o'clock arrives, the curtain lifts, and the play commences. The play holds my attention. I find it visually pleasing and enjoyable to the ears. My favorite parts of the play, however, have nothing to do with the play itself but with the audience, when they applaud. I envy the performers on stage. Night after night, they get to step onto a stage, the spotlight shining on them, people cheering for their words. The performer inside me wants that.

I enjoyed the words of encouragement I received from Arthur, Mitch, Barbara, and Leigh, but I'm thinking of praise on a larger scale, my work eulogized daily, the spotlight on my face. I sit in my sanctuary night after night and type. No one watches. No one claps. No one whistles or cheers. It is only me, my laptop, a plethora of ideas thrown onto a page.

I envisage myself alone on the stage before me, sitting on a stool, the laptop on my lap. I start to write. The auditorium is packed; they came to see James Frost, the renowned writer. Every few minutes, the audience breaks into thunderous applause, whistling and cheering and clapping for my talents. I feel loved. Totally. Purely. Loved. At the end of my typing performance, I stand and bow. The horde goes wild, gives me a standing ovation. I lift my head to them, sucking in the praise, letting it fill me up—then, waving, I walk off the stage with my laptop.

Only it doesn't end there. The clapping, whistling, and cheering is unrelenting, and I have no choice but to go back out onto the stage and give them the encore. I sit on the stool once again and start typing. I hear "ooohs" and "ahhs" from the onlookers, their projected amazement. I stop, then write, stop, then write again. The suspense leaves them gasping. I close my eyes, hands stopped over the keyboard, then I pound at the keys rapidly, so quickly that they can't keep up. I continue like this for five minutes, then, without warning, come to a dead stop. One person claps. Followed by another. Then everyone joins in, a booming applause. I stand, laptop cradled by my side, and bow. I march off the stage and to my amazement, they're still applauding. They want more. I walk onto the stage for a last time and give them the notorious curtain call. I bow, blow kisses, wave to all sides of the auditorium.

In reality, however, I'm just part of the audience.

CHAPTER NINETEEN

Though Christmas is for many people a time of joy, it hasn't been that way for me in a long time, ever since Dad and Mom divorced and Sis and I took sides and went our separate ways with our parent of choice. Our entire family hasn't been together for Christmas since then. Thus, instead of joy on this day, I find sadness. Sadness for what I once had and don't have anymore. Sadness for what our *family* once had and doesn't have anymore.

I receive presents from Mom and Sis each Christmas, but that's not the same as having them here at the house. Last year, for instance, I got a sweater from Mom and a wristwatch from Sis. The year before, they gave me a gift certificate for the movies and a pair of sunglasses. Searching for some correlation between the gifts, I thought about wearing the glasses to a movie but decided against it. I was convinced that if they intended for me to look like a blind person, they would've sent a walking cane. All of these presents, and all the gifts before, I'd give back in a heartbeat if, for once, they could be here for Christmas. They wouldn't even have to bring anything, just themselves and my niece.

That's a utopian idea, unfortunately. In this reality, I have Dad, who's sitting on the floor before the Christmas tree. In about an hour, Leigh will arrive, and I'll have her as well.

I stand from the couch and join Dad on the floor, my legs crossed Indian-style. We open presents, this Christmas morning, the two of us in the living room. I get several books and DVDs I've been wanting and also an iPod, 30GB, black and sleek, accompanied by an iTunes gift card so that I can download some music and a movie or two. I thank him for the gifts. Dad gets a sweater, blue and white stripes, hip for a man his age. It took me an hour to pick that out at Macy's.

"This is nice," he says, holding the sweater up to his chest. "Sure it won't look too young on me, though?"

"You'll look cool."

"And this isn't just for younger people, right?"

I give the sweater a look. "Dad, it'll look good on you. Trust me."

"Okay, okay."

"It'll last you a long time and you can wear it on dates. The ladies will like it." I smile. "It's stylish."

Dad also receives a new winter jacket, a gray Columbia that cost me one hundred twenty-five bucks.

"That will last you a long time, too," I say, watching his stolid face, his hand limply holding the jacket.

Dad sets everything—the crumpled wrapping paper, the boxes, his gifts—on the carpet beside him. "There's something I've wanted to tell you, James."

My blood pumps. "What is it?"

"I've been trying to think of ways to tell you but I'm not sure there's a good way to break it to you."

Cancer? Some other life threatening disease? "Is it something bad?"

He's pokerfaced. "Not necessarily."

Okay. Not cancer. A curable tumor? "Well, what is it? Spill it."

He heaves a sigh, then folds his arms over his chest. "I'm not sure how much longer I'll be staying in New Hampshire."

Leaving on a jet plane? "What are you talking about?" I ask.

"I'm tired."

"Of what?"

"Of living in New England, of pushing the same mop and broom day after day, of shoveling snow, of the lack of sunshine, of only a few months of warmth. Of paying almost fifteen hundred dollars a month for a house that I don't even like." His eyes are morose. "I don't wanna be here much longer. It's time for a change."

I shiver. I had once thought he would do janitorial work until the day he died. I guess I'm not much of a fortune teller. "How long have you been thinking about this?" I ask.

"Month or two."

"Where would you go? What would you do?"

"Idaho sounds nice. There's more sun out there, and housing is much less expensive than these parts." He's done his homework.

"But there's nothing in Idaho. What are you gonna do? Become a farmer?" I mock the idea because I hate it.

"There's California, too." His face lights up. "I've been looking at San Diego. According to a couple Web sites, that part of California is one of the nicest places to live in the United States. The *most* sunshine, the best average temp."

"What would you do there? Become a surfer?" I can see him now, enclothed in flowery board shorts, shirtless, chest shaved, holding a board, a *gnarly-dude* hairdo completing the package.

"Very funny," he says. "I'm not sure yet. There's a ton of jobs over there. It's the eighth largest city in America, if I remember correctly. One thing's for sure, I don't wanna clean up after people anymore. I've done that my whole life. I'm tired. You understand?"

I'm terrified. "I guess."

"I could always work for the Padres. They have plenty of job openings. I'd sell hotdogs if I have to. Whatever I gotta do to pay rent."

What about me? What am I gonna do for work if you close down your company and leave? Where am I gonna live? "There's no way you'd consider staying in New England?" I ask.

"I don't see it happening."

I think of Mom and Sis, how they live so far away, in Nevada. I can't bear the thought of Dad moving across country, too. "I'd miss you," I say. *Now, please, reconsider.*

"I know you would." He doesn't return the sentiments.

I wanted him to say, "Ooops, that's right; I can't leave you behind. What was I thinking? I was being selfish. Sorry about that, James."

Dad speaks. "We're both adults here. We can make it on our own." He implies that he's done his part, his job, and enough is enough.

"But I don't know if I can make it on my own," I say.

"Why not?"

"First of all, if you leave, I won't have a job. Second, if you leave and I get another job, I won't be able to find one that pays as well as you pay me. And third, if you leave, I could work two jobs and maybe live alone, but then I wouldn't have any time to write, and you know that's what I want to do with my life."

He shrugs. "Well, I could leave you the company . . . but I know how you feel about cleaning."

I don't say anything.

He says, "That's what I thought."

"What about Christmases?" I ask, tears mounting.

"What about them?"

"Will I get to see you or will I just get presents in the mail?" *Sunglasses and movie tickets . . .*

"I don't know," he says calmly, like he's not even going to pretend that he gives a crap.

* * *

Dad left ten minutes ago to go to a friend's house to exchange Christmas gifts. I hear a knock at the door but don't answer. Instead, I sit on this floor, holding the iPod Dad bought, staring vacantly into the screen, pondering our previous conversation.

A knock at the door . . .

Another.

Another.

I'm paralyzed. My world is about to turn upside down. I don't think Dad was bluffing. He wants out of this place. He desires to go out and *live*. And honestly, I can't blame him. He's worked so hard. He needs to find some happiness, right?

I hear the door handle jiggle. The door opens, and Leigh appears holding gifts. "You didn't hear me knock?" she asks.

I set the iPod on the floor. "I'm sorry," I say, eyes on her troubled face.

"You're white as a ghost." She places the presents in front of the door, approaches me, bends over, puts her hand on my forehead. "You don't feel hot."

She sits next to me. I tell her about the conversation Dad and I had.

Now *she's* white as a ghost. "But what about *us?*"

"I'm not going anywhere." I empathize with her fear.

"You wouldn't move to California with your dad?"

"And leave you behind? No way."

She half-smiles. "Good."

Then we trade presents; I give her two boxes from underneath the tree and she hands over the two she brought with her. I open gifts first—a leather jacket, black and smooth, and a collage of photographs from different points in our relationship. I tell her that I love the gifts, and I thank her.

"I'll want to add more to the collage, so you'll need to stick around," she says, serious.

I smile, tap on her first gift. "Your turn."

She unwraps and opens the box to a framed Bible verse. I went to a Christian bookstore, asked about a Christmas gift for a woman her age, my girlfriend, and the owner led me to this one.

She reads the passage: "'Charity suffereth long, and is kind; charity envieth not; charity vaunteth not itself, is not puffed up, doth not behave itself unseemly, seeketh not her own, is not easily provoked, thinketh no evil; rejoiceth not in iniquity, but rejoiceth in the truth; beareth all things, believeth all things, hopeth all things, endureth all things.'" She looks up at me, her face radiant. "This is one of my favorite passages," she says, smiling. "How'd you know?"

"I didn't."

"Love withstands everything," she says, setting the frame on her lap. "Do you believe that?"

I nod. Within the chasm of my soul, however, I'm uncertain.

CHAPTER TWENTY

Ten. Nine. Eight. Seven.
   Six. Five. Four.
   Three. Two.
   One.
   Happy New Year!
   Leigh and I hug beneath the firework-lit sky. We cheer and clap, blending with the crowd on this snowy hill overlooking the bay. I revel in this moment, kissing her deeply and passionately.

* * *

   I'm sitting at my desk, about to dive back into my rewrite. I open the file and stare absently at the screen. Another year has rolled in. Last year, at this time, I certainly didn't think I'd be reworking *The Forsaken World* after receiving twenty rejections and kudos from not only Mitch and Arthur but from Barbara Johnson, the former head of creative writing at UNH. Also, at this time last year, I hadn't yet received the letter from Robert Frost, the one over my left shoulder, and I hadn't met Leigh, and I definitely didn't know that Dad was going to start looking for a new place to live and work. Wow, what a difference a year makes!
   I wish I were psychic, like a palm reader, only one that isn't a fraud. Then I would know what to do next. In the meantime, I can

set goals for myself. I open a blank Word document and begin typing the goals as they roll into my head. No particular order:

1. Get this rewrite done.

2. Keep flossing and brushing my teeth twice a day.

3. Get engaged? See where things go with Leigh. Time will tell. Always does.

4. Somehow get a literary agent to give me a chance. This might come before the engagement thing. Who knows? Or I won't get engaged and I won't get an agent to look at me. Ooops . . . these are supposed to be goals, positive reinforcements. My bad.

5. Get published? Forget the question mark. GET PUBLISHED! Exclamation mark instead.

6. Marriage?

An unusual number of goals, six, but that's how many I have. Lofty? Yes. Realistic? Perhaps and perhaps not.

* * *

Last week, I bought Boston Celtics tickets, nosebleed seats deep in the balcony. Leigh and I are on our way to Boston, in my car. She would have driven, but she expressed her fear of driving in big cities. I respect that and told her I would be glad to drive. This is my chance to take the wheel, to give her a break from driving; she does the bulk of it in our relationship.

"Hopefully we'll see a good game. Last night the Celts weren't so hot." I blend with the traffic, foot tapping at the brake.

Leigh watches the road, tense. "Yeah," she says.

"Yeah" this and "yeah" that; I'm uncertain of her today. Why so quiet? The radio is off—because I don't like the added stimulation in traffic—but I had it on most of the ride because the silence between us became awkward and I needed something to fill the empty space.

"Are you feeling okay?" I ask.

She comes out with her favorite word. "Yeah."

I don't believe her. "You're not excited?"

"I am."

"You don't look it."

"I don't?"

"No. And you're not acting like it, either."

"I'm thinking."

"About what?"

"Nothing."

That's what she says when she's thinking something but doesn't want to reveal what that "something" is. "You can't be thinking *nothing*," I say.

"It's a nice day. Sunny. Cold but sunny." She provides a weather report, clearly her way around the topic.

We arrive at TD Banknorth Garden, the home of the Celtics and the Bruins, and I park in a garage near the arena. We walk across the street, yards apart, passing snow bank after snow bank, no holding of hands, no touching of any sort, alienated from one another. We come together near the entrance, where I hand her a ticket, and ask, "Are you sure you're okay?"

"Yeah." Her vocabulary doesn't differ. She steps in line, ticket in hand. "Nice day. Sunny. Cold but sunny."

I step into line behind her, detached. One wouldn't realize we are in a relationship. "You're not acting yourself," I say. "Are you—"

She snaps over her shoulder. "Quit asking me, all right?"

Her words stab into me. "Okay. Sorry."

A ticket taker—a person who takes tickets for a job, and definitely has a life outside of this—rips our tickets and leaves us the stubs. Leigh and I find our seats, two chairs in the most pitiful place in the Garden. The ball players look insignificant and nomadic from up here. Hard to believe they stand over six feet, each of them.

"This view is going to make me dizzy," Leigh says, arms on the rests, looking down on the players, those ants, watching their warm-up.

"I'm sorry," I say, as if I've committed a crime. "These are the best I could get." I feel my face flush.

The game begins, after the announcing of the Celtics players and a brief show of lights. I can't concentrate on the game, thinking of her abnormal behavior, wondering if there's anything I might have done to cause this estrangement. I glance over at her, this woman I don't understand. She ignores me, eyes on the game. The fans cheer. Leigh and I don't.

I'm tired of our lack of touch, our lack of connectivity. I sneak my hand onto her armrest and subtly touch her forefinger with mine. She doesn't respond, not so much as a look in my direction or a twitch of her finger. It's like she's been freeze-framed. This is not the Leigh I've grown to enjoy, to love. This lady is an imposter. I move my finger onto the top of her hand, start rubbing in a circular motion. No response from her. I slip my hand into hers and she pulls away, a mannequin coming to life, shocking me. She scratches her face, as if she truly has an itch. I feel rejected, unwanted.

Halftime arrives and we don't stand, we don't speak; we simply observe our surroundings, the dancing cheerleaders, the mascot—a fake leprechaun who uses a trampoline in front of the hoop to propel himself high enough to slam dunk—and a guy who tries to hit a three point shot for five grand but misses.

I had high expectations for this game, this event for the two of us, a time to grow closer, to have fun together, to do something out of the ordinary, but it's flopping, as are the Celtics.

An idea comes to mind, one of the oldest flirtations in the book, a way to touch her nonchalantly. You see it in the movies. The guy yawns, raises his arms over his head, pretending to stretch, and smoothly lands an arm over her shoulders.

I mimic the movies.

She slouches and looks oddly at me—like girls from the past—out of the corner of her eye. Her face grows bothered. Considering her obvious displeasure, I pull away, crestfallen.

CHAPTER TWENTY-ONE

Leigh and I see one another only three times in the month of February, hardly a serious association. We go through the motions of a relationship—talk on the phone a few nights per week, discuss our jobs, nothing meaningful. Our relationship is hollow, owing to deficient communication on her part and mine; I bury myself in writing, and she in her work, which leaves us minimal time to focus on us as a couple. I assume she's afraid I may leave (follow Dad, if he goes), thus she's only going to get close enough—and put forth as much effort as necessary—to maintain the relationship. Nothing extra.

Valentine's Day is uneventful. We go out to eat at TGIF and swap presents; she gives me a Bible and I present her with a plain silver bracelet I found on clearance. She doesn't let me touch her—no hugging, no kissing. I become standoffish toward her, angry, passive aggressive. I pick up the Bible from time to time, skim through pages, but mostly use it for a doorstop. She asks me on several occasions whether I've been reading it. "No. No, I haven't," I say, my voice petulant.

* * *

The snow banks diminish and Daylight Savings Time isn't far. Leigh and I are at the Boston Museum of Fine Arts, which was my idea. Leigh has expressed her liking of museums before, and I thought this would bring us closer. The plan doesn't seem to be working. I'm dead tired after a late night of intense writing, and I can barely keep my eyes open. I need five, ten, twenty energy drinks. Now.

We come to the Egyptian exhibit. The air is stale, dry. Ancient artifacts sit in cases on all sides of us—a sculpture in granite of the head of the goddess Bat, a wall tile of a Nubian chief, a sarcophagus of Queen Hatshepsut, a sandstone statue of King Tutankhamen's head. I try to start a conversation with Leigh.

"That's cool." I point to a mummified cat behind glass.

She glances at the cat but is much more interested in the glass-encased ancient bowl she's been eyeing. This doesn't make any sense to me; a dead, bandaged cat is much more fascinating, in my opinion. I join her at the clay bowl, examine its red exterior, its yellowish interior, its curvy lines and strange symbols.

I read the description below the glass. "This thing's been around like eighty times longer than us."

"I know," she says, jaded.

I go to hold her hand, to touch her. She stuffs her hand in a pocket before I can follow through. The refusal gives me a boost of energy, the equivalent of at least two or three cans of Red Bull.

"*That's it*," I say, bearing teeth like a cornered fox. "I can't take this anymore. What's wrong with us?"

Her eyes move around the room. "Umm . . . can we do this somewhere less public?"

Screw that. "I don't care if people hear us," I say. There's only one other couple in here. They're heading toward the exhibit's exit, holding hands, smiling, goading me into jealousy.

"I *do* care," she says.

We watch the couple—*the Perfects*—leave. "Tell me what's going on," I command, as though I have power in this relationship. "We can't keep acting like this, pretending nothing's wrong."

She slants her head, acting Bush-dumb. "Huh?"

"You won't let me touch you."

We gravitate to the middle of the room, near a case full of idol statues.

She frowns. "I've been doing a lot of thinking."

"About what?" I tuck a hand in my pocket.

"We rushed into this relationship."

"Are you having regrets?"

She wags her head. "Not regrets, per se."

"Then what?"

"My parents."

"What about them?"

"They don't approve."

"No crap." No sugarizing of the moment. "You've been thinking about *that*?" I ask.

"James, what if we were to go further with this relationship? I don't know if I could handle the animosity forever."

"They hate me?" I ask, for some reason acting shocked.

She takes her time. "Pretty much."

"Why, though?"

"They say you're not marriage material, and you're not the type guy I should be with." She pauses. "Mom says you won't be able to support a family. They think you're a starving artist and always will be."

My veins pop. *So the Grim Reaper and Uncle Sam think I'm undeserving, eh . . .?* "You don't believe that, do you?"

She doesn't verbalize an answer.

"They don't even know me," I say, anger boiling my blood. "They only know what I appear to be—a janitor, a starving artist. They don't *know* me." I watch her unexpressive face. "Look at what they're doing to you, Leigh. Look at the power they have over you. The influence. You're being controlled!"

Unmoving, freeze-framed again, she doesn't say a word.

I do: "Think about it. What have they always done when they don't approve of the things you do?"

After a second, she conjures an answer. "They make it difficult." Her face looks surprised, like, *Wow, I amaze myself.*

"And don't you see how messed up that is? They manipulate you."

She's speechless, like, *Wow, James is right and I don't want to admit it.*

I'm not without words: "They don't like what you're doing, so they make it so unbearable that you feel you have no choice but to submit to their wishes."

She doesn't want to hear this, changes the subject. "I've been looking for a new job, James, and I don't know where I'm gonna end up."

"Is that why you've been so cold to me?" I ask. "I don't know where *I'm* gonna end up either. . . ."

She looks at the floor, speaks in a feeble voice. "I don't know what to say."

* * *

Winter vanishes like a healthy relationship with Leigh. I'm roughly halfway done with the rewrite of *The Forsaken World.* Unfortunately, it's not easy focusing on my writing, sitting here at my desk, because of the chaos around me. For starters, Leigh called me last night and totally shocked me:

"I got a new job, James!" she said, ecstatic.

"Where? Doing what?" I asked.

"In Portsmouth, the seacoast."

Oh man. That's an hour away. "Doing?"

"I'll be working for a management company."

Furthermore, I've been thinking all too often about my future, what I'm going to do if Dad leaves, where I'm going to live, and whether or not Leigh and I will be able to sustain our relationship.

Something else that doesn't do my writing any good is the little time Leigh and I spend together. This should be positive for my writing because I have free time on my hands, but the sadness I have for our loss of intimacy depletes my creative juices. We are still in a relationship, technically, but because we see barely any of each other, and because of our lack of communication in general, it doesn't feel like we're dating, let alone that we're friends. In effect, these days, we're acquaintances.

* * *

This afternoon, Leigh will move into a small apartment in Portsmouth—the New Hampshire seacoast, the place of her dreams and of our earliest times together. I offered to help, but she said it would be best if I left it to her father and brother. I can understand where she's coming from; she doesn't want or need moving day to be more stressful than it already is, and her father and I clashing would definitely create additional stress.

I try to write but can't stop thinking about Leigh and her new apartment. I'd love to be there with her, instead of her father and brother. She and I could get her moved in, then go out and celebrate, do dinner and a movie, touch and caress and kiss in the back row of the theater. I miss the way things were between us in the beginning— hugging, kissing, holding hands.

* * *

She calls me on the first night at her apartment, scared.

"I feel so alone," she says, as if she's a castaway on a deserted island.

"Want me to come over?" I ask. "I can keep you company."

"I'm not used to this bed."

"I can be over in about an hour."

"I keep hearing weird creaking sounds."

"You're in a new environment," I say. "It'll take a few nights to get used to it."

"I miss home, my mom, my dad."

How's *that* possible? "Let me just throw on some clothes."

"But I'm already in bed."

"You don't want me to come over?" I ask, wounded.

"It's late."

"But it's better than talking on the phone . . ."

"I have work tomorrow."

"How early?"

"Eight."

"You have to start at eight?"

"Need to wake up at six-thirty."

"Are you gonna be okay?"

"Please, stay on the phone with me. I need to hear someone's voice."

"Okay."

I feel used.

* * *

Working at the school is like chewing on broken glass. A kid decides to vomit in my designated area. Guess who has to clean it up? Me. It's mud season and the kids don't wipe their feet before entering their classrooms. Guess who has to clean it up? Me. A kid urinates on the bathroom floor. Guess who has to clean it up? Me.

I'm exhausted with playing janitor. No, beyond exhausted. *Want-to-hit-something* exhausted.

* * *

It's Leigh's first weekend at her new place, and she doesn't invite me over. I haven't even seen her apartment yet. Yesterday she phoned me. We didn't talk long, about ten minutes. Work is going well, she said, she's adjusting to her new environment, which she's beginning to enjoy. Then she went on to tell me about this guy named Tim who she ran into at the grocery store. She explained that she knew him from before she moved to Portsmouth, from her younger days; he used to go to the same church as she and her family until he moved to Portsmouth a couple years ago, after landing a good job. He's the pastor's son at her parents' church. Anyway, her running into him worked out great in her eyes because she's been looking to meet friends in her area.

This weekend, instead of hanging out with me, her boyfriend, she's spending time with Tim, her so-called friend.

I'm highly offended.

* * *

I'm at the school, taking my fifteen minute break from cleaning. I call Leigh. Six rings and she picks up.

"Hey. I'm on the other line with someone. Can I call you right back?"

"Who are you talking to?" I ask.

I hear her smack her lips. "Tim, if you must know," she says.

"Oh."

"So can I call you back?" she asks, unflustered, like this isn't a big deal.

"Sure."

She doesn't return my call until the next afternoon, when she's on her lunch break and I just woke up because I wrote into the wee hours of the morning after a work shift.

"What have you been up to?" I ask. "We haven't talked much lately." I don't touch the subject of her not returning my call, blowing me off, in a sense.

"Tim and I went to the ocean last night. We've been doing a lot of catching up."

Jealousy makes an appearance. "After or before you talked to him on the phone?" I ask.

"Before."

So she went to the ocean with him and had to call him to say goodnight afterward. She didn't call me to say goodnight! "What's going on?" I ask, frightened for what she may say.

"What do you mean?" she says, flabbergasted, oblivious to my feelings.

"You've been spending an awful lot of time with Tim. There isn't anything going on between you two, is there?"

She chuckles like a schoolgirl. "We're only friends."

I want to chuckle and say *I'm only going to kill him.* "What'd you do on Saturday?" I ask, chuckle-free.

"Me and Tim went to his apartment, watched a bunch of movies, cooked dinner together, and we fell asleep."

"You fell asleep at his place?" I say, animated.

"Calm down. Nothing happened. I slept on his couch. It was too late to drive home."

"But can you see why I'd be a little weirded out about this?"

Silence, then she says, "I guess so," but I think she really means, *No, not really.*

"Wouldn't you be weirded out if I went to some girl's house and fell asleep there?" I ask, thinking of Erica, not that I'd actually sleep with the Wicked Witch.

"I don't know. Maybe." Leigh pauses. "Okay. Yeah."

CHAPTER TWENTY-TWO

Leigh has been extremely noncommittal about having me over to her place—and noncommittal in every other facet of our relationship—but finally, today, Saturday, I get to see her apartment. The apartment complex is tucked in between a cheese and wine shop and a flower shop, and she's on the ground floor. I stand in the hallway and knock at her door.

"Coming!" Her voice echoes from within her apartment.

I hear the faint sound of a man's voice.

"Hey, you," she says, opening the door, "come on in."

I step into her home, expecting to see Tim wrapped in a towel, lingering near the bathroom, or lying in her bed, nude, the drama you see on soap operas. Tim isn't here; it is, I notice, the TV from which the man's voice is coming.

Leigh doesn't lay a finger on me, not a hug or a kiss, which is expected by now (I'm diseased and highly contagious, I suppose), then she goes straight to the remote control, and turns off the television.

"Have a seat." She points to the couch, then sits.

I join her, scanning this living room/kitchen. The walls are painted in tones of blue. She has everything set up nicely—a black kitchenette table sits against the far wall beneath a mirror; the TV is mounted on the wall; a seascape painting hangs above the couch. I ask her where she got it. She says she purchased it at the mall for two hundred dollars.

"It's good to finally see this place," I say, "and to see you."

Her head bobs. "It's been a while, hasn't it?"

"Have you missed me?" I ask.

She skirts the question. "I can only spend a couple hours with you," she says, "because Tim and I have some plans for later."

My heart stops. *I guess she didn't miss me.* "But I love you," slips out. *Crap. That sounded desperate.*

"You *love* me?" She doesn't return the statement.

I want to break down and cry. "What are you two gonna do?" I ask.

"He just got a new car and wants to go cruising."

"What kinda car?" I'm working hard to keep from collapsing.

"A Beemer. It's sweet, from the sounds of it."

I'm threatened by Tim and his fancy car. "I bet his parents bought it for him, didn't they?"

"Actually, no. He makes good money and bought it himself." Her tone has attitude.

I'm your boyfriend. You should be cruising with me! "But I traveled all the way out here. I thought we were gonna spend the whole day together," I say, desperate yet again.

"I know. I should've told you. Sorry."

"Are you sure there isn't anything going on between you two?"

"I told you before, we're *friends*."

"Are you attracted to him?"

She doesn't say no and she doesn't say yes. I wish I hadn't asked.

* * *

I'm driving home from her apartment, grieved. I don't get to see Leigh all week long and when I finally get to see her, she cuts our time short because she wants to hang out with Tim, a guy who sees her practically every day of the week. Is she serious? I picture them in his Beemer, windows down, sunroof open, Leigh's hair blowing in the wind, he smiling at her, she smiling at him.

I weep, tears streaming down my cheeks. I glance at the passenger's seat, the void Leigh has left behind, where she once sat. My windows are down, my sunroof broken. I'm going home to nothing.

I don't know why, but I see them at a beach, hands interlocked, as ours once were, hugging and kissing, as we once did, and I bawl. I don't want to lose her, the woman I love, but I feel I already have. She's attracted to Tim. I know it, feel it inside.

I imagine her mother and father sitting her down at their kitchen table, the table where I was ostracized. They discuss Tim vs. James as though it's a boxing match.

"Tim is everything we want in a son-in-law," her father says. "You should really think about dating him." There's one punch to my face.

Her mother says, "Think of it. He's the pastor's son. He has a high-level job, can support you and a family." Another wallop, this one on my nose.

Again, her father: "But then there's James. He's everything we don't want." *Bam!*

Her mother: "So which one will it be?"

Leigh doesn't need to give it much thought. "Tim," she says. A right hook. *Pow!*

Her father smiles, claps his hands together in glee like a cartoon villain. "We knew you'd come to your senses one of these days," he says. That's the final blow. It's a knock out in one round. Hold up your hands, Tim. Ladies and gentlemen, introducing the new heavyweight champion of the world!

* * *

I sit at the kitchen table, poking at my food like Leigh's mother. When I finally push myself into taking a bite, one tiny piece of chicken, I find the food flavorless, as though my taste buds packed up and went on vacation. I set my silverware down, sobbing alone, tears pouring on the plate, wondering if I'll ever have a desire to eat again, thinking about Leigh and Tim gazing into each other's eyes, their long, flirtatious phone calls, their lengthy car rides in his Beemer. These thoughts knot my stomach.

* * *

In bed, at night, I can't lie still. The sheets are too tight. Then, after I kick them out, they're too loose. The room is too warm. Then, with the help of a fan, it's too cold. There is no comfort. On top of the latter, I cry every few minutes, deep, unrestrained sobbing, flashing on Leigh and Tim at the mall, our old stomping ground, and she and him spending exorbitant amounts of time at his apartment, watching movies in the dark, touching, holding, falling in love.

* * *

Writing is virtually nonexistent. I don't desire to write about magic of any sort, or to write. Period. It takes enough work to bathe, to shove a couple saltines down my throat and to throw down a glass of water from time to time. I can't possibly imagine being creative at this point.

* * *

I pass by the Robert Frost letter, stop, and stare at the text. I'm letting him down, wherever he is. He frowns, eyes narrowing. "You should be ashamed to carry the Frost surname," he says.

* * *

At work, I barely function. A constant haze swallows my mind. In the past, I've done a respectable job cleaning, but this week I forget to collect the garbage from four trash cans total. I also somehow overlook the vacuuming of two classrooms on two separate occasions.

Dad approaches me outside the janitor's closet. "You're not yourself these days. What's wrong with you?"

If you were around once in a while, you'd know. "Nothing," I say. "Is that you saying you don't want to talk about it?"

No, it's me saying it's too late to come swooping in asking questions about my life when you've shown practically no interest before. "Sorry," I say. "I'll try harder." I wish he would say the same.

* * *

I've lost five pounds from a body that can't afford to lose any weight. My hair has gotten long, inches beyond where it usually falls, and I'm taking a break from wallowing in despair to get my hair cut, of all things. There's a chance I might see Leigh later today (she said she may have some time), and I want to look as attractive as I can for her. In that case, I should go home and stuff my face with food, despite my non-appetite, because I need to gain some of this weight back. And fast.

My hairdresser, Phyllis, starts snipping my hair. "So what's going on in your life?"

I have that stupid bib over my body and I'm sweating underneath. "What *isn't* going on in my life?"

"That much, huh?"

"Yeah." I don't look at myself in the mirror, instead look down at my lap, watching peripherally as the hair falls from the side of my head.

"Last time, you said you were seeing a girl. What was her name again? How's that going?"

Can I plead the fifth? Ah, screw it. "Leigh. And things aren't going well."

"What's wrong?"

I don't have anyone else to discuss this with, so . . . "She moved to Portsmouth because of a new job and she's been hanging out with a guy named Tim all the time instead of with me. Her parents hate me. And when I say hate, I mean *hate.* I'm the last person they want their daughter with."

"That's not good. How'd she meet Tim?"

"Bumped into each other at the grocery store. She recognized him. She knew him from before."

"How'd she know him?"

"From church back home. She used to go to church with her mother and father. He's the pastor's son."

"Interesting."

"Why?"

"She's religious?"

"Yeah. *So?*" I don't know what she's getting at.

"Do you go to church?"

Oh, here we go . . . "No." I look at her in the mirror.

"You need to watch out, then."

"Why?" I've asked this too many times already.

"I can understand what you're going through, I think." She circles me, cutting hair here and there.

"You can?"

"Before I married Emerson—what, twenty years ago now?—I was engaged to a guy named Paul. He was a good guy. Went to church each week with his family. A real straight-edge. Treated me really well. But his parents couldn't stand me, thought I was the devil or something because I didn't believe the things they believed and I didn't go to church with Paul and them. About a year into the engagement, our relationship changed. Paul stopped calling as much as he did before and we weren't spending much quality time together. Come to find out, his parents had been speaking ill about me behind my back the whole time and they didn't want him to date me anymore. I know this because he told me."

"So what happened?"

Phyllis is still cutting; I watch her reflection, her fingers wrapped around the scissors. "He broke off the engagement," she says. "He said he needed to find someone that his parents didn't hate and be with that person. A year later, he was married."

"To whom?"

"To some woman his mommy and daddy picked out for him. Last I heard, he and his wife were miserable." She pulls her hand away from my head, gets rid of the loose hair around my neck with a brush. "How do you like it?" she asks, standing behind the chair.

I look into the mirror. "Pretty good," I say, thinking that Tim is likely more attractive.

* * *

I'm in the car after the haircut, driving, thinking about the conversation I had with Phyllis. I flip open the cell phone and dial Leigh. She picks up, says "Hi," and I don't waste any time. I ask her right away, "Is everything all right between us?"

She pauses, the most horrific silence possible. Then: "Well . . . no, James. We need to talk, but not on the phone."

"Why not on the phone?"

"Because this is the type of talk that should be done in person."

I pull to the side of the road, fear washing over me. "You can't give me some clue as to what you need to talk to me about?" I think of Phyllis, her engagement turned sour.

The line is silent for a second, then she says, "I don't know if we should be together, honestly."

I want to vomit. "Does this mean you're breaking up with me?"

She pauses. *This* is the most horrific silence possible. "Would it be okay if I came over tonight?"

"Why don't you want me to come over to your place?" I ask.

"Because that wouldn't be right."

"What wouldn't be right?"

"What time is best for you?" she asks.

"Anytime."

"Five?"

"That works."

"Okay. See you there."

Call ended.

CHAPTER TWENTY-THREE

Oh boy, what is it that she needs to talk to me about? Is she going to reveal that Tim had sex with her, that she's fallen for him, he and his Beemer, his job, his apartment, his status as pastor's son, his appeal to her parents, and she wants to be with him and not me?

I'm outside the house beneath a quilted sky because I can hardly breathe, and inside the house, warm and stuffy, isn't the place to be when you're on the verge of hyperventilating. Leigh will be here in about thirty minutes. Why didn't she want me to come over to her apartment? She said it wouldn't be right. What does that mean?

I can see it now:

She arrives, and we sit down in the living room to talk.

Leigh: I can't be with you anymore.

Me, hyperventilating: Because?

Her, indifferent: Because Tim's a better fit. My parents love him. He's what they want in a son-in-law.

Me, dying inside: So this is it. Are you gonna leave me now? Is this why you wanted to come over here instead of me coming over to your apartment?

Her: Goodbye, James.

Me: But goodbye is something you only say to people you're never going to see again.

Her: Exactly.

I hope I'm wrong about those thoughts. I hope the conversation doesn't happen like that. I pick up a rock, an inch long, and hurl it across the street; it strikes a tree trunk, makes a *thud*. I choose another rock at my feet and chuck it even harder; it skims through the woods, hitting one, two, three trunks like a pinball game. I bend over again to select another rock to throw, to help ease some of this anxious energy, but prior to doing so, I hear a voice I haven't heard for a while.

Tim's everything a guy should be. Brad has returned with vigor. I picture him standing in front me, grinning. *Tim has a better car than you. He has a better job than you. He has a better place to live in than you.*

* * *

Leigh and I sit down on the couch, her on my left. Dad's gone. What's new? I'm trembling slightly, worked up about the possibilities: What's she going to say? What does she need to talk about? I could cut the tension in this living room with a knife, or I could cut myself with the knife—if she decides that breaking up with me is what she wants to do. I would slash and slice and dice and scream, after she leaves, that is, and Dad would eventually find me on the floor, lifeless and bloody. Brad would be straddling my carcass, invisible to my father, as always, and Brad would be leering at my remains.

Then my Dad, standing over my body, would cry, but eventually, in a week or two, would get over it, keep womanizing, leading a selfish life. Then he would move away, some place far from here (San Diego?), somewhere that does not remind him of me.

I look into Leigh's face, the features I've fallen in love with. "Let's just sit here in the silence. Let's stay in this moment. *Please.*" I don't want to be in agony. I don't want to cut myself.

"But we need to talk," she says.

"I don't wanna talk," I say, stubborn. "I know what you're gonna say."

"You do?"

"You don't wanna be with me anymore. You wanna be with Tim."

"Tim doesn't have anything to do with this."

Please. I don't want to talk. Talking is evil right now. It means you're one step closer to telling me something I don't want to hear. "I know you like Tim, Leigh. Your hesitation when I asked you if you thought he was attractive told me."

She folds her hands over her lap. "I don't think I can keep going on with this relationship."

I picture a knife, a long serrated blade driving into my heart, drawing blood. "Why not? *Please*, we can make it work."

"I don't know. There are too many things going against us."

"Like what? Your parents? That I don't read the Bible as much as you'd like me to?" I get progressively louder. "That I don't have a nice car or a place of my own to live in or a fancy job and I'm not a pastor's son? *Give me a chance.* I'll try harder."

"But, James . . ."

"No buts," I say, voice raised. "I'll do what it takes. I'll fight for this relationship. I believe in this relationship. We're supposed to be together. We met because of fate. Remember? Destiny!" I want to grab her by the shoulders and shake some sense into her. "Is or isn't love supposed to withstand everything?"

"It's supposed to," she says gently, "but—"

"No! Please, no! No buts. You can't break up with me. You can't end it here. It can get better. We can be great together. We can have it all. I know your parents don't like me, but that doesn't have to end us. Don't be with Tim because it's the popular thing to do!"

She stands, hands flailing. "Stop assuming things!"

I stand, inches from her face, a coach arguing with an umpire. "I love you! Can't you see that? Can't you see that we're meant to be?" I put my hand on her shoulder. "Please, let me keep it here. Please, for once, let me touch you."

She doesn't pull away. "Why are we meant to be? Tell me!" She starts to shake. I wonder how long it will be until she throws me out of this game.

"Look at the day we met. On the day I was rejected by the publisher. You were there for me. You helped me through. You supported me. You accepted me when I needed it. Leigh, you saved me! You're the most amazing person I've ever known. Intelligent and beautiful. So unbelievably beautiful in every way." I fog up.

She does too. "I didn't know. I. Meant. So. Much. To you."

I place the other hand on her other shoulder. "Is loving you such an evil thing? Does my love hurt you? Can you not sleep because of it? Can you not eat? That's my life. I love you so much!" Tears are dripping.

"James, I'm . . . I'm . . ." Her eyes burst with tears.

"Tim doesn't love you like I love you. He can't. No one can. It's . . . impossible." Her tears are uncontainable; she puts her hands on my hips, bawling. "Give me a chance," I plead. "Please, give me a chance."

She comes closer, wraps her arms around my waist, crying into my chest. Her voice is muffled, "I . . . I . . . don't know . . . what I want . . . what I need."

"You've *gotta* want me." I put my hand in her hair, brush it through. "We need each other. Love withstands everything," I say with a strained voice. "Love withstands *everything*."

We hold each other close, the warm touch I've been longing for. Eyes glistening, she looks up at me and says, "I have so much to think about. I don't know what to do."

I take a step back, my hands remaining around her. "Do the right thing. Make the right choice. I know you have it in you." I smile at her, tears still flowing. "I love you, and I know you love me," I say, heart squeezed, "and that should be all that matters."

* * *

I call her the next day. She doesn't answer. I call again. Again. Again. The calls go straight to her voicemail. I try to sleep, can't sleep, stomach hollow, heart heavy, a shell of myself.

Brad won't shut up; he's standing just beyond the edge of my bed, creeping me out, feeding me all sorts of doubt.

I call her the following morning, afternoon, evening. I get her outgoing message every time. I start to think about when I told her, "Do the right thing. Make the right choice. I know you have it in you." Maybe she decided that the "right choice" didn't include me.

I still can't eat much—crackers, a snack here and there, no big meals. I'm looking more and more like Leigh's mother, the Food Poker. I cry at bedtimes, in dreams, at work, every time I'm in a situation that provides me with an opportunity to think, to feel, to hurt. To hurt.

I have enough of crying, enough of feeling myself wither away. I get angry at her like never before. I hate the power I've given her.

I hate her.

I love her.

I start leaving messages on her cell. I tell her in one message that I deserve to be loved, that I can't go on like this much longer; it's too unhealthy. I'm wasting away. Inside, I don't really believe that I deserve love, don't believe that I deserve much of anything. I'm bluffing, which is scary because I'm no good at poker.

In another message, I tell her she has to figure things out soon or I'm going to step out of this relationship, find someone who won't hurt me so much, someone who loves me regardless of their parents' stance. After I end the call, I feel empowered. So empowered. So scared. *What have I done? Oh my goodness, what have I done?* I go to the knife drawer, take out a knife, contemplate, contemplate, contemplate, the blade hovering over my wrist.

I listen to Brad/Doctor Kevorkian. *Just do it already, will you?*

Those words cause me to think of the time when I was in the ninth grade and Roberto Sanchez and I were talking in the locker room. Roberto was saying something about his life sucking and he said that maybe he should kill himself, then Brad came out of the shadows and said, "Just do it already, will you?"

I break down into tears, thinking of Roberto, and of myself. Then I decide against the deed, and drop the knife to the floor. I'm worth more than this! Am I, though? Am I worth more than this? I'm not sure.

I walk slack-jointed out of the kitchen, fall to my knees in the living room, alone. I know this for certain: I don't want to die. I'm worth enough to not die.

I want to live!

Tears gushing.

I want to live!

* * *

On yet another hopeless night, as I'm in bed listening to Brad berate me, I hear a knock at the door. Dad's home, for once, so I rush to the door to quiet down whoever is out there; don't want to wake Dad. I open the door, wary, squinting into the darkness. Leigh emerges, arms outstretched, teary.

"What are you doing here?" I don't ask this in a stern manner but in a tone of jubilation.

She dives into my arms. "I'm so sorry. I'm *so* sorry! You were right. You've always been right. They've controlled me my whole life."

I walk her into my bedroom, an arm over her shoulder the entire way, and say, "I'm so glad you're here. So glad you're here." I close the door behind us and we sit on my bed.

She continues: "They want me to be with Tim so badly. They push me and push me and push me and push me. I can't take it anymore. Every night, Mom calls me to make sure I haven't seen you or spoken to you."

"She does *what?*" I take Leigh's soft hand into mine.

She sobs. "I've been so confused. Ever since I can remember, they get inside my head. I'm fed up with it! Every aspect of my life. I was only allowed to go to the high school they wanted me to go to. I was only allowed to go to the college they wanted me to go to. And friends—my parents dictated who I had as friends. Now they're trying to tell me who I should and shouldn't date. Who I should and shouldn't love. I don't want to be confused anymore. I don't want to be controlled. I want to make my own choices and live with them!"

She looks on me, wet-eyed. "I choose you, James! Tim is everything *they* want but not anything *I* want. I was never attracted to him for myself; only for them."

My eyes well up with tears. "Oh, thank you, Jesus." I glance at the ceiling. "Oh, thank God Almighty."

"It took being away from you and spending time with Tim to see how special you are, James. He was superficial in every sense. When we talked, it was about his car and his job and all the things that don't matter in life. He never complimented me. Never made me feel like you do: alive and free. I'm so sorry. James, I'm so sorry. Please forgive me."

I take her into my arms and we roll over on the bed; I'm on top, she's on bottom. "I love you," I say. "I love you so much. *So* much."

She smiles and initiates a kiss, the warmest, most amazing kiss I've ever experienced, even beyond our earliest lip-lock. I feel love radiating through our lips, through our bodies as they connect, through our hands as they touch, and for the first time, as she pulls away from the kiss, I hear her say the three magical syllables: "I love you."

* * *

I sit at the kitchen table, devouring my food. I take a bite of chicken and find the food flavorful, the taste buds having returned from vacation. It doesn't take long to start gaining weight back. Thankfully, I won't look like a skeleton with hair.

* * *

In bed, at night, I lie still. The sheets aren't too tight. They aren't too loose. The room isn't too warm and it's not too cold. There is comfort. I remember how to sleep.

* * *

I desire to write about magic. To write. Period. Thus I do, nightly, once again, slapping at those keys.

* * *

I pass by the Robert Frost letter, stop, and stare at the text. I'm making him proud, wherever he is. His eyebrows arch and he smiles. "I'm proud to have you carry the Frost surname," he says.

* * *

At work, I function well. I do a respectable job cleaning, not forgetting to collect the garbage from any trash cans, not overlooking the vacuuming of classrooms. Dad has no reason to approach me.

* * *

Leigh and I are talking on the phone when she gets a beep. She pauses, then says, "Someone's calling me."

"Do you need to take the call?" I ask.

"No." She sighs loudly. "It's Tim. I told him not to call me anymore. I don't know what he's thinking."

"You don't want to talk to him anymore?" Time for a party.

"I'm talking with the person I want to be talking with."

PART THREE

CHAPTER TWENTY-FOUR

I'm en route to join Mitch at DJ's once again, strolling past stores of various types that line either side of the street, and as I pass one of the gift shops, a poster hanging on the inside window catches my attention. I stop, mouth gaping, transfixed in front of the window, experiencing a tingling sensation on my spine. I reread the poster:

The 14th Annual Book and Author Luncheon
To benefit the Moose Acres Public Library
Where: Pine River Colony Club, Moose Acres, NH
When: June 2nd at 1:00 PM
Cost of admission: $20
Featured guest: Pulitzer Prize-winning, New York Times *best-selling author Meranda Erickson*

* * *

Mitch and I are at DJ's, eating and conversing in a booth.

"Remember Meranda Erickson?" I ask.

"Yeah, untraceable ole Meranda." Mitch sips some milk.

"I wouldn't go as far as saying she's untraceable," I say, stabbing a fork into a piece of blueberry pie.

"And why not?" Mitch bites into a piece of his own pie.

I take a bite, smile while chewing. "Because I found her," I mumble.

He swallows. "Get out! *How?*"

"FBI."

"No, *seriously*. How'd you find her?"

"I know people in high places."

"Stop pulling my leg," he says.

"I'm not pulling your leg. I really found her."

Then I tell him about the poster at the gift shop. His eyes enlarge and he starts laughing. "You're screwing with me. You've gotta be screwing with me."

"Nope. No screwing here."

"Then you know what this means? You need to go to that luncheon!"

"Got that right."

"How far along are you in your rewrite of *The Forsaken World?*"

"Three hundred eighty-four pages."

"Does that mean you're almost done?"

"If all goes well."

"You amaze me," he says, then turns to a male voice—"Mitch!"—coming from a couple tables away.

A man with an obvious comb-over wig and a lined face waves at us and saunters to our table, a woman in the same age range, wrinkles similar to her partner, trailing him.

"Good to see you!" Mitch shakes the man's hand. Then Mitch eyes me and says, "This is my accountant, Dan."

"Have you met my wife before?" Dan asks.

Mitch shakes his head.

Dan motions to his wife, who stands at his side. "Melinda," he says, "meet Mitch Ermont."

Melinda gives a quick wave, and Mitch says, "I'd like you two to meet one of the best up-and-coming writers around, James Frost."

My face gets warm. I take a fleeting look at Dan's hair and think: *Why, hello, Trump.* "Nice to meet you," I say, hands perspiring.

"What kind of writing do you do?" Dan asks.

"James is a novelist." Mitch smiles, proud.

Dan looks astonished. "What books have you written?"

"*The Forsaken World,*" I say.

"What is it about?" Melinda asks.

"You'll have to buy it when it comes out," Mitch says.

Dan crosses his arms. "When will *that* be?"

"That's still being determined." Mitch winks at me without them seeing.

"Well, we'll keep an eye out for it," Dan says, and I swear I see his hair move, like it's not a wig at all but a shaggy creature of sorts, and it's going to attack. But then I realize, glancing upward, that someone in this joint turned on the ceiling fans and Dan's hair is merely reacting to the wind current.

"*The Forsaken World* by James Frost?" Melinda puts her arm around The Donald. "I'll have to remember that," she continues.

Mitch grins. "You might want to get his autograph now, before he's famous and untraceable."

* * *

After lunch, I stand with Mitch at his car in a sun-drenched parking lot. I'm wearing sunglasses, and he's wearing sunglass clips on his regular spectacles.

"Have I ever told you about my child?" he asks.

"You have a child? I thought you two weren't able to have kids."

"When we were newly married, we were expecting. . . . We went out and bought a larger house, set up a baby's room. We went all out. Got the best crib available. Painted the walls with nursery rhyme characters. We were set to go."

"So what happened?"

"One morning she was having horrible cramps. She went into the bathroom and noticed she was bleeding. She was on the toilet when she called out my name. I came rushing in there and she grabbed my hand, squeezed and screamed. I was a young man and didn't know what was going on. I didn't know if that was normal or if there was something wrong. I watched her face, my beautiful wife's face, and it was contorting every which way. 'Something's wrong, something's wrong, hon,' she kept saying."

I don't know why Mitch is telling me this.

He slips a hand into a pocket. "My instincts told me to get her off that toilet. She shouldn't be on that toilet. That's not her place. I didn't listen to that instinct. Next thing I heard was a splash." His speech is slowing. "*Please be poop. Please be poop*, I remember thinking over and over again. *Please make it be poop I heard splashing.* She looked down in the bowl and I knew from her scream, from her tears, from her wailings . . . it was our child. Dead." Mitch stops, face tight, controlling his emotions.

"I had no idea," I say. *What do I say to that?*

Mitch doesn't leave additional room for comment. "It took us four years after that," he says, "four years to give having a child another try. Nothing worked. We went to the doctors. They told us to try this and try that—stand on your head, do it hanging from a tree, whatever. Once again, nothing worked. We tried for years after that, but no luck."

"I'm so sorry, Mitch." *Still don't know why you're telling me this.*

He looks up at the sun, smiling, then eyes me. "Sometimes it appears as though we've been denied an essential piece of life, like a child, for instance, but then God has a miraculous way of giving us what we need." He halts, pats me on the back. "You probably didn't know this, James, but you're God's gift to me." His bottom lip quivers slightly as though he's about to cry. "I'm proud of you . . . *son.*"

* * *

I'm finally able to see the light at the end of the tunnel with the rewrite of this novel. The tale is far ahead of where it was months ago. The characters are so real, I expect them to step from the pages any minute now.

I could sit each of them down and talk to them separately.

First, with Stephen, the protagonist, the mistreated underdog:

Me: Thank you for putting up with me, the god of your universe, all along, even when things seemed bleak and hopeless.

Stephen, his jet-black hair frowzy: You know, it hasn't been easy. For the longest time, I couldn't see you. I had a feeling you existed but you weren't in front of me, in view. There were days when everything seemed chaotic, as though nothing and no one had control over things.

Me: You're a true hero. I love you, my creation.

Stephen, his blue eyes lively: There were days when I thought you had forsaken me. I was thrown into circumstances that I loathed, situations that no one should have to endure. Why'd you do that to me? Why'd you put me in those places?

Me, smiling: You needed to grow. You weren't going to do that without some hardships and roadblocks to persevere through.

Stephen: There were days when I hated you for not intervening. When Dreco murdered my mother and father, I hated you passionately. You were an enemy.

Me: I was there with you from the beginning, loving you. I saw the end before you were born. When you thought I wasn't intervening, that's when I was.

Stephen: I look at myself, my face scarred by Dreco's blade, and wonder how I made it. How'd I make it here?

Me, grinning: Love withstands everything, Stephen. Love withstands everything.

Next, with Dreco, the antagonist, the murderer:

Dreco, his bald head polished, eyes bloodshot: Why have you brought me here?

Me: Justice.

Dreco, voice dithering: What kind of justice?

Me: You're a murderer, aren't you?

Dreco: Yes, but I'm sick.

Me: I've taken that into account.

Dreco, his lips curled downward: Will you forgive me for my wrongdoings?

Me: You admit you've done wrong?

Dreco, tone sincere: Yes. Please forgive me for my trespasses.

Me: I was there with you from the beginning, loving you. I saw the end before you were born.

Dreco: Then you knew I'd murder but you still created me?

Me: You were part of an overall plan.

Dreco, pleading: Please forgive me.

Me: You are forgiven, my creation.

Dreco, lips curled upward: Thank you. Thank you so much. Despite all of my wrongdoings, you still found it in your heart to forgive me.

Me, smiling: Love withstands everything, Dreco. Love withstands everything.

CHAPTER TWENTY-FIVE

Leigh and I are eating at Mario's, an Italian restaurant five minutes from her apartment. I have fettuccini alfredo and she has lasagna. In between bites, we chat.

"After this, do you want to go to the gym with me?" she asks. "I'm allowed a free guest with my membership."

The excuse: "I'm not really the gym type."

"You don't want to go?"

The real reason: "I'm too skinny and pale."

"No, you're not."

I take a drink of cola. "Have you seen the guys that go to those gyms, all big and full of muscles—and tan?"

"That's not true."

I don't listen. "I'm not gonna go stand next to one of those guys and work out." I lift an arm over the table, tap at the bicep. "Look at this thing. It's too skinny."

"You have nice arms. I like them."

I lower my arm. "No, you don't. You're just saying that."

She rolls her eyes like her mother. "I'm not just saying it. I *do* like them."

"If I were any whiter, I'd be clear."

"That's not true. I like your skin."

"Maybe you should get your eyes checked. You're obviously not seeing correctly."

"It's *your* eyes that need help," she says. "Just go with me, James. You'll see it isn't bad at all."

"If I were to go, there would be no wearing of sleeveless shirts."

"*I* can't wear one?"

"I'm referring to myself. I don't need the whole world to see Mr. Transparent's skeletal arms."

"Would you quit the self-deprecation already?"

"But it's how I feel."

"Well, forget that. Your mind's distorted."

"No, it isn't."

She smiles, pressing on the message, "James, I like the way you look."

* * *

We're at the gym against my better judgment, and I've never seen this many mirrors. Mirrors hang on walls near the bench presses; they hang near the free weights, next to the treadmills, the elliptical machines, everywhere, like a funhouse. There are busy bodies far and wide. Buff men—a cluster of Fabios—lift the dumbbells, gazing adoringly at their reflections. Average-looking men lift the same weights, few smiling. Skinny men—a group of corpses—struggle with the bench presses, pain written across their faces. A mixture of men and women run on treadmills, shirts doused with sweat, faces determined, pushing for a gold medal in a nonexistent sport.

"I'm going to go stretch," Leigh says as we stand next to the water fountain. "You should too."

"Yeah, I should." We go over to the mats, stretch for about ten minutes, stand.

"I think I'll do some running." She glances at the treadmills.

I look at the skinny men. "I think I'll do some lifting."

"This isn't what you expected, is it?" she asks, an *I-told-you-so* moment.

"Well, they aren't all Fabio. That's a plus."

"You fit in, *see?* You need to stop assuming things."

"I know, I know . . ."

* * *

Leigh and I have run approximately one mile on Atlantic Avenue, a road situated near the Atlantic Ocean. *Go figure.* Huffing, we slow the pace to a jog, to a brisk walk, then, as our breathing quiets, we stroll. Mansions encased by endless gates tower on each side of us. Multimillion dollar homes, no doubt. I marvel at them as a window shopper who can't afford to buy.

"Tell me about your dreams." I take her hand into mine.

She says, "When I was a kid, I wanted to be a teacher."

"What happened to that?"

"Grew out of that phase, I suppose."

"What about now? Any dreams since then?"

She smiles. "I'd love to own a café."

"That sounds nice. Where would you want it to be?"

"On the beach, somewhere tropical."

"What will it look like?"

"I don't know."

"You *should* know."

"I should?"

"How will you see it through if you don't know what it's gonna look like?"

"I don't know . . ."

"Work with me here," I say. We pass an extravagant garden that sits at the edge of a front lawn. "What do you see?"

"Flowers," she says sarcastically.

I chuckle. "No, *crazy*—away from the garden." We stop on the side of the road. I tell her to close her eyes. "*Now* what do you see?" I ask, releasing her hand. I stand directly in front of her, watching her face contort.

"Bright walls," she says.

"What colors?"

"Orange and yellow."

"What else?"

"Umbrella tables out back. In front of the ocean. People sitting beneath the umbrellas, reading, sipping our finest iced coffee."

I have her open her eyes. "Do you believe in what you saw?" I ask.

"Yeah . . . *in my dreams,*" she scoffs.

"You don't dare believe in it, do you?"

"No."

"Why?"

"I don't wanna be let down," she says.

"What's wrong with dreaming big?"

She shrugs. "It feels too far away."

"Then you need to map out the idea. You've conceived it. Now figure out exactly where it's going to be. Exactly what you're going to serve. Exactly what it'll look like. Bring it to life. That's what I did with *The Forsaken World,* and all of a sudden it doesn't feel far away anymore." I hold her hand again. "Don't you believe God will give you the café?"

"Half and half."

"I don't believe in half and half. You either believe or you don't."

"But I don't want to lie and tell you I completely believe."

"Leigh, did you ever think that maybe God is the one who gave you the idea for the café?"

She flushes. Her eyes water. "You think?"

"You'll have a café someday on the beach, with umbrella tables, and people will sit at them and drink your iced coffee. But you have to believe it first."

She rubs her eyes, smiling. "I'll work on it."

* * *

"Just so you know—there's a very good possibility I'll be moving to California. I sent my résumé to five companies in the San Diego area. All of them are customer service positions. Not exactly what I want to do but definitely a lot better than cleaning up after people."

I dunk the mop in a bucket. "That would be nice, Dad." I don't, in truth, think it would be nice, forsaking me.

Dad unclips the bulky keychain from his belt, holds the keys in his palm. "I wouldn't miss dealing with this school." He glances over my shoulder, down the hallway. There is no one in proximity.

"Me neither." I slop the mop down on the floor.

"I don't know about you but once I leave this place, I'm never coming back. I'll never set foot in this building again."

"Will you come back to New Hampshire to visit?"

"You could come out to California to visit, you know."

"So *you* wouldn't visit?"

"There's nothing for me here." Dad idly separates a key from the rest, his eyes on me.

I start to mop. *What about me? Hello . . . Dad, what about me? Have you forgotten about your son? I'm nothing to you?*

"New Hampshire is an area I'd like to forget," he says, thoughtless.

* * *

I put the finishing touches on the rewrite, click the SAVE button, and stare in awe at the screen. I started with a blank page lifetimes ago. Now I have page upon page of filled space. I jump to my feet, dash away from the desk and out of my room. High on this feeling of victory, I hurry outdoors, pumping a celebratory fist. "I did it. I did it!"

In the cover of night, shaking, I laugh and cry, laugh and cry . . . schizophrenic.

Ten minutes later, I call Leigh. She's been sleeping, so she sounds groggy as she answers the phone, but after I fill her in on the news, her voice livens up: "I knew you could do it, James! You're amazing."

* * *

For the first time in months, I call Sam's cell. He doesn't answer. Nothing earth-shattering here. I've been thinking about him lately, wondering about his new existence in a land far, far away. It's time to find out. I call his parents' house. His sister picks up. I ask her when Sam is coming home for break. She explains that he won't be coming home, that he plans to stay in Pennsylvania for the summer, renting an apartment with one of his friends from college.

"Which friend?" I ask.

Her small voice says, "A guy named Fred."

I pause, envision the Gucci man, anger present. I go on to thank her for the information. We end the call.

Time told, eyes moistening. *Goodbye, Sam. Goodbye, my brother.*

* * *

I drive beneath a brilliant lapis sky, windows down, music playing, feeling successful. Final destination: Leigh's apartment.

I'm doing fifty in a forty zone. I play with the radio, changing stations, attention alternating between the knob and the road. Find a song that I like, give full attention to the road. I'm coming to a four-way intersection. There are no cars in front of me in this lane, just a set of lights, currently red. I tap at the brake pedal. I'm not slowing down. I tap at it again.

The vehicle isn't slowing!

I stomp on the pedal, hands tense, clutching the steering wheel, heart spanking the inside of my chest. The pedal hits the floor with no resistance. I'm still going fifty. Vehicles are passing through the intersection—SUVs, cars, trucks. I let off the brake, try pumping it.

The pedal hits the floor again. The vehicle isn't stopping!

I think of Leigh, her beautiful face, her soothing voice, her silky hair, her accepting nature, her bravery. I think of her embrace, her kiss. I see my text-filled pages, the characters, Stephen and Dreco, and they're dying. The world will never know of their existence.

I can't die. I'm too young to die! It can't end like this, not after things are actually getting good. An idea crosses my mind—the emergency brake. The light is still red. I hold the hand brake, that lever, and pull up slowly, careful not to snap it.

The car is slowing. Finally, the car is slowing! I think of the mechanic, the manager from months and months ago who told me I needed new brakes, and how he couldn't believe I wasn't going to fix them.

I release, pull, release, pull, release, pull the lever, slowing more each time. Five feet before the lights, I fishtail and come to a complete stop, blood rushing to my head. The light turns green. I start laughing. The irony.

I crawl through the lights, going five, hand on the lever, coast into the parking lot of a gas station, and use the e-brake to stop. I call Leigh.

"Are you okay, James?" She responds to my trembling voice.

"I almost died."

"Where are you?"

I tell her the name of the station. "Can you come pick me up?"

"Of course."

* * *

The car is in the shop, towed as it was, and Leigh and I are driving to her apartment in her car.

"I didn't want to have to spend that much money," I say.

"You're fortunate to be alive. You heard what that mechanic said. You could've crashed."

"But I can't afford to have it repaired. I'm gonna have to throw the expenses on my credit card. I hate debt."

"It could be much worse. What if you died, James?"

"I thought I was going to."

"Where would you go if you died?"

"Where would I go?"

"Do you know where you're going when you die?"

"No. Who does?"

"I do."

"Where?"

"To a place with no tears, no sadness, only perfection and happiness. A place where there are no cars and chances of dying in one. A place where there is no death. Period. A place with no war or sickness. That's where I'm going."

"Heaven?"

She nods. "The Kingdom of God."

"That sounds like a place I want to be."

"I want you there, too."

We get to her apartment and sit on her couch. She pulls out her Bible, thumbs through the pages, and stops on a passage.

"I want to read this to you. Do you mind?"

Why not? "Go ahead."

"'Jesus answered and said unto him, Verily, verily, I say unto thee, except a man be born again, he cannot see the kingdom of God. Nicodemus saith unto him, How can a man be born when he is old? Can he enter the second time into his mother's womb, and be born? Jesus answered, Verily, verily, I say unto thee, except a man be born of water and *of* the Spirit, he cannot enter into the kingdom of God.'"

"What does *that* mean?"

"To be born again is to be saved. I've mentioned that term to you before, being *saved*." She points to the page. "It doesn't have to be a raising-your-hands-in-the-middle-of-a-field kind of moment or anything. Faith is a process . . . If you want to see the Kingdom of God, you do that by believing in Jesus. First, let me read this to you." She turns the pages, finds a new spot. "'For all have sinned, and come short of the glory of God.'"

Okay? I'm unaccustomed to seeing Leigh in preacher form.

She proceeds. "Then Romans goes on to say this, which explains the consequence of sin: 'For the wages of sin is death.'"

"So if you sin, you die? Doesn't everyone die?" I'm acting like a raging skeptic, and I know it.

"If you sin, and don't accept Jesus Christ as savior, you're condemned to death."

I grimace. *Lethal injection or the chair?* "Ouch."

She turns the pages again. "The Book of John says this: 'For God so loved the world, that he gave his only begotten Son, that whosoever believeth in him should not perish, but have everlasting life. For God sent not his Son into the world to condemn the world; but that the world through him might be saved. He that believeth on him is not condemned: but he that believeth not is condemned already, because he hath not believed in the name of the only begotten Son of God.'"

Goodbye, Death Row. Hello . . . "Everlasting life. Immortality." I smile. "Through Jesus, the Son of God."

She closes the Bible. "For centuries, people have been searching for ways to achieve immortality. The Fountain of Youth. The Philosopher's Stone . . . They were looking in the wrong places, devoting time to the wrong causes."

I chuckle. "But you're saying immortality was under their noses the whole time?" I'm beginning to understand, to see the picture.

"Yes." Her face glows. "Believe in Jesus and you'll live forever." She closes the Bible, sits it beside her on the couch, and we hold hands.

I rub her back. "*Then* will I be with you in the Kingdom of God?"

Her smile doesn't perish. "Forever," she says.

* * *

The next night, Sunday, I sit down, curious, with the Bible that Leigh bought me for Valentine's Day.

What do you think you're *doing?* Brad asks.

That question makes me think of Chris Williamson from high school and how he used to carry a Bible, and I think of one time when I crossed paths with Chris in the hallway and asked him what he liked about the Bible the most, and Brad happened to walk up behind us as we climbed the stairs, and he asked, "What do you think *you're* doing?" I turned around and he continued with: "You're not gonna turn into one of those Jesus Freaks, are you? Christianity is unoriginal crap . . ."

I picture Chris and the look of hurt I saw on his boyish face, and this time, *now*, unlike before, I tell Brad to shut up. Just shut up. For some reason unknown to me, he actually listens.

Leigh told me the best way to start believing in Jesus, to indisputably believe in him, would be to read the Gospels, which she said are the Books of Matthew, Mark, Luke, and John. She also said that it would be a good idea to read the Gospels because we should strive to be like Jesus, and the Gospels are full of his actions.

This Bible provides in depth analysis of virtually every verse of every chapter in the form of footnotes. Because of this, naturally, the tome is over two thousand pages in length. It's heavy, about three or four pounds, I think, and it's spread over my lap as I'm sitting up in my bed, the bedside lamp casting a yellow glow over the pages.

I start somewhat reluctantly at the beginning of Matthew, learn about Jesus' birth, the angel that came to Mary's husband, Joseph, beforehand and said that the child inside her was from the Holy Spirit—which I learn, through footnotes, is an aspect of God. Then the angel prophesied that Mary's son, whom she was to name Jesus, would save his people from their sins.

I flip through the pages, intrigued.

I come to when Jesus was baptized by John, and as soon as Jesus came out of the water after being submerged, the heavens were opened and God descended like a dove down to them. And a voice from heaven declared Jesus his beloved son.

Then I arrive at Matthew chapter four, where Satan the Devil takes Jesus to an exceedingly high mountain and offers Jesus all the kingdoms of the world. Jesus doesn't take Satan up on the offer, which amazes me because if I were presented with power like that, I'd probably cave and accept the proposal.

Then I find myself, after tossing through a few more pages, at the Sermon on the Mount, where Jesus taught about the Law, about lust, anger, divorce, vows, retaliation, prayer, loving your enemies, giving to the needy, money, worry, and many other things. My favorite part of the Sermon is Matthew 6:25–34, which basically says that we shouldn't be worrywarts, since God promises to provide us with what we need.

I'm enthralled by Jesus at this point—his wisdom, his Voice of Power. Another one of my favorite passages, as I continue to read, is about criticizing our fellow human-beings and how if we judge others, we'll end up being judged, too.

I smile, spellbound by this book, the lyrical language, the unparalleled wisdom. Jesus spoke those words. I'm in awe of him.

I read on, reach the miracles—how Jesus healed a person of leprosy, the AIDS of that time period; how he healed a paralyzed man, made it so that the man could walk again; and how he healed the blind and mute, and more.

Then I jump ahead to Jesus' parables, which I also find outstanding. Afterward, I read about when Jesus supernaturally turned five loaves of bread and two fish into enough food to feed about five thousand people.

It has been five hours since I began reading this Bible and I can't put it down. On every page, there is some aspect to be learned, to discover, to understand. Jesus walked on water. At one point, he even healed all those who touched him. Being a writer of fantasy, this book is especially delightful. I don't dare to begin comparing *The Forsaken World* to the Bible in terms of quality, but the fantastical elements exist in both, like the transfiguration of Jesus on the mountain, for example; the prediction of his own death; the healings and miracles, obviously; and greatest of all, his ability to conquer death!

It goes like this: Jesus was betrayed by Judas, one of his followers who Satan possessed (now that's a story!), then Jesus was arrested by the authorities, because Judas turned him in. Eventually, they crucified Jesus on a cross, the most horrific type of death. Jesus was a substitute for us when he died on that cross. Three days later, he rose from the dead with a restored body!

Stuff like this couldn't have been invented. These accounts were written by different people in different time periods, and these writings survived many centuries to find their way into this Bible sitting on my lap. With an open mind and heart, I believe what I've read is genuine. Jesus, the Son of God, followed through with his death so that we could live forever, so that everyone on earth that believes in him can have everlasting life.

I end my reading on the part of the Bible, in the Book of Matthew, when Jesus gives what is called, according to the footnotes, the Great Commission, where he says that he's been given all power in heaven and in earth, and I think: *Wow, Jesus is all-powerful. Puts the Man of Steel to shame.*

I close the Bible. I know there's still much more I need to learn; I have only grazed the surface of this enormous book, the Word of God, as it has been proclaimed. I am mesmerized. Fascinated. Rapt. Captivated.

However, in the back of my mind, I wonder if Brad was right all those years ago about Christianity being unoriginal. I shake my head, teeth clenching, think: No, Brad—Christianity *isn't* unoriginal. Jesus himself was *unconventional* with his thinking, his preaching and ideas. That's why the masses hated him. He didn't fit in. He was an outcast. Like me. Like Chris from high school. Jesus dared to be unconventional in a world full of conventionality. He told the people of his time about the dangers of anger. He spoke about lust, how it can destroy a person. He touched on divorce, how one should never use that vehicle to satisfy his/her longing to marry another. He said that instead of retaliating when someone hurts us, we should do good to them, love them, and forgive.

I can still remember the day I watched in the distance, from my locker, as Chris, while curled up in a ball on the hallway tiles, face showing anguish, tried to use that philosophy with Brad after being walloped in the stomach. Chris said, in a weak voice, "I forgive you," then Brad laughed, punched him again, and said, "Forget forgiveness."

I hold the Bible tightly. What Brad said is what the world as a whole has been saying for centuries . . . even now. Jesus taught about loving your enemies. He even forgave those who crucified him. He actually forgave his killers! He urged people to love God and not money, to trust that God will give us what we need. But even greater, he lived a life of selflessness. Absolute, utter selflessness, even to death.

Christianity isn't some clone-ish religion. Instead, true Christ-followers strive to be like Jesus and make every effort to live out his unconventional teachings . . .

Finally, I see Jesus as more than a ghost or a phantom; I picture him on that cross, arms outstretched, long dark hair, an olive complexion, bleeding from head to toe, wearing the crown of thorns, nails spiked through his palms, and he's wailing in agony, shouldering the sins of the world. My sins included. I've lied, therefore I'm a liar. I've stolen (when I was younger, but it still counts), thus I'm a thief . . . and I wonder: How does all of *that* make me a good person, which everyone seems so keen on declaring themselves? With a nauseating feeling, I realize that it doesn't make me good, and I feel sorry for my lies and for my thievery, and I wish I could take it all back, but I can't, and there's only one who can.

I look into Jesus' eyes, the Son of God, recognize the pain, the sadness he has for the world, and for me. I tell him that I'm sorry for my sins. *So sorry.* I want to cut him down from that cross, to bring him somewhere safe, to sit down and eat with him, ask him all the questions my heart desires, but I know he must follow through with this. The world needs him. *I* need him.

The worst physical pain I've endured in my life came when I broke my leg in the sixth grade during a baseball game. Not quite on the same level as crucifixion, admittedly. I remember diving into home plate and hearing a snap, then wincing as pain stabbed through my leg. It was horrendous. Comparatively, though, my pain was nil next to Jesus'. I can't fathom being in his place on that cross.

CHAPTER TWENTY-SIX

I step through the door of the post office, clutching, with both hands, my novel, this chunk of papers, at my waist. At the counter, I ask the mail clerk for a box. He wants to know what size box I need. Double-handed, I hold up the block of papers to give him an idea. He nods, ducks below the counter, then reappears with an unassembled box. He puts it on the counter. No line behind me, so I set my manuscript on the counter and assemble the box here. The clerk watches as I neatly slip the pages into the box, then print Arthur's address on the front.

I hand over the package, the manuscript, my child, to the clerk. He sets it on his scale, gives shipping options—standard, priority, overnight. I choose overnight with signature confirmation. He slaps a special sticker on the box's face, jots something onto a paper smaller than my palm, sets the box aside. I pay him.

"Here's your tracking," he says, handing me the small paper.

I glance at the slip, put it in my pocket. "Take extra care of that package, please." I can't step away, leave the box out of sight.

He nods and smiles. "It'll be safe with us," he says, reassuring me, the apprehensive father. Clammy Danny Tanner fretting over little Michelle's first day of school.

I take two steps backward, grinning. The clerk scoops up the package, and as he walks out of sight, the box in hand, I think: *Be safe, my child.*

* * *

Leigh and I step into the stuccoed church, holding hands. We're immediately greeted in the entrance by a man clutching literature, a brochure of sorts. He hands us each one, smiling, and says, "Welcome." Leigh smiles in return, as do I, and we thank him for this—bulletin, it appears to be, now that I'm looking inside of it, walking past the greeter. Big bold letters that read **WEEKLY BULLETIN** on the inside flap give it away.

Next, we walk down the center aisle. I close the bulletin, examining this place of worship. Pews fill both sides of us, about half of them loaded with worshipers. I'm not underdressed, to my surprise, in a pair of khakis and a collared shirt. I only spot a handful of men in suits. I find comfort in this discovery. Evidently, dressing up for God isn't *in* anymore. Continuing down the aisle, my vision moves to the side walls, which are adorned with stained glass windows of various colors depicting: Jesus walking on water; Jesus with his hand on someone bowing in deference before him; the nativity scene; a dove with spread wings; and crosses, big and small.

My focus drops down to Leigh's backside. Not her buttocks. The center of her back.

She turns to me, stopping at a pew four rows from the stage. "How are these?" She motions to the row.

I nod and shrug. "This works." We scoot into the pew and sit on the hard wood. I'm in the aisle seat and she's to my right.

I put my arm around her, smiling, and whisper in her ear, "Thank you."

She pulls away, grinning. "For what, crazy?" she whispers.

I'm starting to feel syrupy. "You've played a big part in this. Without your influence, I wouldn't have arrived at this conclusion."

"What conclusion?"

"That this is where I'm supposed to be, a place of worship for Jesus, my unconventional savior." Overflowing with belief.

She doesn't stop smiling; neither do I.

"You're welcome," she says.

The service starts a minute later. Pastor Anderson, as his name says in the bulletin, begins with a word of prayer, his voice magnified from a microphone clipped to his shirt. After the prayer, he tells us to open our hymnbooks to page one hundred two. The pianist begins. The congregation starts singing *Amazing Grace* as one, and I just stand here, listening, taking it all in like a teenage Kirk Cameron.

I've heard this song before on TV, I believe. It never made as much sense as it does now. *Oh, Jesus, I was once lost and now I'm found.* Thank God Almighty for finding me, this wretch. An image comes to mind: I'm walking in the dark, aimless, alone, angry and fearful. Then, suddenly, a luminous hand reaches out for me, the softest touch I've ever felt. I don't pull away, don't reject the presence. Without warning, arms close around my body, an embrace of infinite warmth and love. Then a face appears—Jesus' glowing countenance, smiling. I've been found. Unconventional Jesus has found me in this game of hide-and-seek.

We close our books, smiling, everyone in attendance. I've never in all my years seen this many smiles. One would think they discovered coupons for free Botox. In truth, though, these people appear genuinely happy, unconcerned with any of the negativity of this world, shielded by Jesus' love. Leigh looks like she could cry, eyes on me, the boyfriend who believes. This sight makes me want to get on my knees and weep. I love her. I love this moment, this precious, precious moment.

Pastor Anderson prays again, asks us to be seated. We sit. His sermon is about joy. He explains that joy should be part of a Christian life, that the Bible commands us to be joyful. In fact, Pastor Anderson goes on to tell us that in Philippians, Paul, while imprisoned, was filled with joy. Initially, I find it odd that a person in prison could find joy, but then Pastor Anderson explains, gesturing to us spectators: "Paul was able to find joy because he believed that regardless of what happened to him, Jesus was in control and would be with him . . ."

I think of a prison cell, bars containing a nondescript man. I don't know exactly how it went for Paul, but I see a man sitting on the cell's floor, not dejected but joyous—smiling as he's given scraps to eat, smiling as he's beaten by the guards, smiling as his life is threatened. I'm in awe of this man from my vision and his faith for Jesus. I wish that I could have faith of such magnitude.

I ponder my life, the times I thought I had it so bad. My parents' divorce, up to more currently: the rejections and performing janitorial work. Paul had all his freedoms taken away and could've easily sulked, but instead he found joy through Jesus. Of course, he had something to be joyous about, his faith. That's something I didn't have until recently.

* * *

I call Arthur to see if my novel made it to him safely; I misplaced the tracking number. He comforts me, says it made it to his house. I talk to him about maybe lowering his hourly rates for editing services because I haven't been doing well financially—with the car repair especially. After a brief pause, he offers to edit the current draft at no cost. "Think of it as a gift from one friend to another," he says. I get choked up, clear my throat, thank him repeatedly for his kind gesture.

Then I inform him of the Luncheon. He expresses interest.

"You should come with me," I say.

"Offer a time and a place and I'll be there, my protégé."

* * *

Leigh and I read our Bibles together on a blanket at the beach, in the café section of Barnes & Noble, at her apartment, at Dad's house in my bedroom, at the park. We study together after riding our bikes, after dinners, before dinners, after long and meaningful conversations about God. We study over the phone. We grow closer, discussing the passages we read.

One night, as we're reading, I imagine Jesus on a white horse, hooves kicking up dirt, and Jesus is chasing after Brad—the bully who has molested my mind—with that spiky blond hair, those cruel grins. Jesus, my savior—my unconventional savior—corners Brad near a pit, then Jesus points to the great hole, and Brad, as though moved by an invisible force, suddenly finds himself spiraling down into the pit where he can no longer hurt me. . . .

Leigh ends up giving me a book of Christian theology. I read it when I'm alone, learn about the Holy Trinity—the Godhead: Father, Son, and the Holy Spirit. I dive head-first into Theology Proper, Christology, Christian Anthropology, Harmartiology, Angelology, Demonology, Eccesiology, Eschatology, and lots of other *ology* words.

I like learning about God the Father, about Christ and his nature. I'm fascinated as I learn about the nature of humanity, about the effects of sin. I'm captivated as I learn about the angels, the mission of the church . . .

The learning never ends.

CHAPTER TWENTY-SEVEN

Tomorrow is the Book and Author Luncheon at the Pine River Colony Club. I contact the coordinator of the event, Cindy Smith, via e-mail asking about the dress code because when I mentioned the Luncheon to Leigh the other day, she said she thought the dress code would be formal attire.

I receive Cindy's e-mailed response. Leigh was right; I'll need to wear a blazer, which I guess is a kind of suit jacket. Of course, I don't own one. Subhumans don't usually attend events at which you need classy jackets. I call Mitch, the only person I know who probably does own a blazer. We meet up quickly at the post office an hour later (he has some mailings to do for his business), and he hands over a gray jacket, and even throws in matching slacks and a white dress shirt and tie.

"I want you to look your best for Meranda," he says.

The clothing is lying over my arms. "This will be the best I've ever looked." I grin.

When I get home, I check my e-mail and spot another message from Cindy. She writes that my name sounds familiar, asks if I attended Langwood High School. I write back and tell her that I did indeed attend. She comes back with yet another message, this time explaining that she thinks she had me as a student. I keep the correspondence going—send her another e-mail telling her that I don't recall having her as a teacher. We go back and forth, back and forth, until she figures out why I can't remember her; she wasn't married back in those days and went by the surname Wolfe instead of Smith. Cindy Wolfe—Mrs. Wolfe, that's a name I remember. She was my tenth grade English teacher.

She keeps the messages flowing—wants to know why I'm interested in the Luncheon. I tell her about my writing, my novel *The Forsaken World*, and I explain the story about Mitch trying to track Meranda but how he couldn't and how I spotted the poster inside the window months later.

She writes: *So you want to meet Meranda Erickson? That can probably be arranged. I was one of the people who talked her into the appearance. Actually, she owed the library, the establishment that will reap the benefits from this Luncheon. She promised an appearance long ago to support our library, and this year, the committee called her on it.*

I write back: *So you're friends with Meranda?*

She responds: *I wouldn't go that far. I don't believe Meranda's one to hold friends.*

* * *

In a bathroom at the school, I spray the toilet seat with disinfectant. I think of Paul from the Bible and his imprisonment. I tear a square away from the paper towel roll and wipe the seat clear of bright yellow urine. Once again, thinking of Paul, his smile, his joyous nature, I squirt acid bowl cleaner into the toilet, the blue liquid that smells of mint, then I use the infamous oversized toothbrush to scrub away the black ring of residue around the bowl.

I flush the toilet, grab the window cleaner from my cart, and start spraying the mirror. I take another square from the towel roll and with it clear the mirror of splattered soap and an assortment of gunk. I look at my reflection, imagine myself wearing a black and white striped jumpsuit, a badge of numbers across my breast, and I smile. If this is my prison, then I need to keep smiling. Jesus is with me. He loves me.

I, the eccentric convert, love him as well.

* * *

Light drizzle falls against my windshield from the dome called sky. I pull into Pine River Colony Club's parking lot, anxious. I step out of the car, one of Meranda's Pulitzer Prize-winning novels, *Entangled*, held at my side (in place of the Bible, my book of choice nowadays), the Luncheon's ticket in my pocket. I adjust my tie and hike up an incline to the Club's entrance. A line of people snakes around the building. I get into line as an alien amid refined beings. The extraterrestrial who can't phone home.

I subtly search for Arthur in the sea of people. I can't find him, my Master in Writing. The line starts moving. I peek ahead and notice tickets being collected at a table inside the Club. I take my ticket out of the pocket and hold it in my left hand. The line slowly dwindles, and I make my way inside the Club. I approach the elongated table, hand the ticket to the Taker.

"Thank you," she says. "Enjoy your lunch."

I boomerang the "thank you" and follow people into the dining hall. Contained in this eating area are about fifty circular tables with white tablecloths and fine china on each, a podium, people scattered over the room, some sitting, some standing, most talking. Near a far wall, before a painting of pine trees and hills and rivers gushing, with the words *Pine River Colony Club* over the scene, sits a table with copies of *Entangled* spread out on its surface, lying in stacks, upright on stands, as well as dozens of copies of two of Meranda's other hits, *Perplexed* and *Say it Loudly*. Other than the books, the table is empty.

I scoot to a table that looks out over the adjoining golf course. The fairway is lush, well kept. Alone, I take a seat in front of the windows, smiling, hands folded neatly on the table. I'm worried. *Where is Arthur?*

A couple in their late forties comes to the table, asks if they can sit with me. "Sure," I say, and they sit across from me. They jump into a conversation with one another about Meranda Erickson this and Meranda Erickson that.

12:50 according to my watch. Ten minutes until the official start of this Luncheon. The mass of people are slowly filling the seats. I'm trying to keep the seat next to me clear by resting my arm over the backing. So far the plan is working.

Where is Arthur?

12:55 according to my watch. Five minutes until start. Virtually every seat is occupied except the one I'm protecting. Arthur appears in the doorway. I wave him down. He approaches the table in a corduroy blazer of sorts. He sits in the seat I've been guarding, apologizes for his tardiness, and lets me know that something came up and he won't be able to stay for the entire Luncheon. I tell him it's okay, that his presence, even if only for a few minutes, is greatly appreciated. I want to continue talking but a woman's voice booms over the speaker system. I look to the podium, spot Cindy Smith, my teacher of old, behind the microphone. She introduces herself, thanks us for coming to support Moose Acres Public Library, gives a brief story regarding past luncheons, closes with a line about us being friends of the library, then steps away from the podium and sits at a table with three other people. One of the people is Meranda Erickson. She looks exactly the way she did in the newspaper clipping Mitch showed me— silvery, mushroomed hair, large Coke bottle eyeglasses, weathered face, petite.

Servers provide us with our lunch, a fancy chicken dish with miniscule portions and far too much parsley on the side. I thank Arthur for coming, for showing me support. He smiles, says, "You're welcome," digging into his food. I turn my head a tad to the left and watch Meranda Erickson, the legend, eat. Her hand visibly shakes as she lifts the forkful to her mouth. She chews like a real person, swallows like a real person, and wipes her mouth with a napkin like a real person. Wow, wouldn't you know it, she *is* a real person. She reaches for her wine glass, takes a swig, and sets it down. Takes another bite of chicken. Takes another drink of wine. Feeds herself more chicken. Back to the wine, she knocks the rest of it back, and gets a server to pour her another glass. She digs into the chicken, hand shaking a little more as she slips a piece into her mouth. Again, she drinks and drinks and drinks. She is so enmeshed in her meal—especially the alcohol—that she doesn't have time to talk to anyone at her table.

I look away, concentrate on *my* table, on *my* plate. I need to eat. What seems like ten bites later, my plate is clear. The couple across the table suddenly becomes vocal. They ask Arthur what he does.

Calmly, Arthur says, "I edit a few magazines, some non-fiction, and fiction." He shakes the couples' hands. "Arthur Pennington," he says. They introduce themselves as Bob and Emery Sindel. Arthur turns to me. "And this is one of my clients, James Frost, one of the best writers around." He nods at the podium. "He'll be up there one of these days."

Heat rushes to my face. They eagerly shake my hand, tell me how nice it is to meet a young writer. I laugh inside. They don't know that this suit was borrowed. They don't know that after this Luncheon, I'll peel off this posh outfit and clothe myself in ripped carpenter jeans and a tee shirt. They have no idea that after I dress in that tattered clothing, I'll go to the school to clean up after people. But then again, I have no idea what they'll do either.

"I've been editing the newest draft of James's novel," Arthur says. "We'll be putting it out there with agents before long."

They nod and seem impressed. I'm enjoying this inflating-of-my-head moment.

"Have you been published?" Bob asks.

Cindy's voice sounds over the speakers, cutting our conversation short. She introduces Meranda Erickson, the Pulitzer Prize-winning, *New York Times* bestselling author, then calls her to the podium. Meranda sets her wineglass aside and walks carefully, somewhat off balance, tipsy, it seems, to the podium, where she takes Cindy's place at the microphone.

Meranda speaks slowly, hand unsteady on the podium: "The good news is I'm calm." She pushes her glasses up the ridge of her nose with a forefinger, scanning the audience, me included. "The bad news is I'm feeling woozy." She chuckles at her state.

A gentle titter rolls over the room.

One woman in the crowd holds up a wineglass and announces, "Cheers!"

Laughter breaks out, fills the space between these walls.

I wonder if anyone else is alarmed by this sight, a Pulitzer Prize-winning, *New York Times* bestselling author with a buzz. I'm not laughing and I don't find her semi-drunkenness amusing. Nothing funny about that.

Meranda holds out her hand to the audience. It's still shaking. "I can assure you that I don't have Parkinson's, despite what some of you may be hypothesizing," she says, lowering her hand to the podium.

Giggling, chortling, and sniggering courses through the occupied tables.

As before, I do not unite with the laughter.

"Okay, okay," she says. "I'm told I have to talk for a while . . ." She does, voice occasionally wobbly; gives a glimpse into her childhood by telling us about her family growing up. Her father was a factory worker; did factory work to earn a living, the way I see it. Her mom was a stay-at-home mother (she didn't have any talents and wouldn't have known where to start in the world of work, Meranda explains) who took care of the children (which is actually work in itself, she says), Meranda and four siblings, all of whom live abroad nowadays. Meranda's mother also looked after the house and prepared and cooked the meals for the family. Meranda reveals that when she was a young girl, seven or eight, she began writing stories. For the first story—and she chuckles while telling us this because, well, we learn that even when she was a young girl, she had a twisted imagination—her protagonist was a rabbit that was trying to stop a coyote bent on eating the rabbit's family for dinner.

"Gruesome, I know," she says, her voice flattening out. Her hand is not visible anymore; I wonder if it is still shaking. "I shared the story with some of my peers and they found it fascinating," she says. "By the time I was nine, if I'm remembering correctly, I had turned that heroic rabbit into a series of short stories."

Meranda Erickson, one of the greatest writers of all time, started her career writing about a valiant rabbit?

Meranda hops to her adult years, discloses information regarding the first novel she penned, *Say it Loudly*. It was literally penned in those days; she didn't own a typewriter, and computers were a thing of the future. From start to finish, it took her three years to write *Say it Loudly*. Sixty-two rejections (she says)—right on with the quoted number from the clipping I read—and the sixty-third agent to read her material chose to represent her work, thankfully. The debut novel went on to win the Pulitzer Prize.

A man in the audience raises his hand. She calls on him, jokingly says that this isn't the question and answer segment of the show but to shoot away, nevertheless. He asks, "When do you plan on publishing your next novel? Nine novels just aren't enough." He grins.

She releases a short laugh. "Can someone hand me my glass?" She points to her table, to the wine. "Need another swig." People out here in Spectator Land express amusement at her dry sense of humor—laughing, chuckling, assorted renditions of the two. Once the crowd calms, Meranda leaves the man's question in limbo, discusses the books following her debut tome. . . . The writing time for her novels went from the original three years to pen one book to about six months each, with years of down time from book to book. Right before she started writing her third book, she bought her first typewriter, deserting the pen except for when she needed to jot quick notes for herself on the run. By the fifth book, she switched to a word processor. The writing process became considerably easier. Saving to floppies was a nice upgrade from whiteout and became her savior; gone were the days of retyping a single page dozens of times. "Now that was progress," she says, smiling. She wrote her seventh novel with an Apple—the computer, not a fruit, she makes sure to clarify, as if we do not know what an Apple is. "It was a real piece of crap, looking back, but in those days, a computer was a computer. I was thrilled to have a monitor. Every time I sat down to write, I felt like Scotty from *Star Trek*. I cannae hold 'er together much longer, Captain. I don't have the power." Yes, she tests the Scottish-American accent. Not quite a match but funny, funny, funny. I laugh. Arthur almost chokes over his drink, laughing.

After the raucous din stops, Meranda goes off on a tangent. "I never took any classes on writing. Didn't see much reason to. There wasn't anything there that could be taught that I didn't learn on my own."

I think of my visit with Barbara, her opinion that attending classes on writing isn't always necessary.

Meranda says, "If you're thinking about taking a course or two on writing, don't waste your time and money. Expressing yourself on paper can't be taught. You either have it or you don't."

I like this woman, find her intriguing. She could do without the booze, but still, I like her.

As Meranda continues to talk, Arthur leans toward me, cups a hand over my ear, and whispers into it. "I need to get going. We'll talk soon, okay?"

I nod at him, whisper another thank you. He stands quietly and walks soft-footed past the mesmerized audience, out of the room.

Meranda takes a moment to clear her throat. She glances at her wristwatch, then back up. "My time's up," she says. "Thanks for listening to this old goof." She looks to Cindy, who's sitting with hands clasped over the table. "Oh," she says, an afterthought, "and thanks for supporting the Library." A couple hands shoot up out of the throng, but she responds to them by saying, "I'll be signing after. I need another drink. Can you save your questions for when you meet me? Thanks." She looks to her table and the wineglass, then steps away from the podium.

We applaud. A man from somewhere hoots; I don't know where exactly, can't see him. Meranda crosses paths with Cindy on her way to the table. Cindy approaches the podium.

"Meranda Erickson, everyone!" Cindy, behind the podium, extends her arm toward Meranda, who's tipping back merlot. People clap again, laughing and chuckling. She finishes the glass and smiles at the applauders.

I don't know why people find watching someone drink so enter-taining. She obviously has issues, and it hurts to watch, reminding me of Dad, the lush version, and Gramps.

Cindy thanks us again for joining in on this event and reiterates that there will be a signing after lunch. She points to the table in the back with Meranda's novels on its surface. I must go there. I must meet Meranda Erickson at that table. But first, dessert. The servers give each table a platter of chocolate cookies, chocolate-covered strawberries, and slivers of chocolate cake, everything chocolate. I grab a cookie, nibble at it, watching Meranda eat a piece of cake, quaking.

I'm the camera-less paparazzi, and I don't let her out of my sight.

* * *

The servers take our plates. People stand and scatter. Cindy es-corts Meranda to the signing table. I stand, say "goodbye" to Bob and Emery; I'll never see them again, I'm sure. Bob nods. "Nice meeting you." Emery waves, cloning her husband's halfhearted farewell. I walk away from the table, clutching *Entangled*, toward the signing area. Meranda is sitting in a chair behind the table, stacks of books sur-rounding her, gripping a pen. A line begins to take shape in front of her.

Cindy walks in my direction. I try to wave her down. She looks beyond me, through me, then toddles by. I turn. She twists around, does a double take. "James?"

"Mrs.—"

"Cindy's fine." She steps to me, shakes my hand.

"It's been a long time," I say. Our hands part.

"Are you ready to meet Meranda?"

"Sure." Adrenaline kicks in. This is it.

"Follow me," she says. I trail her past the forming line and we end behind the table. Meranda is two feet away, signing a book for a fan. Cindy tells me to wait a second. I wait at least fifteen, then Cindy gets Meranda's attention by stating her name.

Meranda looks to Cindy, then me. "Who's this?"

Cindy nudges me forward. "I want you to meet someone very special. This is James Frost, one of my old students. He's a great writer and wanted to meet you."

A great writer? Cindy hasn't read my current work. "Very nice to meet you." I hold out my hand.

Meranda stands, faces me, level with my chest, ignoring the people in line. Our hands hug. She asks, "What have you been writing?"

Cindy says, "I'll leave you two alone." She walks away.

Meranda appears unstable on her feet, leaning on the back of her chair. "What's your preference? Short stories? Novels? Poetry?"

I adjust my tie, nervous. "A novel called *The Forsaken World*."

"What a true title that is. Which genre?"

"Fantasy."

"Oh, I've read a few of those in my day. Tolkien is my favorite. Is your novel complete?"

"Yeah, just recently."

"Do you have a publisher lined up."

"No, ma'am. Any recommendations?"

"All sorts. But none of them accept unsolicited material." She takes a quick look at the line. "We'll have to finish this conversation later."

I glance at the impatient faces.

"Here." Meranda hands me a business card, which contains her snail mail address and e-mail address.

"So I can e-mail you?" I tuck the card in my breast pocket.

She nods. "Do you want me to sign that?"

I remember *Entangled*. "Oh, yeah. I mean, sure, that'd be great." I hand her the novel.

"James, correct?"

She remembered my name! "You got it," I say. *Meranda Erickson remembered my name!*

She sets the book on the table, and starts her pen moving on the first page she opens. She presents the book to me. I take it and thank her for her time.

"It was my pleasure, James," she says.

"I'll e-mail you," I say, shaking her hand again.

"I'll look for it."

I leave the table and open *Entangled* as I'm walking. In scrawling handwriting, her inscription is difficult to read: For James, Looking forward to one day seeing your name in print!

I hunt down Cindy, thank her profusely for being the matchmaker.

She says, "I'm glad I could be of service."

* * *

On my ride home, I call Leigh at work and tell her about the exciting meeting with Meranda—the business card, the inscription, Meranda's request to finish the conversation through e-mail.

Then I call Mitch.

"That's my boy!" he says. "You're on your way to the big leagues."

"I hope so."

"Contact her as soon as you get home. You want to catch her while your name is still fresh in her mind."

"Good plan."

"Take her to lunch or dinner. Make her remember you."

CHAPTER TWENTY-EIGHT

At home, I change out of the suit and tie and into my shabby work clothing. *Back to reality—the subhuman world.* I sit at my laptop and write Meranda. I know she met a lot of people today, so I remind her of who I am, what she wrote in my copy of *Entangled*, the name of my novel, and that she told me she wanted to continue the conversation by e-mail.

A day passes. I don't get a response.

Another day goes by. Not a word.

Three, four, five days ensue. Nada.

I write her another e-mail, reiterating what I wrote before.

* * *

A Friday night. I'm sweeping the gym. Dad enters, asks if I have a minute. I tell him I do. I lean the broom handle against a wall.

"I wanted to let you know that the house is being shown tomorrow morning at ten."

"What are you talking about?"

"I'm trying to sell the house."

"I didn't even know you put it on the market."

"It was only yesterday."

"How quickly are you looking to sell it?"

"As soon as possible."

"How long do you think it'll take?"

"Not sure. Could take a few days, a week, a couple months."

"Talk about having to be on high alert."

"It's the way it goes. . . . Oh, and can you do me a favor and be somewhere else while they show it? The realtor doesn't really want anyone around."

"Ummm . . . okay."

"Thanks."

You're not welcome.

* * *

Halfway through the work shift, on my break, I phone Leigh and tell her the news. I ask her if I can stay at her apartment tonight because I can't be at the house for the showing tomorrow. She says she would be happy to have me over.

"I get off work at midnight."

"What time can you be here?"

"After one."

"I'll leave the door unlocked for you."

"Thanks, Babe. Love you."

"Love you too."

* * *

I leave the school two minutes before midnight. Driving, I think of sabotaging the showing tomorrow: *I could make an appearance at the house at ten o'clock, tell the people who are looking not to be alarmed by the doors slamming by themselves and the echoing voices and the apparitions . . .*

I could go on: Oh, and beware of the bugs. Termites, I believe they're called. You'll see them from time to time. They also come with the place . . .

Then I could go even further: Just so you know, the neighbors aren't the type of people you'll want to invite over for dinner. Mr. Gardner, the guy across the street, do not be alarmed by him. He really was in Vietnam and when he shrieks and shoots off his gun at random, whether at four in the morning or eleven at night, that's him recreating the war. No biggie. Mrs. Canker. Don't fret over her either. She has what the professionals call Tourette syndrome, so when you're walking to the end of the road to retrieve your mail, just ignore her when she's sitting on her deck swearing like a sailor. That really is normal behavior for her.

Overall, it's not a terrible place to live. You'll get used to it.

* * *

I open the door to Leigh's apartment. I'm greeted by darkness.

"Is that you, James?"

"It's me, Babe. Don't worry." I shut the door behind me, scoot through the living room, eyes working to adjust, hands groping through the curtain of darkness. Leigh's bedside lamp flickers on. She pulls her hand away from the lamp and sits up in her bed.

"I missed you," she says, rubbing her eyes.

"Missed you too." I stand by her bed.

She yawns. "Do you want anything to eat? Anything to drink? You haven't had dinner, have you?" She starts to get up.

"You don't have to. I can get it myself."

"No, it's okay." She gets out of bed and walks past me. She's wearing a blue tank top and boy shorts. "I can make you a sandwich," she says. "Is ham and cheese okay?"

With *that* outfit, she could make me a maggot and cheese sandwich and I'd be all right. "Ham and cheese. That'd be awesome." I join her in the kitchen. "Thank you."

She stands at the counter, while I lean against the sink beside her. As she makes the sandwich, we talk.

"How are you feeling?" she asks.

"Kinda angry, honestly."

"*I'd* be angry, too."

"It's like Dad isn't even including me in his decision," I say. "Do I not factor into this?"

"You're his son. You should." I love that she's agreeing with me.

"He's more concerned about himself than anything else. He knows my situation. Where am I supposed to go if the house sells and he moves to California and closes down the business?"

She spreads mayonnaise on the bread. No maggots. Honey ham and Swiss. "Have you started looking for a new job yet?"

I've been caught with my pants down. "No," I say, aware of how that must sound.

"You need to jump on that." She closes the sandwich and cuts it in half like my mother.

"But what if I can't find a job? What do I do then?"

"You come live with me."

"You wouldn't mind?"

"I wouldn't let you live in a cardboard box, James."

"You're a good person," I say, in awe of her, the woman who would turn her home into an orphanage.

Blushing, she walks the plate to the black table and sets it down. We sit on opposite ends.

I take a bite and swallow. "Your parents, though. They'd hate me even more . . . if that's possible."

"If you moved in here?"

"Yeah. They wouldn't want you living with your boyfriend."

"Well, if it's either that or you live on the streets, they can deal with it. I love you and want to keep you safe."

"You're amazing."

She goes red in the face again. "Just care is all."

"It *would* look really bad, you know. Me living here with no job. I'd be the boyfriend who mooches off his girlfriend . . . I need to find my own way in order to retain any amount of dignity."

"Then what are you going to do?"

I take another bite. "As much as I don't want to, I guess I'll have to start looking for a new job."

"What would you want to do? Any ideas?"

"Be a novelist."

"Well, yeah. Of course. But other than that?"

"I'm good with computers. I'm a fast typer."

"You might be able to do some data entry. It's tedious work but you're used to that."

"If I had to, I guess."

"You might have to."

* * *

The next day, while the house is being shown, Leigh and I gather newspapers at Barnes & Noble and sit with them in the café section of the bookstore. We're at a round table. Every so often blenders blend, machines—microwaves and coffee/espresso makers, I think?—beep, and cell phones ring. The air smells of espresso, with a hint of chocolate chip cookies.

"What about this one?" She speaks through the unfurled paper held over her face. "Customer service position for a—Oh, wait, never mind. You need an Associate's degree."

I turn the page of my paper and set it on the table. "Engineering. Good pay. Bachelor's degree required. Next . . ." I'm beginning to see why people sell their bodies for sex.

"How about this?" Leigh says, then immediately: "Oops. Forget that. College degree necessary." Male gigolo—that will be me at this rate.

I come across a position dealing with passports. "This looks good." I read the ad further. "Scratch that. I don't wanna work third shift. Second shift has been bad enough. Plus, I want to be able to see you, and working third shift wouldn't help that cause."

"Pass on third shift . . ."

"You don't want a vampire as a boyfriend?" I chuckle. "You know—hissing at the light?"

"No thanks."

* * *

Two days later, Arthur calls my cell and informs me that the editing is going swimmingly.

"How far along are you?" I ask.

"Page one hundred and eleven."

Move faster, Arthur. I need it back so I can query agents. I need to get that novel published! "How do you like it?" I ask him.

"From what I've seen thus far, the story is vastly improved. Good job, James."

"Thanks."

"I'm proud of you."

"Thanks." *Hurry up, Arthur. Hurry.*

* * *

I go on the Internet to different career Web sites, create a fresh résumé and cover letter, find an ad for a job working for a newspaper in Portsmouth, e-mail my cover letter and résumé to the editor. I find another ad for a data entry position. Matches the hourly rate Dad gives me, first shift, and you need not have a college degree to apply. I send them a cover letter and résumé. A day later, I hear back about the data entry opportunity. The position filled. Two days thereafter, the editor from the newspaper responds—writes that he's searching for someone with experience in journalism. He goes on to say he doesn't have time to train.

In a sense, I'm relieved because I didn't really want to land either of those positions. I didn't really want to work for a newspaper—the chaos, ridiculous hours, unsteady income—and I didn't especially desire to sit before a database for eight hours per day, typing letters and numbers into fields that mean nothing to me, a twenty-first-century android.

In another sense, I'm scared. If I can't land *these* positions, then what am I going to be able to land? What am I going to do? I don't want to have to live with Leigh, although seeing her daily is certainly an appealing notion. Her apartment is too small for the two of us, for starters, plus, living together would lead to temptation. There are times when all she has to do is move a certain way, wear certain clothes, smile a certain smile, talk a certain talk, and I feel like I'm going to explode. Sleeping in the same bed night after night, holding each other, kissing, hugging, I would not be able to take it. I can't live with her. Not now. Not before saying "I do."

Leigh's parents. I can hear them now.

Her mother: James is a bum. I told you he couldn't support a family. Look at him, he can't even find a job. He's a leech.

Her father: You should've listened to us. You should know better than to get with someone who has no future, someone who has to live on food stamps and has to live with his girlfriend because he has no job, no money, nothing. You should've chosen Tim!

I want to play pretend on paper for a living. This will start by getting my manuscript back from Arthur, making the corrections needed, and querying agents once again. The agents will read my revised work, see the potential in it, decide to take a risk on me, the never-before-published writer. The agent that chooses me will land a deal with one of the largest publishing companies in the United States and that will be it. Visualization. I've heard it's powerful stuff.

I don't want to be a journalist. Don't want to slap at keys for a database. Don't want to have to work at a supermarket, a mall, and a convenience store at the same time. Don't want to get up in the morning knowing that I've given up on my dream, that I don't have enough time to dream. That I'm working sixty, seventy, eighty hours a week and I'm still poor, eating oatmeal for breakfast, lunch, and dinner, unable to purchase spices, or toilet paper to wipe my butt, toothpaste and mouthwash and floss to tend to my rotted teeth, soap to clean my body, to wash my hands, shampoo to wash my hair, detergent to wash my clothes.

* * *

Lying in bed amid the pall, I pray. *God, I need your help more than ever. I don't know what I'm going to do. What do you want me to do? I can't hear you. I can never hear you. Are you giving me answers and I'm not listening? Why can't I hear you speak? My ears are open. I'm waiting for your voice. I'm open to you. Please help me. Please.*

I'm a beggar who doesn't get the hint.

* * *

Dreaming—and I know that I'm dreaming because I can't see anything. Can only hear.

Test one, two, three. Can you hear me? Is this thing on? A voice rumbles through my brain.

<Who are you?> I find it rather unusual that I don't feel my mouth move.

You know.

<God, is that you? Are you going to tell me what I should do?> Seems like a reasonable question.

You know what to do.

<But I need to hear it.> Even Magellan had a compass.

Why?

<To be sure.>

You need to keep writing . . .

<I knew it.>

Of course you did.

<So is this God?>

No.

<Then who are you?>

I'm you.

CHAPTER TWENTY-NINE

I open my e-mail, expectant, and spot a message from Meranda Erickson: *James Frost, I rEmembre you. Thanks' fro you're emales.* Just like that, misspelled, grammatically incorrect, and hasty. I sit with her response for a minute, tapping at my desk with uncut fingernails, then I type and send her an e-mail asking if she would be up to meeting me for a cup of coffee. I tell her I would gladly base the meeting time around her schedule.

A couple hours later, after reading thirty-two pages of *Entangled*, I check my e-mail again. I find another message from Meranda: *9:00 tomorough AM @ Perk Up Café. Be theyre.* My mind flashes on her sitting at her computer, a wineglass—the same one she held at the Luncheon—in her hand, tipsy, seeing two screens, cracking jokes to herself, laughing. Honestly, though, I can't understand a prize-winning writer typing such ludicrous e-mails.

Maybe it isn't her at all. Maybe Brad is on the other end of cyberspace, cozy in a bedroom with his buddies, laughing aloud, with booze and Grateful Dead posters and bongs all around, and he and his friends are poking fun at this hopeful writer known as James Frost, wanting me to think that I've come in contact with Meranda Erickson. They want me to believe I have a chance of getting to know her, and that someone who has written the greatest literature of our time actually desires to speak with a person aspiring to do the same.

That's impossible. Well, not entirely. My imagination is running wild. I need to quit it. I'm being crazy. It's Meranda. It has to be Meranda. She handed me this business card, the one sitting on my desk next to the keyboard. She gave me this e-mail address.

Maybe Meranda isn't wearing her glasses and she doesn't know how to type without looking at the keys. That could explain her sloppy e-mails. Or she could be a sleeptyper. There are sleepwalkers, people who walk in their sleep, and there are sleeptalkers, people who talk in their sleep, so there must be sleeptypers, people who type in their sleep, right? I can see her with her mushroom haircut, no makeup on, groping at the keys, her glasses remaining on her nightstand. I like this much better than the idea of her sitting at her desk with booze, drunk out of her mind.

I don't put a stopper on my imagination. I can picture myself going to Perk Up Café, waiting there, waiting, waiting, and waiting, and she doesn't show. She doesn't remember the e-mail she wrote me. She's in bed dreaming and drooling while I'm at the café, glum and forgotten. I wait some more. Three, four, five hours. I finally leave the café. I am unseen once again. I write her another e-mail, ask her where she was, I was waiting for her at the café, and she doesn't respond, ignores my message as though we never met, as though we never agreed to finish our conversation at the Luncheon via e-mail.

Okay, okay. Enough assumptions. I should've learned my lesson by now, not to assume things, like when I assumed Leigh wanted Tim and I later found out she never actually wanted him but really only thought she did—or something like that—because of her parents. I allowed that assumption to fester and it threatened to fracture our relationship.

I can't allow assumptions in with this Meranda situation. She could very well be at the café when I get there. She could have already ordered a coffee and be sipping it by the time I spot her in a booth and sit down with her. She could remember our correspondence clearly. She could want to get to know me, ask in-depth questions about my novel, then speak elegantly in general, not stumbling over a numbed tongue.

I have a fervent desire to go meet with her. Tomorrow. 9 AM. Perk Up Café. Be there.

I should.

I will.

I must.

God and his mighty hand maneuvered everything into place. I trust in him, and believe he didn't bring me to this point only to crush my hope, to laugh and poke fun at me like Brad from my reverie. Mitch revealing that newspaper clipping, me bumping into the poster, going to the Luncheon and meeting Meranda and her handing me the business card—none of this is coincidence. I don't believe in coincidence. We aren't floating around aimlessly like a bunch of hobos. I believe in Jesus and in order and in reasons behind every aspect of my life, and everyone's lives.

Perk Up, here I come.

There is a reason.

* * *

Perk Up Café. 8:55 AM.

Never been here before now. The walls are brick, festooned with art of sorts . . . the logo of Perk Up Café, an unoriginal silhouette of a cup of coffee with steam rising from the cup and with the café's name in cursive letters printed over the illustration; abstract paintings of chairs, tables, and cups of coffee; and framed prints of people sitting around tables, drinking from cups or laughing with mouths open, heads tilted back. Mirrors span the entire ceiling and form one giant mirror, which is practical if you're looking for an aerial view of yourself. The floor is checkered black and white, a giant chess board. A neon sign that reads *Fresh Eats, Lovely Treats* blinks from the wall behind the counter area and makes me grateful that I don't have epilepsy. Tall red stools surround numerous square, rectangular, diamond, and circular tables, which people burden.

I think of Leigh's café, the dream of hers. Where are the umbrella tables? Where is the ocean, the iced coffee, and the vibrant walls? I scope out the crowd, don't spot Meranda amid the faces, then find, after a minute of strolling around the café, craning my head all about, the only vacant table, a square table that hasn't been cleaned. I sit on one of the provided stools. A female worker (late thirties?) approaches and says she can wipe down the table if I don't mind. "Thanks. That'd be great," I say. While she follows through with her offer, I wonder how Meranda will tell me apart from this crowd, and I begin to worry that she won't be able to.

My watch reads 9:02. She's late. The worker says, "All clean." I thank her and she walks away with the damp cloth and gets lost in the sea of bodies. In my mind: Meranda walks in the café, looks for me, can't see me, decides I've stood her up, thinks *screw this*, leaves, and I've missed my chance.

I stand, trying to make myself more visible. I would leave the table and stand next to the front door, but then this table would get stolen and when Meranda arrives, we would have nowhere to sit and engage in conversation. Well, I guess there's always the floor . . .

I wait—9:15—and wait—9:30. I wait, 10:00, wait, 10:15, remaining in my standing position, eyes peeled, and wait, 10:30. Finally, I sit. Is she sleeping, drinking, doing whatever sixty-something prize-winning writers do, other than meeting a young person who wants to write for a living? I order a coffee from a pimple-faced waiter, drink slowly from the cup, prolonging my stay, pretending that her tardiness doesn't bother me and that I enjoy coffee. I look down at the cup, stir in a few more packets of sugar, attempting to make this bitter coffee experience a bit more tolerable, then . . .

I hear the voice of Meranda Erickson: "Good morning . . . "

I nearly jump from my seat. My attention flies upward. "Morning!" If this were anyone else showing up almost two hours late, I wouldn't be quite so energetic. Guaranteed.

Her hair is unkempt, she's wearing a stained white blouse, and she has a pocketbook slung over a shoulder. "Sorry I'm late, I think, probably," she says. "It was a night and a half, I'll tell ya." She sits on the stool across the table, and I can smell whiskey, I think it is, on her—from her breath, her clothing, her skin? Her attention darts around the room.

"Are you okay?" I ask, then take a cautious sip of coffee.

"Oh, yeah, yeah." Her bloodshot eyes finally rest on me. "I'm dandy," she says. "So what am I doing here?"

"You don't remember the e-mails?" I set the cup on the table, but I really want to chuck it across the room, discontented about the brew.

"Perk Up Café," she says. "Sometime in the morning. Jimmy Frost. Care to fill me in on the rest?" She chuckles hollowly.

I envision her as I did yesterday, at her computer holding a wineglass, trashed. "You told me to meet you here at nine o'clock," I say. I can't get over the booze aroma floating this direction, devouring all available untainted air. I look around, try to tell whether anyone else notices her stench, if anyone from the multitude is remotely aware. No one is checking us out.

"Well," she says, "what does an old lady have to do to get a coffee around here?"

"Oh . . . right," I say, then flag down our waiter. He comes to the table.

"Chad, how ya been?" Meranda looks up at the pimpled, greasy waiter.

I'm appalled that he's allowed to serve food or beverages or edible items of any kind. "I'm pretty good," he responds. "The usual, Meranda?"

She nods. "And make it snappy, got it?" She smiles.

"You got it," he says, chuckling. I want to tell him to forget the coffee and bring a vat of perfume instead, so we can douse her in it, but he disappears from the table.

"You come here a lot, huh?" I ask.

She says, "I enjoy my daily routine. Coffee is part of it."

"What else?"

"Getting personal, are we?"

"I'm sorry. Didn't mean to intrude."

She laughs. "I do a whole lot of nothing these days. The Internet is an entertaining time killer—and that's what I use it for, killing time. I go for walks. I used to run back in the day. Hard to believe, I know." She reaches for her pocketbook, sets it on her lap. "Staring into nothingness is a hoot. Very enjoyable. Ever try it?"

"Can't say it's a hobby of mine."

She laughs again. "TV's a hoot, too. Those soap operas are wonderful. No thinking involved. Can watch them numb, the way I like it."

"When do you find time for writing?"

"*Come on*, not more of *this*." Her voice sharpens. "I write e-mails and grocery lists. . . . You probably expected a glamorous answer?"

My head bobs. "I just didn't know if you wrote anything to keep you busy," I say meekly.

"I'm busy enough, *all right*? All I ever did was write and go on book tours. Enough is enough." She stands abruptly, holding the pocketbook by its straps. "If you'll excuse me for a moment, Jimmy, I need to take care of another part of the daily routine."

"Sure. Not a problem," I say, and she walks away from the table and into the crowd.

Did I say something to offend her? I went too far with the questions. Must have gone too far. Where's she going? What's she doing? What is the other part of her daily routine? Is she coming back? If she was offended, telling me she needs to take care of the other part of her routine might have been a polite way for her to ditch me. Instead of: *Jimmy, you're an intrusive idiot and I don't want anything to do with you, so I'm ditching you now. Don't know why I ever invited you to meet me here in the first place. Must've been really drunk last night. Couldn't have thought it through. Have a good life, nosey boy . . .*

Five minutes pass. Chad drops off her coffee. A couple seconds after his visit, she appears and sits. The booze smell is more intense than before. She sets the pocketbook on the table and speaks unhurriedly, "Much better."

"What was wrong? Are you feeling better?" I notice a metal flask poking out of the top of her pocketbook. This is an assumption, but it's one based on decent evidence: She doesn't have juice in that container.

"What were we up to?" she asks.

I don't dare bring her writing back into this. "Your routine," I say.

She struggles to speak clearly. "Yes, that's right. I like Internet checkers and backgammon and chess and solitaire—again, a hoot." She drinks from her cup.

"Do you get out much?"

She peers over the top of her thick glasses. "Yes, Jimmy. Believe it or not, I *do* get out. I'm not Salinger. Remember the Luncheon?"

"Of course." I nod.

"That was me getting out. . . . I grocery shop, too. Yes, re-nowned Meranda Erickson buys cheese and meats and frozen dinners and toilet paper and paper towels and—liquor. Mind-boggling, right?"

I cock my head.

She says, "And you won't believe this: Sometimes renowned Meranda Erickson goes to theaters and watches movies. Inconceivable, right? Humanizing. She eats, sleeps, bathes, pees, poops, listens to music, to CDs, to the radio, watches the news, tools around on the Internet, gets hammered, gets angry, gets sad . . . drinks coffee." She holds up the cup, smiles, and winks. "It's your turn now. What do you do?"

"Everything you mentioned, except for getting hammered, and add writing to the mix," I say.

"You don't drink?" Meranda sounds horrified, unable to imagine a world without inebriation.

"No, I don't drink."

"Why not?" she asks, shaking her head as if to say, *Shame on you for not being a drunk.*

"Alcohol doesn't interest me."

"Ah . . . you're probably better off that way."

I watch her hands begin to shake. "Yeah. Better off."

"Your friends don't drink either?" she asks.

"My friends are gone. I have a girlfriend."

"A girlfriend is a friend."

"Good point," I say. "I'd rather write and spend time with Leigh than drink."

"Your girlfriend?"

"Leigh." I nod. "That's her."

"I used to feel that way."

"What way?" I ask.

"Would rather spend time writing and with Eddy."

"Your husband?"

"That *was* him." She stands, eyes watering behind her specs. "I'll be back in a minute. Save the seat for me, will ya?"

She vanishes with her pocketbook, that flask, and returns after ten minutes, staggering, her eyes glossy, her body and breath and clothing, her presence in general, reeking of whiskey even worse.

She parks on the stool, leans her elbows on the table, hands trembling. "Thank the man above for that," she stammers. "Where would I be? How would I feel?"

My mind wraps around Randy and Gramps and Dad in his drinking days. Meranda is all three. The Trinity of Lushes. "Are you feeling okay? You look really pale," I say.

"I'm okay. Really . . . okay," she says loudly.

Her hands don't stop shaking. "Are you sure?" I ask.

She begins to sway on the stool. "Forget the feeling. Forget . . . feeling, all right?" Her voice raises an octave. People notice.

"Okay, okay," I say, reaching for her.

Her eyes roll into the back of her head. The swaying is out of control. She loses her balance, falls off the seat.

Down she goes.

She hits the floor, as does the stool, both on their sides.

People notice.

"Meranda!" I jump off my stool, stoop to her, see that she's unconscious, her eyes closed, mouth gaping.

Chad materializes at my side, his pizza face fearful. People crowd around us, chattering, shouting, "Call 9-1-1!" I hear Meranda's voice in my mind. *You won't believe this: Sometimes renowned Meranda Erickson passes out. Astonishing, right? Humanizing.*

CHAPTER THIRTY

I follow the ambulance, its whiney siren, its flashing lights, weaving in and out of traffic, through sets of lights, down a narrow street, a right onto a wide road, bumping over potholes.

I pass a man stumbling on a sidewalk. He's wearing a dingy sleeveless T-shirt, blue jeans that hang from his waist, cowboy boots, and in his left hand is a bottle of some sort of alcohol—it has to be alcohol because look at him stagger on that sidewalk, drunk, disastrous. I give him another look from the rearview mirror and notice him muttering something to himself.

Concentrating on the road, on following the ambulance, I think of Meranda lying in that box-shaped van, out cold as when they lifted her into it. She's unaware that they just drove by her double. How long before *he* collapses? How long before *he* winds up in the back of an ambulance? That could have been me walking unsteadily on the sidewalk, a bottle of beer or whatever in my hand, tanked, and mumbling. That could have been me slurring my words at the café, passing out, crashing to the floor.

My heart swells at those thoughts. I want to turn around and go after that guy, grab the bottle from his hand and chuck it, hear that vessel of self-destruction shatter on the sidewalk, watch the dumbjuice wash over the road, shake him by the shoulders, tell him to smarten up, to find some other way to cope. I want to take him off the streets, bring him to his house, warn him that he is going to find himself in the back of an ambulance heading to a hospital one day if he doesn't quit drinking now. *Now!* I want to scream in his face for Meranda and for Randy and for Gramps and for the younger edition of Dad—"Wake up! Don't you see what you're doing to yourself? Don't you understand where you're headed?" My mind flips to Gramps, to his lifeless body spread over the couch, the beer bottles on the floor.

The ambulance takes a left. I follow.

* * *

My cell rings. I flip it open. It's Leigh.

"Hey, hon."

"Have you thought about what you wanted to do today?" she asks.

"I don't know if we're gonna be able to get together."

"Why not? Are you all right?"

"Yeah, I'm fine, but Meranda isn't."

"What's wrong?"

"She passed out at the café, and now I'm sitting here."

"Where is *here?*"

"The ER. The waiting room. It's already been about an hour. Still no word from the doctor."

"Was it a heart attack?"

"No."

"Stroke?"

"No."

"Were you scared?"

"Yeah."

"Are you still?"

"I'm nervous, yeah. The ER isn't a good sign."

"Don't worry about hanging out with me. I certainly understand."

"Thanks. I feel like I'm supposed to stay here for her."

"Aw, take your time. I'll find things to do around the apartment."

"Talk later?"

"Sounds good," she says. "You'll have to fill me in on the details."

"I will. Love ya."

"Love ya."

We end the call. A doctor in a white coat appears before my chair, clipboard in hand.

"Doctor Gillman," he says, holding out his free hand, impassive, detached.

"James." I stand, shake his hand, attaching us. "Is she gonna be okay?" I let go.

"Your grandmother should be all right." There's no comfort in his voice, like he's speaking of a nonentity. He's a cyborg. Wires instead of veins. A motherboard instead of a heart.

My grandmother? He assumes because I'm young, she's old, and I'm here waiting for her, that I'm her grandson? I roll with the presumption: "Is she awake?"

"Yes. She's conscious. She's undergoing observations for acute alcohol poisoning. I'll keep you updated regarding her progress." The Cyborg speaks in a monotone.

"What type of observations?"

"She'll be observed until she's deemed clinically sober and we've determined that she has no complicating injuries or illnesses. I did notice some inflammation on her left hip due to the impact of a fall."

"When can I see her?"

"I'll keep you in the loop, James. Hang in there, okay?" says the Cyborg, almost human. He shakes my hand again and, with a swish of his coat, he is gone.

I sit, glance at the woman sitting adjacent from me—the only other person in this room. She has short, wavy blonde hair. Her face is round, and she has the outline of a mustache. *Smack, smack, smack.* Chewing gum, reading *Good Housekeeping* (some woman who I've never seen is on the cover, smiling, wearing a straw hat). The lady blows a bubble, then pops it handless. Tongues the gum back into her mouth, blows another bubble, and pops it again. I find something about this unsettling.

My eyes redirect to the TV hanging on the wall to the left of her. It is tuned to The Weather Channel. Tomorrow, a high of eighty-five degrees. Mostly sunny. Who cares? People agonize here. Die here. I start to wonder why anyone waiting in the ER would be interested in the weather. *Hey, Johnny's dying but let's keep tabs on the weather . . . Marcy just OD'd but tomorrow is supposed to be mostly sunny with a high in the eighties . . . Phillip just had a heart attack but hey, who cares? High of ninety tomorrow . . .*

My eyes fall from the screen, run along the white wall, sweep across the room of blue plastic chairs. I examine my chair. One would think hospitals could afford seats with more comfort—the millions upon millions they make. They could do better, could supply the weeping with cushioned seats.

I look on the table to my left, the one full of assorted magazines—*People, Star, US Weekly, Seventeen, Time, Newsweek, Sports Illustrated.* I scan those magazines, thumb through the pages. Celebrities over-glorified. Page after page of superficiality. Buy this cologne, this MP3 player, these sneakers, this car, this handbag, this watch. Purchase this plasma television, this DVD. Get this cell phone, your choice of pink or blue or green or silver or black. You will be cool. We promise. You will find enlightenment. This actress is dating that actor. He called her stupid, and she fired back, calling him arrogant and dull-witted. Everyone, hold your breath, the world is coming to an end. So and so broke up with so and so. He's cheating on her and she's cheating on him. Pop diva went off the deep end. Will she recover?

All the while, Meranda Erickson is lying in a hospital bed. Why hasn't anyone shown up yet? Doesn't she have family? Doesn't anyone care other than me? Did the ER receptionist—or whoever—inform her family of this incident? Honestly, I'm partly, and selfishly so, I admit, relieved none of her family members have arrived, because I would then have to explain why I am being referred to as her grandson.

I close my eyes. In this reverie, I'm in the hospital bed instead of Meranda, tubes stuck in my arms, one jammed up my nostril. I wear a hospital gown, a slit in the butt region. My face is covered with wrinkles, my hair grey, and I'm sixty-two-years-old. I write for a living. My father is dead. My mother is dead. My sister is a grandmother. She lives in Nevada, and doesn't have much to do with me. I lie here and hope for a call, a visit from anyone, proof that someone in the world cares for me. The doctor—a cybernetic organism—and the nurses are the only familiar faces.

I open my eyes and rub them with sideways fists. Meranda deserves a familiar face, one that isn't soulless. I will be that presence for her. I will stay here for as long as it takes.

* * *

A nurse wakes me. I glance at my watch. I must have fallen asleep. I missed lunch and dinner. My stomach rumbles, and I feel slightly nauseous. I run a hand through my hair. Per Doctor Gillman's go-ahead, the nurse tells me that I can visit my grandmother if I would like, and that Mrs. Erickson should be ready for release in about an hour.

I stand, smiling. "She's doing okay?"

"Recovering nicely. Yes," the nurse says.

"Please, bring me to her."

"Right this way."

I follow her out of the waiting area and through several corridors and doors until we finally arrive at Meranda's room, her temporary abode. We stand outside the door.

The nurse says, "She's been asking for you."

"She said my name?"

"Jimmy. Yeah." The nurse drifts away from the door. "I'll leave you alone with her. Take your time." She twists around and walks away.

Hesitantly, I stride into the room.

Meranda is sitting up in the bed. "There you are, Jimmy!" she shouts across the room.

I approach the bedside. Color has returned to her cheeks. "How ya feeling?" I ask.

"Embarrassed." She speaks clearly. "You waited here all this time?" She looks up at my face.

"Yes."

"You don't have anywhere to be?"

"I was supposed to spend time with my girlfriend but I decided to stay here." I hope she doesn't spot brown on my nose.

"Why would you do that?"

"You don't want me here?"

"I didn't say that," she says. "I'm asking—why did you stay?"

"Because if I were you, I wouldn't want to be alone in this hospital."

She looks down at the blanket covering her legs. Her tone hardens. "I don't need your pity, Jimmy."

"I'm not pitying you."

"Then why'd you *really* stay?"

"Like I said, I didn't want you to be alone."

"What do you want from me?"

"I don't follow . . ."

"You must want *something*."

"Why do you say that?"

"A twenty-something young man doesn't forfeit time with his girlfriend for some old bag unless there's something he wants in return." She pauses, turns to the tray of food next to her bed. "Will you be driving me home, *Grandson*? You're all I have."

"Uh . . . sure. Yeah. Not a problem."

She picks up a Snack Pack pudding from the tray, hands it to me. "Here. This is what you get. Your compensation." She smiles impishly as I accept the pudding, then hands me a spoon. "Consider us even," she says. "Now explain to me how it is that the staff here is under the impression that you're my grandson?"

I shrug, my face warm, pulsing. "I didn't tell 'em so. Honest."

"That's funny, seeing as how I never had children."

I smile, my attempt to soften the mood.

She changes the subject. "Doctor Gillman said I had alcohol poisoning. I tried to tell him I didn't drink much, but he wouldn't buy that. I didn't drink much, did I, Jimmy?"

I rock my head, say nothing.

"You think I'm a drunk, don't you?" she asks.

Yes. The Lord of all Drunks. "You passed out. You must've had too much to drink."

"Okay, so maybe I have a slight problem."

I make sure to wear a deadpan face. "I was worried about you. Everyone was worried. I'm glad you're doing better."

Her eyes glisten. "Doc said I'll have to stop drinking."

"That's not a bad thing," I say, but then I remember who I'm speaking to.

"It is when you need relief."

"Relief from what?"

"Thoughts. Life. Pain."

I surprise myself and tell her about my grandfather's demise.

"Good gravy, what are you insinuating?" she asks.

"To stop drinking is probably a wise idea." I'm the mascot for Team Sobriety.

Doctor Gillman enters. Chalk-faced Data from *Star Trek*. "Hello." He walks past me, looks her over with a critical eye, asks how she's feeling. "Fine, Doc," she says. He deems her ready to return home.

"The next time I see you, Meranda, I want it to be for your annual physical, not because of getting carried away with the whiskey, all right?"

She rolls her eyes. "Sure thing, Doc."

He points to the clothing—a folded pile on a chair, near the end of her bed—she was wearing when she came to the ER. "Get yourself dressed and we'll send you on your way."

"About time." She dispenses attitude.

Data and I leave the room. He shuts the door behind us, and we start walking down the corridor.

"You'll need to take care of your grandmother. She needs your help . . ."

CHAPTER THIRTY-ONE

We approach the red covered bridge, headlights shedding light on the road, then the bridge itself, the MOOSE ACRES, N.H. sign posted to the top of its entrance. I pass through the bridge.

From the passenger's seat, Meranda says, "A couple miles from here."

I nod, randomly think of the parking lot at Perk Up Café. "What are you gonna do about your car?"

"You'll help me pick it up tomorrow."

Two miles later, she has me take a left into a lengthy gravel driveway; a mailbox at the entrance reads ERICKSON. Trees line either side of the drive. The tires crunch over the gravel. My body jiggles slightly from the bumps in the road. At the end of the driveway, it opens to a spacious lot, about the size of half a football field. There are no cars parked here. To the lot's north sits a two-story scarlet Colonial on three or four acres of grass, six windows on each story facing us, a screened-in porch, a four-car garage flanking the house. She orders me to park in front of the garage. As I obey her command, motion lights beam down on us from the top of the garage, and I prepare myself for an alien abduction.

I step out of the car, shut the door, walk around the tail of the car, and open Meranda's door. I hold out my hand to her. She takes hold and says, "Well, aren't you a gentleman." I help her out of the car, close the door, and I put my arm around her waist. She smiles at me. We slowly hike her cobblestone walkway, our eyes squinting through faint light. We come to her porch and another motion light powers on, this time from a lamp over the screen door. She takes the lead, walks up the steps, unlatches the door and opens it. I walk in behind her. The door snaps shut. I glance at my wristwatch—9:02.

Inside her house, standing in the entrance, I see the place hasn't been vacuumed or dusted in a long while; dust bunnies float all over, and the carpeting is covered with dirt. I guess this is the sort of stuff people who clean for a living notice.

She says, "I need to use the little girl's room. Make yourself at home. There should be something to eat in the fridge."

She scurries away, up a set of stairs to our left, and calls down, "Just don't go stealing anything!"

I let out a laugh. "Don't worry. I won't!" I walk out of the entranceway, to her living room—a blue couch, a recliner, a nineteen-inch TV next to a picture window. I step to her couch, linger at its base, gazing at the framed photographs ornamenting the wall above the sofa—a younger version of Meranda shaking hands with President Kennedy, a fellow Pulitzer Prize winner; locking hands with Reagan; posing with *Entangled* on *The Johnny Carson Show*; walking onto David Letterman's set; her headshot on the front of *Time* Magazine, *People*, and *Newsweek*.

I sit on the blue fabric, prop my right arm on the rest, thinking: *What hasn't this woman done?* I sink in the puffy couch, and suddenly become ravenous. The refrigerator. She said it would be all right if I get myself some food. I stand, mosey into the kitchen, open the refrigerator, and spot a couple packaged cheese sticks. I remove them both from the fridge, devour the first and second, remaining hungry. With my hand holding the door ajar, I scope out the rest of the refrigerator. The top shelf holds nothing but milk and fruit juices and colas. The second shelf is empty. The third level contains an expired carton of eggs. The door is packed with condiments—two bottles of mayonnaise, a bottle of ketchup, mustard. My stomach screams at me.

I insert the cheese stick wrappers in a front pocket, close the door, and notice an antique piece of furniture—a stained oak cabinet with detailed carvings—tucked next to the refrigerator. I pull open the cabinet's doors. I lean in toward the cabinet, see bottles of whiskey and wine, one of each. This is no ordinary cabinet meant for dishes. Doctor Gillman's words rush through my mind: *You'll need to take care of your grandmother. She needs your help.*

I glance over my shoulder. Meranda is nowhere to be seen. *Must still be in the bathroom. Is she okay? Long bathroom trip. Should I check on her?* I remove the bottle of merlot from the cabinet, get rid of the cork with a corkscrew I find in the cabinet, and walk with the wine to the sink. I pour the dumb-juice down the drain of the dish-cluttered sink. *This is for your own good, Meranda. This is me helping you . . .* I toss the bottle in a trash can next to the sink, enjoy the sound of shattering glass but worry that she may have heard, fret over how she will react.

Take care of your grandmother. She needs your help.

As in a trance, I go to the cabinet and grab the whiskey, unscrew the cap, and deposit it into the sink, smiling. I can't have her passing out at a café again, staggering down the street like that guy I saw, dying like Gramps, unaccompanied, with exception of her bottles. I don't wish for her to show her face to Doctor Gillman before her annual physical. I don't want to read her obituary in the newspaper, to read about her untimely death on the Internet.

"What in the—what is *this?*"

I whirl around, catching Meranda's horrified face, a look reminiscent of when she learned about my non-drinking philosophy. "You can't drink this stuff anymore, Meranda." I hold up the whiskey bottle, gutsy.

She steps to me, hand flailing in the air. "I leave you alone and this is what you do?" She grabs the bottle from my grip, looks in through the top, and begins sobbing. "Where'd it go? What did you do with it?"

I give a fleeting look at the sink.

She pushes me aside, leans over the sink, stares at the drain. "Why'd you do it, Jimmy?" She marches to the cabinet, stands in front of the open doors, her back to me. "What'd you do with the merlot, Jimmy? Where's my merlot?" She faces me.

I nod at the sink.

"*You little—*"

"What happened to you?" I ask softly.

"Eddy happened to me. That's what happened, you ignorant jerk!" She lunges at me, trips over her own feet before I can move, and falls to the tile. She sits herself up, crying. "He wasn't supposed to die. We were supposed to grow old together. He left me, Jimmy. Got shot in the head!"

I kneel next to her, preparing to comfort.

She speaks through the pain. "He wasn't supposed to go down that alleyway. He wasn't even supposed to be in the city . . . Give me a drink. I need a bloody drink!" She grabs my collar, pulls me close, sniveling.

"No! Don't you see what you're doing to yourself? Don't you understand where you're headed?" I picture the man stumbling down the road in his cowboy boots.

"Why do *you* care?" she asks, letting go of my collar.

I focus on her sodden eyes. "You're my grandmother."

She wipes her face with a hand. "I don't have a grandson."

"You do now," I say, "and I don't want my grandmother to die." I stand and present a helping hand to her. She latches on, and I pull her to her feet.

Her eyelids look heavy behind her glasses. "I need to sleep. I want to sleep. I need to shut down, Jimmy."

"I get it, Meranda. That's fine."

She folds her arms. "Be here tomorrow morning at ten. I want my car back."

"You got it."

On my ride home, I flip open my cell and call Leigh. I have a lot to tell her.

* * *

9:49 AM. I knock on Meranda's door and she lets me in. We talk in the entranceway.

"You came." Her eyes appear refreshed.

"Of course."

"I didn't think you'd show."

"Why not?"

"I'm a complete embarrassment. After yesterday, who would want to help me?"

"Your grandson would." I smile.

She looks like she's going to grin, but she holds back. "Let's get going. I want some coffee," she says.

"Wait." I look at the pocketbook slung over her shoulder. "The flask?" I hold out my hand.

She rummages through her bag, and hands it to me. I say, "Thank you," and walk past her, to her kitchen. I dump the remaining whiskey, and set the flask on the counter.

She cringes. "Throw that abhorrent obsession away . . ."

I pick up the flask, walk with it to the wastebasket, and glance at her for confirmation. She gives a nod. I drop it into the basket. She takes a profound breath.

* * *

At Perk Up Café, we sit at the same table as yesterday. She orders a coffee and I order milk. Chad, the acne wonder, is nowhere to be seen. Maybe he took the day off to buy some Neutrogena.

"Tell me about your girlfriend," Meranda says.

I explain about MySpace.com, how it works, and tell her about our first date, the same day as my rejection, tell her that I love Leigh, would do anything for her, that she is a great woman. I tell her about Leigh's parents, the dislike they have for me but that Leigh, after drama with Tim (I explain the back-story), decided against her parents' wishes and chose me. I tell her that I'm a new member of Christianity, the religion of unconventionality.

"Your girlfriend is a lucky woman," Meranda says.

"How so?" I ask.

"She has you."

"Thanks," I say, stunned by her sudden warmth, sentimentality.

"So you believe in Jesus?"

An unflinching, "Yes. What about you? What do you think?"

She takes a drink from her cup. "I'm thinking where was Jesus when Eddy died, huh? Was he sleeping?"

I grimace.

"No offense," she says, "but I can't believe in a deity who overlooked my husband's murder."

"But what about living forever? Don't you want that?"

"Not like this."

"How about if things were perfect?" I ask.

"Perfect in comparison to what?"

"No death, no murder, none of that junk. What would you say to that?"

"I'd say you're fulla fecal matter, Jimmy." She takes another drink.

Silence falls over us for a minute; I hear the chatter of others around us.

"I'm sorry if I offended you," she says. "You probably think I'm a horrible person, huh?"

I shake my head. "No."

More silence comes forth, then she says, "Hey, would you be interested in earning some money? I need my lawn mowed sometime this week."

Servant mode kicks in. "Sure," I say.

"Don't you want to know your pay first?"

"Nah, that's not important."

She tilts her head. "Forty dollars for the whole shot."

I shrug. "Okay."

"What do you do for work otherwise?"

"You won't judge me, right?"

"No, Jimmy."

"I work for my dad's janitorial company."

"That's nothing to be ashamed of, young man. My mother was a maid."

"Like that chick on the *Brady Bunch*?"

Meranda nods and cracks a smile. "Mother was stinkin' proud of it, too." She finishes her coffee. "Are you in college?"

I explain how I spent my time after high school, and that college isn't for me.

"That's all right," she says. "Most kids go to college to figure out what they want to do with their lives. But if you already know what you want to do, then disregard college."

I smile.

"Do you work forty hours?" she asks.

"Yes."

"*And* you write?"

"Yes."

"You must really love it then," she says; I nod. She continues, "What does your work schedule look like?"

"Normally, I start at four o'clock, end at midnight."

"All right. Then an evening is out of the picture. How's Tuesday morning at, say, ten?"

"That'll work," I say, preparing myself to become Meranda's maid. Without the blue outfit, of course.

CHAPTER THIRTY-TWO

Tuesday.

I took one of Dad's AA brochures this morning, the one regarding the Twelve Steps and the Twelve Traditions, and I plan on giving it to Meranda today. I arrive at her house at ten o'clock. With the brochure in my left hand, I knock on her door with my right. A Mormon preparing to preach. She does not answer. I call out her name. Knock again. She does not appear. I wait on the porch for five minutes, sitting on a white chair, the brochure on my lap. I open the brochure to the note I left inside the pages, read it to myself. The note ultimately says that I believe AA could help with her drinking problem, and I encourage her to explore the brochure, to read it once, twice, as many times as it takes, that the hardest step is the first, admitting that she's powerless over alcohol and her life is unmanageable . . .

I nod, close the brochure on the note, step to the door, and this time pound on the wood. I press my ear against the door, hear nothing, then push the door open. I walk through, close the door, and I call her name again. I scan the kitchen, the living room, sit down on the couch, set the brochure on the middle cushion, stand, walk to the stairs, peer up the flight, wonder if she's asleep, if she's okay, if I should go upstairs to check on her; I think that's where her room is. I'm unnerved by the silence of this house. I hope she's here. She could have forgotten about today. My eyes dart along the ceiling, along the walls. I hope I don't sound an alarm.

I can see it now: the police arrive, push the door open, guns raised. They throw me to the ground, read me my rights, and next thing I know, I'm sitting in a jail cell with a guy named Big Boy who considers violent sex with inmates a wonderful pastime.

I jet up the stairs. *Please, Jesus, no alarm. Please, God, don't let an alarm go off.* Once upstairs, I notice all the doors are shut except one. I walk to the open door. "Meranda. I'm here to mow!" I enter the bedroom. Meranda is lying on the bed, reeking, hair messy, eyes closed, vomit on her chin, her neck, and her sheets, a bottle of whiskey on her nightstand. She must have purchased more. I dash to the bedside, grab her shoulder and shake. "Wake up!" I consider calling 9-1-1.

Her eyes flutter open. She gasps, vomit spilling from her mouth. "Get it away, dammit! Get it away!"

I pull my hand away. She gags, leans to the side of the bed opposite me, and throws up on the wooden floor. "Just take it away. Take this away!" She hits the nightstand; it tips onto the floor, and I hear a smash. I pray it's the whiskey bottle. I race to the other side of the bed and confirm that it was the bottle.

Meranda moans. "I'm sorry, Jimmy. I'm so sorry. I couldn't help it. Basket!" She points to the attached bathroom. "Get the basket! I couldn't help—" She vomits again.

I zip to the bathroom, find a wastebasket next to the toilet (it's empty!), and hurry back to her. I hold the basket to her face as she hurls.

Ten minutes later, she's done heaving. "Sleep. I just need sleep," she says. I take the basket away and set it on the floor. She lies back and closes her eyes. "Sleep. Give me sleep."

A minute later, she's snoring. I go into the bathroom, find a towel, scoop it up, and run water over it. While she sleeps, I wipe her face and neck clean of the vomit. Then I pull the sheets off her and throw them at the foot of her bed, away from the pile of puke. She is curled in the fetal position, clothed in a white nightgown. I don't see any discharge on the gown. Apparently, it's one of those self-cleaning articles of clothing.

Five minutes later, I'm downstairs searching for disinfectant and a sponge to use for cleaning her floor upstairs. *I guess my janitorial skills* can *come in handy.* I look underneath the kitchen sink and find what I need. Twenty minutes later, the wooden floor of her bedroom is sanitized, the glass from the bottle picked up, and I'm carrying around her sheets (which are balled tightly to make sure no vomit leaks out), hunting for a washer and dryer downstairs. I find a door. It's a closet. I find another door, open it. Steps lead downward. I flip a light switch on the wall, carefully descend into the basement, and find the washer and dryer. . . .

I check on Meranda periodically to make sure she's still breathing, to make sure she doesn't throw up while sleeping, and that she doesn't choke on her own vomit and die. As 11:30 rolls around, I figure she's safe, merely sleeping off the drunkenness. I do the dishes, search for a vacuum, find one and use it on the first floor. *It won't wake her. She's in a deep sleep.* I search for Endust, find a can, use it and a towel to wipe away the dust. I'm officially Alice. I feel bad I haven't mowed Meranda's lawn yet. I go outside and begin my hunt for the mower. I check the garage (which, to my surprise, is unlocked), and find it there next to a tower of boxes. I roll it outside, to the front lawn.

After two hours of mowing in sweltering heat, forfeiting lunch, I put the mower back in the garage and eventually wind up in Meranda's bedroom. I step to her bed. A floorboard creaks.

She opens her eyes. "Good kid, Jimmy," she mumbles, then her lids close again.

I have to get home, eat, and go to work. I look at her one last time. She appears to be sleeping soundly. "Sleep tight, Meranda."

I go downstairs with an idea. I seek out a pad of paper, find a pad of Post-its on a stand beneath the wall telephone. I write her a note:

Meranda,

I mowed the lawn for you. I hope you like it. Don't worry about the money. Free of charge. You can do me a favor, though. The next time you feel the urge to drink, call me. Night or day. Doesn't matter. Call me and I'll be here. By the way, your sheets are clean in the washer. I didn't get around to drying them. Sorry.

Sincerely,

Jimmy
555-6789

I stick the note on the phone, second-guess that idea. How often does she receive and make phone calls? She may never spot the note if I leave it here. I think of the most conspicuous place in the house to leave the note. The couch comes to mind. I can see her sitting there often. I stick the note on the brochure's cover.

I pray: *God, please be with Meranda Erickson. Amen.*

* * *

Wednesday. I don't hear from Meranda. My mind goes mad. I wonder if I should have called 9-1-1. At home, I come across a newspaper, open to the obituaries, holding my breath. Her picture, her name, neither is listed. If she died, would they post the article that quickly anyway? I don't know how it works. I wonder if she got my note, if she has had the desire to drink, if she's simply too prideful to call and ask for help. I wonder if she's read the brochure, if she's read it and read it and read it. Did she find solace in the brochure, or anger and fear? All three? Did she tear it up, toss it in the garbage?

I wonder.

* * *

Thursday.

Still haven't heard from Meranda. Is she drowning in her sorrows? Too drunk to pick up the phone? At work, I carry my cell phone in my pocket, just in case. I told her to call me day or night. I need to be ready to follow though with my offer. Jimmy of Team Sobriety—ready to pounce.

* * *

Before work on Friday at, say, eleven, my cell rings. I flip it open, expect to hear Meranda's voice, but a person introduces herself as Sasha, and she wants to know if I have time to complete a brief survey. I tell Sasha I don't have time. I tell her to take me off her list, and that I don't ever want to hear from her or her company again. Then I say "thank you" really politely.

At 4:30, I gather the garbage from the classrooms, wonder if Meranda even saw the brochure I left behind, and think the gesture may have been too strong. I may have pushed her away, like someone pointing out a sin: *"Hey, you have a drinking problem, Meranda, and you need help. Repent, you evildoer!"* Why couldn't I have waited for an opportune time to give her that brochure? Why couldn't I have held off until the brochure could be presented to her in person? I hope she didn't find the included note offensive.

My cell rings from my front pocket. I drop the garbage bag, pull the cell from my pocket, open it, press it against my ear. "Hello?" I hear static.

"Jimmy . . ." More static.

"Meranda, is that you?"

"Jimmy . . ." My name is faint, choppy.

"Are you okay?" I ask.

"I need you." Meranda's voice comes through clearly.

"I'll be there," I say. "Don't do anything you'll regret. I'll be there. Do you hear me?"

I close the phone, throw it in my pocket, walk briskly out of the classroom, up the hallway, to Randy's cleaning area, and past the room he is vacuuming. I hear him say, "Useless kids. *Slobs*," as I turn a corner. I shake my head at his anger, think: *What are you doing to get outta here, Randy? You hate cleaning here. You hate the kids. Do something about it* . . . I scurry along the hallway, past the principal's office, the secretary's office, picking up speed. All the students and teachers are gone for the night. I get to Dad's cleaning area, the end opposite from my cleaning zone. I hear Dad's vacuum, follow the sound to the classroom he is vacuuming. I stand in the classroom's doorway. Dad's back is to me, his right hand pushing and pulling the vacuum over the brown carpet, in between desks. I step into the room, flip the light switch off and on. He whirls to the door, to me, powers off the vacuum, and holds it upright by his side.

"What's going on?" he asks.

"I need to leave."

"*What*? Why?"

"Meranda needs me."

"Who's Meranda?"

I shake my head at him. "Don't you remember?"

"Am I supposed to?"

I nod. "She's the writer I told you about. The lady I met at the Luncheon."

"Oh, yeah. Meranda Stetson, right?"

"Erickson."

"Close enough." His grip tightens around the vacuum handle. "And why does she need you?" He doesn't let me respond. "I need you *here*."

"I'll come back after and finish. Promise."

He groans at the inconvenience. "All right. This one time. You better come back, though. I don't wanna be stuck with your work."

"I won't stick you with any work, Dad."

I'm about to say "see you later" when he starts the vacuum and turns his back to me. He goes over the carpet with quick, short strokes, his body tense.

Go, James. Go. He said you could. I leave the classroom, sprinting down the hallway like a superhero about to shed his civilian clothing.

Meranda needs me.

* * *

I knock on Meranda's door. She doesn't show her face. Is this a repeat episode? I bang on the door. Zero response. I throw the door open, hurry through, shut the door. I sprint up the staircase, straight to her room, expecting the worst—her inert body sprawled on the bed, whiskey bottles scattered on the floor, her mouth hanging open. I peek inside the room, give it a quick scan. The bed is made. There are no visible bottles of whiskey or bottles of any type lying on the floor or sitting on her nightstand. She isn't here. "Where are you?" I yell. *Come out, come out, wherever you are . . .*

I run out of the room, down the stairs. I look in the kitchen, don't spot her there, check the living room, and see her sitting on the couch stiffly, wearing her nightgown, eyes vacant, blank-faced. She's holding a pocket-sized photograph on her lap. Four transparent bottles of whiskey sit on the table in front of the couch. They are full, the caps screwed on. Also on the table is the brochure fanned open. The one placed by Jimmy the AA delegate. The Post-it note I left is stuck to the glass top coffee table. I sit on the cushion to her left. She flinches but doesn't say anything. I sneak a peek at the photograph. The man in the photo is wearing a Navy uniform, smiling, with a docked ship as the backdrop.

We sit in silence for about five minutes. Then flatly, without turning her attention to me, she says, "It would've been our thirtieth anniversary today . . ."

Suddenly, I understand. "Is that Eddy?" I point to the photograph.

She looks down at the picture, expressionless. "You know, it's kinda funny. Not funny ha-hah, but funny as in ironic." She shakes her head. "He survives a war but not New York." She releases a laugh. "What kind of a sick joke is that, huh?"

I watch her toss the photo on the cushion to her right.

"But who even cares?" Meranda asks, finally looking at me. "My friends didn't." Anger flashes across her face. "They told me I should get over it and move on with my life. Six months after his death and they thought I should move on . . . You know what I said to them?"

I shake my head.

"I said *burn in hell*. You don't know what it's like. You haven't walked in my shoes. And do you know what they did?"

I wag my head.

"They left. Just like that. Gone."

"They stopped being your friend?" I'm appalled.

"They stopped calling," she says. "They stopped visiting. They stopped writing. They stopped caring." She crosses her arms. "Betsey died last year. Bertha, the year before. I figure I'm next."

"It doesn't have to be like that."

"You don't understand, Jimmy. I need a drink so much."

"What good would that do?"

She looks away, toward the picture window. "I wouldn't have to feel. I don't want to feel it."

"Drinking isn't helping you. You know that. It's controlling you. I know you can be stronger than that."

She sighs and shakes her head. "I don't know, Jimmy."

"You drink, and so what? It's just a Band-Aid. You get smashed tonight, the feelings will still be there tomorrow."

She nods at the brochure. "I've been doing some reading." She slowly turns to me.

"And?"

"Every page I read, I'm full of rage, Jimmy." Her voice grows angry. "It was never supposed to be this way." She picks up the brochure and examines it. "At first I was peeved that you would give this to me. AA is for the diseased, I thought, and certainly I'm not diseased. I'm Meranda Erickson . . . But then this *thing*," turning a page, "started to make sense and that's when I realized—I'm an alcoholic." She starts to cry. "I don't know if I can do this, Jimmy. I don't know if I'm strong enough."

"What do you want? To be held captive by whiskey the rest of your life or to be free?"

"I want to be free."

"Go to a meeting. Just go," I say. "You won't even have to say anything there. You could just listen, feel out the situation."

"How do you know?" she asks, tears rolling down to her lips.

I explain my father, his past drinking problem, how AA helped, and how he divulged, on many occasions, the specifics of AA meetings—names excluded, of course. "It helped *him* and it can help *you*."

She flips a page, points to the third step, which talks about turning your life over to the care of God. "The care of God . . ." she says, face tensing, sobbing. "I don't trust his care."

I put my arm around her, look into her wet eyes. "God didn't do *any* of this to you." I glance at the bottles on the table, then back at her. "Tell me, whose care would you rather be in? God's or whiskey's?"

The strength of her sobbing grows. She doesn't speak, couldn't do so if she wanted. The tears consume her. I say, "God *didn't* do this to you." She lets me hold her. I say, "You're gonna kick the habit. Just hold on."

When the crying halts, she wilts in my arms. I rest her on the couch. She's sleeping. I set the brochure aside, then decide I should move her upstairs. I carefully lift her petite frame, walk to the stairs, balancing her body in my arms, and climb the steps. I get to her room, breathing heavily, lie her on the bed, and drape the sheets over her. I lean in and touch her forehead. She opens her eyes, dried tears on her cheeks.

"I'll be here tomorrow morning to check on you," I say.

She works to smile. "Maybe I'm already in God's care, after all," she says.

"Oh?" I cock my head.

"He gave me you," she says. A second later, her eyes close. She drifts to sleep.

I stand at the edge of her bed, grinning. "Goodnight, Meranda," I say, then I go downstairs and collect the whiskey bottles. I slowly pour them down the drain and toss the bottles in the garbage.

I love to hear the *smash*.

* * *

I arrive back at the school at about 1:15 AM. I let myself into the building and punch in the company's security code. I call Dad at the house and tell him I'm at the school and he doesn't need to worry—I'll get the work done. He says, "Good." I start to explain why I had to go over to Meranda's house. I want to divulge the happenings there, but he interrupts, tells me he wants to go back to bed.

He hangs up the phone.

I finish taking the garbage out of my cleaning area, clean the bathrooms at rapid speed, vacuum and mop the classrooms, sweep, mop, and buff the hallway. My work is complete at six o'clock. I leave the school, drive with windows down, chewing on a piece of gum, listening to blaring music to keep me awake, over and over and over again replaying the conversation I had with Meranda.

CHAPTER THIRTY-THREE

I arrive at Meranda's house after only three hours of sleep. I knock. She comes to the door immediately, lets me in. She asks if I want some coffee.

I say, "Milk, please," then: "No Perk Up Café this morning?"

"I want to stay away from my routine, if you know what I mean," she says.

I smile. She brews a pot of coffee. Gets me my milk. I tell her how nice a day it is.

"It's gotta be eighty already," I say. "Not a cloud in the sky."

After we're done drinking our beverages at her kitchen table, I ask if she'd like to go for a walk. She agrees to it and we head outside, hook up with the dirt road. We walk leisurely, trees hanging over us, standing beside us, Jiminy Cricket and his kin chirping from the thickets.

I stare at her, our feet scuffing the dirt.

"You were right," she says softly, "God didn't do any of this to me."

We stop in the middle of the road.

"I'm gonna go to an AA meeting," she says. "I'll sit and listen, feel out the situation, as you said. I need help." There's a tremor in her voice. "I'm an alcoholic and I need help."

* * *

Leigh and I order Chinese from her apartment. An Asian man delivers the food, two bags. Leigh starts devouring the meal without a word regarding her weight or what she should or should not eat. We chat over lunch. I explain the breakthrough I had with Meranda. "I don't want her to die," I say. "I don't want her to wind up like Gramps."

Leigh sets the fork down, grinning. "I love you."

I chuckle. "What was that for?"

"You make me proud."

* * *

Each weekday morning, before work, I visit Meranda. The days resemble one another: She answers the door sober, smelling of perfume instead of whiskey. We don't go to Perk Up Café; instead, we stay at her house. She tells me about her most recent AA meeting. She says she hates the meetings, that she dreads going but feels it to be a necessity to her staying sober, and she wants to stay sober. "I need to face this," she says often. "I don't want to die. I want to live. I want to be free."

We go for walks, and one day, a Monday, she says that she feels diseased. Entirely diseased. She talks about the slang used in AA, how the redundancy sometimes angers her. Some of the most common phrases and words, she explains, are: Newcomer, which she is; Running and Gunning, which relates to active drinking; the Big Book, which is basically AA's Bible; Normie, AA's description of non-drinkers; Higher Power, the label many of the members use for God; Stinking Thinking, thoughts that lead to drinking. She says, "Going to Group is like being part of a secret sect; they have their own language, their own beliefs, they're separate from society, and they're shadowy. Anonymous. The fact that the meetings are held in basements of churches adds to the feel of secret sect." She says they use the Serenity Prayer at the beginning of every meeting, and this makes her want to cry every time.

When we are together, she smiles often, laughs frequently, and begins implementing AA language into our conversations. There are no dirty dishes in her sink. The house is dust-free and vacuumed without my assistance. "Gotta stay busy," she says. She tells me that she still has the desire to drink, that some nights she wakes drenched in sweat, needing and wanting whiskey, feeling the urge crawling beneath her skin. Some nights before going to sleep, when she's alone, she gets bored, but then she thinks of me, and our upcoming time together, and the AA meetings, and she knows drinking isn't worth the temporary numbing of feelings.

On a Thursday, as we sit on her porch, listening to the birds sing and watching them fly, she points to one of them and says, "I want to be like that. I want to soar."

I say, "You are, Meranda. You are."

She explains how different she feels lately, more awake, with heightened senses. She likes where she's headed, toward sobriety. She talks about the "Chip" one of her fellow AA sect members received last meeting. "And I'm not talking about a potato chip," she says. "They gave it to him to mark thirty days of sobriety." She tells me that she wants to get a Chip, too, dammit. "I don't expect a Normie like you to understand what I'm talking about, though," she says.

I chuckle. "Don't use that AA slang on me, young lady."

She laughs, and I ask her if anyone from Group has spoken of AFGO yet. She winks and says, "Yeah . . . *A flippin' growth opportunity* . . . that's what this is."

I continue the playfulness, tell her to stay away from the thirteenth step. She says, "What are you talking about? There are only twelve steps."

I tell her there are actually thirteen. The "thirteenth step" is when you date someone from Group. She assures me that won't happen, that the others are too crazy for her, and quite frankly, they remind her of herself too much.

* * *

I walk to my mailbox, flip the lid, reach into the box, and pull out the mail. Mixed in with the rest of the parcels, I discover a notice informing me that I need to collect a package from the post office. Roughly thirty minutes later, I'm at the post office, at the counter, showing the notice to the postmaster. He takes the slip from my hand, walks out back, and returns with a large, bulky envelope, which displays Arthur's return address. The postmaster hands me the package, nods, and says, "There you go, son," and I cradle the envelope at my hip and depart the building into the noonday sun, grinning.

I take the manuscript home, scour it for Arthur's queries [comments and suggestions made within brackets], find two in the first chapter, three in the second, one in the third, and so forth. I read fifty-five pages before work, find his editorial skills superb, as usual; he's incredibly talented at spotting inconsistencies and minor flaws and resolving the problems or at the very least, explaining how to resolve a particular blemish. I call him and thank him for his fine performance.

"You're very welcome, my young protégé."

"You're a good friend," I say. "I'll never forget this."

At work, my body is busy, but my mind focuses on the novel. Eight hours scream by. I come home, eat a microwavable dinner, and submerge myself in *The Forsaken World*, not for an hour or two or three, but all night, through the hooting of owls and creaks from swaying trees and talking crickets, I read and read and read. The sun ascends into the sky, announcing a new day, and I'm still sitting at my desk, staring into the laptop.

At ten o'clock, I tend to Arthur's final query, which pertains to pacing and suspense. I correct the problem by adding three paragraphs, nearly a full page of text, which slows the pace and consequently builds suspense. I save the file, turn off the laptop, and crawl into bed, wired and exhausted at once. Back of my head on the pillow, legs stretching to the end of the bed, I think of my next move: Tomorrow, after I wake from this nap in five hours, and after another night of janitorial work, I will formulate a general query letter to send to new literary agents regarding *The Forsaken World*.

* * *

Inside the janitor's closet, as I'm filling the mop bucket with water from the hose attached to a faucet, I get a feeling like someone is watching me, maybe a secret admirer. I spin toward the door. Dad is standing in the hallway. Definitely not my admirer. I turn off the faucet and step out into the hall.

"Do you have a minute?" Dad asks, hands in his front pockets.

I shrug. "Sure."

He leads us to the library and shuts the door. We sit opposite each other at one of the square wooden tables. He wastes no time. "I'm going to be moving to San Diego," he says.

I shiver. "Really?"

He nods twice. "The house sold and I got a new job."

I let out a sigh as though Jackie Chan just roundhoused my gut.

"Are you all right?" Dad asks.

I try to force composure upon myself. "When are you moving? What's your new job?" My tone speaks of worry.

"We'll need to vacate the house by September first," he says matter-of-factly. He pauses, reaches in a pocket, and pulls out a stick of gum. "Then I'll move in with a friend for a few months." He tosses the wrapper onto the table and smacks the gum. "I'll be moving to California the first of December," he says, virtually expressionless.

"And your job will be?"

Impassively, he tells me it will be a customer service position for a five-year-old company.

"When did you interview?" I ask.

"A week ago, over the phone."

"And they gave you the job just like that?"

"Based on the résumé I sent them and the phone interview. Yes."

"Who are you gonna stay with until December?"

"Candace."

"I didn't know you knew a Candace."

"I didn't until a couple weeks ago."

I curl my upper lip.

"What?" he asks.

"You're going to move in with someone you met only two weeks ago? Where does she live?"

"*Boston.*" His passive tone turns aggressive. "And I can make whatever decision I want, thank you."

"Why are you getting so defensive?"

"I knew you'd react like this."

"*How else am I supposed to react?* My dad sells the house I'm living in out from under me, says we need to leave it by the first of September, says that he's going to move in with a woman named Candace, whom he's known for two weeks, and doesn't once mention his son in the equation! Where am *I* in all of this?"

He shakes his head. "I thought you'd be happy for me."

I toss my hands up. *You thought wrong.* "What are you gonna do for work until December?" I ask, vehement.

"I've saved plenty of money. I'll be fine for a few months."

I *only have four hundred dollars in* my *account!* "So, then, you're closing this business when?"

"As of August 25, the last day of the school's summer vacation. I'd like you to stick it out if you can."

I issue a laugh, not one of glee but out of nerves and anger.

"What's so funny?" he asks.

"Who knows where I'll be," I say.

I think he senses my resentment, because he quickly overcompensates with uncharacteristic optimism, "James, look at it this way: You never liked cleaning the school anyways, so pretty soon you won't have to. That's good news, right?"

He's treating me like a child, and I'm not amused. "Sure, Dad." *Whatever you say.*

* * *

The movie ends, and the credits scroll down the screen. From Leigh's couch, she and I speak over the faint music, lying intertwined on our sides.

"That movie didn't help take my mind off anything," I say. We sit up and face one another.

Leigh grabs the clicker and turns off the television, eyes steady on my face. "Talk to me," she says.

I ease into conversation. "There was a time when I thought Dad was gonna be doing janitorial work until the day he died." I pause, then chuckle. "I'm the one who was supposed to get out of cleaning the school, not him. I'm the unconventional one."

"You're *going* to get out, and your dad, too," she says. "Your dad's business won't exist after August . . . What are you gonna do now that your dad's leaving is a reality, not just conjecture?"

"I wanna write. That's what I'm good at. That's what I love."

"Be rational, James. What are you gonna do for work?"

"I told you. I wanna write."

"And *I* told *you*. Be rational."

"Rational from whose perspective?" My voice rises.

She shrugs and shakes her head. "It won't be the end of the world if you have to work two or three jobs. People do it. They survive."

"I don't want to merely survive, Leigh. I wanna thrive . . . I wrote a new query for agents. I'm gonna send out that letter to a bunch of them." I pause, collecting my thoughts. "Think outside the box, Babe. Why are you so afraid of doing that?"

"I don't want to have unrealistic expectations. It hurts too much when things don't work out," she says. "I don't want to see you get hurt again. I saw what happened the last time things didn't work out as planned with your writing."

"My expectations *are* realistic. To *me*. It's not like I sit in a closet, dreaming, doing nothing to fulfill the dream."

"You truly believe writing is what you're supposed to do?"

I think about her question. "It's where I wanna be," I say, eyes locked on her, unblinking. "It's where I *need* to be. If I'm not writing, where will I be? Working at a grocery store? A gas station?" I halt, take a breath, body tensing. "Why'd Dad have to go ahead and pull this? It pisses me off!"

Her eyes widen. "You're not at all happy for him?" she asks.

I lack a response.

She says, "You've told me how selfish you think your father is, but, James, you're being selfish, too." She places her hand on my shoulder. "Be happy for him. Forgive him. Accept his decision. Love him."

"Don't you understand? Once he leaves, my whole family will be gone. Nevada and California. Across the country, Leigh."

"Your whole family won't be gone." She smiles, rubbing her thumb over my palm. "*I'm* here," she says.

* * *

On a Friday, after a long discussion about AA, Meranda says, "I've got to be honest with you." Her right arm lies on the couch's armrest. "I don't know if the longing to drink will ever go away completely."

I lean back on the couch. "You've gotta stay busy."

"But I can't clean my house and go to AA meetings round the clock."

I grin. "How about writing?"

Her focus plunges to the carpet. "It's been so long. I wouldn't know where to begin."

"Yes, you would. You're a great writer. That's not something one loses."

She raises her head, eyes on me. "I miss Eddy so immensely, Jimmy. He was a great man. You would've liked him." She pauses. "He would've liked you."

"What do you miss the most?"

Eyes dampen behind her glasses. "His adoration for me and for life, and his absolute belief in my writing."

"Then don't you think he would want you to write?"

She takes a deep breath. "I know he would."

"Then you owe it to him."

"I'm scared, Jimmy. What if it isn't good enough?"

"What if it *is* good enough?"

She laughs. "What am I going to write about?"

"*You're* the award winner." I smile.

She parallels my face and says, "I'll need to be inspired . . . I should start reading again. That may help."

"You could go to the library . . ."

"Nah."

"Why not?"

She beams. "I'm blessed to have you in my life, Jimmy. And just to think, I almost didn't go to the Luncheon." Fondness arrives in her eyes. "Why haven't you asked me yet?"

My eyes shift in my head. "I don't quite understand."

She speaks at a snail's pace. "*You* write and *I'm* looking for something to read. Do you see a connection here?"

"You wanna read *my* book?"

She laughs. "I thought you'd never ask."

CHAPTER THIRTY-FOUR

I present Meranda with *The Forsaken World* the following morning. She places the stack of loose sheets on the kitchen counter.

"Thanks for doing this," I say.

She's holding a broom. The kitchen is the cleanest I've ever seen it. *She's* Alice now. "Reading your book is the least I can do for you, Jimmy."

* * *

All of the next week, throughout five visits to Meranda's house, she doesn't utter anything relating to my novel. Rather, she tells me about AA, as usual. The first visit, she tells me that yesterday she spoke for the first time at Group. "I said 'Hi, I'm Meranda, and I'm an alcoholic' and afterward, everyone greeted me in unison like you see on those stupid TV parodies." She tells me that she told them her life story, and they listened well. At the end of her speech, a guy spoke using "I" statements, which is common with AA. He said, "I can relate to losing a spouse and allowing that to affect me. I lost my wife five years ago, and that's when I started to drink. I've been sober for sixth months."

On the second visit, Meranda tells me she's proud that she's been Cleaning House. "And I don't mean literally cleaning the house," she says, although she has been.

"I know," I say. Cleaning House, in AA slang, means that one is getting their life in order. "I'm proud of you, too, Meranda."

The third visit, she tells me that the man whom she told me about before—the one who lost his wife—is now her Sponsor. A Sponsor, in AA terms, refers to an alcoholic who has experienced progress in Group and recovery and shares his or her experience with another alcoholic. She says they met last night for dinner and shared experiences. "I like The Sweet Widowed One," she says. "When I talk to him, I don't feel so alone in this process. I feel like I'm not the only one diseased."

The fourth visit, she tells me that she has fallen into some Stinking Thinking lately. "I don't want to relapse," she says.

The fifth visit, she says, "I met with The Sweet Widowed One again last night."

I ask her how old he is.

She blushes. "I'm two years his elder."

"I sense a crush."

She giggles. "I'm not ready for the thirteenth step," she says.

Silently, I wonder if I should take her silence regarding my novel as a sign that she dislikes my story.

* * *

Sitting on my bed, I tear open an envelope from one of the agents to whom I sent my newest query letter. The agent says he doesn't have room on his list for *The Forsaken World* but that he wishes me the best of luck. I call and thank him for the good wishes and tell him that I'm sorry he chose to pass on my novel.

I worry that soon Brad could find his way out of the pit.

* * *

The FOR SALE sign on the front lawn vanishes. Around the house, cardboard boxes appear. They sit stacked in the living room, in the kitchen, in the basement, each box full of Dad's belongings. I never see him pack any of his things, which leads me to believe that he fills the boxes while I'm at Meranda's house or while I'm with Leigh on the weekends. Perhaps little leprechauns do the grunt work while we sleep . . .

* * *

The first Saturday morning of August turns up. I travel thirty-five minutes to Staples, purchase moving boxes and bubble wrap, return to the house, and start packing. Moving is imminent like the Second Coming of Christ. I remove from a wall the collage Leigh gave me, and from another wall, Robert's letter. I wrap them in bubble wrap and set them in a box. Next, I box my books and my DVDs . . . After three hours, I've packed all my possessions, save the bed, the desk, and a few other stationary items.

I stare at the boxes, my life in cardboard.

* * *

I pray nightly. *God, I need one of these agents to respond favorably. I need to have one of them scoop me up as a client. I need a publishing deal, God. I'm trying to have faith in this. Trying to believe you won't let me fall. Don't let me fall, God. I've paid my dues. I'm ready. I'm so ready, God. I couldn't be more ready . . .*

* * *

I receive another rejection slip, rip it up and immediately toss it in my wastebasket. Jesus, with his long hair, wearing a white robe, stands above the pit, looking down at Brad, vigilant. I fear that it won't be long until Jesus grows tired, desiring a rejuvenating sleep, and Brad finds a way out of the hole.

* * *

Leigh sends me e-mails containing links to job Web sites. Stubbornly, I don't follow the links. I reply to her e-mails with gratitude but then delete them. I have my own way and that "way" doesn't include hunting down more tedious jobs.

* * *

Another rejection lands in my mailbox. The letter then finds itself in the garbage. *God, please. Where are you? I can't afford to fall.*

* * *

On Tuesday, the second week of August, two more rejections come in the mail. I think I see Brad climbing up the rocks in the pit. Jesus' eyelids are heavy, and he's looking away from the chasm.

What else do I have to do, God? Are you hearing me? I'm ready. I love you. I'm trying to be patient, to smile in the middle of this chaos, like Paul. Why aren't you listening to me, God? Don't you see me struggling? Didn't you see me packing my life away? Don't you know I need you to come through?

I'm scared.

So scared.

* * *

More e-mails of job links load my inbox. The fear is getting to me. What am I going to do when Dad leaves? What am I doing? I give in, click on one of the links, an ad for a custodial job at an office in Portsmouth, the seacoast. I stare at the ad.

Decent money, it looks like. But I'd be stuck, once again, cleaning up after people . . . But I could live on my own. Not easily, but it could be done. I could eat. Not easily, but it could be done. I could afford toilet paper to wipe my butt. Not easily, but it could be done . . .

I walk to the mailbox, open an envelope addressed to me. A fresh rejection letter smacks me in the face. I imagine Jesus is sleeping now, curled up at the mouth of the pit, dreaming of the Last Judgment. Brad will step out of the hole any minute.

* * *

Meranda and I sit on her porch. We discuss AA yet again.

"The Sweet Widowed One hit on me last night," she says.

"Do I dare ask what you did?"

She tells me that she doesn't know how it happened, but they kissed. She hadn't expected it, didn't even know if she wanted it, but they kissed. "We pulled apart and I was scared," she says, "and angry at myself."

"Why angry?"

"Angry because I feel guilty for enjoying The Sweet Widowed One."

"Why do you feel guilty?"

She can't look at me directly. "I feel guilty because when we kissed, I stopped thinking of Eddy."

"Does The Sweet Widowed One make you happy?" I ask.

No hesitation, "Yes."

"Eddy would want that for you," I say, "and you know that."

Her lips quiver. She starts to cry.

I say, "Let go."

She says, "I don't know if I can."

I stand, walk to her chair, bend down, lean in, hug her as she cries. "Let go," I say. "Let go."

* * *

Leigh and I walk barefoot along the beach, beneath an overcast sky. The ocean to our left is choppy and rumbling. The smell of seaweed fills the air. We dodge clumps of seaweed as we move over the sand.

"Have you been submitting your résumé to any of the employers I pointed you to?" she asks.

"Yes."

"Which ones?"

"The custodial job in Portsmouth. I don't know what else to do. It's what I'm qualified for." I hate myself for thinking of this as an option.

* * *

Meranda and I take another walk. We decide on a different route this time. Instead of walking on the road, we walk through a path carved in the woods. In the winter, she says, the path is for snowmobiles. Birds shriek and sing and chirp. We see a moose in the distance. We stop. It stops and stares back at us. It has a full rack—as in *antlers*. It's one of the biggest creatures I have ever seen—as in *body mass*. I whisper to Meranda, "Don't move." She doesn't. The moose looks away, then slowly departs from our area. We take a right, start walking down a separate, connecting path. This path is wider, more plush. Watchful for other moose, we start to talk.

She says, "I think I'm ready for the thirteenth step, Jimmy."

I scan our surroundings—the trees, undergrowth, squirrels, birds, tiny orange salamanders, rocks. "But what about step twelve?" I ask, glancing at her.

She frees a laugh, adjusts her hefty glasses. "The Sweet Widowed One makes me happy. I want to be happy. You were right, Eddy would want that for me. I know he would want that for me. I've spent too many years in self-pity, too many years oppressed by grief. I'm ready to be happy."

"Then you should be with him," I say.

She nods, changes the subject, tells me about another member of her Group, "DUI-er." She says DUI-er, he's about my age and he started Group yesterday, so she's not "the baby" in Group any longer, which she likes. From what she says, he got a "Nudge From The Judge"—was court ordered to attend AA—after a reckless driving charge. She says she's glad to have met him. "He reminds me of you, Jimmy—an alcoholic, driving-while-under-the-influence copy of you." She smiles.

It's my turn to change the subject. I ask her if she's had a chance to read my novel. She tells me that she hasn't had a chance, but not to worry. "I've been writing my own novel," she says, then winks.

I stop, and face her. I tell her that Eddy would be proud. She says, "I know, Jimmy. I know."

I arrive home (*home* for the time being, that is) from Meranda's, get out of the car, sweating, and crying. I want to be happy. Why can't *I* be happy like Meranda? I throw my hands toward the sky, the cottony expanse. "Where are you, God?" With tear-filled eyes, I watch the clouds float. I scream beneath my breath: "Show yourself to me! For once, show yourself! I've done everything I can. If you can part the Red Sea, create the sun in the sky, *create the universe*, you can do this for me, God! You have the authority. *All* authority. I've given myself to you. How about some divine influence?" I'm unstable on my feet. "Where are your hands to catch me? Where are your hands, God? Hold them out for me. Let me find myself in them. SHOW YOURSELF TO ME!"

* * *

On the night of August 21, after more cleaning, I pass by my landline phone. The answering machine blinks 1. Exhausted, I play the message. A person claiming to be the Facilities Manager from an office in Portsmouth says that he looked over my résumé and he would be very interested in interviewing me for the custodial job. He provides his phone number and extension and would like me to call him tomorrow to set up a time and date for the interview, if the job is something I'm still interested in.

I sit on my bed and sigh. The question of all questions—am I interested in the job? The answer is no, I was never truly interested, but I have to eat and I need a place to live. I think of God, balling my fists. Where is he now?

I watch Brad as he pulls himself from the pit. He grins, stepping over the sleeping Jesus, then he says, *That's right. I'm back, sissy.* I put my face in my hands. I don't want him to be back. I want him isolated in that pit, moaning and suffering.

* * *

I pick up the phone, hating myself. I dial the Facilities Manager's number. He picks up. I give him my name, tell him that I'd like to interview and that I need a job quickly. The first part is a lie; I wouldn't "like" to interview. I would "hate" to interview, actually, because that would mean that I'm interested in more cleaning. More mindless tasks. That would mean that I'm one step closer to becoming conventional—working fifty, sixty hours per week, dreamless. The Manager asks if tomorrow at twelve-thirty would be good for me. "Yes. That sounds fine," I say. I hate myself for agreeing to interview.

After I hang up the phone, I realize that I don't know the first thing about interviews. I've never been on one. I start to hyperventilate. What type of questions will he ask me? I want to be prepared. Are there standard questions asked at interviews? I force myself to take a deep breath.

I laugh. This is what my life has come to: I'm worried about interview questions for a custodial position.

* * *

I drive to Portsmouth, nerves mounting. I arrive at the office, park my car in the lot. I don't exit the car right away. I sit and look around the parking lot, which is full of expensive cars. My car is by far the ugliest out of them all. The car parked directly to my right, a black Mercedes, gleams in the sun. The car to my left, a red Porsche, looks like a vehicle out of a *James Bond* movie.

I step out of my car, legs like rubber, hands shaking slightly. How did I get here? I don't remember the drive. This is a mistake, a big mistake. I shouldn't be here. This is not what I envisioned for my future, for life after Dad's janitorial business. I walk across the parking lot. With each step, I want to turn around, get back in my car, and drive away. I come to the entrance, grab the door handle, and pull. The door doesn't budge. I pull harder. It must be locked. I let go of the handle, step away. This is definitely a mistake. I shouldn't be here. I can't even get in the building. I should turn around and walk—no, *run*—away. Never look back. Never stop. I should get in my car and drive. See where I end up. But I can't move. I stare at the door.

Is this *my destiny?*

I take another step back. I'm about to turn and start walking away when the door opens and a man in his mid-thirties appears. "James Frost?" he asks.

I nod. He tells me to come inside. "Sorry about the door," he says. "We keep it locked for security purposes." He goes on to say that he told the secretary to keep an eye out for me, but she went home sick and he just got out of a meeting. I step inside the building. We shake hands in the vestibule, then enter into the lobby together. He asks me if I found the place all right. I say that the building was easy to find and thank him for asking. We walk past the secretary's desk—ten feet long, rectangular, sleek and black, devoid of a secretary, covered with papers, a computer, pens and pencils, folders.

He brings me to a conference room. "Have a seat. We'll get started right away." I pull out a chair before the conference table, heart jumping. He sits across from me, my résumé on the surface before him. He reads parts of it aloud, says that I'm undeniably qualified for the job, but he wants to get to know me a bit more. He wants to know why I want this job. I lie to him, say that I like performing janitorial work, that I like the feeling I receive after I've cleaned up a really big mess.

He nods, writes on the paper. "Why don't you want to work for your father's company anymore?"

I set my hands on the table. "He's closing it down."

He nods again.

"And you won't mind the commute from Moose Acres?" he asks.

I tell him that I'm looking to relocate. He asks several other questions. Quick, intrusive questions. I answer each question vaguely like I'm a member of the Mob and my existence is top secret. He nods a lot, doesn't say much.

He stands, and I follow suit. We shake hands and he says, "I'd like you to work for us."

I force a grin. "Okay."

I feel like one of those Goths interested in self-mutilation who roam around with a *life sucks* mentality. Black mascara. Dyed black hair. Black clothing with chains. I'm full of self-hatred.

CHAPTER THIRTY-FIVE

On Friday, August 25, at the school for my last day of cleaning on behalf of Dad's company, I bring him into the library, and ask him to have a seat. We sit at one of the wooden tables.

"I've been looking at apartments in the seacoast area," I say, trying to get him involved.

"That's where you're going to move?"

Perhaps. "I want to live closer to Leigh."

"What are you gonna do for work? Figure that out yet?"

I hang my head, eyes on the table, fire in my chest. "I took a custodial position at an office in Portsmouth."

"Is that what you want to do?"

I look at him, like—*You jerk, your decision to leave is doing this to me.* "No, it's not what I want to do, but I need to eat. I need to have a place to sleep . . ." And you're giving me no choice.

He says, "Well, you have plenty of experience with cleaning. You'll be fine."

I stand suddenly, emotions growing. Can't let him see me cry. I say, "I have to get back to work."

He nods, gives a long, "Okay?" as if to say, *What was the point of this?*

We exit the library, Dad walking in one direction, I in another. I stride down the hallway, into a bathroom near the gymnasium. I enter a stall, looking down at the toilet, tears pouring like rain into the bowl. No, Dad, I won't be fine. Why are you doing this to me? How can you decide one day that it's time for you to pack up and leave? How can you toss your son away and do whatever it is you want to do?

I wonder if he even loves me, and if he has ever loved me. Then I think: *Why would he? I'm worthless. Nothing. Less than nothing . . .*

Ten minutes later, I leave the bathroom, eyes dry. I walk by the gym and see the bald guy from the past, the person who, in front of the children, said, "Don't worry, it's just the janitor." Summer basketball practice is going on, kids dribbling, shooting at the hoops, running up and down the court, and the bald guy (who looks like a basketball) is watching, his back to me, leaning against a wall near the gym's entrance.

The guy's voice echoes in my mind: *It's just the janitor . . .*

My body tenses. My jaw clenches. I'm *not* just the janitor. Dry-mouthed, I watch the bald man for about a minute before I decide I should approach him, tap him on the shoulder, and tell him what I think of his statement.

He spins around, looks at my hand pulling away. "What do *you* want?" he asks, fiery.

Puffing out my chest, ready to swing if need be, I say, "I'm James Frost, not just a janitor. I bet you didn't know that I wrote a novel, did you?"

"*No,*" he says freshly.

"It's going to be published someday, and I'm leaving this place." I pause; his nostrils are flaring. "Someone else will come in here and perform janitorial work in my stead, and you won't know him, either. You won't know what he does outside of this building. You won't know his aspirations. So don't *ever* think you know him based on what you see him doing here, because I can guarantee you, that's not him."

He folds his arms over his chest. "Are you done yet?"

That wasn't quite the reaction I was hoping for, and it throws me off. "Uh—well—yeah, umm—I guess . . ."

"Sign any big deals with any publishers lately? I'm sure you're having to beat them off with a stick." His tone bursts with sarcasm.

My cheeks fill with warmth. Meekly, I say, "No. No big deals."

He laughs. "A janitor who writes . . . What's next? A garbage man who sings opera?"

I don't know how to verbally respond to that, so I shake my head at him, then turn around, before I humiliate myself further. As I start to walk away, I hear him say, "Good luck with the publishers. I'm sure they can't wait to sign a—janitor." He busts out laughing.

I keep walking despite my desire to drop that guy where he stands.

Body tense, I enter my end of the school, the hallway I have swept and mopped for the past few years. I go into the janitor's closet, taking deep breaths, composing myself. I grab the broom and sweep the hall one last time. Afterward, I retrieve the mop bucket from the closet, roll it into the hall, and mop the floor one last time. I find solace in the fact that there have been many one-last-times to-night: I scrubbed the toilets one last time, cleaned the sinks, vac-uumed, and mopped the rooms. One last time.

I finish mopping the hallway, place the mop in the bucket, bring the bucket into the closet, and rinse out the mop in the sink one last time. Ten minutes before midnight, I peek inside the rooms, say goodbye to each of them, walk out of my designated area, into Randy's.

He turns off his vacuum and stands it at his side. "So what's next for you, bro?"

My face feels hot. "More cleaning. In Portsmouth."

His eyes show delight. "Yeah, that feels about right. Writing's not for you . . ."

I shake my head at him. I can't believe he said that. "Goodbye, Randy." I will never have to see him again.

I go into the gym (which is empty now) and say goodbye to the floor, the walls, the basketball hoops, the bleachers. I go into my fa-ther's end of the school and say goodbye to the rooms as he buffs the hallway.

At midnight, I step out into the vestibule and say goodbye, my heart rejoicing. I throw the doors open and depart the building. One last time.

Beneath the joy, however, exists the heart wrenching truth that I will continue to clean, not here, not for my father, but somewhere else.

Once again, I'm scared.

* * *

August 30, I rent a small U-Haul and drive it to Dad's house, Leigh with me; she took the day off from work, using accrued vacation time. By mid-afternoon, Leigh and I have the U-Haul loaded with my possessions. Dad pulls into the driveway, and parks next to us.

"I'll wait out here," Leigh says, opening the U-Haul's passenger's-side door. "Take your time."

I nod at her, leave the dutiful girlfriend behind, greet Dad as he gets out of the car, and follow him into the house.

He tosses his car keys on the kitchen table. "So this is it, huh?" He lingers next to the table.

I step toward him. "Yup. Start the new job tomorrow." I scan the room—the kitchen table, boxes upon boxes, Dad's life in cardboard, the television in the living room, the couch. "Will you need any help with this stuff?" I ask.

He shakes his head. "I'll be fine. I hired a moving company to help."

We stand in awkward silence for a minute, lost in this hollow house.

He excuses himself. "I need to hit the bathroom. Can you stick around for a minute?"

Hardly an ideal time for a dump. "I'll be here," I say.

He walks away, into the bathroom positioned across from my sanctuary. He shuts the door. I go into the ole bedroom, gaze at the room devoid of any sign that I once occupied this space. I look to the spot where my desk once sat, picture it still there, me sitting before it, the laptop on its surface, my fingers poking at the keys, the sound of clicking. From across the room, I watch the backside of James Frost, his foot tapping on the carpet, his body steady as he scribes *The Forsaken World*. I watch James, my heart aching, standing in my used bedroom two days before my father leaves for Boston, getting ready to depart before he can leave me, before he pulls the house out from under my feet.

I will always remember this room, the sanctuary from a conventional world, the place where dreams were born, where my relationship with Leigh hatched from a few messages passed over the Internet. Where I once lived.

Goodbye, dear sanctuary.

I'm rampantly crazy, talking to all these inanimate objects.

I think I hear Dad cry in the bathroom, a faint weeping sound. I leave the bedroom and knock on the bathroom door. Either he's feeling emotion or he's passing a kidney stone. He blows his nose and says in a weak tone, "I'll be out in a minute . . ."

I go to the kitchen table, heart heavy for him, sit there and wait. I hear the bathroom door open, and Dad appears at the table. I stand as his equal, man and man, no longer man and boy. Eyes puffy, he says, "Good luck, James."

"You too," I say, opening my arms to him. He appears baffled; leans in toward me, raises his arms waist-high, then lowers them so they dangle. Leans back, raises them again, unsure of the procedure for hugging, a Martian to affection. I lean in, place my arms around him, the teacher giving a lesson. I wait for his response. Several seconds into my embrace, his arms come alive and fold around my back. I hold him tightly, not wanting to let go.

"I understand your decision," I say, and in this split second, I genuinely do comprehend: Our parting is inevitable, and he's been searching for a woman, like a quest to find the Holy Grail, because once I'm gone, he doesn't want to be alone. I feel like crying, thinking of his desperation, and all the times I felt so angry about his seemingly selfish actions. *Are we* that *different? What would my life be like if*

I didn't find Leigh? I picture Dad alone in a beat-up apartment some-where, and that's not what I want for him. I wish for him to have someone, like I have Leigh. Fighting my desire to cry, I continue, "I stand behind you, I'm happy for you, and I love you."

We pull apart. He looks at my face. His eyes water. "I . . . love . . ." He swallows some air and can't continue.

Why can't you say it, Dad? For once, why can't I hear it?

"I'm . . . proud of . . ." He turns his head, hiding the emotion, ashamed.

Why can't you say it?

He turns to me again, wet-faced. "You'll be . . . missed," he says, eyes downcast and dripping.

I walk to the door. He comes along, eyes on the carpet.

"See you later, Dad," I say, lips quivering, my back to the door.

He looks up. "See you later, James," he says, and touches my shoulder.

CHAPTER THIRTY-SIX

It's my first night at the new apartment in Portsmouth, and I can't fall into a deep sleep because I hear something skittering across the kitchen floor. I turn on the bedside lamp—a lamp that came with the apartment and closely resembles a manikin's leg covered by a shade—and I stumble toward the kitchen in my half-sleeping daze. I rub my eyes, look down at the faded and peeling brown linoleum floor. No creature in sight. Becoming more aware, I scan the studio, one end to the other, and see no trace of any critter. I wonder if I was imagining the sounds. Perhaps I was. I walk to my bed, climb aboard, wrap myself in the clean sheets—the only part of my apartment that is clean, it seems—and shut off the lamp. I try to fall asleep, but I can't.

The skittering sound returns. I sit up in bed, reach toward the lamp but decide not to turn it on. I continue to listen to the claw-tapping sounds coming from the kitchen floor. I slowly and silently get off the bed, creep toward the kitchen, expecting something furry to rub against my bare feet. I don't feel anything. Suddenly, I don't hear anything. I run my hand along the nearest wall. There is a light switch here somewhere. I've used it once or twice before. My index finger locates the switch. I hear a squeak. Another squeak. A third squeak. I flip the switch. Light fills the studio. On the linoleum, sure enough, I spot a rat, its worm-like tail dangling behind its plump and furry body. The rat stares up at me, doesn't move, petrified. I don't move either. I come to the shocking realization that my apartment is a rat's nest. Literally. Of course, I didn't know that when I signed the lease. My eyes dart along the studio, searching for something with which to flatten this rodent. The worn-out rocking chair? No. Too loud. A book? No. Far too messy. My alarm clock? No. I'll need that for work. A sneaker? No. I'll need that for walking. The broom? Perfect. One problem presents itself, however; the broom is leaning against the side of the refrigerator and the rat is standing upright in front of the refrigerator like he wants to do a trick. I don't think I'll be able to cross paths with the rat without it scurrying away. I take my chances and leap toward the fridge. The rat kicks into reverse, does a cookie, falls on its butt, jumps to its feet. I grasp the broom, take a swing, hit the floor, miss the rat, and watch helplessly as the rodent dives beneath the refrigerator.

I get down on my knees, poke the broom handle through the opening between the floor and the fridge. No contact made. I stand, then push the fridge away from the wall. I walk behind the refrigerator, eyes on the ground. The rat does not reveal itself. I take a step back, notice a fist-sized hole in the wall, a wormy tail swinging from the opening like a pendulum. I shove the broom handle in the hole, hear high-pitched squeaking, then nothing. I step away from the cavity, but see no movement inside.

I smile, return the fridge to its original position against the wall, lean the broom on the side of it, and revisit the bed. I throw the sheets over my body, feeling a sense of accomplishment from defeating the insignificant rat. Five minutes pass and my eyes close, my body relaxes, and I start to drift off to sleep. Wonderful sleep.

The sudden sound of tiny feet pattering inside the wall at the other end of the studio causes my eyes to open. I glance at my alarm clock. I need to sleep. The feet keep moving in the walls. I wonder if there are more rats or if I somehow missed my target. I hear squeaking. More squeaking. Crunching. Clawing. Scratching. Squeaking. There has to be more than one. Did the rodent decide to call a meeting with his fellow rats? I can see it now: Fievel and family plotting to oust me from their home. I don't belong here. They know it. I know it. But this is what I have, what I can afford.

This is my life.

* * *

There are accountants here, customer service representatives, managers, engineers, directors. I overhear men in power suits talking about growth rate and customer satisfaction and profit. Three people work in Human Resources. Seven in Marketing. Twenty in Sales. High-paying, important jobs galore. I know their names (they're posted on the cubicles), but they don't know mine, don't bother to ask. I've been here for three days. My hours are nine to seven, a fifty-hour workweek. I clean the bathrooms and the lunchroom. I vacuum around the cubicles as people shuffle out of the office at the end of the day. I clean the hallways, upstairs and downstairs. I ensure that supplies are stocked in the lunchroom—paper plates, plastic ware, napkins, condiments, soap, paper towels. For the bathrooms, I make sure that there is plenty of toilet paper, paper towels, soap. It is also my job to see to it that there is ample paper available for the copiers and printers. Sometimes this means walking out to the warehouse with a dolly, returning to the office with over a hundred pounds of paper. I do little boring jobs, like the one from the other day, when I installed metal cubbies above select cubicles in the Sales Department during their weekly meeting, which they held in the Conference Room upstairs.

It's two o'clock and time to collect the garbage. I start in the Sales Department, where people always look agitated and stressed, never smiling. I step to Adam's desk with a back pocket full of trash bags, say hi. He says hi in return, but doesn't look at me, doesn't make eye contact, fingers striking the keyboard. I take his garbage, toss it in the trash bin on wheels I've been rolling around, install a fresh bag in his can, and move on to the next person in line, Tom. I ask him how he's doing. Tom says he's pretty bad, actually, and he doesn't look at me, would rather I didn't exist, I guess. I dump his garbage, insert a new bag in the can, advance to Ingrid's cubicle. I greet her. She mumbles something, tosses a candy wrapper at the garbage, misses the garbage, doesn't care to pick it up off the carpet, eyes focused on the database-filled computer screen. Her fingers hit the keyboard. I stare at her, wonder if she knows that she missed the can, wonder if she's taunting me, if she's seeing how far she can push the janitor before he snaps. I breathe. Compose myself. I want to tell her that she's being inconsiderate. That I am a human being and I should be respected just like any other person. Instead, I bend and pick up the wrapper, take her garbage, adorn her can with a clean bag, and walk away.

Fifteen minutes later, with a rolling trash bin packed with garbage, I head toward the door, surprisingly catch my name ("the janitor") from the lips of one of the employees. I stop and stand behind a partition, eavesdropping. Marcy is saying that the janitor is far too talkative, overfriendly. Virginia laughs, says that she just tries to stay away from making eye contact. I cringe, walking away from the partition, beaten and furious, hands clenching the bin's handle.

I dispose of the garbage, go into the bathroom, into a stall, shut the door and lock it, hiding from the world I've gotten myself into. My heart hurts. Why did I do this to myself? I feel anger toward Leigh, since she directed me to this job. I want to blame her for all of this, but I remind myself that I have no right to blame anyone else. I was scared. I made a choice based on fear. A bad choice. One that placed me here.

I lean against the wall, shaking. I hate myself. I've always hated myself. The suicidal thoughts, the self-sabotaging behavior . . . it all makes sense. Deep down, I feel that I don't deserve anything good in life.

I hear Brad: *That's right. You're not good enough.*

And I still think he's right. I'm *not* good enough. Even when I found Leigh, I didn't think I was worthy of her, didn't understand why she wanted to be with me. The years working for Dad . . . why didn't I get out? Why couldn't I walk away?

I imagine Brad saying something like: *Because you wanted to be unconventional, you idiot. You strive for that. You live in pain, love the pain, feel you deserve the pain.*

I could have gone to college, could have taken out a loan and gone. I could have been an unconventional college student, could have chosen to stay away from alcohol, parties. I could have chosen to study. At least then I wouldn't be standing here in a bathroom stall as a custodian. But college would have been too easy. Brad's right. I love pain, feel I deserve pain. *I am pain.* I don't want it anymore. I don't want to hurt anymore. I want to feel good.

I'm worth something. I have to be worth *something.*

* * *

I go to the grocery store, calculator on the cart's seat. I need meals—breakfasts, lunches, dinners. I walk to the frozen aisle, select several one-dollar microwavable meals, throw them in the cart, add the amounts to the calculator. I walk to another aisle, pick out the cheapest, roughest toilet paper they have, essentially sandpaper, and add it to the calculator. I need more toothpaste. I go to that aisle, get a tube of Crest. I also get mouthwash, the store brand, and floss. I stock up on Dial hand soap, Lever body soap, Head and Shoulders shampoo, Tide laundry detergent. The total on the calculator is more than I can afford. I sigh, return the Crest, get the store brand, recalculate. I return the Dial for the store brand. I do the same with the Lever, Head and Shoulders, and Tide. Recalculate. I can afford this. I have enough left over to buy some mousetraps. I pick them off the shelf, smiling. I don't want to live in an apartment full of rats. For once in my life, I want some comfort.

I arrive home. *Is that what this is? Is this really my home? Do Dad and I really live apart?* I set the traps with plenty of cheese. Leigh calls me. She says, "I don't care about those rats you told me about. I want to spend some time with my boyfriend in his apartment, rats or no rats." I invite her over.

* * *

We cuddle on the couch. This is one of the very few good things about taking the job: I'm able to see Leigh nearly every day after work.

As the sun sets and my apartment darkens, I hear the snapping of traps. Leigh chuckles. I laugh. I'm tired of living in pain.

I will not live among rats.

Farewell, Fievel.

CHAPTER THIRTY-SEVEN

I go to a local bookstore, research the writing market, purchase books (with my credit card, of course. Will the debt ever end?) that are supposed to help hone the art of query writing. At home, via the Internet, I research the names of agents and editors taking on fresh literary voices. I write five, ten, twenty drafts of a query letter. Trash them all. I write twenty-five, thirty, thirty-five drafts. Trash those, too. I write the thirty-sixth draft. I stare at the laptop's screen, and laugh. Thirty-sixth time is a charm.

I send the letters to fifteen agents, then pray God will hear me.

* * *

I miss Dad. Miss him so much. He never calls me. I call him once a week. When he picks up, I do the bulk of the talking. I mostly talk about surface topics—my job, my apartment, the weather—without any mention of my feelings. This is the type of relationship we have. I'm learning to accept it. I love my father, always have, always will. Unconditionally.

During one of our calls, he surprises me and asks if I've learned anything from this experience. I say, "Yeah, I've learned that when you work fifty hours a week, you can still dream . . ."

* * *

I talk with Meranda on the phone every other night. I ask, "What have you been writing?" She says, "*The Diary of an Alcoholic.*" She tells me that The Sweet Widowed One is still sweet, and she says that she's been drinking inordinate amounts of coffee lately to replace the whiskey, if that's possible. She tells me that she started reading my book. I hold my breath. She says, "I think you've created fantastic characters with great dynamics among them." I want to cry and laugh at the same time. She apologizes for taking a while to get started, especially after she requested the novel. "I needed to get some things in order before I could give your book the attention it deserves," she adds.

She tells me that someone from AA relapsed recently, and she worries that she will do the same. "The urge never ceases. I want to drink, Jimmy, so much. Drink and drink and drink. But I don't want to fall into that trap again, don't want to slip back into my old self-destructive ways." I tell her that she doesn't have to relapse, that she doesn't have to live in pain, love pain, or be pain.

She says, "I don't love pain."

I say, "Yeah, you do."

She says, "No, I don't."

I say yeah you do for a final time and explain: "You love alcohol, right?"

"Umm, well, not really, but . . ."

"Admit that you love it. I know you do."

"Okay, yeah."

"And what does alcohol do to you?"

She pauses, then chuckles. "Causes me pain."

* * *

Leigh and I spend time all around Portsmouth. We visit the Jackson House (a local museum), Market Square (the heart of downtown), The Music Hall to see a play. We take a steamboat cruise to the Isles of Shoals (she pays), see the forlorn, castle-like Portsmouth

Naval Prison along the way, Lunging Island, the Portsmouth Harbor Lighthouse, Smuttynose Island, Star Island, The Wentworth Hotel, Whaleback Lighthouse, and more. We spend time in an independent bookstore (window-shopping) and a music store (again, not buying anything) that features thousands upon thousands of new and used CDs and DVDs. We go to the mall (just to look around).

* * *

Frail leaves float aimlessly to the ground.

Rejections find me. One rejection, two rejections, three, four.

I don't know what to do. How much longer can I go on like this? Where are your hands, God? I'm still waiting for you to reveal them to me. I need you. Jesus, where are you? Unconventional Jesus, where have you gone? I go to your church every week, pray to you constantly, love you, even through doubts that you'll let me crash to the ground. I don't want to live in pain, love pain, be pain anymore, God. Take the pain away. Please.

And I think that maybe he won't take the pain away, because part of me still loves it. I'm like one of those sick and twisted masochists. *Yeah . . . bat me upside the head. Again and again and again. Feels wonderful!*

* * *

I receive a call from Arthur's sister, Mindy. With an unstable voice, she says, "I don't know how to tell you this. I'm not sure how to say . . ."

My heart descends. "What is it?" I ask.

She gulps. "Arthur, he, well . . . he died three days ago."

I fall to the floor inside my apartment, shocked, scrabble to find the phone. I ask her how he died. She tells me it was a heart attack, that he was dead when she found him. She begins to cry. I can't help myself. I start to cry, too. "No," I say. "No, no, no, no. This can't be happening." She assures me, in an uneven tone, that yes, he is dead, and this is happening. Her brother is dead. She says, "He spoke of you all the time. You don't understand how important you were to him." I tell her no, I didn't realize. She gives me a time and date for the funeral. She asks if I'll be there. "Yes," I say, still on the floor, "I'll be there."

I think of Arthur's sign, the first time I saw it. I imagine driving by the sign now.

Tears pool in my eyes.

I think of him standing in the doorway of his house, greeting me, of him and his encouraging words, of him offering to edit my book for free.

I cry. Pain. More Pain.

* * *

Arthur's service is small, intended only for close friends and relatives. The sky is milky, the grass damp. I stand bleakly in the cemetery, Arthur's sister at my side. Bleary-eyed, I look to the casket suspended over a hole in the earth. One of his friends gives the eulogy. I cry throughout the entire tribute.

A breeze blows over the cemetery.

I swear I hear Arthur's voice float by. "There's my ferociously ambitious protégé," it says. Then I picture Brad in my face, smiling at my misery, and he says, *How do you feel now? Your master is dead. You're pain's protégé now.*

* * *

I read the Bible in my apartment to find comfort. I don't find any. All I want to do is weep, so I do, everywhere I go, including work, in the bathroom stall, the custodian's closet. I weep in my car, on my way to work, on my way to Leigh's apartment after work, on my way back to my apartment after spending time with Leigh at hers, speaking fondly of Arthur, telling her about the times we had together, his kind and generous nature. I cry in bed, as I take a shower, as I make myself breakfast, lunch, dinner, all the while not eating much of any meal. Every time I look at my manuscript, I can't help but think of him. He's scattered within the pages. This is his story, as it is mine, and I miss him.

I hate myself for not calling more often. Why couldn't I have picked up the phone while I had the chance? I stare at my phone, pick it up, dial his number, unsure of this action. It rings and rings and rings. The answering machine picks up. I hear his outgoing message. I weep, hang up. I call again, listen to the message, cry.

One evening, after work, Leigh and I travel to the cemetery in which he was buried. I drop to a knee, place flowers at his grave. I say, "It's me, your ferociously ambitious protégé." Leigh stands behind me, places a consoling hand on my shoulder. I talk to Arthur, my vision of him. I tell him I miss him, wish he were here, wish we could spend another day together. I tell him that writing won't ever be the same without his helping hand. I tell him that I cry whenever I read my book because I know that a part of him exists within it.

Leigh and I drive by his house. The sign is gone. It vanished as he did, without notice. I look to the front yard, and see its replacement—a FOR SALE sign. I cry and tremble. Leigh holds me, whispers into my ear, "It'll be okay, James. It'll be okay."

I walk to the front door, and knock, Leigh behind me. I think I hear footsteps from inside the house. I knock again. I want him to open this door, to stand in the doorway, to greet me, but he can't. He's gone. Leigh hugs me. We walk away from the house. I stop, turn around, give the abode one last look.

Goodbye, Arthur.

I'll miss you.

Goodbye.

* * *

Weeks pass.

In my apartment, inside a cardboard box I threw in my closet after the move, I uncover an old friend, the Robert Frost letter. I place it on the wall above my bed. He can look over me this way. I tell him about the new things in my life—the move, Dad living in Boston, Arthur's death, my new job at the office. I ask him to forgive me for waiting so long to put him on my wall; I've been busy. I imagine that he says it's okay.

Rejections number five, six, seven, eight, nine, ten, eleven, twelve show up. I ask God for his hands. I want to know where they are. I tell him that I'm tired of living in pain. Can't he see that? I read the Bible, searching for answers, find none. The Bible doesn't touch on publishing matters. It doesn't let me know whether or not I should give up on writing, dive into work instead, increase the weekly hours to sixty, seventy, concentrate on that overtime pay, become a workaholic.

CHAPTER THIRTY-EIGHT

Leigh and I revisit Prescott Park in Portsmouth. We sit on one of the many benches facing the Piscataqua. The cool air smells of seaweed and fresh salt water. The amount of seagulls has lessened since our last visit. A few orange and red leaves are scattered at our feet.

Leigh zips her jacket, staring out at a pier lined with fishing boats on one side. I hold her hand. Watching her, I can tell she wants to talk about something important because she keeps opening her mouth and closing it, and people don't do that when they're on the brink of discussing a painless topic. I think I might know what she wishes to talk about.

I bury my free hand in my jacket pocket, expecting that Leigh will turn to me any second. When she doesn't, I try to get her attention by playfully saying, "Hey, let me see that face of yours."

Leigh looks in my direction with somber brown eyes. "Better?"

I nod and begin to caress her thumb with mine. "It's your parents, isn't it?"

Her head bobs.

"Your visit didn't go well?" I ask, unsurprised.

She shakes her head.

I'm rubbing her palm with my thumb now. "What happened?"

She opens her mouth, then closes it.

I encourage her. "It's okay. You can tell me."

Leigh runs her fingers through her long, wavy hair. She opens her mouth, speaks, "I just wanted to spend some time with my family. Was that too much to ask for?"

I provide a sympathetic smile. "No."

"When I pulled into the driveway, Dad was busy working outside, and he was his usual self. He just said hi as I got out of the car, and he didn't hug me, of course, even though I wanted him to. . . . I lugged my suitcases into the house, which weighed a ton, and right away I spotted Mom in the kitchen . . ." Leigh's voice turns bitter. "I put my suitcases down and went to give her a hug, but she wouldn't hug me either, so I told her it was *nice seeing her too* really sarcastically, then I went into my bedroom to drop off the luggage. . . ."

I can't think of anything to say other than, "I'm sorry, Leigh."

She acknowledges my caring words with a nod, and continues, "At lunch, Mom and Dad barely spoke to me, but they were more than happy to concentrate on my brother, who *still* can't make a right choice to save his life, by the way. They joked with him and chuckled and were being playful, and that disgusted me, James. They asked all sorts of questions about *his* life, and they refused to ask anything about *my* life." She lets go of my hand. Her face takes on a red hue, and her breathing quickens. I can hear the resentment in her tone as she says, "Then Erick told them that Heather, his girlfriend, was coming over. Dad patted him on the back and was like, *Oh, good, she's a nice girl,* but the thing is, James, she *isn't* a nice girl at all. . . ."

I've never seen her this angry. Her brown eyes are piercing me.

She goes on, "Here I had traveled almost two hours to see my family and it was like I was invisible to them. I wanted them to ask *me* about *my* life and chuckle with *me* and be playful. I wanted them to smile as I mentioned your name in passing, but they glared at me instead." I watch her jaw tighten. "My brother can do whatever he wants, whenever he wants, and they continue to treat him the same, but when *I* make a decision they don't approve of, they treat me differently. Like this one time, about a month after I graduated from college, I got home late after spending time with a friend, and the outside lights were off and the doors were locked." Anger flickers in her eyes. "That was their lovely way of telling me that they disapproved." Sad eyes replace the angry ones. "The truth is, James, I can never please them. My brother makes all these bad decisions and they treat him like gold. I make all sorts of good ones and they treat me like crap. What's wrong with this picture?"

I tell Leigh to come here and let me hold her. She leans in, and I wrap my arms around her. I say, "*A lot* is wrong with that picture."

She pulls back so that I only have one arm around her. "I don't understand it," she says.

I ponder the situation, and from out of nowhere, I remember Leigh's words from ages ago: *They want me to be with Tim so badly. They push me and push me and push me . . . I don't want to be controlled. I want to make my own choices and live . . . I choose you, James!*

"*I* understand it." I take a moment to gather my thoughts, then, "First, they're overcompensating for the fact that they know your brother has made some really bad choices and they know they didn't do the best job raising him. Second, they're giving you the silent treatment for a reason."

"But why?" she asks desperately.

"Because being vocal and pushing you doesn't work anymore, and they've chosen to revert back to what they did to you with turning those lights off and locking the door."

"Which is?"

"They're *showing* you their disapproval."

"What should I do?" Leigh asks, wet-eyed. "I want my parents to love me."

"They do. Ever hear the expression *tough love*? Of course, I'm certainly not saying I condone that method . . ." Then I explain that she needs to take action, and that she can't expect things to change if she doesn't show them that *their* actions are unacceptable. I tell her that up until this point, she has allowed them to manipulate her, and she keeps going back to them regardless, which shows them that it's okay to treat their daughter poorly.

"What next?" Leigh's lips quiver.

"The next time you go to see your parents, if they treat you poorly, pack your things, tell them you're leaving because the way they treat their daughter is unacceptable. Then leave."

* * *

Mitch invites me to his two-story lake house. I drive almost two hours to see him. His house is gray, and his yard full of leaf piles. He appears at the door, bald head shining in the sun, waves me inside, away from the cold, tells me to come with him to his office. He takes my coat, hangs it in a closet. We enter his office, a room off of the kitchen, and he shows me one of his new inventions. He smiles and says, "It's amazing what a little belief can do."

We leave the office and enter the living room. The walls are decorated with photos of he and his friends smiling, holding bass, trout, salmon; with he and his wife on their speedboat, their yacht; with magazine covers of he and his inventions. Shelves beside the couch contain signed baseballs of Ted Williams, Willie Mays, Carlton Fisk, Manny Ramirez, Ken Griffey Jr., Pete Rose, Pedro Martinez, Nomar Garciaparra. This place is a museum. The shelves hold numerous sports, fiction, and non-fiction books as well. This museum is also a library. Crackers and cheese and soda sit atop the coffee table. I smile, sit on the couch. He sits on the couch, smiles in return. We eat and talk, eat and talk. On his mantel, I notice a framed photograph of the Varsity baseball team Mitch coached; I'm included in the photo, as are my former teammates.

"Those were the days," he says.

I nod, eyes remaining on the photo. "Good times," I agree.

"You were good. Really, really, *really* good."

I fidget in the seat. "Nah . . . I was all right."

He tells me, "Listen up, son. You were good. You could've gone far with baseball."

I'm silent.

"Why'd you throw in the towel?" he asks.

"I wasn't good enough."

"But you *were* good enough . . . like your dad," he says.

My eyes are boring into him. I don't understand why he's bringing this up. "But I *wasn't*, all right?"

"In your mind, yes, you're absolutely right; you weren't good enough."

"What do you mean?" I ask.

"You had no self-worth. You didn't feel you deserved success."

I can't speak. A grandfather clock chimes from the dining room.

"Write those agent and editor letters until your hands bleed," he says. "You *are* deserving of success. You're worth it, all right? You're worth success, son." His eyes smile behind his glasses.

* * *

Rejections thirteen through fifteen turn up. I read them, yell into them, cry into them. Brad won't leave me alone. Over and over again, I tell him to shut up. Just shut up. Please, just shut up.

He doesn't listen. *Can you hear that?* he asks. *It's Arthur from beyond the grave, laughing at his stupid protégé . . .*

* * *

At work, alone, vacuuming around the cubicles, I think of Arthur. I can't give up on my novel; he lives within the pages. Then Mitch's encouraging words come to mind: *Write those agent and editor letters until your hands bleed, son. You* are *deserving of success.* Mitch is right. I am deserving! I've worked so hard, for so long. I need success.

I'm so tired. I want to put this vacuum down and lie on the floor and not think about any of this, sleeping until all my problems disappear. Then I can get up, only I won't be here in this office; I'll be at a book signing, surrounded by fans. I'll have a pile of my books stacked before me on a table, like Meranda at the Luncheon, and I'll take comfort in that because it is my payment for all of my writing and hurting. Fans will greet me, smiling, and they'll ask how I did it. My answer will be that I finally realized I deserved something good in my life, finally admitted to myself that I'm worthy of success.

Finally became a self-help guru.

After work, I sit on my bed, the laptop on my lap, Robert looking over me, and I compile a new list of agents and editors from the Internet that are actively seeking fresh talent. I think of Arthur and cry. I think of Mitch and smile. I open a Word document, spend hours upon hours writing a new synopsis for *The Forsaken World*. I pray to God, ask him to guide my fingers on the keyboard, help me to find the correct words. I find some comfort in this. I finish the synopsis, read it ten, twenty times, revel in its excellence.

* * *

The next night, after visiting with Leigh, I form a query letter around the synopsis. I'm pleased with it. In my mind, I see Arthur at his front door. I stand before him and he tells me to keep going, to send those query letters out, to be the ferociously ambitious protégé he's come to love. He puts a hand on my shoulder and says that he's sorry he had to die. He didn't want to die. He wanted to live forever. I cry and tell him that he *will* live forever . . . within the pages of my book. Everyone who reads it will unknowingly catch a glimpse of him. His presence will fill each room, each beach, everywhere *The Forsaken World* is read.

CHAPTER THIRTY-NINE

I mail the letters. Brad says, *You don't stand a chance.* I try not to listen to him. Meranda calls, slurring her words. She says that The Sweet Widowed One is now The Nasty Widowed One.

"Are you drinking?" I'm the concerned parent figure, raising his voice.

"I couldn't take it any longer." She mumbles. "I couldn't take all this."

I tell her to put that whiskey down and to step away! I inform her that I'm coming over and I'm going to talk some sense into her. *She's cruisin' for a bruisin'.* I hear her swallow, then she says that she wants to get trashed and be numb again. I say, "Put. The. Whiskey. Down. And. Walk. Away."

She gulps again, taunting my efforts. "Ahh, this feels so good, Jimmy."

"I'm hanging up the phone now, and I'm gonna get in my car and come over. Right now," I say, putting my foot down, parental.

She says, "Forget The Nasty Widowed One. *Forget* him. I love this stuff. I need this stuff. I am this stuff." She is one with the Alcohol.

I hang up the phone, grab my keys. I throw on a pair of jeans, a sweater, boots, and a thick jacket. I travel about an hour and a half to her house. Flurries fall. Wind gusts knock the car around on the road.

I pound on her door. She doesn't answer. I knock again. No answer. I open the door, walk through. The first thing I notice is my manuscript open to page one hundred twenty-one on the kitchen counter. From the sight, I gather that she hasn't been reading my novel very much. I turn a corner into the living room, see her lying on the carpet by the coffee table, eyes open, a bottle of whiskey in her right hand. She looks up at me as I stand over her.

"Give it here," I say, holding out my hand.

She shakes her head, eyes glazed. "No. It's mine. Forget The Nasty Widowed One."

"Give it here!" I shout.

"No!"

I grab the bottle from her hand. She tries to stand but staggers and falls to her knees. Her forehead creases. She curses and curses at me, trying to stand. "Give it to me. Just give it back!" she yells.

I shake my head. "No."

"Yes."

"No."

"Yes."

I leave the arguing behind and walk briskly to the kitchen, perform my famous pour-the-whiskey-down-the-sink-drain routine. I toss the bottle in the garbage, hear it smash, walk back over to her, look down at her. She is sleeping. I leave her there, sit on the couch, then lie on the couch. I wait for one hour, two hours, three hours. Her eyes open. She sits up, puts a hand over her forehead, and says, "I feel horrible."

I stand. "It's understandable that you would."

She hangs her head. I sit next to her on the floor. She says that she couldn't control herself, that The Nasty Widowed One breaking up with her brought up those past relentless feelings of loss.

I say, "You're worth more than this."

She looks at me, head tilted. "Worth more than what?"

"You deserve better than this."

"Better than what?"

"Whiskey," I say, "and The Nasty Widowed One."

She starts to cry, puts her head on my shoulder. I run a hand through her hair, tell her repeatedly that she's worth more than this. Her crying grows stronger. I put my arms around her, and hold her tightly. Not letting go.

* * *

Two days later, Meranda phones me, says that she joined a new AA group away from The Nasty Widowed One. "I'm afraid that I may relapse again if I have to see him," she says, "so hopefully this works." I commend her for joining another group, tell her that she needs the support. She says, "I should've stayed away from the thirteenth step." I tell her not to beat herself up over the relapse, that it was a mistake and it doesn't have to happen again.

I'm like a motivational speaker.

* * *

She calls on another night, says that The Nasty Widowed One has been leaving nasty messages on her answering message. I ask her if she's all right. "The messages were okay at first," she says, "but after the third message, he started saying that he wished he never met me, that dating me was a complete waste of his time, and he should never have been my Sponsor."

"He sounds crazy," I say. "I bet he's been drinking . . ."

"I don't know, but he's making *me* crazy," she says. "I'm so angry and sad and lonely, all at once, and I don't know what to do with these feelings." Then she explains that Group isn't helping much, that starting with a new mess of people is making everything even more difficult than it was when she was in the other group. "I feel totally vulnerable in all aspects of my life and I want to drink," she says. "I'm going crazy. I swear, I'm going insane."

"You're a recovering alcoholic," I say. "Don't be so hard on yourself. You're not going insane."

She pauses. "I don't know if I can handle more messages from The Nasty Widowed One."

"Call him and tell him to stop calling you," I say. "Tell him that his cruelty caused you to relapse and he needs to respect you, and tell him that you're worth more than this, all of this, and you deserve better than this and he better not call again or you'll call the police."

Or I'll sic Team Sobriety on him.

* * *

The next week, I call her on Monday. She doesn't pick up, so I leave a message saying hello and ask her to return my call when she can. I don't hear from her.

Tuesday passes without a word.

I call her Wednesday, and get her answering machine. I'm worried about her, and my voice, as I leave a message, comes out shaky. "Meranda? Are you there? It isn't like you to not pick up. I hope you're okay. If you need anything, feel free to give me a call, all right? I'm here for you."

I don't hear from her on Thursday.

Nothing on Friday. I wake four times Friday night, nervous for her safety. I hope she hasn't been drinking. Please, Lord, I hope she hasn't been drinking.

I call her again on Saturday morning, get the machine, ask her with fear in my voice if she's okay. I tell her to please pick up, please pick up. I wonder if she's been screening her calls, wonder if I said something to offend her, if I did anything to offend her. I ponder our previous conversations, searching. I can't think of anything I've done, anything I've said that would make her not want to talk with me.

Sunday appears, and I call her early in the morning before church with Leigh.

Ring.

Ring.

Ring.

Ring.

I hear the machine. "This is James again. Why haven't you called me back, Meranda?" My tone reveals frustration. "If I've done anything to upset you, please know that I didn't mean to. Please call me back. I'm worried about you." I pause, hoping that she'll answer. She doesn't. I flip the cell shut.

At church, I can't concentrate. I keep moving around in the pew. Leigh puts her arm around me, asks in a whisper if I'm okay. I look into her brown, concerned eyes, shrug and fake a smile. She scoots closer to me in the pew, smiles, removes her arm from my shoulder, places it on my leg. I face the pastor, try to listen, try to focus on him, but to no avail. In my mind, his words are replaced with *"Meranda"* and *"Is she okay?"* and *"Did I do something to offend her?"* and *"She's been drinking again. I bet she's been drinking again."*

I decide that I can't sit here any longer. I whisper into Leigh's ear that I'm going to the bathroom. She nods, her eyes on the pastor. I stand, scoot past the other people in the pew, and walk to the bathroom. I stand before the mirror, fiddle with my tie, stare at my reflection, tell myself to get a grip, to calm down. I look into my blue eyes, see fear in them, horrifying fear. Something is wrong with Meranda. I know something is wrong. I'm having premonitions. I remove the cell from a pocket, turn it on, call voicemail. No messages exist from Meranda. I put the cell away, look into the mirror at my fearful eyes. I take a deep breath, and pray. I ask God to help me make it through the service, to help me sit still, to help me listen to the pastor. I leave the bathroom, return to my seat, try, try, try to listen, can't listen, can't pay attention, can't sit still, but I do make it through the service.

I drive us away from the church.

"What's wrong?" Leigh asks. "You've been acting weird."

My hand tightens on the steering wheel. "Meranda hasn't been answering my phone calls, and I'm worried about her."

"You should pay her a visit then," Leigh says.

I think on the recommendation, then nod. "I'll go after lunch."

Leigh and I eat lunch together at her apartment—grilled ham and cheese sandwiches with sour cream and onion potato chips and cola. I thank her for making the sandwiches. She tries to make conversation. I can't focus enough to hold a conversation. At the end of lunch, we move from the table, and she gives me a hug. "It'll be okay," she says, smiling. I don't believe her. I kiss her anyway, tell her that I love her.

I drive the longest drive of my life to Meranda's house, the heater blasting, the sides of the road before me covered with snow, scenarios playing out in my mind: I'll get to her house and she'll greet me at the door and apologize that she didn't return my calls yet. She'll point to a suitcase in the house and tell me that she went on a mini vacation to get away from The Nasty Widowed One's messages and that she just got my messages a couple minutes ago when she walked through the door for the first time in a week.

Or: I'll enter her house and find her drunk on her bed with puke everywhere because she relapsed the day after we last talked and she's been drinking ever since in an attempt to kill the pain.

Or: I'll get to her house and knock on the door and she won't answer and I'll knock again and she won't answer and I'll knock again and she'll open the door a crack and tell me to go away, that I'm not welcome, that she doesn't want to talk to me ever again, that I offended her, and I'll tear up and my shoulders will drop and I'll tell her that I need my grandmother, that I've always needed a grandmother and she has filled that void and I can't walk away. She'll tell me to step back or she'll call the cops and I'll ask her what I did or what I said. She won't say anything other than step back, and she'll shut the door and I'll stand frozen on the porch and I'll start to cry because I'll never see her again and I'll miss her and I love her and I need her and I invested in her and I believed in her.

CHAPTER FORTY

I arrive at Meranda's house, exit the car, shivering, tiny snowflakes falling upon me. Boots crunching through crusty snow, I come to the porch, proceed inside, to the front door, then knock with a gloved hand.

She doesn't answer.

I knock again.

She doesn't open the door.

I grab the handle, twist, open the door, step inside, fretful. I smell something vile, like a dead rat, but much, much worse. I holler her name, hear nothing in return. I walk into the kitchen, don't see her there, walk upstairs, see no trace of her anywhere, go back downstairs to the living room.

I don't want to believe what I see. I close my eyes, open them, close, open, close, open, attempting to purge them from this image.

I don't want to believe.

She can't really be sprawled across that couch, empty whiskey bottles on the coffee table, a pile of paper on the floor beneath her dangling hand.

I don't want to believe.

I inch toward her, the smell of death growing, and my eyes follow her dangling hand down to the mound of papers, my manuscript, *The Forsaken World*. I hover over her body, the stench overwhelming. I want to throw up. I look down at her ghost-white face, shocked, terrified.

I don't want to believe.

I remove my gloves, toss them to the floor. I place my hand on her arm. Cold. She is so cold. I stare at her closed eyes, wishing they would open. I want them to open behind those glasses and I want her to wake with a start and smile and tell me she was just kidding. I want her to stand from the couch, sober, and glance down at my manuscript and tell me how good it is and how much she has enjoyed reading it and tell me it wasn't the story that drove her to drink and pass out. I want her to apologize for the foul smell of her body and to explain the odor—she ran out of soap or her shower doesn't work.

I lift her dangling hand and place it palm down on her stomach. I kneel before the couch. Her eyes don't open. She doesn't wake or smile or tell me she was just kidding. She doesn't look upon *The Forsaken World* and tell me how good it is and tell me that it didn't drive her to drink. She doesn't apologize for her odor.

I don't want to believe.

I remove her glasses, set them on the coffee table, battling the urge to puke. I lean over her body, my face an inch from hers. I examine her face, the eyes that won't open. No matter how much I want them to, they won't open. I pull my face away. I pray, tell God to open those eyes, to bring a smile to her face, to stand her from the couch, because she can't be dead. I tell him that she was so close to recovery, that this isn't fair, that AA was supposed to help her get away from alcohol. I stand, can't look at her anymore, look at the photographs above the couch and cry.

I ask God for his hands.

She fell.

Where were your hands?

She fell.

Why didn't you catch her?

She's dead.

Tears run like a river down my face.

She's dead. Meranda Erickson is dead.

Meranda is dead.

Where were your hands?

I step back from the couch, and walk out of the living room, bawling. I need to inform the police of her death. They need to know Meranda Erickson, one of the most talented writers of all time, is dead. I come to her phone, spot the answering machine blinking. I remember my messages. I was angry at her for not picking up. How could I be angry at her? She was dead. I was leaving frustrated messages to a dead person. I shake my head, tears dripping to the floor. I push the machine's play button, expecting to hear my messages. Instead, I hear an angry message from The Nasty Widowed One, and I know it's him because he's telling her that he's not going to leave her alone, that her scare tactics—telling him to stop calling or she'll call the police—won't work. He laughs at her, calls her a foolish old drunk. He pauses. Suddenly, I hear a break in the message, then Meranda's voice. She says, "I told you to stop calling. *Please*, I can't take this. You're making me want to drink. I can't drink. You know I can't. You know what it does to me," and the message comes to an end.

Another message plays. The machine's voice says that the message was left a day after the previous rant. It's The Nasty Widowed One again and he tells her to pick up, just pick up this time, because he wants to talk, then he'll leave her alone, he promises. I don't hear a break in the message. Meranda doesn't answer. I wonder if she was dead during this message.

My messages play. I can't stop crying. What if she was alive—drunk, but alive during these messages? I could've saved her. Why did I have to move so far away? I could've been here, talked some sense into her, taken those bottles and dumped them down the drain. I could've saved her.

The messages end. I reach for the phone, go to dial 9-1-1, but stop. I don't want to call them yet because I know that when they come they'll take her away and I'll never see her again and she'll be thrown into a box and lowered into a hole in the ground and she'll disappear forever and I can't have that.

* * *

Mourning.

I'm so tired of mourning.

I go to work and I mourn Meranda and I mourn Arthur. I have tears in my eyes often, but no one at work says anything because no one there looks into my eyes and no one there would care even if they did look into my eyes. Each morning, I consider calling in sick, but I know that I can't because I need the money. I would rather stay in bed than go to work. I want to slip into a coma and sleep everything away.

I spend a lot of time with Leigh hugging and holding and talking about Meranda. I cry and smile, and Leigh listens and smiles sometimes and cries sometimes, too. She doesn't know what to say to stop my pain, but I tell her that her presence is all I need from her, that I don't need her to lie to me like *Pinocchio* and tell me that everything is going to be okay.

I come across obituaries and articles about Meranda Erickson's tragic demise on the Internet, in newspapers, magazines. I flip through TV channels and watch frowning reporters talk about her death and all of her literary accomplishments throughout the decades. I hate all of this coverage. I feel like they're exploiting her. When she was alive, they didn't care that she was alive, and now that she's dead, people are coming out of the woodwork sad and puffy-eyed and I think it's sick, so unbelievably sick.

We go to Meranda's funeral. From what I've heard, she didn't have a will so her estate was escheated to the State of New Hampshire, which means they own the rights to everything of hers now—including her funeral. Hundreds of people attend. People I've never seen before, people who weren't her friends—all wearing winter apparel. Everyone sulks, pretending to care. I want to throw my hands toward the sky and scream, "You idiots didn't know her. She wouldn't want you here. Walk away. You're not welcome here!" Instead, I stand quietly in the rear of the crowd while a famous preacher gives the eulogy.

Leigh wraps an arm around my waist.

I mourn.

She holds tighter.

I look to the casket suspended over a cavity in the soil (the only nearby area without snow, it seems), and I mourn my deceased grandmother. Why couldn't she have heard me when I told her that she was worth more than the self-destruction she poured upon herself? She deserved good things, deserved success. Why couldn't she see that?

I mourn.

I didn't kill her, I work to convince myself. *The Nasty Widowed One drove her to drink. He drove her to lift those bottles to her lips and drink and drink and drink until she died. He did this to her and I hate him. He did this to her.*

My legs are shaking. *I tried so hard. I tried to save her. I did what I knew how. Where are your hands, God?*

Where are your hands?

I feel like I'm going to fall.

CHAPTER FORTY-ONE

I receive my latest rejection two weeks later. It's the same old: Dear James, You suck at writing. Sincerely, Critic who didn't actually read your manuscript.

I'm tired of living in pain. I deserve better. Brad keeps at me virtually everywhere I go. He tells me often that I don't deserve better, that I will always be rejected.

Work is totally monotonous. I hurt all over. My arms hurt from vacuuming and mopping and sweeping and lifting boxes and shoveling snow away from the doorway of my apartment. My feet hurt because I'm on them constantly and my worn-out sneakers offer zero support. My teeth hurt because they're decaying despite my efforts to keep them clean. My eyes hurt because of constant crying. I want it to end. Brad reminds me that it will never end, that James Frost lives in pain, loves pain, and is pain.

I go to church with Leigh, tortured by God's absence. I've been waiting so long for his hands. He won't reveal them to me. It's like he's stubbornly holding back. The pastor speaks of faith. He says that when we have doubts about our life that we are in fact doubting God and his power. He says that we should cast our worries upon the Lord. I feel like all I've been doing is casting them upon him and he just keeps throwing them back.

At the apartment, I read my Bible, reluctant, feeling betrayed by God, demanding that he show me the way, show me how I can move past the pain. Tears fall on the pages. I'm desperate for God's help. I need him. I can't work through the pain without him. I come to the part in the Bible where Jesus speaks of loving your enemies. I stop on the page, crying, and think: *That's the ultimate in forgiveness, isn't it?*

Brad's face swims into view, and I hear him say, *Forget forgiveness* as he did after punching Chris (the persecuted Christian from high school) in the hallway, years ago. I wipe the tears away with my sleeve, look down at the pages, and it dawns on me: Brad is my enemy, always has been my enemy, and I've hated him with all of my heart and I've wanted him to suffer and to disappear. And the more I hate Brad, the stronger he gets, the harder he pushes with his hateful words. Brad adds so much pain to my life, so much nearly unbearable pain, and I've been feeding him with what he knows best and what he thrives on: hatred.

I stare at the page. Everything becomes unambiguous. *Love your enemies.* I close the Bible, stand from the bed, shut my eyes. I see Brad standing before me—spiky hair, angry eyes, fashionable clothing.

I hold out a hand to Brad, then smile. *I found the answer. I'm not going to hate you anymore. I'm no longer going to wish ill upon you.*

Brad tilts his head like a confused dog.

I take a step closer to him, and say, *I'm not going to give you what you want anymore.*

Brad lunges at me, then tackles me to the ground as he did with Chris. I lie pinned beneath Brad's body, his face hovering over mine, expecting a punch on my nose. I stare into his dead eyes, smiling. *I'm not going to give you what you want anymore.* I won't throw him a bone.

Brad stands, and I don't stay on the ground like Chris did; I spring to my feet, invincible as the Road Runner, and I keep smiling. *I forgive you*, I say, the bigger man.

Brad's eyes expand as from under a magnifying glass. *Forget forgiveness*, he says.

I think of Chris as I observe Brad. *I love you.* I open my arms to Brad. *I forgive you.*

Brad begins to laugh, but I persist with another *I forgive you*, and it's like he gets shot in the heart with those words; he's holding the left side of his chest, wincing.

I step to him, place a hand on his sweaty forehead, and he doesn't take a swing at me. He just stands there, weak and submissive, wobbly on his feet, and I wish Chris could see him now because I think Chris would get some redemption from this scene. *I love you*, I tell Brad, and I must really mean it because I feel genuinely sorry for him, watching him struggle like this.

White light suddenly seeps from his face. I let go, step back. He stumbles away, screaming, thrashing, hand still on his chest. Light shines from his torso and his legs. The light engulfs him, then implodes, and in an instant, Brad is no more.

* * *

The snow piles dwindle.

Four more rejections (i.e., hate mail) emerge.

I don't hear from Brad.

I still think of Meranda and Arthur. I miss them. I miss them so much, but I know that they would want me to be happy.

Brad is silent, Satan locked away for a thousand years.

* * *

The snow fades away.

Birds, sun, warmth, rain, grass, plants, bugs, flowers, leaves, they return. I open and tear up six rejections. I make an effort to swap negative thoughts with affirmations: *I'm a good writer. I deserve success. I'm worthy of success.* The more I focus on these self-esteem boosters, the more I start to believe them.

Leigh went home two days ago. She tells me that her parents treated her shoddily—ignored her—and she finally got up enough courage this time to pack her overnight belongings, tell them that they were treating their daughter unacceptably and that she wasn't going to stand for it any longer. They wouldn't apologize, so she headed toward the door, and they followed. Then she told them, "If you want to talk to your daughter, *you'll* have to call *me*. And if you want to see your daughter, *you'll* have to visit *me*." Her mother glared, and her father shook his head, and Leigh left the house. She tells me that she felt stronger at that moment than she ever has. I hug her, tell her that she is very brave, and that she should be proud of herself for standing up to her parents. She shrugs, looks down. I tell her to keep that chin up. She looks into my eyes. I smile, tell her I love her. She smiles back.

She waits for their phone call. One day passes.

Two days pass.

She says that she's been second-guessing herself. I remind her that she did the right thing.

She waits.

Waits and waits and waits.

* * *

It's been two weeks and a day since she left their house and she hasn't received a call. We go for a walk along her street, and she starts to cry. We stop on the side of the road. I ask her what's wrong. "I just wanted them to love me," she says. I hold her. She buries her head in my chest, sobbing. "They *do* love you," I say, "and maybe that's the hardest thing about all of this . . ." I tell her that she's very brave, and that they were abusing her and she's better off without their abuse. "I know it hurts," I say, "but you're better off." I tell her that she deserves better.

She cries, letting go of her parents.

CHAPTER FORTY-TWO

Enthusiastic Editor Lady calls four days following as I step out of the shower. She reminds me of the query letter, says that she would really love to see the entire manuscript, says that I can send *The Forsaken World* via e-mail as an attachment, if I would like to. I chuckle, shivering, wet, a blue towel covering my waist, then say, "Of course I would like to." She provides her e-mail address, tells me that she'll keep an eye out for the manuscript and she'll look forward to it. I thank her and thank her and thank her. She laughs, says, "If the rest of your book is as good as the three chapters you included with your query, I'll be the one thanking you."

After the phone call, I fall to my knees, chuckling. An editor wants to read my manuscript. This means that there's a chance I may actually get published.

* * *

I take Leigh out to a Mexican restaurant, and it's not Taco Bell. We sit outside on a deck beneath a party tent overlooking the Piscataqua River. Just beyond the deck, tugboats float through the water toward a vessel, seagulls circling above the ship in the noonday glare.

Mexican music plays softly from a speaker overhead. Droning chatter ripples through the heavily peopled tent. The smell of chimichangas, tacos, burritos, nachos, and refried beans fill the air.

My stomach growls. I reach across the table, take Leigh's hand into mine, smile. "I have something to tell you," I say.

She leans forward. "What is it?"

I tell her about the editor requesting the manuscript, fill her in on the rest of the short conversation.

Leigh beams, squeaks elatedly, looking like she's going to jump up from her seat. "That's great!" she says. "You deserve this!" Her excitement doesn't bring us any attention from the others.

I stare into her eyes, those remarkable brown eyes. "I think I'm starting to believe that."

"You'll make it. I just know it." Her smile remains. A tugboat whistles in the distance.

"I don't want to jump to any conclusions just yet, though. There's still ample time for rejection." My focus falls to the table as our waitress drops off the nachos.

Leigh tells me to look at her. I do. She says, "Listen to me. You taught me this. You *deserve* to be published."

* * *

I wait for Enthusiastic Editor Lady's response. One day, two, three . . . A week, two weeks, two and a half. I shoot her a short e-mail, ask if she's had a chance to read the material. Still no response.

I feed myself encouraging words. *Be patient. Good news will find me. I'm a good writer. I'm worthy of success. I deserve success.*

I can't concentrate at work, constantly focusing on what she may say, if she ever says anything at all. In my thoughts, I see her in an office at a desk somewhere in Manhattan. She starts on the fourth chapter and shakes her head at the computer screen upon reading the first page. She summons her colleagues to the desk, shows *The Forsaken World* to them, laughing, and they all poke fun at the prose, the corny magical elements, the archetypical characters, the author who scribed such overwrought nonsense.

In an alternate scenario, I see her reading the manuscript at her desk, only this time, she realizes that she requested material from the wrong person. The man who she meant to contact has a name closely resembling James Frost. She laughs at herself, the honest mistake, deletes my file, immediately phones the person who she had originally intended to contact.

Sleeping doesn't come easily. I count sheep. That doesn't work. I take sleeping pills. That doesn't work. I need an answer from her one way or the other—to publish or not to publish.

Soon.

So I can sleep.

So I can concentrate.

So I can live.

* * *

June begins.

Heat, thunderstorms, sun, humidity, air conditioners, fans, tans, barbeques, beaches, parks, shorts, skirts, bathing suits, trunks, sandals, T-shirts, sun, humidity. Leigh in a bikini!

Enthusiastic Editor Lady becomes Mysterious Editor Lady once I read an e-mail from her. She apologizes for her lack of communication and wants to let me know that she's close to completing the manuscript and that she'll contact me with her thoughts shortly.

Apparently, the scenarios I conjured before were inaccurate. She wouldn't apologize for her "lack of communication" if she thought my work was garbage and if she and her colleagues poked fun at it. If she confused me with another writer, I would have been notified by now about her unfortunate blunder.

I remind myself to be patient, that I'm a good writer. That I'm worthy of success. That I deserve success. That she'll contact me shortly, whatever that means.

* * *

June 16.

Mysterious Editor Lady transforms back into Enthusiastic Editor Lady when she calls and we talk for forty-five minutes. She first talks about the "wonderful aspects" of my book. She says that I've produced great characters, that she loved the beginning, the honesty of it, that the pacing was superb, that I kept a perfect amount of conflict flowing through the story, that the ending was both heartbreaking and inspirational and she couldn't help but cry and smile at the same time.

That's exactly what I do after she expresses herself, cry and smile. She asks if I'm okay. I tell her I'm fine, just very pleased that she enjoyed my book. Then she talks about the aspects of my book that need improvement. She tells me that the book needs a little work on sensory stimulation—infusing the story with descriptions of smells and sounds and sights and tastes. She then asks me to work on sensory stimulation in the novel as she starts the book through the acquisitions process.

I agree to her terms, my heart running, hands shaking, smiling.

* * *

June 24.

I've imbued the tale with descriptive smells, sounds, sights, tastes, and I'm pleased with the improvements.

Enthusiastic Editor Lady calls and tells me that my novel will go before the acquisitions committee tomorrow and that she will certainly contact me with any news. I ask her what she means by "acquisitions committee" and she says that it can also be referred to as the "editorial board" or the "publishing committee" and it approves the acquisition of a book or denies the acquisition of a book. Jokingly, I ask her to give me the members' names so I can shower them with gifts and other briberies. She laughs.

* * *

Sleep.

Is.

Not.

Something.

I.

Can.

Do.

It's two o'clock, the sun has yet to rise, and I open my laptop from bed and stay busy writing random, nonsensical thoughts into a Word document the night before my book is brought to the acquisitions committee, the night before people I've never met, all faceless, play God in my life and decide whether or not my work is worthy of publication, whether or not I can quit my job as custodian, and whether or not I can move out of this seedy apartment I've had to call home.

Nerves. Anxiety. Fear. Excitement. I try to block all of this as I write and write and write.

Not sleep.

Write.

And wait.

* * *

Enthusiastic Editor Lady calls after work as I'm driving to Leigh's apartment. She says that she spoke with the acquisitions committee and they were extremely excited about my book. Based on the excerpt that they read, they thought the characters were extraordinarily realistic, that the story was fantastic, and the writing splendid.

I shift, ask her what this means for me. She says that she'll phone me shortly with an official offer. I think, *There she goes again with her favorite word: shortly.*

The remainder of the car ride passes in a blur. I'm so happy, I could fly—Peter Pan thinking happy thoughts. I end up in Leigh's parking lot, go inside, tell her, with hands raised, about the recent conversation with Enthusiastic Editor Lady and Leigh gives me a huge hug and says, "I'm so proud of you!"

* * *

August 6.

Enthusiastic Editor Lady phones me with amazing news: The acquisitions committee approved *The Forsaken World!* She goes on to make an offer for my novel. I chuckle, think she's joking about the amount. The offer is a large offer. More than I currently make per year, which isn't much to some, I suppose, but *I'm* thrilled. I thank her, thank her so much, tell her that I've been waiting for this for so long, she doesn't even know.

I run outside my apartment, raise arms toward the cottony expanse. Tears of happiness fill my eyes. I thank God for his hands.

For finally revealing his hands.

Smiling, laughing. This is my payment, my wonderful payment for all of my writing and all of my pain. I think of Arthur, who lives within the pages, and I flash on Meranda, who died among them, and I cry and think *this is for them.*

CHAPTER FORTY-THREE

The best autumn of my life.

After over a month of contemplation, I approach the Facilities Manager and give my two-weeks notice, explaining that I won't need this job anymore because of my recent book deal.

His face shows shock, then he says, "I don't require you to stay with us for the next two weeks. I prefer that this be your last day."

I can't help but smile. "My last day it is," I say, watching him roll his eyes.

I understand that my decision to give my notice probably appears foolish to society. Here I am with a steady job and I'm tossing it for my art. I say, let pessimists—like the supervisor standing in front of me— think whatever they want. It's okay. Really, it is. Since when have I listened to them anyway? Plus, a couple days ago, I received my first check from the publisher. And there are many more to come. . . .

I clean, smile, clean, smile. This is my last day of cleaning. I clean the bathrooms one last time. I go to the warehouse and retrieve paper one last time. I enter the Sales Department with the rolling garbage bin, come to the first desk, tell Ingrid to look into my eyes and see me, not this custodian but this person who writes, this person who is never going to clean for a living again, this person who instead is going to play pretend on paper for a living because he worked hard, worked so tirelessly and that is his reward, his payment for the pain. She smiles, extends a hand, introduces herself for the first time, her eyes locked with mine. I shake her hand, smile in return, and she says, "It's nice to meet you." I collect her garbage one last time.

I roll the bin to Tom's desk and I give him the same treatment as Ingrid. He turns from the computer screen, hands off the keyboard, eyes on me, and he nods, wishes me good luck with the writing. I chuckle, thank him. I take his garbage one last time.

I walk to Virginia's desk, tell her to look into my eyes, ask her if I'm talking too much, ask her if this makes her feel uncomfortable, ask her what's wrong with being friendly. Her eyes bulge. She's speechless. I grab the garbage one last time, depart her area.

At the end of the day, I vacuum around the cubicles one last time. I sweep the hallway, mop the hallway, buff the hallway one last time. I say goodbye to the mop, the buffer, the broom, the rolling garbage bin, the cleaning supplies, the vacuum, cleaning as a whole. I'm finally able to say goodbye to cleaning! I say goodbye to the Sales Department, not the people but the cubicles and the empty space. I say goodbye to the building, goodbye, goodbye, goodbye, and I leave the office one last time.

ONE.

LAST.

TIME.

CHAPTER FORTY-FOUR

I decide to purchase—with play-pretend-on-paper-for-a-living money—a modest cottage by the seashore, fifteen minutes from the rundown apartment. The home—kind of a fixer-upper—consists of granite counters in the kitchen, cherry cabinets in the den (which I plan to transform into my writing office), an in-need-of-repair fireplace in the living room, two small bedrooms, one bath, central air, and so forth. The mortgage fits my tight budget perfectly, and I love this place, can picture myself here for a long time to come.

I stand alone before the fireplace in the unfurnished living room. This is my home. I earned this. Next week, I will move my belongings from the apartment and formally graduate from the studio to this house. Leigh has no knowledge of this acquisition (I haven't even started packing, so as to remain inconspicuous), and for good reason. I pull a jewelry box from a pocket, open the lid, and marvel at the white gold princess-cut diamond, the dazzling combination. I want to spend the rest of my life with Leigh. I want to have children with her and I want us to smile, smile, smile, and be happy. I want to wake up next to her and look into her eyes and tell her I love her and I want us to make love. I want to be able to call her my wife and I want her to be able to call me her husband and I want us to know that we are one and we are pure.

She deserves this.

I deserve this.

We deserve this.

* * *

I call Mitch, and he tells me that he still can't get over the fact that I'm going to be published. He says he's been telling everyone he knows that he's so proud of his son, so proud!

I thank him, feeling his warmth, then I say, "There's some place I want to go, and I want you to come with me."

We visit Robert Frost's house in Franconia, walk the leaf-littered trail, stop at the plaques, reminiscing. Before we leave, I walk to the gray mailbox, remove a folded note from a pocket. I open the letter, double-check the words:

Dear Robert,

Thank you for your letter. You were correct; I was on the right road all along.

Your friend,

Mr. Lonesome

I fold the letter, smiling. I look around. It is only Mitch and me. He watches as I open the mailbox and insert the sheet.

* * *

"No peeking," I say, hands on Leigh's hips, walking beside her, guiding the way.

"Where are you taking me, James?" she asks, giggling, her hands covering her eyes. "My arms are getting tired," she says.

My hands leave her hips. I excavate the keys from a coat pocket. "Don't you look, Leigh," I say. "Don't you look . . ." I unlock the door, return my hands to her hips, and prod her inside the cottage, away from the brisk air, to the living room, before the fireplace. "Open," I say.

Facing the fireplace, she lowers her hands. "What is this place?" she asks.

"I know it's not perfect," I say, cracking a smile, "but it's our house."

She quickly examines the derelict living room, then her attention reverts to me. "*Our* house? But when?—how?—I mean—"

She silences as I drop to one knee, my heart throbbing. I pull the jewelry box from another pocket, hand tremulous. I gaze up at her, open the box, and hold it upward, arms wobbly. "Leigh, will you marry me?"

She ogles the glimmering ring, its small but beautiful diamond, and her eyes dampen. After ten seconds, she says yes, crying and smiling at once.

I stand, relieved. She holds out her hand. I take the ring from its box, and slip the rock—or pebble, as some would say—on her finger. "I love you," I say.

Her face lights up. "I love you too."

We kiss, my arms locked around her and hers around me, the walls of our future sanctuary, this home, surrounding us. I let go after a minute, step back, tell her I have another gift to give.

She smiles. "There's more?" Amazement dwells in her voice.

I nod. "Wait here. I'll be right back." I leave the room, return thirty seconds later with a cardboard box, three quarter-sized holes on the lid.

"What's in there?" she asks, smiling.

I place the box at her feet. We stare at it, and it begins to wobble. She starts to laugh, gets down on her knees, removes the lid, looks into the shaking box. Her smile deepens, and she begins to cry. "You remembered . . ." She looks back at me, grinning, damp-eyed.

"What will you name it?" I ask.

Smiling, she lifts the black and white cat from the box, holds it in her arms, and stands. "This is Hope," she says softly, her hand brushing over its back. "This is our cat Hope."

* * *

We elope the following month to Wailea Beach, South Maui. It sounds glamorous, and quite frankly, it is. But it's still unconventional, that's for sure. Plus, I figure we'll save a significant amount of money by omitting a guest list. *A traditional wedding equals about $25,000. A guestless wedding on a tropical beach equals about $7,000. Hmmm . . . tough decision, right?* The wedding takes place on a grassy knoll fifty yards from the ocean, tropical fauna all around, palm tree thickets ringing the powder-white gazebo from which we give our vows at sunset. After the ceremony, as one flesh, we have pictures taken, holding one another, before the ocean, a pond, a waterfall, and a tree.

We dine at the resort's five star restaurant, just the two of us, she in her gown, I in my tuxedo. We eat, smile, talk, laugh, flirt, Hawaiian music playing in the background, a lone candle lit at the center of the white-clothed table, and I think: *Maybe good things* can *fall into your lap . . . you just need to be in the right seat.* I stare into her eyes, my elbows on the armrests of the seat I've chosen. I tell her that I love her, and that I'm a lucky man. A very, very lucky man. With a smile, she tells me she's a lucky woman. A very, very lucky woman.

* * *

Our honeymoon. We enter our room on the beach, smiling. I close the door, take her into my arms. I kiss her at the door, at the dresser, at the window with a backdrop of the ocean reflecting a three-quarter moon. I whisper into her ear, "This is the beginning of eternity together." Tears roll from her eyes, worrying me. But then she smiles and I know that they are tears of joy.

I lie her on the bed, kiss her cheeks, her lips, her neck, and slowly, with her assistance, remove her gown. I gaze at her body covered sparingly with lingerie. She smiles. I smile. She, with my help, removes my *James Bond* tuxedo, revealing a pale, skinny chest above plaid boxer shorts. *Not quite 007.* She tells me that I look great, that she loves my arms, my chest, my skin, everything. She kisses my chest, my arms, my skinny, skinny arms. I kiss her belly, her flat belly, tell her that she looks amazing, that I love her belly, everything. She smiles, and says, "I've been looking forward to this my whole life." I smile in return and say, "I'm a lucky man. A very, very lucky man."

The next morning, I wake up next to her and tell her I love her. We go down to the beach before breakfast. She wears a tight, revealing bikini. I wear trunks below a shirtless torso. We lie on a blanket, soaking in the rays. We stroll the length of the shore. We laugh, the sun warm against my bare back, the sun kissing her perfect body. We wade in the water, even though I'm fearful of water.

And we do all of this, of course, without her parents tagging along.

CHAPTER FORTY-FIVE

One year later, on a chilly and blustery fall day, I'm driving in my Camry. I see a car (an Accord, perhaps?) broken down on the side of the road and the backside of a man looking inside the open hood. I turn around, stop, climb out of my vehicle, and walk toward the man, the lifted hood blocking his face from my view.

"Need some help?" I walk past the rear.

"Battery's dead," says a familiar voice.

I come to the front, and the man's appearance leaps out at me—it's Brad, not in my mind but in flesh, with his hair combed to one side, not spiked. He aged a bit since school, especially around the eyes, and he now wears a well-groomed goatee without a nasty grin.

"I remember you. Frost, right?" He speaks with a shocking amount of gentleness in his voice.

I nod. "Brad, isn't it?"

His head bobs. "Do you have jumper cables, by any chance?"

"Yeah, I think so. Lemme look . . ." I go back to my Camry and find the cables in my trunk, chuckling at the situation. A couple minutes later, I pull my car up to his and park so that my front is parallel with his hood. I pop my hood, leave the Camry, and stand next to Brad again, cables in hand.

"So what do you do these days?" Brad asks as I give him the clamps.

I smile, perfectly white teeth visible, the result of countless visits to the dentist. "I'm a son, a brother, a husband, a child of God . . ." I pause. "And what do I do for work? Is that what you're asking?"

He's connecting the cables. "Yeah."

"I play pretend on paper for a living."

Brad's focus is on his battery. "How does that work?" he asks curiously.

"I'm a published author."

"Wow." Brad sounds genuinely impressed. "You've done well . . ." He steps away from his gleaming Honda and hands me the cables. I attach them to the Camry, thinking: *What happened to the malicious Brad from Langwood High?* Brad turns the ignition on his car. It starts immediately. We get out of our cars and meet beside them.

"Do you live around here?" I ask.

"Yeah . . . over on Mercy Lane."

Silence. I chuckle inside. *Mercy Lane. Is that next to Forgiveness Street?*

Finally, I speak. "So, umm, what do you do? I mean, who are *you* nowadays?"

More troubling silence, then he smiles. "Who am *I?*" He puts his hand into a pocket, pulls out his wallet, and opens it to the photograph sleeves. "I'd say this about sums it up." He points to a picture of a blue-eyed, blonde bombshell and grins—but in a way that isn't wicked at all. "This is Alexandra," he says tenderly, eyes brightening. "We got married a couple years ago. She's wonderful . . ." Then he taps on a photo of two children, and his smile expands. "Frankie and Katherine. Our prides and joy."

"You have a beautiful family, and you've done well for yourself, too," I say, reaching into my pocket.

"Thanks." He beams, closes the wallet, and returns it to his pants.

I take out *my* wallet and, over the course of about two minutes, show him photos of Leigh, saying all sorts of great things about her. At the end of Show and Tell, I put my leather money-trap away. Brad stares into my eyes, and I can't help but stare back. We don't move, caught in this connection. I start to chuckle, then blurt, "So, I guess you should be okay, huh? Your battery's probably juiced up just fine by now . . ."

He laughs, then agrees that yes, his car is most likely ready to go. We remove the cables and shut the hoods.

"Thanks, James." He holds out his hand.

I take his hand, pump twice, and let go. "You're welcome, Brad. Maybe I'll see you around."

He smiles. "Maybe."

"Take care of yourself . . . and the family." I start toward the Camry.

"Hey, James . . ."

I turn back to him. "Yeah?"

He's still standing by his Accord. He inhales and exhales loudly, like he's about to have an Asthma attack or something. "I was young and stupid in school," he says, "and I want you to know that, well—I guess what I'm trying to say is—I'm sorry." He begins to breathe normally again.

His statement catches me off guard. *Did the bully really apologize? I thought this only happened in movies.* I reply to his apology with a smile, then: "It was good seeing you again, Brad."

His head bobbles like one of those sports figurines. "Same here."

We enter our cars and drive in opposite directions. I'm glad I could help Brad, and it's good to know that he's happy and that he isn't suffering or moaning or sitting in a pit, and this makes me smile.

I arrive home. Leigh greets me at the door, Hope brushing up against her leg, purring. Leigh's belly is plump beneath a baggy shirt. She hands me a paintbrush. "Let's go, Dad," she says, winking. We enter the baby's room, Hope following, and continue working on the mural of clouds and the sun, flocks of birds, trees, grassland, and bushes. As Leigh strokes the wall with her brush, she says, "I decided where I'd like the café to be."

"Oh yeah?" I add detail to a tree.

"Laguna Beach," she says.

"With umbrella tables?"

She smiles. "With umbrella tables outdoors and bright orange and yellow walls inside. People will sit beneath the umbrellas, reading, and sipping our finest iced coffee."

"I'll make some calls." I grin.

After almost an hour of painting, we part ways and I go to a book signing. People line up before me. A fan steps to the table, *The Forsaken World* in his hand, and he asks me how I did it, how I became a successful author. I tell him I finally realized that I deserved something good in my life, finally admitted to myself that I was worthy of success. "And I can't forget God and his helping hands," I continue. "I can only imagine where I'd be without them." He thanks me for my answer, hands the book my way. I open it, flip to the dedications—*To Arthur A. Pennington, who lives within these pages; and Meranda Erickson, who died among them*—and I smile at the text. I turn the page, autograph below my printed name, give the kid one last pointer: "Adopt unconventionality. It'll bring you places."

Over fifty autographs later, hand aching, I return home. Leigh is taking her daily nap. I go into the den/office to write, receive an e-mail from my editor, open it and read:

James, Have you figured out what you're going to write next?

I ponder the text. For weeks, I've tried to answer that question. I thought of devising a sequel to *The Forsaken World*, but couldn't see how that would work. I thought of writing a story about time travel, but I kept thinking *Back to the Future*. I even considered jumping outside the fantasy realm to delve into a comedy piece, but I'm not a comedian.

Today, I'm determined to find inspiration. I open a new Word document and stare into the blank screen, allowing my eyes to go out of focus and my mind to wander where it pleases. Nothing transpires from the daze, not a single word typed on the page. I look on the wall above the laptop, eye the hanging Robert Frost letter, and see Robert's visage nod in my direction. I think of the online writer's program that I plan to launch next month. I'll make sure it's free to all registrants. I flash on Mitch and me at Robert's house, then at the diner when he gave me the letter. I think of Arthur and I think of Meranda. Then, in the back of my mind, I hear Mitch's voice, and what to write next becomes clear.

I laugh, heart fluttering. I can't believe I didn't think of this sooner. Smiling, I lean in toward the laptop and start typing:

The greatest and most inspiring achievements are not produced by those who conform to society's idea of normal, but by those who courageously adopt the unconventional.

ABOUT THE AUTHOR

Photo © JLeigh

J. J. Hebert is a writer. Surprising, huh? He has written fifty-two nov-els, including the immensely successful, award-winning *Willard's Heart*. J. J.'s also an archaeologist, and he recently unearthed an an-cient religious scroll in Jerusalem that, in time, will prove absolutely nothing about anything important. He presently resides in Yemen, where he enjoys being the richest man in the land.

Of course, the aforementioned isn't true (except for the "J. J. Hebert is a writer" part), but you found it entertaining, right? Per-haps just a little funny?

Honestly: *Unconventional* is J. J. Hebert's debut. Currently, he lives alone in New England, home to some of the greatest sports teams in the world (for now), where he's at work on his next novel.

You can visit J. J. on his Web sites: www.jjhebert.net and www.jjhebertblog.com.

Breinigsville, PA USA
09 October 2009

225555BV00001B/15/P